BLOOD
and SALT

BLOOD
and SALT

BARBARA SAPERGIA

COTEAU BOOKS

Edited by Geoffrey Ursell
Cover and text designed by Tania Craan
Typeset by Susan Buck
Printed and bound in Canada at Friesens

Library and Archives Canada Cataloguing in Publication

Sapergia, Barbara,
          Blood and salt / Barbara Sapergia.

ISBN 978-1-55050-513-9

          I. Title.

PS8587.A375B56 2012   C813'.54   C2012-903823-7

Also issued in electronic format.

EPUB ISBN 9781550507171
PDF ISBN 9781550505351

10 9   8   7   6   5   4   3   2

2517 Victoria Avenue
Regina, Saskatchewan
Canada   S4P 0T2
www.coteaubooks.com

AVAILABLE IN CANADA FROM:
Publishers Group Canada
2440 Viking Way
Richmond, BC, Canada
V6V 1N2

Coteau Books gratefully acknowledges the financial support of its publishing program by: the Saskatchewan Arts Board, the Canada Council for the Arts and the Government of Canada through the Canada Book Fund.
          We also gratefully acknowledge the financial support for this book of the Canadian First World War Internment Recognition Fund.

   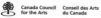

This book is dedicated to the memory of the men, women and children who were interned in Canada during World War I.

PART 1

CHAPTER 1

Going to the mountain

August 18, 1915

TARAS KALYNA sits turned to the window. Nothing to see but his reflection. Ashy skin, tangled black hair, eyes staring into the dark. A see-through man. He looks past this ghost to the banks along the track where the train's lamps cast a faint glow. Ghost land. For all he can tell, the world might end in blackness just beyond the light.

He's travelling west to a place he's never heard of. He doesn't understand how he came to lose his freedom. A week ago he had a job laying bricks to build a school in a small town in southern Saskatchewan. Now it's as if none of that existed. Like the other men in this car, he's a Ukrainian immigrant to Canada. He thinks this has something to do with why he's on this train.

The man beside him, Yaroslav – a railway worker – keeps trying to get him talking. What's your name? *Taras Kalyna.* Are you married? *No.* Where did you come from in the old country? *Bukovyna.*

Bukovyna is part of the Austrian empire. Canada is at war with Austria and Germany. Taras thinks this also has something to do with why he's on this train.

Yaroslav nods, taking in the news that Taras is from Bukovyna. Yaroslav must be at least forty. Grey strands crowd out the brown in his tangled hair and beard. He's skinny and the tendons in his neck stick out like ropes. Now he's talking again.

"They've got no right to hold us." He looks hard at Taras, seems to expect a response.

"No, they've got no right." Taras tries to suck in a deep breath. The hot moist air sticks to him like sweat. He's young, he doesn't know anything about rights. He only knows what happened to him.

It doesn't occur to him that Yaroslav might be trying to help. That he sees a young man who's angry and confused and might need to talk. Yaroslav tries again, says he's from the province of Halychyna – what the Canadians call Galicia – near Lviv, a beautiful old city. Has Taras ever been there?

Taras mumbles that he passed through Lviv once, and turns again to the window. He's not going to say he was running from the Austrian army at the time. Anyway, what's the point of talking? With somebody who looks like a starving hound. Sure, he must look nearly as bad himself. His crumpled blue shirt sticks to him, his armpits sting. He hasn't shaved in a week. Nothing to shave with. He's been sitting in a detention centre in Lethbridge, waiting for the people in charge to decide what to do with him. They put him on this train eight hours ago. It feels like days. Wheels clank against the track and everything gives way to their rhythm. Hard wooden seats dig into his bones.

He keeps asking himself, What have I done wrong? Why am I here?

He counts about forty prisoners in the car, watched by four soldiers. Two sit at each end, rigid as statues, clutching rifles with bayonets fixed. Somebody must think a bunch of dazed, half-starved men are really dangerous. To hell with the stone-faced bastards.

He looks away from them and in a moment he's back at the meeting where the police dragged him away. A meeting to start a union at the brick plant. He never wanted to be there in the first place – only went because his friend Moses asked him to. The local police knew he did nothing wrong, knew he didn't organize the meeting; he's sure of that much. In fact he's pretty sure they didn't want to arrest him in the first place.

He sees the bare room where they interviewed him, hears the

repeated questions. Do you own any firearms? *No, but I snare rabbits sometimes for our supper.* Do you have any contact with the Austrian government? *No, why would I? I left that place.* Just answer the question. Do you belong to any subversive organizations? *I don't understand.* The policeman explaining what subversive meant. *No, I work at the Spring Creek brick plant, and when I can, I help my parents break their land.* Land which is unsuitable for any kind of farming, he'd wanted to add, but didn't.

He thinks the local Mounties believed what he said. But they washed their hands of him and shipped him to a detention camp in Lethbridge, Alberta, where he soon saw that he wasn't the only one arrested. There must have been a hundred other men, most of them as confused as he was.

In Lethbridge it was soldiers who questioned him. Like the Mounties, they asked about subversive organizations. Spying. Sabotage, which apparently meant blowing up bridges, or buildings. They asked their questions over and over, as if they thought he'd been lying and would eventually slip and tell the truth. "No" was always the wrong answer and they kept on asking. Now he's on this train.

He wonders if there *are* subversive organizations in rural Saskatchewan. Where he would even look to find one.

In the darkness Taras no longer has any sense of forward motion. What if the train's just rocking in place and never arrives anywhere? Hunger bites his belly. Nothing to eat since Lethbridge. He's desperate to get off this train but doesn't want to get where it's going. They told him he'd be going to an *internment* camp. Taras doesn't understand the English word, but he thinks it means a kind of prison.

Wheels screech, the car bucks and jolts, and the train enters a curve in the track. The headlamp flashes light on the rails and trees flare into life; darkness swallows them back in a second. Now at least he can feel the forward thrust, his body hurtling into the night.

At the sun's last light he thought he could make out giant shapes against the sky. But maybe he only imagined them because a soldier at the detention centre said he'd be going to the mountains.

"You'll work. But you'll be taken care of." The soldier wouldn't look him in the eye.

He's never seen mountains, but he thinks he can feel them out there. Looming, dark shapes just outside the window, cutting off light.

HALF AN HOUR ago the guards agreed the windows could be opened.

"Christ," Yaroslav said to the nearest guards, "do you think we're gonna jump out the window? Off a goddamn moving train?"

"Watch your language," said a private, gripping his rifle stock so tight his knuckles went white.

"I suppose not," said the sergeant.

"Not yet, anyway," somebody muttered, but the sergeant had the private open one window and the prisoners did the rest.

TARAS CAN'T FEEL much difference. Too hot outside. And the train moves too slowly to create any real breeze. He fingers the back of his seat, scored with the names of people coming to the west. This could even be the same Colonist car that carried him and his parents across Canada to Saskatchewan. He remembers the noise and the clamour of many languages, and the bread and cheese Batko bought along the way. Mama amazed at the idea of *buying* bread. This all happened not much more than a year ago. A few months before the war began.

If they'd stayed in the old country, he'd be fighting in the war. For the Austrians. Because the province of Bukovyna is ruled by Austrians, and every man has to do service in their army.

He remembers when the train dropped them at Spring Creek and he and his parents looked around in what he now realizes must have been terror. Vast, open grasslands everywhere they looked; and nothing resembling a Ukrainian farm. A language that rushed past their ears before they could grab at the few words they'd learned on the train. And just a few months to get ready for what they'd heard would be a colder winter than any they'd known back in the village. *Blizzard* was one of the words they learned on the train.

"I wonder if the *assholes* who planned this trip ever rode a train before," Yaroslav says loudly. "I wonder if these *assholes* ever heard that trains can run late. In this case, five hours late." A few prisoners laugh. Yaroslav speaks in Ukrainian, but he says "assholes" in English.

"Shut up," the private says, "if you know what's good for you." But he can't get much energy into it. He's probably wondering about assholes too. They were supposed to make Castle Mountain siding in late afternoon, but there was never any chance of it. The train was late before it reached Lethbridge, and it stopped three times to let freight trains go by.

"The best thing about this?" Yaroslav says in Ukrainian. "The guards haven't eaten either. Life is seldom that fair." He sees Taras smile and thinks, That's a good sign.

Thinks, What would Ukrainians do without humour?

The sergeant announces that they're getting close to Banff. "Everyone stay in their seats," he orders.

The train whistle shrieks, echoes up and down a long valley. The train slows, wheels squealing. Taras sees warm light on the station platform. The guards jump to their feet, bayonets thrust forward. The idea seems to be, *If you try to escape, this blade's going into your gut.* Would they really do that? Do they really believe the prisoners will try to run for it?

The paying passengers from the sleeping cars step onto the platform. Men in suits and straw hats, women in flowered summer dresses, turn golden in the light and pass in a moment into the station, so quickly Taras could almost believe he imagined them.

The engine shudders, pants like a great beast and heaves them back into the dark.

A voice floats through the car. "No bloody right..."

Taras looks around at the tense faces, the narrowed eyes. He doesn't want to be like these men. He's younger than most of them, just turned twenty. Stronger than most, too. In Bukovyna he worked on the land and in his father's smithy. He can do anything his father can do. He can train horses better than anyone he's ever seen, including the skilled horsemen of the Austrian army.

Or his father, who learned during his time in the army.

But he *is* like these men. Prisoner.

Lightning burns through the trees and in the burst of light Taras sees a tracery of branches against the sky. Thunder crackles like a rifle volley – as if the war's come to him here in Canada – followed by sudden, hard rain. Ferocious rain. Like the rain that fell on Noah when he was in the ark, Taras thinks.

Soon the train will reach the camp and the guards will drive the prisoners out into the wind and rain. It's only a storm, but after a week of not knowing what's happening, of never-ending questions, he feels scared. He flexes his fingers; looks at his sturdy hands. Until now he's trusted their strength and skill to get what he needs. Now nothing is what it was.

About ten minutes later, he feels the train slowing, slowing. Outside the wind picks up and a sudden cool breeze gusts through the car. The train jerks to a stop near a small siding where soldiers hold lanterns against the darkness. The sergeant yells that the prisoners are to get out and follow the path to the camp. At the front end of the car, the guards block the door, while at the back the other guards stand waiting to herd them out into the rain.

Taras's feet have gone numb; his legs are like wood. Men stumble past him down the aisle like sleepwalkers. He flexes his feet back to life and joins the slow march.

In a moment he's on the platform between the cars, and as he lowers a foot to the metal stepping box, the wind hits him, driving rain into his face, his eyes. He feels a push from behind. Lurches onto greasy earth, falls to his knees, pulls himself up again.

Sheet lightning reveals a dirt trail swelled to a flowing creek of men and mud. Guards on either side, soaked to the skin, point the way, their bayonets giving back a dull gleam in the flashing light. After a few steps Taras's boots are heavy with mud. He's been told he'll be helping build a road, the Banff to Laggan road. This must be it. No, can't be. Too rough and narrow. He pulls a foot out of the muck and takes the next step. His clothes are plastered against his body.

Trees thrash in the wind. Thunder explodes like heavy field

guns. A streak of fire rips past his face and heat gusts through him. He's seen thunderstorms before, but never anything like this. There's a loud crack, very close, and he looks up to see a huge pine split vertically from the top down to the ground. The two halves hover in the air like reflections of each other and then move gracefully apart. One half sails, slowly it seems, toward him. He leaps aside at the last moment and the split trunk lands beside him on the path. He smells scorched wood.

For a moment no one moves. Then men swarm over the blackened trunk like ants over a twig. Why not? That tree can't fall again.

Pale white shapes appear through the downpour, and he makes out rows of tents inside a barbed-wire fence that must be ten feet tall. At the gate, a framework of wood and wire, guards shout, herding internees inside like cattle. Taras plods on.

Lightning strikes with a slap of thunder that makes his ears ache and a section of fence bursts into a web of fire, its connecting posts sizzling. As he stumbles through the gate, a prisoner with thin hair stuck to his head shoves Taras off the path and into a guard. A bay-onet snakes out, tears his shirt sleeve and slices a shallow cut in his arm. Taras feels it like the stroke of a whip, and for a moment imag-ines turning on the guard and knocking him to the ground the way the lightning felled the tree. He steps back. Blood mixes instantly with rain.

A crash of thunder rolls through him and in the sudden light the towering mass of Castle Mountain burns itself on his eyes.

A guard grabs his arm and heaves him into a milling line of prisoners. Others shout instructions, hand out sodden blankets and straw pallets, assign men to tents. Ahead of him, Yaroslav stumbles. Staggers to his feet. Asks about supper and is told to go to hell. Now Taras decides he'd like to stick with Yaroslav, even though he talks too much, but the thought comes too late. The guards direct the older man to a tent at the far edge of the compound. Taras is sent to one close by. Light spills out the door.

Inside about a dozen men sit around a coal-oil lamp, as if it's a campfire. Most nod when he comes in. A few don't make the effort. Rain drips through the canvas. He has mud all over his clothes, his blanket and pallet are soaked. He must look like a beggar. He feels like one.

A clean-shaven young man of medium height gets up. "I'm Yuriy," he says in Ukrainian. "I'm a farmer. In Saskatchewan."

"I'm from Saskatchewan too," Taras says. "Well, Bukovyna in the old country."

Yuriy nods as if that's just what he'd imagined. He's maybe thirty years old, has a square jaw, olive skin. Blue eyes, wide cheekbones, and an eager look, as if he's hoping for the best, even as a prisoner in a damp tent in the middle of a violent storm. He finds Taras a place to lay his pallet and blanket. Pats the wet ground. Smiles.

He likes to get things right, Taras thinks.

Several of the men start a card game, playing their cards on somebody's blanket. Others lie down and sleep, or pretend to.

"*Ya* Taras Kalyna. I'm a blacksmith," he tells Yuriy.

"Kalyna? Like the bushes in the old country?"

"*Tak,* just like that."

"Did you know they have *kalyna* here in Canada, only they call it cranberry?"

"No, I didn't —"

"Hey, your arm's bleeding." Yuriy looks worried, as if Taras is an old friend who has come to his door. "I suppose a guard did it?"

"One of them nicked me with a bayonet." Taras realizes it hurts like hell. For a while the pain was just part of the thunder and fire flowing around him.

Yuriy takes a handkerchief out of his pocket, holds it out in the rain until it's sopping. Taras rolls up his sleeve and Yuriy cleans the cut. While he's at it, he cleans mud off Taras's face. Soaks the handkerchief again, wrings it out and wraps it around the cut.

"There," he says, "that's better."

"*Dyakuyiu,*" Taras says. "Thanks." And it is better. Someone has done all that can be done, at least for now.

"What's wrong with the guards, anyway?" he goes on. "The guy just cut me, without even thinking."

"Well," Yuriy says, "they don't like being here. And they figure we must be guilty of something, or *we* wouldn't be here. And also, men keep escaping. The guards have to go out and look for them."

"Look where?"

"Oh, they search along the road to Banff and check all the train stations. But there's lots of sidings where freight trains stop." Yuriy winks. "We know where they are."

There's a *whump!* like a mortar blast and the air flashes white. Taras can't hear for a while but Yuriy keeps talking.

"... actually think we should like it here," he's saying.

"Are they crazy?"

"Some. Most of them just hate their work. And they don't like surprises."

An older man sitting on a blanket speaks from the shadows. "You don't want to make them jumpy, not with those pig stickers on their rifles." The man must be about forty years old. In the soft light, Taras sees glowing black eyes.

"So if I want to escape, I should try to look like I'm not."

"Dobre. Lesson one." The man has black, curling hair and a moustache turned up at the corners, and looks as if he belongs to some earlier time. Taras recognizes him right away as a Hutsul from the Carpathians. Other Ukrainians believe that Hutsuls live a freer life up in the mountains. They say that if you're in really bad trouble, you can run away to the Carpathians and no one will find you.

"Taras," Yuriy says, "this is Ihor the mountain man."

Ihor nods for Taras and Yuriy to sit on his blanket. He fishes in his pocket and brings out three hand-rolled cigarettes. Taras has never been interested in smoking, never liked the smell. Here in this rain-soaked tent, he decides to get interested. The smoke stings his throat and lungs, but it also makes the tent feel like a slightly different place, which seems a worthy goal. It makes him dizzy, too, but who cares about that? In fact, it's all to the good.

"The guards have guns," Ihor says, "so they think they should be able to make us obey. But it's harder than they expect."

Somehow the smoke swirling in his lungs makes Taras calmer, and he feels something let go inside him. The thunder and lightning are moving off, and he's met two men he thinks he can trust. He's got a foothold in this strange world.

The card players throw down their hands, complaining that the cards are too tacky to shuffle. A few men are already asleep. Others struggle to pull blankets into clumsy nests.

"Sleep," Ihor says. "Daylight will be here too soon."

Taras curls up on his pallet on the bare earth. He throws aside his damp blanket but eventually decides he's better off with it than without. He tries not to think about food.

In the darkness he sees his old village, where he could catch a glimpse of Halya almost every day. He imagines her light brown hair flecked with brassy gold; her steady blue-grey eyes and small, firm mouth that sets into a stubborn line when she's angry. He loves her fierceness, the shadow that can come across her face like a cloud over the sun. If he could be with her, he wouldn't care if she was angry all the time. He'd smile, he'd laugh. Thinking of Halya, he reaches under his shirt for a round pendant hanging from a wire. Hides it under the edge of his pallet.

Cold creeps into his bones. Rain patters on canvas. At last his mind drifts into night.

CHAPTER 2

Pokydky

IN THE MORNING he sees the great mountain clearly. Castle: *Zamok* in his language. So wide he can't see it all at once, has to keep turning his head. The cliffs at the top are almost vertical, scored by deep black lines. He tries to imagine being up there, hanging in that blue, clear sky, closer than he's ever been to the sun. Below, the cliffs begin to slope; sparse, thin trees cling to rock. Then denser forest, then the gouged mud of what must be the road bed, a gash in the forest. In the camp the tents make a forest of white canvas. The prisoners are spindly trees.

Taras knows the rolling hills of Bukovyna, his father's fields butting against ribs of forest. But he has no words for this silent immensity of rock flung against the sky.

Ihor comes out of the tent. "Big bastard, isn't it? Not like the mountains at home."

OUT IN THE YARD, staring at barbed wire, the prisoners stand through roll call. At first Taras misses his name, then realizes he's become *Tay*-ris, instead of Ta-*ras*. Ihor has become *Eye*-hor, instead of *Ee*-hor. And Yuriy is *You*-rye, instead of *You*-ree with a soft "yi" on the end.

There must be three or maybe four hundred men here. He wonders how the guards keep track of them all. They shuffle into the prisoners' mess tent to eat bowls of gluey white porridge. A story passes from table to table. Three men escaped during the storm after cutting a hole in the fence. Grins break over the prisoners' faces as word works its way through the tent.

How could they cut through the fence? Or did someone on the outside use wire cutters? Prisoners would have no way of arranging something like that, would they?

Taras saves the last few mouthfuls of porridge, hoping the food won't be so scanty and poor every day. Yuriy catches his eye.

"*Pokydky*. Same old crap." So. Taras would rather not have known that yet.

"What happens next?" he asks.

"It's very simple," Yuriy says. "You won't have to think for yourself at all. You'll eat when the guards tell you to eat, usually some sort of *pokydky*. Work when they tell you to work. Go to your tent after supper. Sleep if you can."

A soldier stops at the table. Taras won't be going out with a work crew this morning. He has to be registered first.

Later he sits at a battered wooden table across from Private Amberly, a skinny yellow-haired boy about eighteen years old. The boy says prisoners have to surrender all personal property, but they'll get everything back when they leave. Taras could snap the kid's arm if he wanted to, but even this boy makes him feel afraid. What'll they do if he refuses? Take it by force. What does it matter any more? But he feels ashamed.

Amberly sees him hesitate. "I'm sorry. You have to turn everything over."

Taras reaches into his pocket and pulls out a watch on a chain, its silver-plated case cool in his fingers, and places it on the table. Moses lent it to him so he could get to work on time. The case is engraved with an elk's head with huge spreading antlers. He loves this watch, more than ever now that he must give it up.

"My friend lend it to me. Comes from his *batko*. His father. I promise I look after it." Taras was wearing the watch when the Mounties came.

"Don't worry, it'll be safe." This guard does look him in the eye. He still believes his story, he's that young. He writes a note in a ledger so that the watch can be returned some day.

Taras feels lighter without the watch. He thinks he'll never see it again.

What is it about a watch? The government doesn't want them to know the time of day? Perhaps knowing the time is *subversive.* Or do they imagine he could turn the case into a weapon? Well, he could if he had the tools from his father's shop. He can make almost anything from metal.

Amberly points him to the lineup for haircuts and shaves. A cheerful man with black hair and a rakish moustache – The Turk, the guards call him – cuts his hair very short, the back and sides clipped smooth. For some reason Taras is allowed to shave himself – with a straight razor. But it could be used as a weapon, couldn't it? As he thinks this, he manages to cut his cheek. Drops of blood red as *kalyna* berries fall on the towel the Turk gave him.

HE'S TOLD TO STRIP DOWN for a bath. The tub looks like a big metal horse trough. Cold water. Scraps of grimy soap. He wonders if they ever change the water. Afterwards their old clothes are gone and each man gets two shirts, a pair of overalls, socks, underwear, boots and a button-up sweater jacket for cooler weather. Taras's shirt is too tight, his boots are too loose, his socks scratchy. The clothes make him feel off balance, a slightly different version of himself. So does the mountain looming over the camp – watching them, or so it seems.

At noon in the mess tent a bored looking guard hands each new prisoner a sandwich made of shredded burnt meat mixed with lumps of lard – more *pokydky* – and a cup of tea with a skin of black sludge on top. Yaroslav sits beside him in a shirt with sleeves that end several inches above his wrists. Taras hardly knows him without the straggly hair. The Turk has shaved his beard off, but left his moustache, trimmed so that it turns up at the ends. It looks almost dashing, fanning out over his skinny cheeks.

Taras considers growing a moustache. He's beginning to realize there aren't going to be many choices for a man to make in this place.

Yaroslav pretends to gag on the sandwich, but he eats it.

With the other new prisoners, he and Taras slog through what feels like a couple of miles of muck under blistering sun. Nobody talks. They reach a work site where trees have been cut in a wide swath to form a road bed, leaving behind a tangle of roots, some thick as a man's arm, others thin as wire. Taras is given a spade and told to dig them up. When he forces the spade into the earth, clods of mud stick to it. He digs, hacks and pulls roots until his arms ache.

After an hour or so, his head pounds. His eyes lose focus. He remembers making horseshoes in the smithy. The hot fire, the glowing iron. The moment when he knows a shoe is ready.

"Pick up the pace, slacker!"

How did the guard get so close without him noticing? He moves a little bit faster. After a few minutes he looks past the gnarled roots to the great trees on either side of the road bed, their shapes repeated as far as he can see. Even if he managed to sneak away, how would he find a way through them? Just as he thinks this, an enormous animal darts through these same trees, grunting and crashing into branches. It leaps onto the road bed and tears across, hooves spraying mud into the air, as if it can't even see the prisoners.

Yaroslav, standing near by, says it's a bull elk. Taras already knows this; it's like the one on the watch.

The elk seems to know where it's going.

Beside the roadbed a tree has been taken down by the storm, its roots spreading to the sky in a great circle twice Taras's height. He wishes he could stop and look at it for a while.

In the middle of the afternoon, the sergeant in charge calls, "Okay! Take a break." Taras limps into the shade and sits; lets the muscles in his shoulders, back and legs go slack. The feeling of being roasted and rendered falls away, a little. He drinks water from a canteen that's passed around and eats a small ration of bread that vanishes almost without chewing or swallowing.

He thinks of his parents, Daria and Mykola, trying to farm a quarter section of dry grassland near the town of Spring Creek. Winter is coming. Harvest, poor as it will be, must be done without him. They came to Canada because *he* had to leave. Now they don't even know where he is. He'll write to them; the skinny boy, Amberly, said they're allowed to do that. They need to know he's safe.

He doesn't feel safe.

He looks up at the mountain and wonders if his parents have heard anything about Halya.

THE EVENING MEAL is thin stew with shreds of stringy beef floating on top, and chunks of rubbery cabbage. And a slice of dry bread with coffee that tastes like charred wood. If he could keep completely still, most of the pain from the work would go away. But every time he shifts in his chair, every time he so much as lifts a forkful of the wretched stuff to his lips, it feels like barbed wire ripples and writhes under his skin. He considers just sitting there but knows he'd faint without food. After the beef and bread comes a dense yellow pudding in which Taras finds three rock-hard raisins that look like small, charred beetles. He eats it all; still hunger gnaws his stomach.

"I see why people want to escape," he says to Ihor as they drink the burnt coffee.

"Food is a good reason. But remember, escaping is dangerous."

"Why? What are they going to do to me?"

The black eyes gleam. "They are going to shoot you."

"*Shoot* me? Just like that?"

"*Tak.* Just like that. And then bring you back."

Taras imagines a bullet slamming into his chest. The pain, the blood. "Do some people get away?"

"Many do. Those who know someone outside. Like the coal miners from the Crowsnest Pass. Their old workmates help them." Ihor explains that although he isn't a coal miner himself, he worked on a ranch in southern Alberta before he came here, and he's met a lot of miners.

Taras's old workmates are far away in Saskatchewan. Moses and some others would help him if he asked. But at least one of those workmates would run straight to the Mounties.

THE BLANKET'S DRY NOW, the pallet almost so, but his muscles scream from all the digging and a thin layer of damp straw doesn't do much against hard earth. Doesn't let him forget his nearly empty stomach either. He remembers laying bricks in Spring Creek and can hardly believe he thought that was work. And in those days he got enough to eat. He turns and turns. As the light fails, the mountain breathes out cold. Men snore, cough, groan. Murmur prayers; curse bitterly; converse in low, intense tones. Can't you shut up, he wants to say, I'm trying to sleep.

One raspy voice catches his attention. It belongs to a man called Oleksa, one of the card players from the first night, who must be about forty-five. Oleksa doesn't seem pleased to have one more man in the tent. He's given Taras a few hard stares, although mostly he looks right through him. You'd think he'd be glad to have a little more body heat in the air, Taras thinks.

"...no damn business putting us here," Oleksa is saying. "We've done nothing wrong." An echo of the voice on the train: "No bloody right."

Oleksa sits cross-legged on his blanket, staring straight ahead, as if he can see through the canvas wall. There's a streak of white in his dark brown, close-cropped hair. His moustache, also clipped short, is a lighter red-brown, the colour of a sorrel horse, that seems to belong on some other face.

"Nothing wrong," he repeats. Taras pays attention. Maybe they're going to explain why they've all been imprisoned.

"Sure we have," says his friend Kyrylo. "We're Ukrainian." Kyrylo's thin lips almost disappear under a thick black moustache turned down at the corners that gives him a permanently gloomy look. A scar runs down his forehead and into one of his bushy dark eyebrows. Saloon fight? Taras wonders. Whatever happened, the thick brow must have saved his eye.

"You can do what you like to Ukrainians," says Toma, a short, stocky man with a quiet voice. "Just ask the Poles, the Austrians and the Russians." Three peoples, as Taras knows, who have fought over, carved up and ruled Ukrainian territories for a very long time. But the other two aren't listening to Toma. ·

"The government likes having somebody close by for Canadians to hate." Something in Oleksa's voice tells Taras he's said these words many times before.

"Why do they want someone to hate?" he asks, forgetting he's not part of their group.

Oleksa looks pained, runs his hand through his stiff hair. "Canada's at war with Austria and Germany. Wars cost money. Men die. The government wants people to keep supporting the war. So it gives them someone to blame. We're what they call the enemy within."

"You mean they think we're Austrians?" Taras asks. "Don't they know the difference?"

"We came here with Austrian passports. That's enough for them."

"The Austrians ruled us, so we're Austrians," Toma says.

Kyrylo pipes up. "I don't know — is that really it? I think it's because there's so much unemployment. They want us off the streets."

"They're afraid of strikes, that's for sure," Toma adds. For no obvious reason, Oleksa looks irritated by this comment. Toma smiles ingratiatingly. Maybe it was something Oleksa was planning to say himself.

"Not like we invented unions," Kyrylo says. His scar seems to crawl across his forehead when he speaks.

"No, but we caught on to them pretty quick." Oleksa laughs, strokes the sorrel moustache. "Besides, there's a lot of radical leaders in Canada, and the government's afraid there could be a revolution."

What's a revolution? Taras wants to ask.

"Well, all I ever wanted was a decent bloody job. Now I'm foreign scum." Kyrylo says.

"Take it easy. Wait till tomorrow. We'll see what we can do," Oleksa says.

"Yeah, yeah." Kyrylo pulls his blanket up around his neck and turns to the outer wall of the tent.

Close by in another tent a man weeps. A gentle voice asks what's wrong.

"It's my little Nasta," the weeping man says. "She's all alone. There's no money. What's to become of her?"

The other man tries to reassure him. Someone will look after Nasta. The Canadians won't let anything bad happen to her. Taras hears uncertainty in the man's voice.

THE NEXT DAY is much like the first, except that it's hotter and the mud has almost dried up. As the long day limps along, Taras thinks about the things Oleksa and his friends said.

They think Ukrainians got sent here for two – or is it three? – reasons. All of them related to the war. Canada is at war with Austria, so the government decides that anyone who was ruled by Austria is an Austrian and therefore an enemy. But can they truly not tell the difference? He remembers a poster in the village tavern in the old country, encouraging people to come to Canada. It was written in Ukrainian, not German. By people who ran Canadian steamship lines and railroads. It seems *they* could tell the difference.

The other two reasons are about unions and radical politics. This puzzles him, because although he was in fact arrested at a meeting to start a union at the brick plant, he was nothing more than a bystander. The people who ran the meeting weren't arrested. And he's never belonged to any kind of political group or talked about radical politics.

Maybe he should have. At least then he'd have been arrested for *something*.

Well, there was one other reason, according to Oleksa. To make people support the war it was helpful to show them the face of the enemy. He is now an enemy alien. The name sounds cold and cruel. An enemy you can't understand, who could do any brutal or barbaric thing.

Taras gets back to camp in the evening with his crew, wondering what slop they'll get in the mess tent. But nobody's there, they're all in their tents. Yuriy explains why. A work gang marched back to camp early after its members, led by Oleksa and Kyrylo, refused to work until they got better food. Their guards tried to stop them, but the park foreman supervising the work supported the men and the guards couldn't just start shooting people.

People not even trying to escape.

Then the commandant, the one in charge of the whole camp, ordered that the men who refused to work would get no supper. Word flashed through the dinner line, and the other prisoners decided they had to support Oleksa and his crew. So Taras is taking part in a hunger strike.

As if he hadn't been hungry enough before.

NEXT DAY AT THE WORK SITE, Yaroslav collapses as he tries to dig out a thick root. His spade drops like a very small tree. The park foreman tells the internees to quit work and go back to camp. Again the guards protest, but he doesn't listen. Neither do the men. They help Yaroslav up, a man supporting him on each side, almost carrying him. Someone says, loudly, in English, that the commandant is an idiot. The soldiers don't even pretend to care.

Later the prisoners hear that the foreman explained to the commandant that men can't work without something to eat. Supper, *pokydky* as it is, is restored. The brief flare of revolt fades, work starts up again: clear trees and brush, grub roots, shift rocks, dig dirt. Some day they'll reach Laggan, whatever that is. Taras doesn't believe it. Still a supper and a breakfast short, he's more famished than before.

"Well, it was something different," Oleksa says in the tent that night. No one bothers to answer.

Taras asks Yuriy and Ihor whether the road they're building is just something to keep them busy or will actually serve a worthwhile purpose.

Yuriy explains that the road will take visitors to a beautiful turquoise lake encircled by mountains. Businesses will grow. Life will be better.

"So, it's not all for nothing. Does that help?"

Taras thinks for a moment. "No."

"When I first came," Ihor says, "the commandant spoke to us one morning. He said, 'This is important work you're doing. You have fresh air to breathe. Beautiful scenery all around.' I think he was expecting us to cheer. He looked disappointed when nobody did, but he didn't give up that easily. 'You are lucky to be in such a fine place,' he said. No one actually spat on the ground until he turned to leave."

"The strange thing about him," Yuriy says, "is how ordinary he seems. You'd never look at him twice. Sandy hair and moustache, pale face with pale eyes. Sometimes he gets this puzzled look, as if he doesn't know what he's doing here."

CHAPTER 3

Well, a potato

SEPTEMBER PASSES into October. Darkness creeps into the tent a little earlier each night. People snap at each other, and they're cold all the time.

One night he walks back to the tent after supper – fried turnips and chicken wings in greasy gravy. He hates turnips, their bitter tang in his belly. Even so, there weren't enough of them. The men from his tent and a few others tried to stay near the mess tent stove a little longer than usual but the guards kicked them out.

In the fading light, Taras lags behind Yuriy and Ihor, staring at the barbed-wire fence. He's grown used to not seeing beyond it, although the big bastard of a mountain is always there. He focuses on the wire itself, wondering if he could make something that would cut through it.

As he puts his mind to the problem, someone bumps his shoulder, hard. He turns and sees that he's wandered into the middle of the twenty or thirty German prisoners of war in the camp. Real prisoners of war, captured in various parts of Europe. Kyrylo, or Scarman as Taras now thinks of him, says the POWs shouldn't be in the same camp with the Ukrainians, who are all non-combatants. But Taras has also heard the guards refer to the Ukrainians as prisoners of war. In this place a lot of things don't mean what you think they mean.

He has no idea who bashed into him. Maybe someone thought he was walking too close to them. Fine. He steps aside.

What the hell? Scarman pops up beside him and smacks into one of the Germans, Eickl. Eickl shoves right back.

"Get out of my way!" Scarman shouts. "Stupid bloody German." Scarman says all this in German. He speaks quite good German, Taras thinks. Better than he himself could manage. The "stupid bloody German" part was really clear.

Taras tries to edge away from them.

Then Eickl says, loudly, in fluent Ukrainian, that a Ukrainian must be an expert on stupidity because he does stupid things all the time; and it's as if a shell explodes between them. Punches fly and suddenly other men join the fight, hammering and flailing until bodies plummet to the earth like heavy birds.

Eickl thumps Scarman on the nose and blood sprays like black rain in the failing light. For a second Scarman can't believe it. Then he kicks Eickl in the knee. Eickl screams.

Guards rush in shouting and shoving, bayonets jabbing the air. In seconds everyone is sick of the fight and it stops cold. At that moment a fist crashes into Taras's left cheek and jaw and he goes down hard. Christ, it hurts. Who did that, for God's sake? He wasn't even fighting. Of course the guards didn't notice a thing. Complete useless tits.

Scarman, bloody but grinning wildly, helps him up, and Taras thinks he could maybe become part of Oleksa and Scarman's group if he wanted to. But he doesn't want to, doesn't even want to get up yet. Somebody might hit him again. In the sudden quiet, the prisoners walk off, some with pulpy lips and bruises blooming on eyes or cheeks. Scarman isn't the only one who looks pleased.

Yuriy and Ihor have stopped to see what's going on. Taras stumbles up to them. "I wasn't even fighting," he says. Yuriy's handkerchief comes out again, wipes away blood where Taras's cheek is cut. Ihor shakes his head like a parent with a foolish child.

ONCE AGAIN Oleksa, Scarman and Toma sit cross-legged on the dirt floor of the tent playing a game Taras doesn't even want to understand. Their eyes track each card that falls as if it matters. Oleksa with his mismatched hair. Scarman with his bushy eyebrows. Toma with his round, almost gentle face.

Scarman started the game in a good mood, but now looks ready to hit somebody. His nose has stopped bleeding, although it still has a mashed look. Like a boiled potato flattened with a wooden spoon.

Taras thinks about a whole boiled potato. Whether he'll ever see one again.

The other card players from the first night stare at the walls, smoking each cigarette until their fingers start to burn, tired of Scarman telling them what to do. Scarman wanted to play for a penny a hand, but Toma, who usually does everything he's told, led a revolt. He said he'd die if he lost all his money and couldn't get cigarettes. Taras was surprised when this worked, but by then the other men didn't want to play any more.

Each man earns twenty-five pennies a day from his work. It doesn't get you much at the camp canteen, but if you're careful you can have, over a week, several candy bars and plenty of smokes.

Taras watches Yuriy read an old copy of the Banff newspaper he found outside. A soldier must have dropped it. He notices Taras watching and reads out loud – a story that explains how the town benefits by selling provisions to the internment camp.

"Good to know we're helping someone," Toma says.

Ihor sits beside Taras, fingers drumming on the ground, and hums a tune that leaps and dips and whirls. A song from another place, of rocks and streams and a life spent on the shoulders of mountains. Oleksa keeps giving him dirty looks, but doesn't say anything. Taras sees that he doesn't quite want to take Ihor on. Doesn't know what might happen.

Taras worries that a fight will start in the tent. Just for something to do. Or to get warm. It probably won't; Yuriy and Ihor are always so calm. Also, Oleksa and even Scarman don't want fights that aren't their idea. Still, you never want to take another man's cigarettes or candy bar. It seems that the less you have, the more you don't want anyone to touch it.

Taras lights a cigarette, but the left side of his face burns and the teeth on that side feel loose. It hurts even to smoke. He throws down the cigarette, watches it glow a moment and sputter out in the dirt. What a waste. His hands and feet ache with cold, even though he's wearing everything he has, in layers. It makes his clothes feel stiff and tight.

He pulls his one blanket closer around his shoulders and looks toward the glowing oil lamp in the centre of the tent. But what he sees is the big clay stove, the *peech,* in his family's house back in Shevchana, that radiated heat all through the night. He tries to call up that warmth.

From the corner of his eye, he sees the card players lay down their hands without a word. Toma gathers them into a deck and ties them with a bit of dirty string. Blows out the lamp. Each man tries some slightly different way to settle against the cold earth.

Taras runs his tongue over his sore teeth. At least he can't taste any more blood, but his left cheek throbs and not even cold drives out the pain.

Tomorrow the guards will look at his face and know him for a troublemaker.

In the mess tent a week later, Taras takes a seat beside Yuriy. Ihor sits across the table. Too late Taras sees Oleksa sit down on his other side, next to Franz Redl, one of the Germans.

Redl and Oleksa hated each other on sight, which was well before Taras came to the camp. Oleksa loudly blames all Germans for starting the war and landing the internees in this place. Redl, a short, swarthy man who doesn't fit the common idea of a German, says the Ukrainians in Canada should have gone back to the old country as soon as the war began and fought in the Austrian army.

Neither man is shy about saying these things.

Redl tries to get up and find a different place to sit, just as Scarman settles himself down on his other side, pushing Redl back onto the bench.

Taras becomes interested in the contents of his plate. A whole potato. Not a very big potato, but still... Meat, who knows what kind, clotted with gristle. Watery gravy. Peas boiled almost grey. Crap, maybe, but he's going to eat every speck.

"Pig," says a low voice. "Filthy, shit-eating sow." Oleksa.

Taras and Yuriy exchange looks. "Well, a potato," Yuriy says. *"Dobre."*

"Tak. Tse dobre," Taras says.

"Turnip face. Cabbage brain." Redl. Not up to the standards of "shit-eating sow."

Taras sees a blur of movement and Redl's coffee spills over his plate and onto his lap.

"Sorry," Scarman says. "That was clumsy of me."

Again Redl tries to get up. Again Scarman holds out his arm. "No need to clean up your mess. Eat. It'll get cold."

For five minutes or so everyone eats silently. It's more than enough time to finish whatever a man has on his plate. You can have a second burnt coffee if you want, but Redl gets up before Oleksa or Scarman can react. Walks quickly out of the tent.

Oleksa strolls toward the door looking bored, hands in his pockets. Sidles out the door. Something thuds against something else. Yells and grunts erupt, more thuds. The other German prisoners try to get out of the tent, but a line of Ukrainians blocks the way. Taras and Yuriy run outside. Already Oleksa is winning the fight, if you can call it a fight. Redl's face looks like a smashed tomato. Blood streams into his eyes. Oleksa has him pinned.

"Get him off me," Redl begs. The guards pull Oleksa away and when he still struggles, one of them knocks him down with a rifle butt.

Redl is taken in an army truck to the hospital in Banff with a broken nose and a swollen eye. Oleksa, whose nose now looks as bad as Scarman's, is sent to the log guardhouse just outside the compound. The hoosegow, the guards call it. From the way they say it, it must be a humorous word in English. Anyway, it's the internees' jail. A small jail beside a big jail.

After everything settles down, Yuriy tells Taras and Ihor that while it's often hard to tell what's lucky and what isn't, this fight contains two examples of good luck. The coffee is never very hot, so although Redl got his face bashed, his private parts weren't scalded. And Oleksa only got a few days in the hoosegow, and a log building, even an unheated one, is bound to be warmer than a canvas tent.

It's quiet in the tent at night. No one goes near Scarman because he's mad all the time. When Oleksa comes back, after getting only bread and water for several days, he doesn't talk either. At night, he sits on his blanket, his back turned to the others, including Scarman.

Shortly after this, the Germans ride out of the camp in the back of a big truck, on their way to an all-German camp in British Columbia. Except for Redl. He's still in the hospital. Scarman hails their departure as a great victory and talks himself back into some kind of better mood. He claims that he and Oleksa "really showed those Germans." He feels pleased enough to give Oleksa a couple of candy bars he was saving for some dark day. Even so, it takes Oleksa a little longer to come around, but before long the card games start up again.

As DAYLIGHT WANES, the sandy-haired commandant makes another decision, explained to the prisoners by the guards: work days will be shortened by one hour a day. But by now Taras is so miserable that he finds it hard to tell the difference. He and his friends are colder, hungrier. Even Yuriy looks dejected.

One night Taras says, "We need to make a plan."

Ihor shakes his head. "Too cold. I don't jump out of the frying pan into the fire." He says the last bit in English.

"What are you talking about?" Taras asks, confused by the change of language.

"Just a little expression I learned from my boss at the ranch. It means you don't leave something bad for something that could be worse."

Still, men who hadn't considered escape before consider it now. Two men do escape. Private Amberly, the kid who took away Taras's watch, is charged with helping them. Taras can't understand why he'd do that, since prisoners have no money for bribes. Is it possible, then, that he *liked* the men he helped? Or that he's in favour of radical politics and thought the Ukrainians were radicals?

Taras doesn't think so. If there's anybody in Canada who knows even less about politics than he does, it has to be Private Amberly.

Another soldier, Lieutenant Sales, is charged with being drunk on duty and using profane and obscene language. This is more understandable. Taras wouldn't mind being a bit drunk himself. But he *can* use profane and obscene language whenever he wants to, because, as Yuriy points out, the guards don't know Ukrainian. Another piece of luck. Up until now he hasn't used a lot of bad language, but if he stays here much longer he might take it up.

TARAS SITS ON HIS BLANKET and writes a letter. It's the middle of October but feels more like December. The guards brought them in from the work site early. Too cold for the men to work, they told the commandant. Sure, maybe they felt some concern for the men, but probably a lot more for themselves. But as Yuriy says, you take luck where you find it. Any time you work a shorter day, you have more time to talk or play cards or write a letter before black night takes you down.

He feels a sob, or maybe it's a scream, trying to tear its way out of his chest. For two months he's been sending letters to his parents, asking if they're all right. Pretending *he's* all right. He writes them and hands them over to the guards. And then nothing happens. For two months he's been asking the guards why he's not getting mail. No one knows. Or cares, as far as he can see. A few men in the camp get letters; most don't. Why?

Taras surprises himself by coming up with an idea. He writes a letter, in English — Yuriy helps him with it — to the commandant. He walks around the mess tent that night and talks to other men who aren't getting letters. Some just wave him off, but quite a few add their signatures to the letter. It says, "We are promised the right to send and receive letters. We have sent letters to our families, but have never received any letters back. We ask you to help us. We demand to know what has happened to our letters."

He gives the letter to Sergeant Andrews, one of the less surly guards, who promises to get it to the commandant. The days drag on until a week goes by. Then a second. He thinks Andrews is avoiding him. Talks to him again.

"I passed your letter on," Andrews says. "His aide told me you'll hear soon."

The first day of November, Taras joins the evening lineup for the mess tent. A soldier he hasn't seen before is talking to Andrews. Taras sees Andrews pointing him out and they come over to the line.

"Mr. Kuh-*leen*-uh," Andrews says, "This is Captain Vernon. He's found out something about your letters." Vernon is younger than most of the guards, about twenty-five, tall and thin, and actually looks good in his uniform. Some rich man's son, Taras thinks. Keeping out of the war in Europe.

"You see," the captain says, "the camp has no official interpreter." Taras looks baffled. "No soldier able to read Ukrainian." What's this guy talking about?

"Perhaps you are unaware, but all letters going out or coming in have to be passed by a military censor." Vernon looks a bit edgy. Taras probably looks desperate. Dangerous.

"Why?" Taras tries to keep his voice steady.

"So no sensitive information is passed on." He sees Taras has no idea what he means. "No information that could hurt the war effort."

"I don't have information like that. Bring my letters, I show you."

"I can't touch your letters. Nobody can."

"I don't understand. Why my letters are not sent?" Taras steps out of the path of men entering the tent. Yuriy and Ihor stop to listen. And Scarman and Oleksa.

"You see, they're written in Ukrainian. So there's no one to read them. The commandant hopes to get an interpreter soon."

"Where are my letters? Where are they?" Taras hears his voice getting louder. None of this makes any sense.

Vernon looks embarrassed. "Sitting in a bag in the commandant's office."

Taras is afraid his head will explode.

"I'm sorry. I don't have anything to do with it."

"I want my letters!" Now Taras is actually yelling.

"Letters written in English are getting through," Vernon says helpfully. "Could you write in English?"

Taras takes a deep breath. "My parents can't read English. They *can* read Ukrainian."

"Oh. Too bad." Vernon's face flushes; he looks like he'd rather be almost anywhere else.

ANOTHER WEEK PASSES, it grows colder, and Taras hears nothing of his letters. The internees begin to believe they will die in their sleep in the freezing cold tents. But a day or two later, Captain Vernon comes to the mess tent and talks to them.

It seems the brass who run this place have decided it's impossible for the men to winter at Castle Mountain. Taras thinks a sensible person would have figured this out back in the summer. There's an edge in Vernon's voice that suggests he might possibly think the same. Oleksa mutters that the commandant would have noticed earlier, except that he has a stove in his private tent.

So the camp will move to a site at the edge of Banff with four large bunkhouses previously used by construction workers. Each holds a hundred men. The word is, they have stoves. Now that's revolution.

TARAS'S BREATH seems to come a little easier as the train glides down the Bow Valley. He's glad to be done with Castle Mountain hanging over his nights and days. Once again he sits beside Yaroslav, who rode with him on the train to Castle Mountain. Yaroslav is even skinnier now. His thick moustache is the only healthy looking thing about him. At Banff station Taras glances around. There really is a town here, and somebody's decided the internees aren't too dangerous – too radical – to be near it. Yaroslav, who used to work on the railroad, names the mountains that circle the town: Norquay, Cascade, Tunnel, Rundle, Sulphur.

"Used to work." At Castle Mountain the men tried to remember who they used to *be;* where they lived, where they worked, what they ate. Who loved them.

The guards march the men right through town, past comfortable houses built of wood and stone. Many have front porches where a man could sit after a day's work. It must be a fine thing to live in one of these houses. People stop and watch them go by. Some look angry, others scared.

One woman looks his way and nods, almost smiles. A woman in a bright green coat that sets off the red and gold mixed in her hair. She holds his gaze, doesn't turn away with that pinched expression Taras often sees on the faces of some of the guards. After three months in the camp, three months of being foreign scum, it brings tears to his eyes.

As they approach the Bow River, Taras sees an enormous castle standing above the town like some fantastic mountain. *"Zamok,"* he says.

"No," Yaroslav says, "it's not a castle, it's a tourist hotel. People from all over North America and even Europe stay there. At least they did before the war."

"From Austria, even?" Taras asks.

"Sure, probably even Austria. Maybe the emperor himself." Taras tries to imagine Franz Josef coming to this place. Leaving the castles you own to visit a make-believe castle in Canada. Well, what could be nicer?

Despite this bitter thought, something about the town feels good. Or maybe just different, a place where there are people who are neither prisoners nor guards, but he finds as they cross the bridge that his pace quickens. Yaroslav gives him a puzzled look. Embarrassed, Taras eases back. For a moment he must have been feeling something like hope.

Beyond the bridge, they turn right and soon reach a small log building guarded by soldiers. They march on toward a place called the Cave and Basin, a hot springs pool Yaroslav calls it, where tourists come to soak. Below it, bunkhouses huddle against the lower slopes of Sulphur Mountain, which Taras imagines as an immense resting animal.

Taras sees Yuriy and Ihor close by and when the guards aren't looking he moves through the mass of men to join them, leaving Yaroslav once again to fend for himself. The guards send the three friends to the same bunkhouse, a long wooden building with one wall higher than the other on the side facing the mountain. A row of small windows near the top lets in light. None of the other men from the tent are sent here and Taras discovers how glad he is to be away from them, especially Oleksa and Scarman. Yuriy smiles, Ihor winks and Taras feels a bubble of laughter in his belly. The building has three stoves in a row down its centre. Taras and his friends find bunks close together near the middle stove. Maybe things will be better.

Supper is no better. Chunks of cabbage with a little meat. Bleached-looking carrots which have somehow been charred as well as boiled. Taras can't look at them if he wants to eat anything.

Afterwards the men turn in early. Although no one's worked today, there's a different kind of exhaustion. The realization that you can never let your guard down. What have these idiots got planned for them now? The bunks are slightly more comfortable than hard earth. Yuriy and Ihor fall asleep quickly, but Taras turns and turns. The pendant he always wears beneath his shirt digs into his skin.

A man with stringy yellow hair and red pimples on his neck walks by. Taras has noticed this fellow staring at him before, lips curled in a knowing leer. God knows why. But maybe there's something familiar about him. Maybe Taras should just ask him what he wants. The man passes on to the corner of the bunkhouse and disappears into darkness.

In the distance Taras hears an amazing noise. Something big crashes through the trees, and calls in a deep voice that makes him shiver. It wakens Ihor, and he sits up to hear it better. He explains that it's a male elk's mating call. Taras listens, wordless; its power and longing call to his heart. He thinks that hearing it is the one lucky thing that's happened to him, except for meeting his two friends, since he became a prisoner.

In his old village, a man called Yarema played the *sopilka,* a handmade wooden flute. He played old songs but also made up his own. They sounded like the birds that flew about the village, or wind in the forest.

The elk's voice brings it all back. He sees that all places have their own songs. With a rush of pain, he remembers the village, the beauty and joy he'd known there and never needed to name.

The elk's call is the mountain's night music.

AT FIRST THE BUNKHOUSE *is* better than the tent camp. For a time it's quite warm. Everyone gets new overalls and woollen mitts. In the daytime they work on many jobs – clearing brush from the town's recreation grounds, building a bridge over the nearby Spray River, or sometimes just shovelling snow off the Banff streets.

Then the real cold comes.

CHAPTER 4

Agitator

November, 1915

TARAS STANDS in a forest clearing strewn with fallen trees and raw stumps, their sharp scent piercing the air. The men in his bunkhouse have been sent out to fell and trim trees for the stoves. He sees tilted, scarred earth before him and a smear of green forest, shapeless except for the nearest trees. Hard white sky touches the ground; mountains dissolve in its pulsing light. The other men appear to float in the whiteness, and when they speak, their words slur and fade, never to be decoded. And yet the whole valley seems to ring, as if the air itself cried out.

Snowflakes begin to drift through the windless air, so many he gets dizzy looking at them. They land on his face and hair, each with its small cold burden. He opens his mouth to let them fall on his tongue and feels a howl building in his gut. How long must he stay in this place?

He knows where the mountains are even if he can't see them, and at times like this he hates them. They are too massive to understand, and every day they cut off hours of the waning light. It seems to him as if this small white space is the entire world, and there is nothing but these men, this moment. They tell time by the slow ebb of light. Small pockets of breath leave their lips like scraps of soul.

The priest back home once tried to help him grasp the idea

of eternity. What did he care about eternity then? Here in the mountains, he's starting to understand.

He lets his axe fall to the ground and considers the forest. If he tried to run away, could he find his way out of this valley? No, but it might be good just to disappear for a little while. It's the coming back that would be dangerous. The guards would think he was escaping, and shoot him.

A HUNDRED YARDS AWAY, another work gang raises and swings axes; beyond them, another, ever smaller images fading into white. Some people say hell is a place where men toil in pain, burned by endless fire. Here ice and snow replace flame.

Not even hard work gets him warm; and there's never enough food. They still don't have winter jackets, only the heavy sweaters they were given in August. In the old country they had sheepskin coats. In Canada Ukrainians are known for these coats. Some people, that's all they see. Walking sheepskin coats. Well, not every Ukrainian owned such a coat. Or a warm coat of any kind.

Back in the village, Taras was reckoned a strong man, but his strength seems to evaporate like water in this dry, frozen air. Along with any clear idea of what's going on in the world.

The guards try to keep war news from them, but it gets around anyway. There's always a guard who lets something slip, or a page of newspaper left behind in the canteen. So the internees know that soldiers still huddle in cold, muddy trenches on the Western Front as they did even before Taras came here. Still die by the thousands and tens of thousands to capture small ribbons of land; a field here, a hill there. He compares this to camp life – where you will be shot and possibly killed only if you try to escape.

Yesterday he heard a guard screaming that it was all the prisoners' fault – the *goddamn hunkies* was how he put it – as if Ukrainians had anything to do with starting or running the war.

The guards still haven't noticed he's not working.

As always, they pace up and down, trying to keep warm. Resettle rifles on shoulders. Wrap scarves more securely. Stare at snow. Taras is getting to know them a little. Not that he likes them, but it helps to know what they might do in certain situations.

Taras doesn't see a thin figure creep up beside him until a swift, hard blow strikes his shins and he collapses in the snow. Pain comes in waves, floods his body, his brain, worse than the time a horse kicked his knee. He can't scream, hasn't the breath for it. If only he could faint and not come back till it was better. A gaunt red-faced man with hair like pale straw grins down at him, runs his fingers over the handle of his axe. It's the one who watches. Zmiya, Taras and his friends call him. Snake.

Blood fills his mouth and he spits into the snow. He must have bitten his tongue when the wooden handle hit. More blood pools and runs down his throat. He spits again and rinses his mouth with snow. Zmiya walks away. For reasons Taras expects never to learn, Zmiya has spied on him since the camp moved to Banff and he ended up in their bunkhouse. Or maybe it wasn't by chance. Maybe Zmiya made sure he got into the same bunkhouse in order to spy on him. Taras sees that he should have confronted the man. Why didn't he? So many things he can't be bothered with in this place.

The guards have seen nothing. The nearest, Bud Andrews, is turned slightly away. In his forties and out of shape, he looks bored almost to despair. His blue eyes and plump, rosy cheeks give him a look of good humour, and he isn't mean like some of the others. But like the internees, he can't leave. He paces the snow with a faraway, almost wistful look. Finally sees Taras on the ground holding his shins.

"Cramp?" Andrews comes a few steps closer. "Just give it a good rub, it'll come round." He smiles helpfully and moves on, utterly failing to see blood. Or to figure out that you don't get cramps in your shins.

Bent over a felled pine, Zmiya laughs soundlessly. Mimes rubbing his shin as if it's the most comical thing in the world.

A second guard, Jim Taveley, stares into the distance as snow glazes his cap and greatcoat. If he's seen what happened, he doesn't let on. Veiled in white, he must think he's invisible. Sometimes when Taveley looks at the internees a pinched look comes over his face, nostrils flared, thin lips turned down. "They're not like us," Taras heard him say once.

The pain is like an acute form of cold. Terrible but also interesting. Taras looks around for the third guard, who was off taking a crap in the trees a while ago. As if Taras's glance has conjured him from snow and air, Jackie Bullard, a stocky man in his mid-thirties, steps out of the forest, red-faced and angry looking. It's no fun trying to pass hard stools while your balls are freezing off. Taras knows.

"Hey!" He spots Taras on the ground. "What the hell are you playing at?" Bullard must see the red blotches in the snow but pretends not to. "Get up! Get back to work."

Taras staggers to his feet, hoping nothing's broken; almost faints with pain. A wash of red spreads over the sky, the snow. He's never seen that before.

"Bloody slackers." Spit flies from Bullard's lips. "Get a move on." He says these words, or something similar, at least once every hour. Maybe it's how he remembers who he is. The prisoners sweep hard eyes over him. Bullard moves closer to Andrews, who doesn't even notice.

"Asshole," Taras says under his breath.

He stumbles to where Yuriy and Ihor are cutting tree trunks into logs.

Yuriy sees blood at the corners of Taras's mouth. "What's wrong?"

"Bit my tongue. Zmiya hit me with an axe handle. Across the shins."

"What the hell?" Ihor puts out an arm to steady him.

"Damn that Zmiya," Yuriy says. "I'm gonna take care of him. Soon." Yuriy doesn't smile as much as he used to.

"Not if I take care of him first." Ihor's black eyes glow, his curling hair and moustache almost invisible under a lattice of snowflakes. He and Yuriy exchange a look. "He won't know what hit him. But he'll get the idea."

"Always some rotten bastard in every village," Yuriy says, as if the camp is a kind of village. "Don't know why that is."

"No," Taras says, "not in my village." Then he thinks of Viktor, Halya's father, who hated him.

Was that how things worked? There had to be one rotten bastard? He'd always thought it was just Viktor, but Yuriy seems to be saying it happens everywhere. No, couldn't be that simple. It *was* just Viktor.

But if Zmiya is the usual rotten bastard, the fact that he picks on Taras may be just a matter of bad luck. Rotten bastards would have to pick on somebody.

He shrugs. He could deal with Zmiya himself, but he just doesn't care enough. Let Ihor take care of it if he wants. Or Yuriy.

At the end of the afternoon each man balances a log, ten or fifteen feet long, on one shoulder and they walk back to camp like soldiers with enormous wooden rifles. Somehow Taras stays on his feet.

AFTER SUPPER he lies on the hard, lumpy bunk, pillow at his back, shins throbbing. When he and his friends got back to the bunkhouse after supper, Yuriy scooped snow into his hankie and Taras has been holding it against the bruises.

Internees sit on bunks built in tiers along the walls or on wooden chairs around tables playing cards. Ihor blew some money he was saving for cigarettes on a new deck but now they don't feel like playing.

Yuriy and Ihor get up and walk slowly to the end of the building where Zmiya sleeps, or feigns sleep. They don't say or do anything, just let him know they're thinking about him.

Close to Taras's bunk, a serious looking young man with a jack-knife whittles a round slab of wood. Bohdan Koroluk finds deadwood in the forest, trims it, and brings it back hidden under his sweater. He shouldn't have a knife of any kind. Anything that could be used as a weapon was taken away when they came to the camp. By now, though, no one cares, least of all the guards, and he carves every evening.

He carves faces. So far he's done Yaroslav the Wise, who began to build the great Saint Sofia cathedral in Kyiv in 1037; Bohdan

Khmelnytsky, the famous Cossack leader; the poet Taras Shevchenko; and several saints Taras has never heard of. In the daytime Bohdan hides the carvings under his bunk. At night he sets them on top of his blanket and people come to look. The faces pull you in, make you long for something you can't name. They are the most interesting thing in the bunkhouse. No, the only interesting thing. There are three other bunkhouses, but only this one has Bohdan Koroluk.

Wind howls and spits snow against the dark windows, knifes a chill gust through the building. Bohdan has begun a new carving, of a woman this time, and Taras watches as her face slowly appears in the wood. She reminds Taras of Halya. Her direct, almost challenging look. The hint of a smile around her lips and eyes. He lets the pain go, lets thought go, and watches work roughened fingers transform the wood. For a while there's only that face, and it eases his sadness.

He's aware in a distant way of marled grey eyes staring at him through hair like thin, matted straw from Zmiya's dark corner. Zmiya looks like a half-starved rat. Or a scarecrow. *Strakhopud.*

After a while he begins to hear the voices around him, swirling through the cavernous room like wind-driven snow. Voices loud or soft, high or low, all speaking Ukrainian. At the table near Taras's bunk, Yuriy's arguing with Myroslav, a schoolteacher in his late twenties, about *hetman* Bohdan Khmelnytsky, the last strong leader of the independent Ukrainian Cossack communities in the seventeenth century. They must have been looking at Bohdan's carving.

Myroslav has straight black hair combed back from a long, pale face. Thick black eyebrows and moustache. Long thin hands and a serious look. In fact at first Taras thought he was far too serious. But his rare smiles transform him. Then he looks like the icon of a saint. His manner is restrained. No harsh or careless word leaves his lips. And yet, Taras thinks, if he were to get really angry, he might be fearsome.

Myroslav says Khmelnytsky made a mistake in allying himself with the Russians.

Yuriy grins. "Maybe so. Anyway, my favourite hero is the one I grew up hearing about. Ustym Karmaliuk."

Myroslav looks puzzled. Taras has never heard of him either.

"Ha! You don't know him, do you!" For a moment Yuriy himself looks like some hero of old, with a vitality drawn from the black soil of *Ukraïna*. "And you a teacher!"

"I teach arithmetic." Myroslav runs a hand through the thick hair. "I don't claim to know all the Ukrainian heroes."

"So I see. Well, our Karmaliuk was a peasant rebel. He had thousands of followers. The Polish and Russian landlords were afraid to take a crap at night."

Ihor comes closer and sits down on Yuriy's bunk. "Don't forget *our* Oleksa Dovbush, the Hutsul hero. Stole from the Polish landlords and helped the peasants."

"Dovbush I know about," Myroslav says. "He's like the famous English bandit, Robin Hood. Stole from the rich, gave to the poor. Yuriy's Karmaliuk also sounds a lot like him."

"Karmaliuk wanted us to have our own country," Yuriy says. "And some day we will."

"I hope we will," Myroslav says.

Yuriy came to Canada as a young man, Myroslav as a boy who'd just finished high school. They both think of themselves as Canadian now, but they don't forget where they came from either. A part of their identity will always be Ukrainian, and until Ukraine is a free country, there will always be a sadness in each of them.

The outer door opens and cold air blasts into the room. Bullard and Andrews come in, followed by Taveley and a new guard, Private Randall. A stocky man of medium height leans heavily on Andrews. His coat is open, his hair blown across his forehead. A bulge inside his torn shirt front must be a bandage. Blood has seeped through to the shirt. Even surrounded by guards, you'd have to say he looks dangerous.

As the small group nears the centre of the bunkhouse, Taras happens to gaze right at the man, into intense dark eyes below peaked black brows. He looks like an infuriated owl; or a dissolute priest. Or a madman. His bright eyes, full of demands, seem to laugh at everything around him. Black hair, salted with silver, hangs in tendrils around his face. A deep cleft marks his chin.

He must have tried to escape. Why isn't he in the guardhouse, then? Must be full already. Or maybe they wanted to keep him away from the men he ran off with.

Taveley and Randall prod the prisoner with their rifle butts, in the direction of an empty bunk, near Taras's. The man stumbles, then turns on them, wild as a summer storm.

"Don't do that," he says fiercely, in lightly accented English. "I'm not going to run away, boys. I've done that now."

"Just keep moving," Taveley says. "Agitator."

"Bloody Bolshevik," says Randall. He looks like he just woke up and has no idea where he is or how he got there.

"Well. You really know your politics," the prisoner says. "Most people don't even know what a Bolshevik is. I, however, am a radical socialist."

"Right there, Bolshie." Randall points his bayonet at the empty bunk. "Your new hotel room."

Will the new prisoner guess that the man who had that bunk died? No one knew Tomak had tuberculosis when he came to camp, but one morning he couldn't get out of bed. Better, Taras thinks, if the radical socialist doesn't know.

Randall tosses a canvas bag and a blanket onto the bunk. Suddenly the steam goes out of him. He glances at the internees who have drawn closer to listen. Taras could swear he looks scared. He must have thought the prisoners would be scared of *him*. Now he doesn't know how to act.

The black-haired man, the Bolshie, sits down, peers around. All the men in the bunkhouse are watching him. The guards would never have given him an audience like this if they'd thought about it. He feels the area over his wound. Blood comes off on his hand.

"Sure could use a doctor, boys."

"Doctor's off today," says Bullard. "Maybe tomorrow." He looks uncomfortable. So does Andrews.

"You're okay," says Taveley. "Fresh blood'll keep the wound clean." He also looks like he can't wait to get away.

"Good to know. Here I thought I was going to bleed to death while you guys were off drinking and playing cards." The Bolshie's dark eyes sweep over the guards.

"I'd shut up if I were you." Angry again, Randall points to Bullard and Andrews. "They know about you. They're not gonna take any chances."

"Be fair," the wounded man says. "Did I hurt anybody? No. Wouldn't you run away if you could?"

"Shut up! We don't care about being fair."

"If you want to see the doctor tomorrow, don't make trouble," Taveley says wearily.

"Me?" The black eyebrows lift to even sharper points. "I'll be a lamb." He's wearing them out with his talk. Even wounded and bleeding, he's enjoying baiting them.

"You'd better be," Randall sneers, but Taras can see he's happy to be leaving. The Bolshie's making him feel stupid.

"Could you just go now," Andrews says. "These are our prisoners. We'll take it from here."

"Yeah sure," Randall says. "But this guy needs to change his ideas."

"Yeah, and it's not your job, it's ours." Bullard looks ready to burst. "Bad enough we're landed with this new guy. I mean, he's obviously a troublemaker —"

"Lunatic, if you ask me," Randall says.

"Didn't."

"Oh." But now Randall can't leave it alone. "Still, how do you tell with these Ruthenians or Galicians, or whatever they are?"

"Yes, well," Andrews sounds very strained, "but crazy or not, we don't hold with bringing in a wounded man who hasn't seen a doctor."

"Come on," Taveley says. "Let's get out of here." He grabs the younger man's arm.

Randall turns to offer a salute to Andrews, but forgets that his bayonet is in the way. Bullard jumps aside, a hand shielding his face.

Taras can't help smiling.

"Private!" Andrews says. "That will be all."

"Sir!" Randall marches for the door. Taveley shrugs and follows him out.

"Christ's sake!" Bullard says. "Asshole almost took out my eye." He and Andrews light cigarettes and look around the room.

Andrews speaks in a low voice, but Taras hears. "You've got your flask, haven't you?"

Bullard points to his coat pocket. "Couple of slugs and we'll sleep like babies." They laugh. "Goddamn it, though, it's starting to give me a pain in my gut."

Interesting, Taras thinks: Bullard in pain. He turns from the guards to the new guy.

The prisoners are silent, unsure how to speak to the newcomer. He catches Taras's eye. Speaks in Ukrainian.

"You want to ask me what it's like, don't you?" Taras can't think how to answer. "Escaping, I mean. Don't you want to know what it's like?"

"I wouldn't mind. What is it like?"

"It's grand." The prisoner laughs, and for a moment Taras imagines a sharp wind and the scent of pine. "You know, just to be alone for a bit. In charge of your own body, your own thoughts. Once we got into the forest, it was like no one else existed. Just us and a million trees. Shall I go on?"

Taras nods. *"Proshu.* Please do. It's...very interesting."

"I've no idea how they snuck up on us. Oleh and Slava were making too much noise, that's for sure, and all of a sudden, Taveley's screaming not to move or he'll stick me with his bayonet." All eyes are on him now and he knows it.

"I suppose I shouldn't have laughed. I honestly thought no one would be that stupid. That unnecessarily brutal. Know what I mean?"

Taras is at a loss for a reply. This man seems to talk for the sheer pleasure of it. Not just to tell what happened, but to pin it down, analyze it.

"You see, then," the man goes on, "how even a wise and experienced person can sometimes be wrong. That pig's fart Randall got mad when I laughed, and before Taveley could even think about moving, Randall stuck me with *his* stinking bayonet."

Again he waits. Myroslav and Yuriy draw closer.

"What was that like?" Yuriy asks.

"It's awful to have your body sliced open! Your blood gushing out! I was terrified. And the pain! Christ! I wouldn't have believed it. I mean, I've been beaten up in my time, but this... Scientifically, I suppose it'll all turn out to be worthwhile, because I've never been stabbed before. So now I'll know."

Again he waits for a response. "I'll know to avoid it!" He laughs. A few people laugh with him, or smile, anyway. But they're a little afraid the guy is insane and will hurt himself with all this frenzied talk. Or hurt someone else.

"Don't worry about me. I'm probably in shock. I mean, I'm so amazed! And outraged! That Randall would do such a thing. Not that I liked him or trusted him up till then, but I never thought... Anyway, turns out the pig's fart never wounded a person before. God, he looked sick when he saw what he'd done. Snuck off and threw up. Oh now, here's something you should always remember. Watch where you chuck up. I mean, he had the whole goddamn forest and he puked on his boots!"

"Excuse me, friend," Myroslav begins.

"Name's Tymko," the newcomer says. "I come from near Kharkiv but I moved to Kyiv and then Ternopil. I've been a miner in Donetsk and worked on a farm in Halychyna. Drove a team to help supply the Austrian garrison at Peremyshl. Spent good money to get a man to arrange Austrian papers for me. Just think, if I still had Russian papers, I wouldn't be in this hole. But how could I tell them I had false papers?" He grins.

"Oh, and in Canada I've worked in a coal mine and on the Canadian Pacific Railway. I'm good at everything I've set my hand to. I've helped organize a union and a strike and —"

"Would you like a glass of water, Tymko?" Myroslav asks politely.

"Who are you then?" Tymko demands.

"I'm Myroslav. I teach school. I mean, I used to."

"Professor!" Tymko smiles. "Excellent! It would be very helpful if you could bring me water." When water comes, he drinks like a man who's been lost in the desert for a week. Or in the woods.

"You can get very thirsty in the woods in winter," he goes on. "Too little water is what turns your shit to stone. That and the lousy food. There's never enough bulk to keep things moving."

"Why aren't you in the guardhouse?" Yuriy asks.

"Too full. And they were probably afraid I'd beat up the other guys for making noise and giving away where we were. But you know what? I wouldn't have. I would only have talked to them about it."

Taras looks around and sees others also wondering which would be harder to take – getting beaten up, or the thorough scolding Tymko would have given them. Not that he's in any shape for beating people up.

Yuriy walks over to the guards, who've been watching Tymko hold court, and asks something. At first the guards don't move. Then Andrews comes over to Tymko's bunk, offers him a hand-rolled cigarette and even lights it for him.

"Thank you," Tymko says in English, and sucks the smoke deep into his lungs. "This will help me sleep." Andrews shrugs and walks away.

"This is the great thing in Canada," Tymko goes on in Ukrainian. "They stick you with a bayonet one moment and offer you a cigarette the next. Keeps you on your toes. Keeps you interested in life."

He smokes the cigarette to a blackened scrap and grinds it out on the floor. Looks around the room as if he's trying to memorize every person and every thing in it. Nods at the men nearest him: Myroslav, Taras, Yuriy, Ihor. Bohdan the carver.

"Good to meet you all," he says. "We'll be friends, I think."

Without another word he glances sideways at the worn and grimy pillow, then at his boots. His head drifts downward, and Taras jumps up and lifts his booted feet onto the bunk. When Taras starts to unlace the heavy work boots, Tymko dismisses him with a wave of the hand.

"I'll rest now," he says. "Tomorrow, we'll see." Yuriy throws the blanket over him. Moments later he's so lost to the scene around him that he could be mistaken for dead, except for his raspy breathing. Taras hopes the man's mind is far away, in some beautiful place of his dreams. He hopes the bleeding's stopped.

Other men turn in and Taras gives up on his letter. Andrews and Bullard take a final look around the room and go out into the night, locking the door behind them. Taras wonders what he'd do if one night they forgot to lock it.

He notices Zmiya, huddled in his bunk at the end of the room, staring out the frosted window at the moon, cat's eyes glinting in the frozen light.

CHAPTER 5

Would you go back?

A WEEK LATER the prisoners notice that Taveley and Randall are gone from camp, replaced by a couple of baffled looking reservists who barely know which end of their rifles to pick up. Word spreads that they've been sent to another camp. Is it because Tymko was stabbed? Tymko says yes: bayonetting prisoners doesn't look good. Ship out the guys who did it. Out of sight, out of mind.

Taras sits on his bunk that evening trying to finish the letter he was writing the day Tymko came. Bud Andrews stopped him earlier in the evening, in the supper line: an interpreter has been found. Mail is starting to flow. At first Taras thought he'd get letters from his parents right away, but Andrews says it won't happen that fast. Huge piles of mail have to be checked.

Taras reads the few lines he's managed to put down, trying to think what to say next. Nothing comes. A dark shadow forms in his gut that tells him his letters will never be received or answered. He wants to cry like a child.

The men clumped around the stove arguing – Myroslav, Yuriy, Tymko, Ihor – are getting louder. They're always arguing. Ihor doesn't say much, but he listens so hard it's almost like talking. Each voice, each vocabulary, is a little different according to the region they come from. Taras understands why they argue. Because it's something to do, because they have such diverging opinions and because it creates something almost like warmth.

Because all this has to mean something.

Tonight they argue about whether Ukraine will ever become a free and independent country. There is no doubt in Myroslav's mind. His eyes look hard and bright as he confronts Yuriy.

"Ukraine *will* be a country one day. No question."

Taras likes his certainty. When Myroslav speaks with conviction, it's hard not to get swept along by him. He speaks well, and by now he's become part of their group and they all know his story. His father was a teacher, so he went to school longer than most children in his village in the province of Halychyna. In Canada he went to university. Not many Ukrainian Canadians have done that, but Myro always knew he would. He is living proof that they can learn and change.

"I'll believe it when I see it," Yuriy says defiantly.

This is how they go on. Yuriy has also told his friends his story. How he grew up near Kamyanets-Podilsky, a town a thousand years old, built on an island of rock high above a river.

"You can only get there one way," he explained. "You have to cross a narrow bridge of rock." He explains that this made it a natural fortress coveted by the Poles, Turks and Russians who have ruled it in turn for a thousand years. The Russians were in charge when Yuriy lived there.

Still, after all that time, all those rulers, people knew they were Ukrainians. So for Yuriy to be so skeptical about a free Ukraine makes you stop and think. Yuriy left his birthplace as a youngest son who would never inherit land. Went to Bukovyna and worked at anything he could get; became a peddler going from village to village. Got married and became an Austrian citizen. Like Tymko, he came to Canada with what turned out to be the wrong papers.

"So that's your answer," Myroslav says. "Ukraine will never be a country."

Yuriy looks embarrassed. "Okay, maybe I do believe Ukraine will be a country. No, more than that – it is a country. I already live in it. In my mind, you know?"

"Lucky fellow," Tymko says. "What's it like?"

Yuriy thinks. "It's solid, my Ukraine. It feels good around me. Like a warm, well-built house." His face relaxes and his eyes shine with tears.

"Excellent description," Tymko says. "Every Ukrainian should have a little poetry in him."

Ihor smiles and nods his head.

"It holds Ukrainians from many territories. Some Polish, some Austrian, some Russian. Different kinds of people, but all of them Ukrainian. Wherever they happen to be. When they meet, they know each other."

Taras tries to figure out what kind of country this would be. A country in his imagination, perhaps. Like a beautiful painting of golden fields, green, swaying trees, pleasant, healthy people. A lovely picture of a country.

"But a country the whole world agrees is a country?" All at once Yuriy looks tired. "I don't know if that's going to happen."

"I believe it right now." Myroslav gets his teacher look.

"Why do you believe this, Professor?"

Tymko puts extra weight on the word "Professor," as if to say that formal education isn't worth a whole hell of a lot in this place. He's recovering well, judging by his fierceness in arguments. The doctor from Banff has been in to stitch up the wound and bandage it properly. Amazingly, Bud Andrews came by one night to give Tymko some extra food. A tin of sardines and a package of English biscuits. He must have bought them in town. He handed them to Myroslav so Tymko wouldn't have to thank him. Good thing, because Tymko couldn't say a word when he saw them. He liked the sardines but said the biscuits were *pokydky*. Of course he ate them all the same. Who wouldn't?

Taras is still getting to know him. He gets puzzled sometimes by Tymko's sudden shifts in topics or moods, but he has to admit it wakes him up.

Tymko knows how to make people listen. Taras wouldn't call him a bully, but he uses his strength, obvious even in his wounded state, and the power of his voice to nudge a man off balance, so he forgets the clever comment he was going to make. Although he's now an atheist, Tymko has admitted that in the old country, as a young man, he was a cantor, singing church services in a deep bass voice.

"*Well,* Professor?"

"*Well,*" Myro says, "I believe this because my heart tells me you can't keep a people down forever."

"Your heart doesn't enter into it, Professor. It will happen, or it won't." Tymko waggles his eyebrows, a mannerism they've all grown used to, designed to put an opponent off balance. Or make him laugh.

"Really? I think it does enter into it. And quit calling me Professor," Myro says, good-naturedly. "I taught little kids arithmetic."

"So what do you think, Tymko?" Yuriy asks. "Will we some day have a country?"

Taras sees Yuriy wants to believe it's possible although he doesn't always side with the professor. Myro is skinny and wears glasses. Yuriy's used to judging people by physical strength as well as cleverness.

"Sure. Absolutely. Free Ukraine, in the service of the people." Tymko's Ukrainian, formed in the east, in Russian-ruled territory, has a harder, more guttural sound. A Russified sound, to the others' ears.

"A socialist state, you mean?" Myro asks. "But would it be a democracy? Like in Canada?" In Halychyna, Myro's dad was a social democrat.

"Canadian democracy. Very good. Look where that's got us. Professor."

Yuriy laughs. "Suppose Ukraine *was* a real country. Free. Democratic. Would you go back, Myro?"

"I would go in a moment. Ukraine would need teachers." Taras likes listening to Myro's voice. Likes what he's saying. "Maybe not to stay, but I would go to help anyone who wanted to learn."

"Tymko?"

Tymko considers. "A real country? All of us together? No more Austrian, Polish, Russian masters?"

Yuriy nods. "It would have to be like that or it wouldn't be a country."

"Sure. I'd go. There'd be so much to do. What about you?" Tymko watches the young man with real interest. Scientific interest, he calls it. He says everything can be studied scientifically. Everything can be understood.

Yuriy looks abashed, as if he hadn't realized the question could be turned back on him. "Once, maybe. To see the old town again. See the river."

"That's all?" Tymko's voice is carefully neutral, but there's a faint tinge of disapproval in the words: *What kind of Ukrainian are you?*

"I want to go back to my farm in Saskatchewan. I can make it a good place." No one speaks. "I'm a farmer now, not a peasant."

Myroslav looks disappointed. "There's a difference?" Yuriy doesn't answer.

Tymko only watches. Taras sees him weighing this information. After all, everything can be studied, and that includes people. He turns to Taras.

"What about you?" Startled, Taras grabs his letter. "Yes, you, the one writing a nice letter to his mommy and daddy."

"What about me what?" He knows but wants time to think.

"Would you go back? If Ukraine were free?"

Taras thinks so long the other men look impatient. He doesn't talk much lately; maybe he's losing the knack.

"So?" Tymko says.

"No," Taras says at last. "I'm never going back."

"Why not?" Myroslav asks. "Wouldn't you want to live in your own country? Your own village?"

"No. I couldn't live there again."

"Really? So tell us," Tymko says. "Tell us your story."

"Yes," Myroslav says. "Tell us why you came to Canada."

"And how you ended up *here*," Yuriy adds.

"I'd like to hear that," says Ihor. *"Proshu."* He moves his chair closer to the group.

Taras tries to laugh it off. Tymko's peaked brows squeeze together as if he can frown Taras into doing what he wants.

Myroslav smiles as he might to a child having trouble with adding and subtracting, Ihor nods wisely and Yuriy's look says, *Come on. Tell us a story.*

Tymko nods: *Begin now.* It seems no one's going to be satisfied until he does.

"It's nothing you haven't heard before –"

"Maybe," Tymko says. "We want to hear it from you."

Taras shifts his weight on his bunk, trying to find a smooth spot. Maybe they really want to hear, God knows why. "All right," he says, but no words come.

The space around him begins to change, seems not quite so cold. Four Ukrainians want to know his story. He'd never have known any of them except for the camp, but they're his family in this place; he hadn't realized until this moment.

He tries to decide where to start. No simple answer to that. Then words come from somewhere, as if they've been waiting to be spoken. He takes a deep breath, sighs and lets them flow out of him.

"It all started the day the big trucks came to the village. Spring, 1914. Drenched Monday. We were throwing water at the girls." The first sentences come out fine. Taras feels them hanging in the air, as if they came from someone else.

"What was your village?" Myroslav asks encouragingly.

"Shevchana, in Bukovyna. Thatched-roof houses on either side of a long lane, trees around the houses. Gardens, orchards behind. Fields all around."

"The usual, then," Tymko says. "Anything else?"

"We had a stave church. Everything wooden. Domes painted bright green. People came from other villages to see it. From the city, even."

"Tavern?" Yuriy asks.

"Of course, what do you think? And a reading hall and a black-smith shop. And a landlord everybody hated. It was the kind of day I'd forgotten about. I had to work hard, but I could walk around as I wished, stop and talk to a neighbour if I wished. I had enough to eat. I was warm. Everyone knew me. Most of the time,

I thought I was free."

The other men sigh. Good, this must be what they wanted.

"So I'll begin?" They all nod. "Well, first of all, did I say that a lane goes through our village, and near the centre of it people often stop to talk?" They nod again, a little impatiently. "And now I'll tell you what was happening there about a year and a half ago. Oh, did I say it was Drenched Monday?"

"Yes!" the others shout, and there's no turning back now.

DOBRE. It was Easter Monday, 1914. A half-dozen young men and boys, their arms around each other's shoulders, shouted and danced in a circle. Several others balanced on *their* shoulders – all of them showing off for several girls who just happened to be in the lane at the same moment. The boys were getting up their nerve for drenching people. Drenching girls.

I was watching them with my friend Ruslan, each of us holding a small jug of water, and we called out to the dancers: "Hey! Danylo!" and "Faster, Roman!" Ruslan was almost a year older than me, and he was already doing his service in the Austrian army. But he'd been given leave to come home for Easter.

A young woman called Larysa strolled by. Larysa is really pretty. She has dark hair, almost black, and eyes that look a little bit blue and a little bit green, with really long eyelashes. Anyway, Ruslan leapt up and splashed her. She shrieked and ran away – but not very far. He ran after her and put his arm around her waist. Larysa opened her hand and held out an egg dyed with a blue-and-red design. She put it in his hand – gently, as if it were a living thing and that life could be crushed in a second.

THE MEN SIGH. He's just described an old Ukrainian custom that must date all the way to pagan times. They've almost all taken part in something similar. Taras continues.

THE DANCERS whirled, building speed until I thought they'd spin off into the sky. Then Danylo in the top row lost his balance and the rest of them tried to hold on, but everyone tumbled to the ground, shouting and laughing.

Ruslan and Larysa moved away a little to talk, and I had a plan of my own. I walked down the lane, the sun warm on my face, and stopped near a house that was a little bigger than the others. Its whitewash was fresher, its wattle fences neater. I looked in the window.

I saw my dear Halya, forming loaves of bread, kneading and patting them until she got the exact shape she wanted. She worked with all the care of our friend Bohdan when he makes his carvings. I've loved Halya since we were children in school, and she looked so serious patting that bread, so neat with her hair braided and wound around her head, that I wanted to hold her and kiss her. Make her forget bread dough.

Halya's grandmother, Natalka, was working at her loom near the *peech*. Natalka wove the best linen, everyone said so, and her movements were still tidy and quick, even though her hands were knotted from arthritis. She raised Halya after her mother died. She's tall for a woman, with a stern look. I think I can say she likes me.

There didn't seem to be anyone else in the house. I decided that Viktor – Halya's father – must be in the fields. *Dobre.* Not even he could watch her every second. Viktor hated me. He wanted Halya to marry anyone else. Well, anyone else with a lot of money.

I crept in the open door. Halya didn't see me at first, but Natalka did. I flung my jug of water at Halya. She shrieked and giggled, and pretended to be cross. She looked beautiful and I can still see the clear drops of water beading on her linen *sorochka*.

Natalka burst out laughing. Halya looked up at a high shelf and I saw a decorated egg. She reached for it.

And suddenly there was Viktor in the doorway. He must have been lurking around behind the house, guessing that I couldn't stay away on this special day. He flung himself at me, shoved me to the floor. Halya screamed. The clay jug shattered.

"Get out of my house!" Viktor yelled. I got up, ready to fight.

"Taras, no!" Halya cried.

Viktor and I glared at each other, hands fisted, and Viktor spat a gob of phlegm on the side of the *peech*. I could see Halya felt ashamed that her father had done such a coarse thing.

And this was the man who thought he was above the others in the village. Who'd be a landlord if he could. A *pahn*.

I saw that Halya wanted me to go, and I slipped past Viktor. In the lane I saw the young people laughing in the square and then I heard a hard slap and a cry. I knew I had to get her out of there. I'd heard that Viktor had been seen lately with an older man from the next village. Lys they called him – fox – because of his pointed chin and red-gold hair. He had a large farm and a fine house and was a widower with no children. A perfect husband, Viktor would think.

I heard a deep rumbling noise and turned to see huge trucks racing up the rough road to the village. I'd seen trucks before, of course, in the city of Chernowitz, but no one in the village had one. The pahn had a motor car, which he sometimes drove to the city to attend a concert, but none of this had anything to do with me.

I knew right away that these trucks had something to do with me.

And then they were in our lane, gears grinding as they slowed down. Four big trucks from the Austrian garrison at Chernowitz, the truck boxes full of soldiers in grey uniforms. Their roar echoed in the lane, slammed against the houses. People rushed to their front doors, including Natalka, Viktor and Halya. In moments the air was filled with a haze of dust.

Now I'd heard rumours in the tavern, about trouble brewing in Bosnia. The Austrians ruled it, but the Serbs wanted it. So did the Turks, because there were Muslims in Bosnia. The talk was that the Austrians were planning to give the Serbs and the Turks a scare and then they'd both back down. War would be averted.

Of course, everyone knew that the Serbs and the Turks might not back down. Ruslan had already told me that people around the garrison believed something was going to happen. Now it felt as if war had already come. As if it had always been there somewhere, like a shadow waiting to find a shape and a colour.

Then the trucks were gone as quickly as they'd come. Dust still hung over the lane. The army must have been doing some training exercises in the countryside. And on the way back to the garrison, I think they wanted to remind people they were around. Let them know things were changing.

THE MEN SIT QUIETLY. Each man remembers a time when he began to realize a great war could happen. But most of them lived in Canada by then, so it wasn't quite as close to them.

"Don't stop now," Yuriy says. "I was just getting interested."

"It's late," Taras says. "Most of the men have gone to bed."

"Tell us more tomorrow, then," Myro suggests. "After supper."

"That's right," Tymko says. "It'll be more exciting if we have to wait."

Taras's friends drift away, but he can't stop the flood of bright images. Moments ago he hadn't known he had a story. Now's he's in a world filled with sunshine, glancing off the people, the houses, his darling Halya. He's living in the story.

He sees himself working at the anvil under his father's eye, shaping a red-hot horseshoe with clanging hammer strikes.

"Why does Viktor Dubrovsky hate me?" he asks, giving the shoe a whack.

"Not so hard! Go too fast, you spoil it." Mykola is tall and powerful and always seems in charge of himself and his life. Others may bluster or rage or brag or drink too much, but Mykola tries to live his life with care, like iron worked until it's right.

"Why does Halya's father hate me? Why won't you tell me?"

"Don't stop! Go too slow, you spoil it." Mykola makes a show of checking the fire in the forge.

"Why, Batko?" Taras strikes too hard and the shoe splits in two glowing red halves. Mykola grabs the tongs and puts the pieces back in the hot coals. Taras waits for an answer.

"Because you're my son." He points to another shoe ready to be shaped. "Work on that one." Taras pulls out the second shoe.

"Why does he hate *you?*" Taras works more carefully now.

"He thinks I'm a dangerous socialist. A revolutionary."

"And are you?" Taras gives his father a serious look.

"Keep your eye on the shoe!" Mykola watches Taras shape the iron. When he's satisfied with the work, he turns the question back to Taras. "What do you think?"

Taras smiles. "No."

"So why ask?" He sees Taras lift the hammer. "Stop, that's just right." Mykola picks up the red–hot shoe, plunges it into a barrel of water. A cloud of steam rises. He pulls out the shoe. "There...beautiful."

"Batko, I love Halya Dubrovsky."

"Do you?" Mykola sighs. "Well, you're young yet...things could change."

"They won't. My love's strong. Like iron."

"This iron's been tested in fire. Have you?"

Taras shrugs. "I've nearly finished training Radoski's horse... I'm going to have a little money soon."

Mykola raises his eyebrows. "Wait until you have the *pahn's* crowns in your hand. Then you can say you've got money."

"When I do, I'm going to marry Halya."

"Yes, well...we'll see. Meeting at the reading hall tomorrow. I'd like you to be there."

Taras grins. "We'll see."

Mykola gives his son a hard look but keeps his peace.

Later Taras leads a black stallion out into the lane in front of the smithy. The animal's Thoroughbred and Arabian lines show in his slim but strong build and arched neck. He moves like living smoke. Taras's foot reaches for the left stirrup and he seems to float into the saddle. The signal to begin is an almost invisible forward movement of his body. They set off down the lane. Taras takes the horse through walk, trot, canter and gallop, smooth as butter. Brings him to a sudden stop, turns him in tight circles and resumes the walk.

Beyond the village they climb a high green hill, and an old trail takes them into dense birch forest just coming into leaf. The horse drifts through the trees, birds sing all around them, and Taras wants the ride to go on and on. But Imperator belongs to the *pahn,*

Radoski. Taras has been schooling the horse for a month, and soon he'll have taught the stallion everything he can. Then he'll have to give him back.

Taras's way of training depends on trust. A lot of what he knows came from Batko, who learned to train horses in the Austrian army, but some of it he figured out himself. Mostly he helps the horse not to be afraid. He learns what the horse needs and how it thinks — which is not the way a man thinks. He's been working all this out since he was a child.

He doesn't want to give this horse back. The *pahn* will ruin him. So he won't talk about the stallion's speed. The *pahn* would think he should whip him to make him go fast. Taras has never hit a horse. He'd be ashamed to.

Anyway, if Imperator ran flat out, Radoski could never stay in the saddle.

Imperator. What a stupid name. Taras takes him through the gaits again and through another series of tight turns, first to the right, then to the left, weaving through the slender trees. Over time their work together has changed the horse. He can do things he would never have done on his own. He seems to enjoy doing them.

Taras loves this horse, not as much as his mother or father or Halya, but close.

He comes out of the trees, reins in the horse and looks down at Radoski's sprawling house and grounds. An old man tends the lawn; its close-clipped blades catch the morning light. Beech and birch show fresh new leaves and a few flowers already bloom. In the distance a motor growls and moments later an Austrian army staff car races up the road in a cloud of dust. The old man jumps back, startled. A dog barks and is hushed as the car skids to a stop. The *pahn* comes out his front door, dressed in an ancient officer's uniform, now bursting at its seams.

The driver jumps out and opens the door for a man in the blue uniform still worn by many older officers. This is the man Radoski brags about in the village. "My brother-in-law, you know — General Loder."

Radoski puffs out his chest as he lunges for the general's hand

and kisses the general's cheek. Everyone knows Loder is not exactly his brother-in-law. Their wives are cousins. In the village there were rumours that Sophie Radoski's family tried to prevent the marriage. Taras can't imagine what she could have seen in him. *Pahns* must have been thin on the ground then. People also say his mother promoted the marriage. Now that she's long dead, though, others question whether Radoski had a mother at all.

With another badly executed bow, the *pahn* ushers the general into the house. Now, why has the general bothered to come all this way for an awkward handshake and a kiss on the cheek? Can this be where the garrison soldiers are practising their skills?

Taras turns Imperator back into the woods.

CHAPTER 6

A horse like living smoke

THE NEXT EVENING Taras's friends grab him right after supper and let him know they wouldn't object to hearing a little more of his story. So he tells them about Imperator and about the *pahn,* and then stops. Myroslav urges him to continue.

"All right, if you want. The next part is about Batko going to the tavern."

"Were you there?" Yuriy asks. Taras shakes his head. "How can you tell us then?"

"From what my father, Mykola, told me. I'm making a story about it."

Yuriy's not satisfied. "But if you weren't there?"

"I can see it all very clearly. Still, if you don't want to hear..."

"I don't know about all of you," Tymko says, "but I could sure as hell use a story to take my mind off this place." They nod agreement, Yuriy included.

MYKOLA WALKED to the village tavern, a plain wooden building down the hill from the church, with his friend Yarema Mykytiuk, a man in his forties with a smooth, round face and blue eyes. His brown hair was carefully trimmed, his clothing neat. He had an agreeable look.

In the lane, laughter and lamplight spilled into the dark.

"Maybe this isn't a good idea," Yarema said. "We won't be able to hear ourselves talk."

"That's all right, they won't be able to hear us either." Mykola threw open the door.

About twenty drinkers sat around a half-dozen wooden tables. Mykola and Yarema found a small table beside an old poster they'd seen countless times, advertising Cunard Lines ships and the Canadian Pacific Railway. And the advantages of moving to Canada.

Isaac Stern, the owner, walked by with a tray of beer and they followed his steps to a nearby table where Halya's father Viktor sat with a man from the next village. Andriy Kondarenko was a tall, taciturn fellow about Viktor's age, known as a capable farmer and a man to be avoided if you had a choice. Now how had they wound up together? Viktor didn't normally come here, in part because no one ever wanted to sit with him, and also because he hated to spend money unless it made him look important.

Isaac placed the beer on the table and Viktor took out his purse.

"Viktor Dubrovsky is buying Kondarenko a drink," Yarema said in mock wonder.

"Who says miracles don't happen nowadays?" Mykola replied.

Two men at the next table overheard him and laughed, slapping their thighs. Pavlo and Lubomyr Heshka, twin brothers in their thirties who shared the small holding they inherited from their parents, looked more than a little drunk.

"Pavlo!" Lubomyr almost choked on his drink. "Who ever thought we'd be present at a miracle?"

Pavlo crossed himself. "Pavlo and Lubo, a couple of peasants. We are blessed."

Viktor saw them laughing. He couldn't have heard their words, but he gave them a dirty look on general principle. The laughter died down, and for a moment Mykola and Yarema could make out the carefully lowered voices of Viktor and Kondarenko.

"I'll need a few days. I have to borrow some of it." Kondarenko.

"Make it quick. I don't have a lot of time." Viktor.

The twins were listening too. "What's Dubrovsky selling?" Lubomyr asked.

Pavlo grinned. "Whatever it is, you know who'll come out ahead. He'd cheat his best friend."

"Viktor has no friends," Lubomyr said. They nearly fell out of their chairs laughing.

"Never mind friends, then. He'd cheat his own mother."

"His mother's dead."

"She was lucky to get away," Pavlo said. He saw that his beer was almost gone and that this would be a good time to go home. "God, nothing ever changes in this place."

Lubomyr noticed Mykola and Yarema reading the railway company poster.

"Yarema," he asked, "what do you think? Should we all go to Canada?"

"Why not? They say the streets are paved with gold." But Yarema looked skeptical.

"I could have almost as much land as Radoski," Lubomyr said. "I'd have respect. I'd be a new man."

"New man!" Pavlo said. "Are you crazy? What are you going to do with the old one?" He laughed as only a drunk person who's made a little joke, and is pleasantly surprised that he's been able to manage it, can laugh.

The twins kept getting louder and Viktor was getting annoyed. He drained his beer and pulled back his chair. "We'll talk again. Right now I want to get out of here. I'm going where I won't have to drink among fools!"

Pavlo and Lubo heard, as they were meant to. "At least we've got friends!" Lubo said, then wondered for a moment if that was really true; they always sat alone in the tavern.

Viktor spoke in a low voice to Kondarenko. "Let me know. Soon."

Lubomyr checked to see if Isaac was watching – not that he'd care – and took down the tattered handbill. He rolled it up and tucked it away under his vest.

"In Canada," he said again, "I could be a new man."

Viktor saw the poster vanish and a look crossed his face, a mix of startled outrage and a desperate need to keep silent. Mykola saw it all, wondered what it meant. Yarema too.

Now why did Viktor care about that poster? And what was he selling Kondarenko?

"I don't understand," Yuriy says. "Why was Viktor in the tavern if he didn't like going there?"

Ihor looks thoughtful. "I think there was something going on that he didn't want his daughter to know. Or Natalka."

"Is there more?" Tymko asks a little impatiently.

"There could be, I suppose," Taras says. But he's willing to stop. It's not as easy as they seem to think to organize all this stuff in his head. He could just stop and smoke.

"I'm curious about that horse," Ihor says. "I sure don't like to see a good horse ruined. What happened there?"

Taras smiles. "All right, I can tell you that part. The day after my father went to the tavern I was working at the smithy, getting ready to take Imperator back to the *pahn*. When I had him saddled, I couldn't put it off any longer and I led him into the lane. At that very moment, an officer from the Chernowitz garrison happened to ride through the village on a bay mare —"

"What? You remember the *horse* he was riding?" Tymko asks in disbelief. Tymko is clearly not a horseman.

"Of course, doesn't everybody?" Taras asks innocently.

"Can't we let Taras continue?" Myroslav says. "I'd like to know more about this officer." Tymko makes a sort of huffing sound, but he shuts up.

"*Dobre.* Well, the officer reined in the mare right in front of me, blocking my way."

"What did he look like?" Tymko wants to know. Probably so he can tell what political class to assign the officer to.

"Reinhard Krentz," Taras settles in to the telling, "was a well-groomed man, tall and muscular, with an air of command. He wore the pike-grey Austrian uniform, and his hat was a kepi, a flat-topped cap with a visor. His blonde hair was smooth, his moustache carefully clipped. He greeted me in accented but decent Ukrainian.

"So what does a peasant need with such a fine horse?"

"He's not my horse," I answered. "And don't call me a peasant." All right, I didn't say the last part, but he could probably see me thinking it.

"Good. I want him."

"He belongs to *Pahn* Radoski. You'll have to speak to him, Colonel." I had a feeling Radoski might not be one of his favourite people, although he was sure to have met him.

"Dobre, it's as good as done."

"Maybe not, Colonel. The *pahn* doesn't like to give up anything he owns."

"Very well, we'll see."

I gave him a pleasant nod, mounted Imperator, rode around the mare and trotted down the lane. Krentz waited a moment, then followed me on the bay. I pretended not to see.

At the crest of the village hill, I saw a dark grey horse in the distance, glowing in the sunlight, tail feathered by the wind. Imperator reared high and when I looked again, the grey horse was gone. I galloped Imperator down the hill. Imagining things. Daydreaming. What would Batko say? I took the trail through the forest and was soon in sight of the *pahn's* yard.

I rode up to the house and dismounted. Radoski appeared in the doorway, smiling in a sneering sort of way. He wore an embroidered vest over a linen *sorochka* and billowing trousers. Sometimes he liked to amuse himself by wearing Ukrainian things. The village women hated making them, but they always needed the money.

"So, young man, what do you want at my house?" He knew very well. "Have you finally finished training my horse?"

"Yes, Pahn, your horse is ready." I remembered what my father had said and imagined for a moment not getting paid. But I had to stay strong, because I needed his money if I wanted to get married. "Please give me my money."

"Not so fast. How do I know he's properly trained?"

"Let me show you." I prepared to remount.

Radoski grabbed my arm. "I'll see for myself. Give me a hand."

I helped him mount. Radoski yanked the reins, dug his heels hard into Imperator's flanks. This was as bad as Viktor spitting on the *peech*. He must have thought he'd spook the horse and then make a big show of bringing him under control. The great rider. He galloped across the lawn, turned back to the house and pulled hard on the reins to stop short. I could almost feel the bit dig into my own mouth. Imperator snorted and pawed the ground.

"He still needs to know who his master is." Radoski dismounted, laughing as though he'd made a clever remark. I felt sick, and there wasn't a single thing I could do. I knew he was planning to say I hadn't done a good job training Imperator – so he could pay me less.

Then I saw a man riding up the road. Krentz, of course, on the bay mare. He came right up beside Imperator. As he dismounted, Radoski waved his hand at me like I was some bothersome fly. "Go away. We'll talk another time."

"Dobre dehn, Pahn," Krentz called out.

Radoski looked startled at being greeted in Ukrainian. Of course, he was wearing Ukrainian clothes, so what did he expect?

"That's a fine horse you have there." Krentz sounded like the perfect Austrian officer, respectful but sure of himself even in the company of a *pahn*.

Radoski puffed up with pride. "Look at that noble head." He said this in German. "This is a horse a prince would be proud to ride. Or a general. Or an emperor!"

"Indeed," Krentz said. "And he's well trained?"

"Oh, uh yes. Reasonably so." I was still standing nearby, so he didn't like to say any more. Otherwise how could he argue for paying me less?

"May I?" Krentz took the reins from Radoski, mounted and rode away over the grass. Led the stallion through turns and stops without visible movement. Took him through various gaits and jumped him over an ornamental pool, then walked him back to the house.

All this time Radoski kept trying to shoo me away, but I pretended not to notice. If the *pahn* wanted to treat me like a stupid peasant, maybe I'd decide to be deaf, too.

"Trained?" Krentz said. "A little girl could ride him." He slipped off the horse.

"You ride extremely well." Radoski almost choked on the compliment.

"I try to ride like a gentleman." The *pahn's* head jerked. Had he just been insulted?

"Now, I need a horse and I haven't seen one I like better. Is he for sale?" Krentz took out his purse.

Radoski turned purplish-red, as if he was trying to pass a hard turd. I could see he wanted to keep this horse so much he could barely breathe. At the same time, he looked longingly at Krentz's purse because he was always short of money, being, as everyone knew, a bad manager. And he always liked to lick the boots of anyone high up in the army.

"I, uh, suppose we could talk." As soon as the words came out, Radoski looked like he wanted to bite off his tongue.

Krentz nodded in my direction. "Why is this young man standing about?" he asked pleasantly.

"He's from the village. An ill-bred fellow. I've told him to go." Radoski was obviously trying to think of a quick and simple way to kill me without anyone noticing.

"I've come to be paid, Pahn. For training the horse." I edged closer. I brushed Imperator's forehead to show him how well we got along, and the stallion touched his face to mine.

"Can't you see I'm busy?" Anger was making Radoski sweat a lot. He had beads of moisture on his forehead and dark patches on the embroidered vest. But he couldn't take the time to make me go. Krentz was after Imperator, but Radoski wasn't sure he wanted to sell.

"Your price would be what? Perhaps..." Krentz named a generous figure.

"That would be...uh...excellent." Radoski struggled to look as though he would have suggested the same figure himself, but it was clearly more than he'd have dared to ask.

"Good with horses, are you?" Krentz chatted to me, while Radoski was thinking.

"I hope so, Colonel."

Krentz turned to Radoski and fingered his purse. "Of course, if there are charges outstanding —"

"Don't worry," Radoski said. "There's nothing this oaf can do."

"Perhaps not. But as an officer of the Imperial army, I must be seen to respect the law." Krentz turned toward the bay mare.

"No, wait." Radoski pulled out his own purse and counted money into my hand. "Now get out of here."

I waited, my hand still out. "The price we agreed on..." With an evil look, Radoski gave me the rest. I imaged Halya watching, saw her smile.

"*Douzhe dyakuyiu,* Pahn. *Dobre dehn,* Colonel." I nodded to each man and began to walk away, very slowly. When I thought Radoski had forgotten me, I stopped and watched.

Krentz opened his purse. "Very good, Pahn. Now, I've taken a liking to your horse, and you've said my offer is 'excellent.' I think we have a bargain."

"What?" Radoski cried. "That was before I paid that lout." He noticed me watching. "Get out, I tell you, or I'll set the dog on you!"

I moved off a little further, but I could still see and hear everything.

"I'm sure the *pahn* would never go back on his word." Krentz looked grave.

Radoski's face got so red I thought his head might explode. "No, of course not." He seemed to be grinding his teeth. He was losing his horse, and looking bad in the bargain.

Krentz counted out the money into the *pahn's* hand. Radoski seemed to be trying not to cry. Krentz took hold of the bridle, stroked the horse's mane.

"You're mine now, my beauty." Krentz led the bay mare up to Imperator and the stallion edged closer to her, nuzzling her neck.

Holding her reins in one hand, Krentz mounted Imperator and took him into an easy walk as the mare kept stride. Called over his shoulder, *"Doh pobachenya, Pahn."*

I began to climb the hill above the house, but I couldn't resist looking back one last time as the *pahn* watched his wonderful stallion walk out of the yard. If I could ever have felt sorry for him, it would have been at that moment. But I couldn't. I admit I enjoyed it. And having the colonel speak to him in Ukrainian must have been the last straw. He kicked at a clump of dirt and smacked his big toe on a rock instead. He waved the toe in the air, holding back curses until it sounded like he was sobbing and cursing all at once. Still I felt no pity.

"My saddle!" Radoski almost strangled on the words. Krentz hadn't paid for the saddle! He looked around for someone to take it out on and saw his gardener.

"Sava!" he yelled.

I had walked almost up to the forest when Krentz caught up to me and asked if I wanted to ride the mare as far as the village. Naturally I said yes.

"I forgot to ask," he said, "what's my new horse's name?"

"Pahn Radoski called him Imperator." I tried not to let on that I thought it was a stupid name.

"Doesn't do him justice. Still, if that's what he's used to..."

We walked the horses through the trees, enjoying the warm sunshine. Back at home, I slid my money between two layers of backing behind the portrait of Shevchenko. Money that would help Halya and me when we got married.

"Douzhe dobre," Tymko says. "It's always satisfying to see a *pahn* thwarted."

"Yes, but wait a minute," Yuriy says. "Why is this fancy officer taking your part?"

"Maybe he hates Polish landlords," Ihor says. "That Radoski sure didn't deserve such a fine horse."

"A horse like living smoke," Myro adds.

Taras feels foolish. "All right, I made a mistake. I said my story started on Drenched Monday. The day the trucks came. I see now that it started before that."

"Aha!" says Tymko. "He tried to trick us. Explain yourself, young man."

"All right, it started more than four years ago. An officer of the Chernowitz garrison was riding near Shevchana when his horse, a grey gelding it was, threw a shoe."

"A grey gelding now, is it?" says Tymko.

"Good beginning," Ihor says.

"Now we're getting somewhere." Yuriy winks and everyone laughs.

"Was his name Krentz?" Tymko asks. "The officer, I mean, not the horse."

"Wait and see. So this officer led his horse into the village, looking for a blacksmith. Batko was in the fields, but I said I could help. I could see he wasn't sure he could trust me. He watched me lead the horse into the smithy and saw how I made friends with him. How quiet his horse stayed while I examined the hoof. He asked many questions to see if I knew what I was doing. I said I'd make a new shoe for his horse and began to build up the fire."

"Why don't you just use the old one?" The officer handed me the cast shoe.

I held it up for him to examine. "Many reasons. First – see these grooves? The shoe is worn and could break, hurting the horse. Also, the pattern of wear could throw his balance off. Then you don't get a smooth ride, and it could injure the horse's foot."

The officer nodded. "So that's it?"

"Also, look at the nail holes. They're too worn to hold the nails properly."

The man smiled. "You're not just saying that to earn more money?"

I was nervous, but I knew I was right. I looked him in the eye. "Maybe I'll earn more today, but you'll save money in the long run. If I put back a shoe that's no good, it's bound to come off sooner than a new one would and, again, it could damage his foot."

"Very well, young man, that sounds sensible." But he seemed to want to hear more.

"Also, I should trim the hoof first, and the old shoe may not fit the new shape."

He smiled. "Enough. I'm convinced. Let me see you work."

I didn't like other people watching me work, but I tried my best to forget the officer. Before I started, I brought the horse a bucket of water and an armful of hay. Then I cleaned and trimmed the hoof and filed the bottom smooth until, with a new shoe in place, I was sure it would match the other three feet and give the horse a balanced, comfortable way of going.

When the fire was right, I put a length of iron on the hot coals. When it was red hot, I grabbed it with tongs and placed it on the anvil. Then I did forget the officer and bent my mind to the fiery spirit in the iron. The smithy rang with sharp, quick blows until I'd made a rough match for the old shoe. I corrected the shape, seeing the newly trimmed hoof in my mind. Punched holes for the nails. I grasped the tongs, lifted the shoe and let it slide into the water. Steam made a small cloud around me.

I lifted the gelding's foot and set the nails into the shoe. The horse stood calmly all the while. I walked him around the smithy, checking his movement. When I saw that it looked right, I led the horse back to the officer.

He paid me and said, "Look here, I'm Colonel Krentz. With the Chernowitz garrison. We can always use men who are good with horses. I've got a new man just now, but I'm afraid I'm going to have to let him go."

I didn't see my father enter and neither did the colonel. "My son is fifteen years old, Colonel. Too young for the army."

Regret showed on Krentz's face. "I can conscript him in a few years, of course."

My father shrugged.

"What about a job then? I could use another man training horses this winter."

Batko nodded. "Perhaps I could spare my son during the winter months."

The bargaining began.

"THAT'S HOW I FIRST saw the city. The Austrian garrison and the Seminarska church and the monastery. The Armenian church and the synagogues. Cafés and pastry shops and clothing stores for rich people. Cobblers, peddlers, tinsmiths, harness makers. All these things were part of the country I lived in, but I'd never seen them before. Endless streets of grand buildings and the theatre sitting in a grassy square. I was out of the village and there was a whole world to see. I saw it, but I didn't forget Halya. I didn't go wild. I saved my money. I knew it would bring closer the day Halya and I could get married. Three winters I worked for the army, training horses and looking after their feet. I shouldn't say it, but Krentz always said I was the best." Taras can't help grinning.

"Yeah, yeah, quit bragging," Tymko says. "Get on with the story."

The smile leaves Taras's face. "Now we go back to 1914, the day after Krentz bought the *pahn's* horse. Several of us young men in the village got notices to report to the army – all of us who would turn nineteen that year. Usually you just had to report some time during the year, but the notice said we should report in two weeks. At first I tried to believe that since I had a job with them I might not have to go. That was crazy, because the army doesn't work like that."

"That night there was a meeting at the reading hall," Ihor says encouragingly.

Taras doesn't want to tell this part. He says he's too tired. The others grumble, but it's late and there will be plenty of other nights to endure in this place.

Yuriy hands him a candy bar and a small packet of cigarettes. They all chipped in to thank him for the story.

CHAPTER 7

Then ask yourselves:
Now who are we?

TARAS SITS ON A WIDE ROCK shelf in a forest clearing with men from his work gang. Fine snow sifts out of pearly sky, settles on coats and caps, eyebrows and moustaches. They keep close together, collars turned up against the wind. Maybe it helps. The weather's turned uglier, dipping down to twenty and thirty below zero. He can hardly believe he ever lived in a warm house with a big clay stove.

The sandwiches are frozen, as usual. He breaks off pieces and warms them in his mouth until he can chew them. He still hasn't had any letters. He shouldn't have thought about that: before he can stop it, a deep sob shakes his chest and he wants to tip over and sink into the snow. A man beside him leans over and pats his arm.

He doesn't want to go on with his story.

The guards seem in no hurry to make the prisoners get back to work. The new man in charge, Arthur Lake, takes his time, but seems to accomplish as much as others do by hurrying. His attitude is spreading to the other guards. Nobody says to pick up the pace or calls them slackers, at least not on this gang. Sometimes, for a little while, it feels as if they're all men together, longing to be free. Longing for hot coffee or tea. One of the internees raises his coffee cup in a mock salute and Taras hears a movement behind him, as Sergeant Lake, crouched behind his camera and tripod, prepares to take a photograph.

ARTHUR LAKE doesn't know why he has to do it. It's partly the way the mountains or the trees or the snow look at a certain time that may suddenly seem more significant than other similar moments in their long days. More important is how the prisoners look. This time it's the way they huddle along the stone shelf, shoulders almost touching, light seeping through the clearing between two wings of trees. The snow looks soft and gentle, but isn't.

He's tall and thin but also big-boned, with large feet and hands. His ears stick out and even his face is bony. Angular. He knows he looks awkward when he reaches to set up the tripod or bends to take the exposure, but his movements are practical and effective. Elegance is for others; but if he starts a task, he finishes it. His wife Winnie calls it his determinedness. Or, if she's annoyed with him, his pigheadedness. He attaches the camera to the tripod and looks for the image that will not only please his eye but will say whatever can be said of this time, this place. He'll know it when he sees it.

An internee glances his way, perhaps wondering why anyone is bothering to photograph a work gang. Many of the guards have wondered the same thing. "Can't you just take pictures of the mountains, for Christ's sake?" was one of the politer questions.

It slides off his back. He likes taking pictures. Especially compared with getting stinking drunk or falling into hopeless melancholy. As a career soldier, he's heard from old hands what combat is like and knows this isn't the worst spot a soldier could be during wartime. This allows him a patience with the world; allows him to look around, see how things fit together, try to avoid trouble. So he's never just marking time. Never forced to live on dreams of when he'll finally be somewhere else. As long as he's here, this is his life, and he intends to live it with all his attention. Besides, a day may come when people wonder about this place, ask questions. When these endless hours everyone wants to forget as soon as possible are remembered and examined.

He's not sorry to have met the prisoners. People have told him that Ukrainians are a hardy and a stoic people who came to Canada because things were impossible in the old country. Too little land, farms carved up over the generations; never-ending debt to former masters; industrial and artisan work scarce. He's heard that they had a desire for an independent country, which under Austrian rule could never happen. A passion for something to change because nothing in the old world was set up for their comfort or advantage.

They are stoic, but everything has a limit. Some Canadians think being stoic means a person lacks sensitivity to pain or hardship. Arthur Lake thinks these are just people, some cleverer or braver or more skilled than others, as in any place you go. They feel pain and loneliness and cold. And injustice.

Since he's here, he has to find a way to deal with it. He tries not to shout or ask for more work than a man can do. When the men come to him, one at a time or in groups, he tries to listen. He is not afraid to walk among them without his rifle.

Some men ask not to be photographed and he respects that. Others don't mind and a few even smile for the camera. Perhaps, like him, they think it's good to have some record of what goes on here. Soldiers or prisoners, they will remember this place the rest of their lives.

Arthur Lake takes the picture.

THAT NIGHT, in the lineup outside the dining hall, Sergeant Lake passes around a recently developed photograph: a long, curving line of prisoners, headed by soldiers and trailed at the end by soldiers, marches through a broad expanse of snow into a band of forest so dense you can't see into it. Taras feels himself pulled into its world. The men furthest away look so small, it rouses his pity, for himself and all of them. Snow falls and the line seems suspended between land and forest, yet driving ahead, soon to disappear, perhaps forever.

Yuriy nudges him. "Hand it over." Taras passes him the photograph and thinks that tonight his friends will ask to hear more of his story. It tells of a world where there are choices, however small, to be made.

IT'S YURIY WHO PERSUADES HIM to go ahead. He says it's helping him think about his own life, and about the old country. And he wants to know about the meeting Taras's father wanted him to attend. So do Myro, Ihor and Tymko.

"The meeting took place in Shevchana's reading room," Taras begins, "a plain wooden hall with handmade tables and chairs and shelves of books and newspapers. People who couldn't read were helped to learn by those who could. People who couldn't afford books or newspapers could find things to read. And sometimes they met to talk about political ideas. I was never interested in that, but my father was."

"Not interested in political ideas?" Tymko says. "What kind of life is that?"

"Anyway," Taras goes on, "there were societies like it in many villages. A portrait of the poet Shevchenko hung on a wall. My father, Mykola Kuzyk, stood in front of it, holding a newspaper. Others sat at tables, facing him. Sitting beside Ruslan's father Teofan, I was proud to see my father standing there."

"Wait," Yuriy stops him. "You said Mykola *Kuzyk*. I thought this man was your father."

"He is my father."

"But your name is Taras Kalyna," Ihor says. "That doesn't make sense."

"It will. Wait and see." Good, he's learning how this storytelling works. "So the meeting was called to discuss an idea of my father's, but people were also worried about their sons. As I said before, young men could be called up anytime in the year they turned nineteen, but they didn't have to report right away or sometimes even in that year. There was time to prepare. Suddenly the army seemed to be in a hurry.

"But the meeting began with my father's idea. He read them a newspaper article about how some villages had started co-opera-tive flour mills. He believed the people of Shevchana could do the same and that this could give the farmers a little more income."

"SEE HOW IT WORKS?" Mykola said. "Each man has a vote in run-ning the mill and gives some of his time. Each one brings his own grain to be ground and gives a portion of his flour to support the mill. No one makes a profit."

Several people nodded. But Lubomyr Heshka looked worried. "Radoski already has a mill. He'll get mad if we start one."

"He's always mad," Mykola said. "Nothing new there."

"*Tak,* but I owe him money," Lubomyr said. "And now he's settling for interest until harvest. What'll he do if I help set up a mill to compete with him?"

Yarema Mykytiuk got to his feet. "We need to work together, or we'll always have Radoski on our backs." When he said the *pahn's* name, it sounded like spitting.

A murmur ran through the room. They liked what Yarema was saying, but wondered, How do you get from here to there – to that better time when the *pahn* isn't on your back? How do you keep yourself and your family from getting hurt?

A very old man in rough, worn clothes, Ostap Vovchuk, stood to speak. His eyes were milky blue, almost blind, but they seemed to see more clearly than the eyes of many sighted men. His long white hair made a blazing cloud in the lamplight.

"You know I was born a serf. When I was a serf, I couldn't see a way to be anything different. But somehow I imagined a time when I might be free." There was a slight quaver in his voice, but the old fellow had their attention.

"Strange, isn't it? I didn't know what being free was."

"All right," Lubomyr said, "we're free now, but it doesn't always feel that way. Not when you owe money and your debt goes on year after year."

I began to wonder how late it was getting. I was hoping to see Halya that evening, at a place in the forest where we'd met before. I'd asked Larysa to speak to her at the village well that morning, and I was sure she'd come – if she could get away.

The meeting broke down into talk about freedom and debt and whether a war was coming. My father saw he wasn't going to get anywhere with a flour mill that night.

"Why do we have to give our sons to the emperor?" a middle-aged man called Zoran asked. "Does he ask us when to start a war?"

"No one asks us anything," Lubomyr said.

"He's kept us out of wars for a long time," said Hryhory, another old *dido*. "To be fair."

"*Tak,* and to be fair, it could all come to an end any time, whether we like it or not," Lubomyr said. He seemed suddenly to see his life in a new way. To see how sick he was of the village.

"I suppose we could always leave," Zoran said. "But how do we know it would be any better someplace else? We don't."

"Maybe not," Pavlo Heshka broke in, "but Viktor Dubrovsky's going to Kanady."

Everybody looked amazed, except for the other men who'd been in the tavern the night Viktor drank with Kondarenko.

I felt it like a blow to the gut.

I saw a bitter look cross Yarema's pleasant face. Kondarenko was going to buy Viktor's land. Land Yarema himself would have liked to buy.

Lubomyr pulled the immigration poster out of his vest.

Smoothed it and held it up for everyone to see. "Look. A man can get one hundred and sixty acres of land. For almost nothing. Why don't we all just sell up and go?"

"That's right," Pavlo said. "Why should Viktor have all the luck?" He tried to laugh it off, but it was obvious he hadn't heard that his brother was thinking about going anywhere. Of course, maybe it was the first time Lubo had thought about it.

"Have you ever got anything for nothing?" Mykola asked.

"Not in this life," Yarema said. "I think we can make things better here."

"Maybe," Lubomyr said, "but rich *pahns* don't sit back and let you take things from them."

"No," said Hryhory, who'd had to live on the uncertain charity of the village since he fell from a hay wagon and broke his leg, "they don't give up what they have."

"Listen to me," Ostap Vovchuk said. "Taras Shevchenko was born a serf. But he became free. He told us always to remember who we are." The old man pulled a book from his vest. It fell open in his hands, so worn it was a wonder it hadn't fallen apart. He held it as if it were a holy icon, and began to read.

Examine everything you see.
Then ask yourselves: Now who are we?
Whose children? Of what fathers born?
By whom enslaved in utter scorn?

The door of the reading hall opened as Ostap was reading the poet's words, and my friend Ruslan came quietly into the room and sat down near his father. Nobody said a word.

Teofan looked shocked, and afraid. There was no way Ruslan should be in this room. He must have left the garrison without permission. My dearest friend, always so neat and reliable, who never made trouble with anyone, had run away from the army. His face was covered in sweat, and he looked desperate.

He and his father whispered together. I heard Larysa's name. I heard him say he had to get married.

We all became aware of a commotion outside, something rhythmic, coming nearer every second. Ostap, who hadn't moved since Ruslan came in, began to read again.

Examine everything you see.
Then ask yourselves: Now who are we?

The door was thrown open. Six or seven soldiers burst in, led by a sergeant I'd seen around the garrison, Werner Schratt, a man nobody seemed to like. The army must have found him useful, though, because Ruslan said he always had charge of the new recruits.

Ostap went right on as though the soldiers weren't there.

Whose children? Of what fathers born?
By whom enslaved in utter scorn?

Schratt grabbed my father's newspaper from a table. "Socialist garbage!" he said. He tore it in half and threw it on the floor. It made me angry, but I kept still.

He was coming closer to us. Ruslan's hands shook, but he held his back straight.

Schratt picked up the immigration poster. "Lies! All lies. You leave here, you lose everything." He crumpled the poster and threw it down too. Ostap began again.

Examine everything you see.

The sergeant grabbed the book and tossed it to the floor. I could see hatred rise from the village men like steam, and Ostap continued from memory.

Then ask yourselves: Now who are we?

Teofan, who is Ostap's son, stepped forward and recited with him.

Whose children? Of what fathers born?

The sergeant tried to sneer, but the old man's dignity sobered him. "Nothing doing here, men," he said and headed for the door. "Just a bunch of peasants who think they're poets." The soldiers didn't think that was funny, since most of them were peasants.

Ruslan brushed off his *dido's* book and handed it back. Ostap held it to his heart.

The sergeant paused by the door and pointed at Ruslan. "Oh, and bring that one with you." The soldiers grabbed my friend. Ruslan struggled to free his arms.

"Let my grandson go!" Ostap shouted.

Ruslan continued to struggle, but the soldiers dragged him out the door. "Please," he begged. "I can't go yet! I'm getting married."

Everyone in the room, except Teofan, looked surprised.

"He *was* getting married!" The sergeant slapped his thigh at his own wit and they marched Ruslan away, Schratt's laughter echoing in the lane.

This was the thing with the Austrians. People said they weren't so bad, certainly better than the Poles. And probably that was so. But they had power over your life. I knew I'd never see them in the same way again.

Soon I'd be in the army, and Halya would be far away. What was I going to do?

"A BEAUTIFUL OLD MAN, that Ostap." Ihor says. "I wish I could have known him."

"What happened to Ruslan?" Yuriy asks.

"Nothing good," Tymko says. "You can bet on that."

"Did you get to see Halya that night?" Yuriy doesn't give up easily.

"All that is coming," Taras says. "But the story goes its own way." He hopes he'll find the right words to tell it.

"That's fair," Ihor says. "Everything will happen in its time."

"So. In a few minutes I came to a grassy clearing in the centre of tall beeches and Halya ran to me like a silver shadow in the moonlight. Her hair smelled like the forest." Taras hears somebody sigh. "We kissed so long we finally had to pull apart to get a breath."

"*Dobre,*" Yuriy says. "Now we're getting somewhere."

HALYA PULLED AN EGG from her pocket. In the pale light I could barely make out the curving lines that spiralled around it. It was the one she'd meant to give me on Drenched Monday.

"Thank you," I said. *"Tse chudoviy."* Beautiful.

"This kind of egg comes from long ago," Halya told me. "Baba showed me how to make it." We were still a bit short of breath and I wanted to kiss her some more, but I knew we had to talk.

"I made something for you, too," I said. I gave her a brass pendant shaped like the sun with slender rays flowing outward.

THIS IS TOO MUCH for the other men. "Where would you get something like that?" Yuriy says.

"They have jewellers in Chernowitz, you know," Tymko tells him.

"I didn't get it in Chernowitz. I made it."

"Made it?" Tymko says. "How?"

"I got the metal from broken harness brass, and I worked on it in the evenings. The sun part hangs from a brass wire that fastens with a loop at the back. It took me a long time to learn to draw out the wire without breaking it."

"I wish I could have seen that," Yuriy says.

"Well then, you can have your wish." Taras reaches under his shirt and pulls out a pendant just like the one he described. "I made one for each of us. Hers is just the same."

"Halya was right," Myro says. *"Tse chudoviy."*

"Thank you. Maybe I could go on now?"

"Please, do go on," Tymko says. "And I'll try to keep these ruffians from interrupting you again."

HALYA FASTENED the pendant around her neck under her blouse. *"Dyakuyiu,* my love."

I showed her my own pendant. We kissed again and held each other close, but in a moment Halya pulled away.

"I don't want them to take you for the army!"

"I know. But Halychka, there's something else. Your father's going to Kanady." She looked at me as if I was crazy. "I found out at the meeting in the reading hall."

I told her what I'd heard, and at first she thought the men who were at the meeting were crazy too. But when I talked about Viktor and Kondarenko in the tavern, she stopped shaking her head. Like everyone else, she knew her father didn't go there, and he certainly didn't buy other men drinks. And the more she thought about it, the more she realized that Viktor had been more secretive than usual lately. Just as if he were up to something.

What on earth could they do?

And then I told her about Ruslan.

We agreed that she'd come to the smithy in the morning. After I watched her into her house, I went back to the unlocked reading room and picked up the creased poster.

"SOUNDS BAD," Yuriy says. "What are they going to do?"

"Taras will have to join the army, and Halya will have to go to Canada," Ihor says.

"Yet he stands before us," Tymko says. "Well, he sits. How can that be?"

"Maybe they traded places," Myro said. "Halya joined the army and Taras came to Canada."

"I hope we'll know some day," Ihor says.

"I hope we'll know a bit sooner than that." Tymko winks.

"I could tell you what happens next, but you'd say I wasn't there."

"No," Myro says. "I don't think you have to worry about that. Just tell it." So he does.

HALYA CREPT into the silent house and heard Natalka snoring in her bed over the *peech*. A rough hand grasped her shoulder and flung her into the room as if she were a stuffed doll.

"You've been sleeping with Kuzyk's son!" Viktor snarled.

Natalka woke with a shriek and almost jumped down from her bed over the *peech*.

"I have not!"

Viktor slapped her face. "Don't talk back to your father!" He got ready to hit her again, but Natalka moved in front of him.

"My daughter's dead," she said fiercely. "I must speak for her child."

"Her child is a shameless slut!" Viktor said, but he looked a little ashamed at the mention of his dead wife. "She makes the whole village laugh at me!"

"No! They laugh because her father's a fool who can't forget the past."

"I warn you —" He stepped toward her, arm raised.

"You'd hit an old woman, would you?" Natalka stood tall. "Coward!"

For a moment Viktor couldn't believe his ears. He took a step toward her.

"Why shouldn't she marry Taras?" Natalka asked. "He's a good young man."

"His father's a revolutionary!"

"Pah! Kuzyk's no radical. Anyway, it's not the father she wants to marry!"

"Shut your mouth!" Viktor slapped Natalka across the face and she cried out.

Halya had been terrified a moment before, but now she stepped right up to Viktor.

"Is this how you're going to treat us in Kanady?" she asked. "When you've taken us away from every thing and every person we know? Every neighbour, every friend?" Her voice was like ice, and her eyes shone with fury. "Then you *are* a coward."

Viktor was stunned. Halya had never spoken to him that way. He'd planned to tell them, of course, at a moment *he* would choose. He'd never imagined it in any detail, only that they would see him as he saw himself. And now she'd taken away a little bit of his power. And made him feel almost guilty. He stomped out, muttering about "damned women."

Natalka was stunned too. What a terrible night, being struck in the face by that bully, and then finding out what he had planned for them.

Halya went to Natalka, stroked her grandmother's hair. "Baba, I'm so sorry."

"Why? You can't help that your father's an idiot."

In spite of everything they giggled nervously. Natalka put a finger to her lips.

"Just one thing. Before you marry Kuzyk's son, he has to promise he never lays a hand on you."

"He wouldn't —"

"*Dobre.* Because I'll kill him if he does."

Halya gave a snort of laughter. "I don't understand. Why is he doing this?"

"Well, I suppose he thinks going to Kanady would keep Taras away from you."

"Why would he need to do that? Taras will have to go in the army."

"Well," Natalka said, trying hard to imagine Viktor's motives, "people do say you can get a lot of free land in Canada. And Viktor's always liked the idea of having more of something than other people have. And also, maybe he thinks he'd get more respect. And he might, until the new people got to know him."

Halya almost laughed. "Isn't there anything we can do?" she said. "We can't just leave everything we know. He didn't even have the decency to tell us."

"What can we do? Well, I suppose we could say we're not going."

But he'd sell the house, the land. They could work for other farmers, doing housework, helping in the fields, but there's not much work for a young woman and her *baba* on their own. Not much money. Less respect.

"THAT WAS A BIT DISCOURAGING," Yuriy says. "Can you tell us a little more? Maybe something a bit happier? Then we can all go to bed."

"I could tell you about seeing Halya the next day. I suppose it's happy and not happy all at once. But it won't take long."

"Good," Tymko says. "That sounds all right. Life is never all happy or all not."

"Well, let's see, she was alone with her *baba* the next afternoon when a messenger came to the door with two envelopes. Viktor wasn't home, so she and Natalka opened them. One contained passports for her father, Natalka and herself; the other, three steamship tickets. They would leave the village in one week."

"That's not much time to get ready," Yuriy says.

"Halya went to the shelf where Viktor had left a folded paper she'd never seen before. She thought he must have left it by mistake, and was dying to find out what it was. He'd driven off in the cart and wouldn't be back until supper, so, she picked up the paper and found it was a map of Kanady, with a circle drawn around a town in a province called Saskatchewan. She copied the name onto a scrap of paper and ran all the way to the smithy.

"I was there by myself, saying goodbye to the place, since I would soon have to report to the army." Taras waits quietly until the other men settle in to listen.

I HELD IN MY HAND a many-times-mended harness which was finally, after all my father's work and my own, beyond repair. The leather felt warm and yielding. Sun filtered through gaps in the roof and wall boards, and through the open door. I had never thought about it before, but now I saw that it was a beautiful place, and I didn't want to leave it. Didn't want to let that light go. This was the place where I'd worked since I was seven years old, at first just watching Batko and fetching things for him, and then slowly starting to learn how to do what he did. And always the light coming in around us. How could I leave?

I had to. I had my notice. My parents would take me to Chernowitz when the day came. But what would happen if there was war? The talk of war might turn out to be just that, but there was a feeling in the village that something had changed. That we young men might be in for something more than training.

And then Halya rushed in, out of breath, and threw herself into my arms. We held each other a long time. She felt so warm against me; I wanted to feel that every day. And I asked myself if there was any way that could happen.

We would never be together if Viktor could prevent it, but there must be some way to get past him. We were young and strong, and he was already getting old.

Halya thrust a scrap of paper at me, pointed to the name written on it.

"Spring Creek, Saskatchewan, Canada," she said. "I think he knew someone from the village who lived there once. Taras, I'll never see you again."

In a moment I made up my mind. "If your father can find this place, so can I."

I held her close, stroked her cheek where the sun striped it gold.

"But no one can get away from the army."

That was what my parents and I had decided. But we also knew that if there really was a war, I might be in the army for years. I could be killed.

I didn't even know what I would be dying for.

"I can't go into the army." My words amazed me. A moment ago I had never so much as thought them. "I'll go to Kanady too, and I'll find you."

Maybe something inside me had been thinking, planning, without my knowing.

We had to tell my parents.

"Did I not ask for something happier?" Yuriy says.

"Well, Taras was showing some glimmerings of social and political consciousness," Tymko says. "That's a cause for celebration."

"What I just told you was about as happy as anything else that happened. I got to hold Halya. I learned where they were going so I could find her again. And we made plans together almost like we were already married."

"I'm sure Yuriy doesn't mean to complain," Myro says. "But maybe tomorrow we could hear something a little cheerier. Something with a little humour in it?"

"I don't know what that could be," Taras says. "But I'll try to think of something."

CHAPTER 8

We were set up, boys

"So..." TARAS LOOKS at his friends. "I tried to think of something cheerier. I hope you'll like it."

"Has it got a little humour?" Yuriy asks.

"I think it does. You'll have to judge for yourself. But I want one thing understood first. I wasn't there myself."

"Fine, fine," Tymko says. "But how do you know what happened?"

"Halya told me — when she came to the smithy. It wasn't all about the two of us, you see. Some of it was about her *baba*. Some of it even made us laugh. Oh, and Maryna told my mother about it later."

"All right, all right," Tymko says. "Enough. You just want us to know you'll probably make a few things up."

"*Tak*. I think that's how stories work."

NATALKA SCURRIED DOWN the grassy lane, holding a loaf of her best black bread wrapped in a linen cloth in one hand and with the other restlessly smoothing her homespun apron against her hips, as if she felt a wrinkle that just wouldn't go away. She came to the gate of a small thatch-roofed house. Oh! There were leaf buds on the *kalyna* bushes, right beside the few berries the birds had left behind. Good, she's always liked spring.

Coming through the gate, she noticed the woven willow fence had been repaired. She knocked and entered the storeroom, even emptier than on her last visit. She passed into the room that was her friend's kitchen, dining room and sitting room all in one.

Late afternoon shadows filled the corners. Maryna stood at the *peech*, a fan of thin-cut noodles slipping through her fingers into a pot of soup. A ray of sun turned her gnarled hands golden as she separated the noodles so they wouldn't clump together. Then she picked up a long wooden spoon and stirred them in as a cloud of steam rose around her, and placed the pot back in the oven of the *peech*.

Well! Natalka couldn't hold back a snort of impatience — her friend knew she was there, of course. Maryna turned to her, a smile pulling at the lines around her mouth. Small and a bit bent, she had all her teeth and her sharp tongue still worked. Not all the wrinkles in the world could hide her playful spirit, her main weapon against a hard life.

"*Dobre dehn,* Natalká."

"*Dobre dehn,* Maryna." Another snort popped out.

"What's eating you? Did the bread fail to rise this morning?"

"Don't be silly. It's —"

"No, of course not. Is that beautiful loaf for me?" Natalka nodded impatiently. "*Dyakuyiu,* just what I need. So what is it, then?"

"I'm trying to tell you. Viktor, that son of a wild boar, has this crazy idea. He wants to take us away —"

"To Kanady." Maryna smiled at her friend, enjoying being one step ahead of her.

"How did you know?" Natalka hated having her forward energy checked. She went to the *peech* and glanced into the pot. Not much in there but noodles. A soup bone, some chopped onion, a few pieces of potato.

"Sorry, it's all over the village." Maryna moved in front of the *peech* to keep Natalka's eyes out of it. "Pavlo and Lubo were fixing my fence. I could have done it myself, but they wanted to help a poor old lady, so I let them. You don't get chances like that too often. Anyway, they heard Viktor talking — in the tavern, of course."

"Those fools!" Natalka exclaimed. "They spend too much time in the tavern."

"Probably eavesdropping for all they were worth. But it's all true. The men talked about it last night in the reading hall."

"Anyway...I'm not going."

Maryna hesitated a moment, then decided to speak. "Maybe you're the fool, then."

"What? You want me to leave my home? My village?"

Maryna enjoyed Natalka's outrage. Really, it was almost comical. A best friend should support you, not undercut you, but Maryna didn't lie to her friends, at least not if the truth might be helpful.

"Why not?" Maryna bent over and tasted the soup, added salt, stirred. "What's so great here?"

Natalka had to pull her eyes away from the spoon, stirring and stirring. She had to get back to her outrage. "You can't mean that."

"Can't I?" Maryna stirred harder, then realized it wasn't going to put meat in the soup and stopped. "Every other coin I get goes to pay off my husband's debt to Radoski."

"But my friends —" Natalka said.

"Don't stay for my sake. I'll be dead soon."

Maryna glanced at two squares of paler whitewash on the walls, where once there had hung a holy icon and a portrait — the kind everyone had, of Shevchenko — both long since sold for what little they could fetch.

"My, I wonder if I'll see my Marko in heaven like the priest says. I wonder if he'll still look old or if everybody gets young again up there. What do you think?"

"Don't give me that, Maryna, you'll be here another twenty, thirty years."

"I don't think so." Maryna's lips twitched. "God couldn't be so cruel."

Natalka looked startled and then started to laugh. Maryna cackled. Then they laughed so hard, deep in their bellies, they could barely get breath. They collapsed on the wooden bench, gasping; lifted their aprons to wipe their eyes.

"Dobre," Natalka said. "I haven't laughed like that for some time. I don't really feel like it with the wild boar around."

"You have to keep watch always. You never know what a wild boar's going to do."

"No," Natalka agreed, "only that it won't be what you want." Her eyes met Maryna's. "There's always so much of what you don't want. Is that what life's meant to be like? I suppose it must be."

"Well well, never mind," Maryna said, "we may as well have some tea. The soup'll be ready soon. And we have good bread." She poured tea from a pot keeping warm on the *peech*. Sliced Natalka's dark rye onto a plate and set it to warm. Steam from the soup twined its way through rays of sun, and the sharp, warm fragrance of the heavy bread mixed with it, turning the room, for a moment, into a haven of warmth and plenty.

Maryna pressed Natalka's rough hand. "What to do, eh? What to do? Every day's the same — same chores, same food. For me, each year just means the soup gets thinner. Maybe if you go, something will change. You'll have choices. Things we can't even imagine."

"Dobre," Natalka says, "I'll be a beautiful *pahna* in a long silk gown with strings of coral and amber around my neck, right down to my apron."

"A *pahna* wouldn't need an apron."

"That's true. Down to my knees, then." Maryna laughed. "Oh, and I'll have soft white bread every day."

"And eat your meat with a silver fork?"

"And wear fine leather shoes and silk stockings."

"Well, we'll see about that," Maryna said. She filled two bowls with hot soup and passed the bread. The scent wrapped around them. Dust specks floated in the slanting light.

There was no butter to put on the bread.

"So THE TENDENCY of this little tale," Myro says, "seems to be that immigration was a good thing."

"Well, a lot of people have had that idea," Taras says. "Or we wouldn't all be here."

"But wait a minute," Yuriy says. "You said Halya told you about this visit, and yes, your mother also, but how could you know what those two *babas* thought? Were you listening at the window?"

Taras smiles. "No. I had to imagine it."

"Make it up, you mean?"

"Something like that."

"I think it sounded quite realistic," Tymko says. "Scientifically speaking."

"Me too," Ihor says. "I felt like I knew them."

"But —" Yuriy begins.

"I'm telling the story, aren't I?" Taras pretends to glower. "Do you want to hear more or not?" Yuriy nods and smiles. As Taras has been telling the story these cold nights, more men have come to hear, sometimes ten or twenty. They listen as if their souls depended on it.

"You know," Yuriy says, "I remember those immigration posters. Men even came up to us in the taverns — to tell us how happy we'd be, if only we came to Canada."

"Agents from steamship companies," Tymko says. "Sometimes they even paid Ukrainian people in Canada to send letters home saying how good everything was here. Even if they lived in holes in the ground."

"Why did they go to all that trouble?" Yuriy asks. "What did they want with us?"

"Labour," Tymko says. "For their factories and mines and sawmills. Most of all, for farming. Somebody had to break up all that land. Chop up all those roots. Who better than a bunch of Ukrainians?" Everyone is silent for a moment, taking all this in. It fits with what they know, but they've never talked about it this way.

"So that's what the government had planned for us all along?" Yuriy doesn't like to believe this, it's so cut and dried.

"That's right. Everything planned in advance. We were set up, boys."

"Set up," Ihor agrees. "As if we weren't really people, just *things* that could be useful to them." He looks sad.

"Or pieces on a chessboard," Myro says.

"But that's not all," Tymko goes on. "The Indians were set up too. And we're part of *that*."

"What do you mean?" Taras asks. "What have we got to do with Indians?"

"Think about it. England finds this whole vast land now called Canada. They want to take it over. Make it their colony. But how do they do that? People live here already. No, not people in cities or on farms. People who move around so they can hunt. Food, clothing, shelter; everything depends on hunting."

"What has that got to do with us?" Taras is still puzzled, but sees understanding in Myro's eyes.

"The land is given to us. We cut trees, break land, build fences. Indians can no longer move freely or hunt on that land. Railroads are built. Every year more land is broken. Trails the animals take through the trees disappear. Suddenly everything you know how to do is no good any more. It doesn't help to be a fine hunter, and know how to make everything you need, if there's no more hunting."

There's a long silence. Taras wishes he hadn't heard this. Tymko says the government has given them other people's land. It makes sense. How else do you have that much land to give away?

"But the land was empty," Yuriy says. "Or almost empty." He has a good farm, or what soon will be a good farm. He wants to be happy about that.

"I didn't say they lived like us," Tymko says. "There weren't so many of them. They didn't fill up all the spaces like we do. But they were here."

"I guess they were."

"How did you come to understand this?" Myro asks.

"When I was working in the mines, I met Indian people. Stoneys. *Nakodah*. They came to town to buy supplies. Flour. Bullets. Clothing. Sometimes we talked."

Silence settles again. This puts what they're living through in a different light.

"Did you have to make us feel even worse?" Yuriy asks.

"Would you rather know the truth or not?" Tymko says.

"If it makes me feel worse, probably not."

"Perhaps Taras will give us more of his story," Myro says. "Just to finish out the evening. Then we can sleep."

"Yes," Ihor says. "We'll have such beautiful dreams."

"Oh well, then," Tymko says, "let's listen. Then we'll all have a good stiff drink and off we go."

"I wonder," Yuriy says, "if we *could* get some homebrew going."

"I've thought about it for months," Ihor says, "but I can't see a way. We don't have anything to make it out of, or any container to make it in."

"I suppose you're right," Yuriy agrees. "But it would be nice. Maybe the cooks would give us some potatoes and a big pot. We could hide it under the bunks during the day."

"Yes," Ihor says. "Along with the pork roasts and the sweet, soft *pampushkas* and the garlic sausage rings."

"And the pretty girls," Tymko says. Everyone looks miserable. "Taras. You may as well go on."

"Maybe a little more, just to finish off this part. But I warn you, it's not all cheery."

"Oh, we're getting used to that." Yuriy manages a wink.

"So you remember I said that I'd realized I didn't want to go into the army. And my parents were going to drive me to Chernowitz – five days after Halya would be leaving, as it turned out. So Halya and I had to talk to them right away, and tell them I was going to take the money I'd saved and follow her to Canada."

HALYA AND I sat on the bench on one side of the table, my parents on the other.

"Taras, think. You'll lose your language, your people," my mother, Daria, said.

"Your country," Batko said.

"I don't need those things." I can hardly believe I said that. I was younger then.

"Stay, my son." Mykola nodded toward the portrait of the great poet. "Help to build *Ukraïna*."

"Don't take my grandchildren from me." Tears slipped down my mother's face.

Halya cried silently. She knew that after I was born, my mother couldn't have any more children. She also knew what it was to be an only child.

"Mama, I have to leave." I held her close, kissed her cheek. "I love Halya, just like you and Batko love each other. And if I stay, I'll have to go into the army."

She looked scared, but she tried to brush it away. "It'll be all right," she said. "You'll do your service, as your father did, and then go on with your life."

My father looked worried. He'd been going over some recent articles in the newspapers that came to the reading room.

"There was no war when I did my service," he said.

"And there won't be now. The Austrians don't want war. What would it get them?" Mama thought this was a good point, and in some ways it was, but Batko wasn't done.

"They've avoided war for a long time," Batko said. "A long time full of grievances, large and small. Alliances made and broken. But now? I'm afraid."

I was surprised to hear him say it. If he admitted this, how could he ask me to stay?

In a moment, Mama was ready for me to travel halfway across the world. But how? There was no time. I had no papers, no steamship ticket.

SOMEHOW this doesn't cheer Taras's listeners up. They do want to know the rest, sometime, but for now it seems they've had enough of the story.

So maybe it's a good place to stop for a while. Later, they'll have time to wonder, *How did he get away?*

CHAPTER 9

Kobzar

December, 1915

IN THE FOREST, trees crack in the cold, pierced to the heartwood. It reminds Taras of gunshots. Today it's too cold to work and the prisoners are allowed to stay in the bunkhouse, except that a party goes out every hour to cut firewood. The stoves have to be fed constantly, and still frost lines the walls and coats the windows in heavy lace. Taras sits with his friends: Ihor the Mountain Man, Tymko the Socialist, Myro the Professor and Yuriy the Farmer. Their card game has come to a halt because Taras can't choose a card. After a few minutes he realizes the others are waiting for him to play. Nobody had the heart to yell at him. He's been staring at his hands, chapped and cracked and stiff from clenching an axe handle. He's never had a landowner's soft hands, but he's never seen anything like this either.

Myro passes around a box of caramels from the canteen. For a while everyone sucks on the gooey candy.

"God, what was that slop they gave us for supper?" Yuriy says, his face a mask of gloom.

"Don't ask," Myro says.

"Be glad you *don't* know." Tymko flicks his cards at Taras. "Play."

Startled, Taras pulls a card from his hand without looking and sets it on the table. Tymko gives him a disgusted look.

"The really pathetic thing," Myro says, "the thing I can't believe?

I wanted more."

Private Barkley, who guards prisoners from another bunkhouse, strides in, followed at a distance by Andrews and Bullard. He grips his rifle with clenched fingers, and stares at Taras's table. Especially at Tymko, whom the guards see as a known agitator. He must surely be planning something. Escape. Sabotage. Spying, although Barkley couldn't say on what.

Tymko waggles his eyebrows at him and Taras has to choke back a laugh.

Barkley tells anyone who'll listen that he wanted to be sent to fight in France. His brother's there, while he has to sit home guarding enemy aliens, losing his chance to be a hero. He walks with a limp, the result, Taras heard Andrews say, of childhood tuberculosis that went to his bones. It's amazing how the guy manages to both limp and swagger at the same time.

Barkley has hair and eyebrows so blonde they look white, and pale eyes like the shadows on ice. His skin is almost as pale as a field of snow. His red lips are the only colour he has about him and Taras finds it unnatural in such a pale man. Of course, if Barkley were someone you could like, he'd never give it a thought. But he isn't, if only because he came up with the stupid idea of sudden bunkhouse inspections. Who knows, he must have thought, what a hundred exhausted men will get up to at night? Sabotage is only one possibility.

Taras has in fact considered burning down the bunkhouse, but doesn't want to find out where they'd end up after that. Anyway, you couldn't do it at night, because they're locked in. You'd have to get something smouldering before the morning's work started. It doesn't seem worth the trouble.

Barkley also boasts that he'll sniff out illicit stills and keep an eye on men spewing dangerous ideas. Thinking subversive thoughts. It's a lot of work watching a man think and guessing what's in his head, but apparently nothing's too much for Barkley. Including bending over to look under bunks.

"If only we *had* some stills," Ihor says sadly.

Myro winks. "We do have a few subversive ideas."

"Yeah – decent food," Yuriy mutters.

"Getting the hell out of here," Ihor says.

The guards continue up the wide central aisle and stop for a moment at Zmiya's bunk. Zmiya's not doing anything, but Barkley gives him a nasty look anyway. After a look like that, who would dare make any trouble?

Now you're getting somewhere, Taras thinks. Find out what that one's up to. But no, they're not interested in crazy people, and they move back toward the stoves. They watch Taras and his friends play a card game with no beginning or end, and no one keeping score.

Again Barkley fastens his icy eyes on Tymko, who does his best not to let on the man's there, and they carry on the game in their own language. "Let's see, what'll I play? I wonder what Yuriy's got. And what's the professor's holding back, hoping I've got nothing left?"

"It's these guards I can't stomach." Yuriy gazes thoughtfully at his cards, flips one carelessly onto the table.

"What do you expect?" Tymko says. "These are the guys even the army can't use." The guards frown, especially Barkley. They don't understand the words, but they do recognize the sound of sarcasm.

Myro nods. "Makes the Austrians look like princes."

"I wouldn't say that," Yuriy says.

"You're right. That's going too far." They laugh.

Barkley moves on, giving Tymko another evil look. The guards head for the door.

"What's wrong with him?" Yuriy wonders. "He can't possibly speak Ukrainian."

"Don't you see?" Tymko grins. "They know I'm a radical social-ist. So now they've decided you're all socialists." He plays a card. "They see you *consorting* with me."

"Oh shit, just our luck," Yuriy says to Myro. "Now I'm a social-ist farmer and you're a revolutionary professor." He plays a card.

Myro plays a card and takes the trick. "I'm not a professor."

"Okay, Myroslav the revolutionary arithmetic teacher." They all laugh.

"Nothing more dangerous," Tymko says. "Socialists who can

add and subtract."

They laugh again but the momentum soon fades. Taras throws in his hand and, after a quick look around, the rest follow. Before he was sent here, each man had things he wanted to do. People he cared about. Maybe even that sneaky bastard Zmiya, who's been watching them all afternoon, had someone. Well, that's hard to imagine.

Months, maybe years, are being stolen. Who among them can know how many days his life still holds? Or what is happening to parents, sweethearts, children, while they wait in this cavern of chilled, indifferent air? Canada has never seemed so foreign and yet so frighteningly like the old country.

Taras hasn't taken up his story again. He hasn't got the heart for it.

"So why do the guards think you're a radical?"

Taras and Tymko are felling trees but have managed to edge a few steps into the forest, away from the eyes of the guards, especially red-faced Jackie Bullard. They are consorting, as Tymko called it, about politics.

"Oh, a lucky guess, I suppose." Tymko fixes Taras with his black eyes. "And because that's what I am." His wild hair sticks out under his winter cap. If he didn't know him, Taras might think: This man could be dangerous. And maybe he could be. But nobody's funnier, either, when the mood takes him. Or kinder when he sees the need.

"Oh. But Viktor Dubrovsky called my father a socialist, and Batko only wanted our village to have a co-operative flour mill. Viktor thought anybody who wanted to change anything was a socialist revolutionary. But that's not really radical, is it?"

"No, it isn't. Lots of people think like that, though," Tymko says. "The important thing to remember is, people in every class are governed by the interests of their class."

"Not my father. He cared about all the people."

"It just seemed that way. He was an oppressed peasant, so he cared about other oppressed peasants."

"I suppose so," Taras says. "But he was also a blacksmith. With his own shop. So we weren't only peasants."

"Oh, all right then, he was a peasant and a *petit bourgeois.*"

"You have a name for everything, don't you? But my father wasn't like the landlord. If people couldn't pay, he waited till they could. Sometimes they never did pay."

"Okay, he was a peasant and a compassionate *petit bourgeois.*"

"If you say so," Taras says, tired of the discussion. His eyes sweep the work site, as men fell trees and guards watch them. Amazingly, no one's noticed they aren't working.

"But what does a revolutionary socialist think? What do you want to see happen?"

"I'm glad to hear you ask that." Tymko pulls at the tips of his bushy moustache. "Curiosity is a good sign in a young man. It leads to change."

"What? What do you want?"

"I want an end to aristocracy and authoritarian rule. I want land for the people. Education for every child. Good food and clothing and shelter for every family." Tymko sees Taras about to break in and forestalls him. "Yes, landlords too, but only their fair share. They'd have to work for it like everyone else."

Taras briefly enjoys a vision of Radoski working behind a plough. Radoski cleaning cowshit out of a stable. Radoski serving beer in the tavern. Of course, he knows how to do none of these things, so he'd do them all badly.

"Oh, and democratic government. Every man voting."

"Every man only?" Taras thinks of his mother, of Halya.

"Sorry. Every man and woman, of course. And every man and woman could be a candidate in the elections."

"Sounds fair. How would you get to this new way of doing things?"

"Any way we have to," Tymko says. "We have to fight."

"Who is 'we'?"

"Peasants and workers. Sympathetic clergy. Ordinary soldiers who join us."

"Who do we have to fight?"

"The government, the landlords, the *bourgeoisie,* the officer class of the army, the rest of the clergy. Anyone who opposes us."

"This sounds to me like a lot of fighting and most likely a lot of people dead. A lot of peasants dead! I suppose I'd have to fight Batko if he's a *petit bourgeois.* Or am I one too, since I'm his son? I guess you'd have to fight me."

Tymko starts to object, but Taras cuts him off. "I suppose you think it would be worth it. Scientifically, I mean. People would have better lives. But how do you know you'll succeed? What if a lot of peasants and workers get killed and nothing changes?" Taras suddenly realizes his voice has been getting louder. But it seems no one's even noticed. Or maybe they have, and they don't give a damn any more.

At first Tymko doesn't answer. Taras sees he's pondered this question before. "It has to change. The forces of history decree it. Natural law decrees it."

"That's almost the same as what Myro said: 'My heart tells me...' You said the heart doesn't enter into it." Taras is proud to have thought of this on his own.

Tymko doesn't waver. "Men will not stay forever in chains. We will seize our destiny."

"Here in Canada too?"

"Everywhere. Nothing can stop it. The Revolution is coming."

"I see. Thanks for explaining. What about the guards? Will we have to kill them?"

Tymko grins. This question's easy. "No point. Wouldn't get us anywhere. We don't move until the time is right. Oh-oh, they've spotted us. Better take a leak."

They unbutton their flies and pee gently into the snow.

Taras wonders if peeing on your hand would be enough to warm it up. Probably not. It would freeze too quickly. And you'd get pee in your mitts. A small laugh shakes his belly.

"Tonight," Tymko says, "it's time for you to go on with your story."

"Do I have to?"

"Yes. Don't pretend you don't enjoy it."

"All right." Taras is actually relieved. Learning how to tell his story keeps him from sliding into darkness and forgetting. He's ready to take it up again.

Jackie Bullard, or *Bullshit* as Taras and his friends have started calling him, appears behind them as they take their time fastening their trousers. He gives a quick look at the two splashes of yellow in a great field of white. "Okay, slackers, back to work."

BUT IN FACT it isn't Taras who tells a story around the card table that night. Myro turns to Taras. "So do you know about this man whose name you bear?"

"Taras Shevchenko? Of course. Who doesn't? We had his picture on the wall, even a book of poems. *The Kobzar.* Everyone in the village had the same."

"I don't mean what everyone knows. I mean, do you know about his life?" Tymko, Yuriy, Ihor all put down their cards. Several others draw close, sensing some interesting talk.

"I know he was also an artist. A great artist."

"He was a very fine artist," Myro says. "He could have been great if he'd been able to do his work in peace. But he couldn't."

"Because he was always getting into trouble," Tymko says. "He talked too much about Ukrainians. Sometimes he trusted the wrong people. People who didn't like his ideas."

"What ideas?" asks Ivan, a young man with soulful dark eyes and soft brown hair and a moustache. He's sitting on a bunk near the card players.

"He thought Ukraine should be a country," Myro says. Taras has always known this, of course, although he can't remember when he first learned about it.

"If he was a painter," Ivan says, "how did he have time for ideas?"

"Interesting question. Most people don't see that a picture has ideas."

"Oh no," Yuriy says, "you're making the professor lecture us."

"So don't listen," Ivan says, "but I'm interested."

"Well. First of all...Shevchenko lived in lands ruled by the

Russians. To be an artist in those times, probably now even, you needed to study in Russia. Right away that tells you something. He had to paint what Russians liked. Rich Russians, that is."

Taras can't keep from asking, "What did they like?" It's like being back in school, only the village teacher was never this intriguing.

Myro smiles. "They liked portraits of tsars and tsarinas, nobles, famous generals and occasionally high-ranking priests. Portraits of beautiful women and girls. Idealized pictures of children, innocent as angels. Famous battles. Extravagant country houses and the life that went on there. Nature, especially with blue sky and swaying birch trees."

Myro has them in his hand. They've never heard anyone speak Ukrainian the way he does. Even when he uses unfamiliar words, he fits them together in a way that helps them understand. He weaves bright pictures, and patterns that shimmer in their minds like *tsymbali* music.

"I see," says Ivan. "They liked pictures that told them everything was going well."

"Yes." Myro beams at Ivan. "They wanted to be shown how wonderful their world was and what a lot of great fellows they were."

"Was that really all they painted?" Yuriy asks.

"People also liked to see bowls of fruit. And icons. And once in a while a painting of peasants labouring, or dancing. Just to remind themselves how things worked. Often peasants would be portrayed with a sort of coarseness about them, to reassure the masters that these must be the people God meant to be doing the hard work."

Tymko laughs. "What was the problem, then? Why couldn't Shevchenko just paint these things, get rich, be respected, marry a beautiful girl?" Taras sees that Tymko knows the answer. He's just trying to feed Myro the next question. They make a good team.

"He couldn't because of who he was. A Ukrainian. A patriot. He couldn't just make idealized paintings for wealthy people. He painted Ukrainians as one who knew them. People with a tangle of thoughts and feelings. People with ideas."

"Hold on, though," Ivan says. "He was a serf. Serfs didn't get into art schools as far as I've heard."

"No. But our Taras had an unusual life. He was orphaned quite young and was raised by his sister. The village priest, who was the local schoolmaster, taught him to read. Yes, Tymko, priests sometimes did things like that."

"Probably expected Taras to cut his firewood for the rest of his life."

Myro smiles but refuses to be diverted. "Perhaps through this priest, Taras came to the attention of his master, Lord Englehardt, who took the boy into his house as a servant. Over time, Englehardt discovered this servant had artistic talent. He found a teacher to help Taras learn, and when the landlord moved to St. Petersburg, he apprenticed Taras, now a young man, to an engraver."

"Wait, that's too much. Why would a landlord help a serf?" Yuriy asks.

"Maybe 'help' isn't quite the word. Englehardt was probably only doing what many masters did – improving the value of his assets. There's a passage in *War and Peace –*"

"In what?" Taras asks.

"*War and Peace* – a great novel by the Russian count, Leo Tolstoy. In it a wealthy man who loves to give lavish parties buys a cook from a friend for a thousand roubles – for his skill at cooking French delicacies."

"*Buys* him?" Taras asks, jaw tense. The others look upset as well. They've always known about serfdom, of course, the bondage of working for someone from birth to death, limited in every action, your life going on at the landlord's whim, but the thought of buying or selling people has never been put to them quite so baldly. Now the teacher's lesson isn't so pleasant and they'd almost like to forget the whole thing.

"So it wasn't that he liked Taras, then?" Ivan asks.

Myro shakes his head. "Taras was a lesser person. Property. In fact, there's a story about the time Taras took down one of

Englehardt's paintings and made a copy of it when the lord and his lady were away for the evening."

"What happened?" Ivan asks.

"The lord came home and found out. He was furious. He had Taras flogged."

"You mean he hit him?"

"No, I mean the next day he sent him to his overseer to be beaten."

For half a minute no one speaks. They feel anger, shame. This is how people like them were treated.

"How do you know all these things?" asks Ihor. "I've heard of Shevchenko all my life, and nobody ever told me such stories."

"I've studied his life for many years," Myro says. "And my father had an uncle at the university in Lviv who spent decades collecting information about the poet, and he passed it down to my father, who gave it to me. But you don't have to believe me. I only thought it would be something we could talk about. To pass the time."

Ihor nods. He might not admit it, but he's interested. The man in the picture everyone has seen is starting to come to life. "I'm sorry," he says. *"Proshu,* continue with the story. I think everyone would be glad to hear it."

"Dyakuyiu," Myro says. "I will be happy to continue." Everyone settles down again.

"You see, in St. Petersburg, young Taras learned many things. He worked hard in his apprenticeship, and whenever he could, he developed his art. At night he'd sneak out of his master's house to a beautiful park where classical statues stood like frozen gods. In the dim moonlight he would sketch them, trying to learn how to draw the human figure. Night after night he worked, until one night someone saw him – a famous art critic and historian, curious about the shabby-looking boy on a cold stone bench, blind to everything but the marble statue in front of him."

Taras couldn't walk away if he wanted to. He's never heard any of this before, but can immediately imagine it, as if he too had ventured into the St. Petersburg night to answer a desperate need.

"The famous man talked to Taras, questioning him about his life and his goals. Few people had ever been interested in him, and Taras poured it all out. The critic — Soshenko was his name — saw Taras's talent and admired the spirit that drove him out into the night. He brought Taras to his house. Showed him his paintings. Introduced him to his friends."

"This feels like some legend or fairy tale," Yuriy says. "It feels like something I should always have known."

"It was the beginning of a great change. Taras began to meet other artists and they became his friends. He entered a new life, filled with the give and take of spirited conversation. He saw that people could sit for hours and talk about drawing and painting. He was in an enchanted place where everyone loved the same things he did. Where he was not a freak because all he wanted was to draw and paint and learn."

Myroslav stops for breath as more men pull up chairs. Pretty soon there are thirty or forty people sitting on chairs or lounging against bunks.

"Yet still there was a barrier between Taras and the others. A barrier to genuine, open discourse, an unspoken embarrassment and horror that could not be tolerated. The young man was still owned by Englehardt. And so, Taras's closest friends, most of them Russian artists, devised a plan to free him. In a generous gesture, one of them — Bruillov was his name — painted a picture and the others sold it by raffle and bought his freedom. I said it was generous, and it was, although not beyond what such a man could fairly easily do for a friend.

"Now, here I must be fair. Many people subscribed to this scheme to free Taras. Generous Russians. They wanted to help a talented young man gain his freedom. These even included some members of the tsar's own family."

"What?" Yuriy says. "Why would they do that?"

"They admired art. They still thought it was fine to have serfs, but they acknowledged that some people's talents might transcend that. They committed a brief kindness which in no way undercut their beliefs."

"But all his ideas about Ukraine being a country —" Ivan says.

"Ah, but those ideas were not well known at this time in his life. That came later." Everyone settles back to listen.

"After that, Taras Shevchenko blossomed in many ways. His friends helped him enter the Russian Academy and his name became known as a painter and engraver. Although he was born a peasant, he was able to enter into middle-class and even upper-class society, had access to fine homes and elegant entertainments. Taras could be filled with joyous and amusing talk. He sang and danced, and recited poetry with fire, with grace. People responded to that, wealthy and talented people. And he was grateful for the kindness of others."

The men try to imagine what such splendid parties might be like. Most have seen the outside of grand homes, but not the inside. Taras remembers the ornate buildings lining the streets of Chernowitz and wonders if the great houses of St. Petersburg looked like them.

"Of course, he couldn't totally shake off what he'd been," Myro goes on. "Couldn't ever be one of them, not for all his charm — and people said he had great charm and an intense, compelling way of talking, especially when he spoke his beloved Ukrainian. Probably too intense for many people."

Everyone gazes at Myro with sympathy when he says "his beloved Ukrainian."

Like Shevchenko, he shows them the beauty of their language.

"Tell us more about his life in St. Petersburg," Ihor says. "Make us see it."

"Make us a story," Yuriy says.

"*Dobre,*" Myro says. "I will try."

St. Petersburg by night looked so lovely, so luminous; it worked its way into his skin, his muscles, his heart. The lamp glow spilling from windows, the pale sheen of moon and stars, touched his face with silver and gold until it seemed his mind was filled with light. It hurt him to know the Russians had created this beauty — a nighttime world so magical, so fine, that perhaps it could only exist next to the poverty all around.

Was that what he was to believe?

How could some have far more than they needed without others going hungry? Was that how it went? He didn't know. But he thought that some day there could be enough for everyone to have a good life and that great works of art might still be created.

Why do we measure value by gold and silver? he wondered. One, because they were rare and therefore costly. But it was more than that; they had beauty of their own, like the sunshine and moonlight they called to mind.

Tonight the count, Alexander Ivanovich Kalnikov, had invited him to a soirée — an intimate party he'd called it. Taras knew by now what that meant: ten or twenty guests, the count's numerous family, and servants enough — serfs enough — to make everything run smoothly. A warm fire, the glow of lamps, the gorgeous colours of the low-cut gowns the women wore, at least the younger women. Young girls waiting for suitable marriages, hair fresh and neat, complexions untouched by hot sun in the fields or fierce, cold winds that turn your face and hands a red that doesn't go away even when you come in the house and sit by the *peech*.

He imagined the moment at the door and almost wished to turn back to his lonely room. No one was ever rude, but the servants' eyes followed him through the elegant rooms. They knew the truth: he didn't belong. He'd been admitted to this glamorous circle of fame, money and privilege because of his talent. It had vaulted him first out of work in the fields, then out of his master's house, and it had bought him freedom. But the servants know he's one of them. He thinks the count understands how bewildering and humiliating it can be, since they've spoken together often and without the reserve he usually feels with the wealthy and highborn. Perhaps his wife and daughters know as well.

He reached the count's house with its tall windows overlooking the street, rang the bell, and there was Semyon, the butler, opening the door at once, as if he'd been waiting. He took Taras's second-hand hat and coat and hung them with the others, and Taras could see him quelling the urge to brush something off them, threadbare but spotless though they were. The thought, "Pretend all you like, you are no better than I," seemed always to lurk in Semyon's eyes.

Most often the servants of the wealthy were happy to see him and exchange a few words. One of their own had been freed and accepted among their masters. This Semyon, though, had a streak of envy and malice. If he must be a servant, why should Taras escape? That must be how he saw it.

He led Taras into the spacious reception room, lit by dozens of candles, the gilded plasterwork reflecting dancing light into a new-comer's eyes. "Taras Hryhoryvich Shevchenko, Member of the Academy of Arts," he announced. Taras was the only man there with no title, no position in government or the army. No land or property, no ancient provenance.

The ordeal of entrance passed quickly. People looked up for a moment, bowed or even smiled in his direction, then turned slowly back, formal and smooth as a figure in a dance, to the people they were talking to before he arrived. As he passed he heard snatches of conversation in the elegant French they'd learned from their nurses and tutors. If there were nothing else, no distinction of dress or good looks or outstanding skill, these upper-class Russians would know each other by this borrowed eloquence. Taras could try to play this game – he'd picked up a basic knowledge of French in his master's house – but he won't lower himself to use it.

It was enough he had to speak to them in Russian, knowing that most of them didn't even recognize Ukrainian as a language. That is, if they'd ever considered the matter at all.

Imagine, he thought. People too refined, too rich, to speak their native tongue. How could anyone be truly admirable who would erase what he really was and affect another country's language and customs? Whenever he was introduced to such people, he'd see that moment's struggle, that slight jolt as they forced themselves to recall and speak Russian.

Kalnikov was different. He looked up with his bright eyes and beckoned him with a nod of the head. Taras approached him, although he sat beside the old crone his dowager mother, who was swathed in dull lavender satin that had seen as many seasons as Taras's own evening clothes. She diverted herself, the count had confided, with planning matches for her many relatives of both sexes with people who could bring them some increase of wealth or position. Now she fussed with the already perfect flowers in the hair of the count's youngest daughter – Tatiana, a rosy-faced girl of fifteen, her low neckline softened by some kind of gathered sheer material. Taras was touched by her beauty and youth. For as pampered as she was, she would soon be faced with the question of betrothal and marriage. If she were a great artist or possessed the ability to manage some grand enterprise, it wouldn't matter. For her there was only one profession, one path.

The count rose and came to him, surely a mark of favour, since it saved him the pain of making conversation with the dowager. He would have liked to greet Tatiana, though, as she was giving him her sweetest smile, not in a flirtatious way, but because she was happy and full of life and had the smile ready for anyone who came along, especially young men taken up by her father.

"Good evening, my dear fellow," the old gentleman said, touching Taras's shoulder, "you're just the person I need to talk to."

Taras bowed and wished him a good evening.

The count's round face seemed to shine with good health, or at least good food and wine. His silvery hair and beard were meticulously trimmed, his clothing was impeccable. He took Taras's arm and walked him over to one of the floor-to-ceiling windows framed in deep blue velvet. Looking out, Taras felt connected once more to the glowing night.

"Do you by any chance know what I'm talking about?" the count asked in a playful tone. "Has some rumour reached you?"

Taras smiled. "I assure you, sir, that your words are completely new and mysterious to me. No rumour of any kind has reached me. Other than that this man Shevchenko is a villain who should be sent packing."

The count laughed heartily. "I think you're safe for the moment. But I see you really haven't heard a word, a rare thing in this town of intrigue and gossip. Well, my dear man, I'm very excited. I have a commission for you."

"I am at your service. What – or whom – would you have me paint?"

"Oh, it's a grand scheme," old Kalnikov said. "A portrait, you know. Just myself with my family. But we want it large as life, and if you should happen to see more beauty in us than the world in general can see, none of us will find it in our hearts to criticize you. Only we also want it to be warm and jolly, so that years from now it will be a memory of all of us happy together."

There could be only one answer and Taras bowed deeply. "It will be an honour. Nature has given you and your family so much beauty that I need only portray, not enhance it. But I hope you anticipate nothing which will interfere with your family's happiness?"

"No. Nothing at the moment. But you know, bad things may happen, even to a fortunate family like ours, and besides, we shall one day or another see our Tatiana leave us. Wish she didn't have to."

"Well, I will accept your commission with great pleasure. I think Countess Tatiana can never look more beautiful than she does now in the bosom of her family."

"Probably true," the old man said. "I don't know where we can find her a husband who'll make her remotely happy, but we'll try. So, Taras Hryhoryvich. It's settled then. Good. Come to me tomorrow – early afternoon? – and we'll decide when you will begin. All the tiresome little details of fees and sitting times and so on."

Taras bowed again. *I* could make her happy, he thought.

"Now, let's go and break up this circle in the corner. I want you to meet my country cousin. He's not at all rustic, by the way. Studied in Paris and Berlin. Has very advanced ideas. He's just freed the serfs on his home estate."

If he could possibly have declined this friendly offer, Taras would have done so. The last thing he wanted was to receive the sympathy or good intentions of this cousin. "But will he speak Russian, sir? As you know, my French is non-existent."

"Ah! Fear not," the old man said. "Not only does he speak Russian, but he can speak your own language. One of his estates is in Little Russia."

Taras felt his cheeks burn, but luckily the count didn't notice, was already touching the cousin's elbow. It's not "little" Russia, he wanted to say. It's not any kind or size of Russia. It is *Ukraïna*.

Yet here he was himself, in Petersburg, among Russians, dependent on Russians. The artists who befriended him. Bruillov, who painted the picture to ransom him. To buy him one last time and then set him free. He was glad beyond measure to have this freedom, grateful too, but still sometimes it was terrifying.

The count was talking about family matters with the non-rustic cousin, who hadn't noticed him yet.

What would be the best thing for him to do now? He could likely make a tolerable living as a portraitist and engraver. He could do well enough to send money to his sister and brother back home, money that would make their lives more bearable. He could manage that. He could perhaps marry. But always his heart asked him to do more. To make something of the gift he had so improbably received. A little bit like the lost prince or princess in a folk tale, he had been restored to his own estate, but he was not yet the ruler of anything.

People were kind to him. Admission to places like this, the patronage of the count and his circle, was immensely useful. These things could help him build a successful career. He could learn to do splendid portraits of counts and countesses, princes and princesses and their retinues of relatives and, who could say, perhaps some day even the Imperial family.

The very ones who considered it reasonable to keep his people in bondage. At home, in Kyrylivka, his sister Yaryna and her family did not own themselves. They belonged and probably always would belong to the landlord Engelhardt.

Across the room, Tatiana sent him a happy smile, no doubt in on the secret of the great project of the family painting.

And now the count was introducing his cousin, Alexei Vasilyevich Maslov, and, unexpectedly, Taras found him both likeable and entertaining. His Ukrainian was very good – and remember, Taras thought, the old count did say "your language," which many people wouldn't do – and his manner was unaffected and friendly. He never once mentioned serfdom in any context at all, but talked of Paris, its art and its people, and the freedom he felt walking its tree-lined streets.

"Perhaps it's only an illusion," Alexei Vasilyevich said, "but as I walked those pavements I felt as if chains slid from my mind. I could forget Russia for a time and believe that art and ideas were the highest good, the passport to all delight. My dear man, you can't imagine their galleries. Oh, they have their academicians too, but it's easier to ignore them. The place seemed to confer permission to experiment or change."

Taras had this freedom too, not as much as this man of education and means, but enough to do many things. A waiter came by with a tray laden with flutes of champagne, golden in the candlelight, and the room changed as Taras helped his new acquaintance and himself to a glass. It felt a little warmer, kinder.

"THAT WAS A GOOD STORY, Myro," Tymko says. "You must be missing teaching."

Myro smiles. "Well, I said I was a teacher. Maybe it was time I proved it."

"Consider it proved. Scientifically. Even this old revolutionary liked it."

"You're not that old." Myro waggles his own eyebrows in a reasonable imitation of Tymko's.

"No," Tymko says, "it just feels that way."

THE STORY SENDS a new spirit through the listeners. Through Shevchenko they glimpse their own place in the history of their country, or the idea of their country – a nation they can neither forget nor wholeheartedly believe in yet. It feels painful, to be sure, but understanding is better than not understanding. Or so it seems at this moment.

CHAPTER 10

It happened far away

THE PRISONERS SIT on benches in the dining hall, which looks like a smaller version of the bunkhouse, drinking coffee at one of the long wooden tables. Taras tries to decide if the coffee actually tastes better than the usual burnt swill, or if he's just imagining it does due to the novelty of decorations. Because the rough wooden walls are trimmed with red and green crêpe paper streamers twined together. A crooked but very fresh pine tree, about eight feet tall, stands in the middle of the room, its spindly branches hung with coloured glass balls. Several prisoners familiar with Christmas trees think it looks pitiful, but Taras likes it. He's never seen one before and it does make some kind of change – Christmas is coming. December 25. Canadian Christmas, the men call it. Christmas won't come for Ukrainians until early January – they use a different calendar.

"So," Tymko says, "Canadian Christmas will be a holiday for both internees and guards. *Dobre.* This calls for analysis."

The other prisoners yawn or exchange long-suffering looks. It seems nothing is to have a simple, ordinary meaning any more.

"Why does it call for analysis?" Taras asks. May as well find out. Get it over with.

"I'm glad you asked me that. Well. Christmas Day – Canadian Christmas, of course – is meant to be a holiday for prisoners and guards. A day of recreation and pleasure, yes?"

It seems safe to nod agreement to this, but of course there's more coming.

"However... This certainly appears to be a contradiction in the case of the guards, since they still have to guard the prisoners. Guarding prisoners is their work. So calling Christmas a holiday for the guards seems to say that guarding prisoners at Christmas is not actually work, but recreation. How can the same actions be work on one day and recreation on another?"

"I don't –" Taras begins.

"On the other hand," Tymko rolls on, "this apparent contradiction may be more complex than it appears at first glance. It may require further examination." He waggles his eyebrows.

"How so?"

"In this way. We know the guards have been *ordered* to put up decorations and install a tree in the dining hall. We may not completely understand Canadian army traditions, but there is a real possibility that this will have been very pleasant – not work at all. It may even have been festive. They have been ordered to enjoy themselves and have done so."

"I wouldn't call that fun," Taras says.

"A perplexing question follows from this analysis," Tymko goes on as if Taras hasn't spoken. "If guarding internees on Christmas day is a sort of holiday, is every day of guarding prisoners actually a holiday? A form of recreation?" He waggles his brows again. "And yet everyone knows the guards are *paid* for these pleasant holidays. Moreover, everyone will have observed that they take little pleasure in them, an obvious paradox."

"That's, uh, very interesting."

"Isn't it? You see," Tymko says, "how important it is to analyze everything in a scientific way? There's so much we can learn. One day we'll understand everything."

It is interesting. But the coffee's gone cold while Taras listened. How did that happen? He'll have to analyze it. When he has a moment.

THE DAY ARRIVES AT LAST. For the prisoners it feels much like any other day you don't have to work, but supper is much better than usual. Turkey and potatoes and boiled peas. Not-completely-grey peas. And an unusual treat: each man receives an extra bun.

Taras gazes at his for several seconds. Of course, it's not the first time he's seen an extra bun. Even on an ordinary day one or two unneeded places may be set. Some prisoner is sick, or in the guard-house, or has escaped. Or maybe the kitchen staff counted wrong. Whatever the reason, you do occasionally see an extra place setting with a bun. Unclaimed, undefended. When that happens there's only one thing to be done, and no one's quicker than Yuriy. Like a fox in a chicken coop, he'll have that bun inside his shirt while the others are only thinking about it.

Today, however, *each* man has been issued a double ration of buns. Good. And there's *also* an empty setting. This time Yuriy captures only one of the extras. Taras has been learning Yuriy's methods and he gets the second. So each of them eats two buns with his supper and carries a third one back to the bunkhouse inside his shirt.

In the bunkhouse they sit and smoke. Each man has been given a Christmas cracker. All over the bunkhouse men pull the ends and wait for the pop.

"Good thing Barkley isn't making one of his sudden visits," Tymko says. "He'd think we were trying to blow up the bunkhouse." Tymko has on a hat of golden tissue paper cut to look like a crown. It suits him. King Tymko.

"I can't believe they'd give us anything containing explosives," Myro says.

"What if we gathered them up and put all the gunpowder into one cracker?" Yuriy wonders. "We could offer it to Barkley and there'd be a huge explosion. What do you think, would it be enough to kill Barkley?" Always practical, Yuriy. "Probably not." He shakes his head wistfully. Blowing up pale, frosty-looking Barkley would be an interesting sight.

"Would it be enough to *wound* Barkley?" Myro asks. Taras starts laughing and can't stop. It's the idea of Myro, in a purple-

and-silver hat, considering blowing anybody up. The crackers are making them silly.

"This is interesting," Ihor says. "It's almost like being drunk." His hat is made of red paper printed with yellow flowers. It looks better on him than Taras would have expected. The dark red colour looks good with his black hair.

They smoke, looking serious in the colourful hats. Taras has a bit of a smile on his face, still picturing Barkley as he pulled his cracker. The tiny moment of surprise; then the realization that he'd just exploded.

"I hate to disappoint you," Tymko says, "but I don't think they use gunpowder."

"Never mind that," Taras says. "Who would pull the other end?" He holds his cracker out to Tymko. They pull but it doesn't pop. He digs around for the hat and finds pleated white paper with gold circles on it. He crumples it in his fist and throws in on the floor.

"What was wrong with it?" Tymko asks. Taras shrugs.

"Oh well," Yuriy says. "It was just a thought." He grows silent and Taras can see he's thinking hard.

After a while he nods his head. "I have a plan. You're all going to help me with it." He takes his bun from inside his shirt and makes an inspection of the woodstoves. Chooses the middle one – it must be the hottest – and places the bun on top to get warm. Comes back to his bunk and starts telling stories. "Once there was a man who had no testicles."

"Sounds like Barkley," Ihor says.

"And also once there was a man with two assholes," Yuriy goes on.

"*Two* assholes!" Ihor says. "Still sounds like Barkley."

"It sounds like many people I've known," Yuriy says. Suddenly his head turns. Taras twists around in time to see a quick movement near the stove where the bun is warming. A blurry figure disappears into the shadows.

"Time for me to get that bun, boys," Yuriy says with a grin. "I'll cut it up for all of us. It'll be a nice way to end the day." He gets up and leads the others to the middle stove.

"What?" he says, "it's gone! How can that be? I put it right here...You know, that reminds me of a story." He winks his broadest, wickedest wink.

Yuriy leads the others down the wide aisle until he reaches Zmiya's bunk in the far corner. Taras notices that it's colder and darker here. Maybe that's Snake's problem; simple physical misery. Zmiya sits up, propped on his folded pillow. He swallows. There's a small bulge under his shirt. His paper hat is still folded on his pillow. Oh no, he had to pull his own cracker. For a moment Taras actually feels sorry for him, but not all that sorry.

Yuriy, Taras, Tymko, Myro and Ihor stand near the bunk. Yuriy sits down near the middle of the bunk and Ihor at the foot. The others drag chairs near and sit around in a partial circle. Zmiya can't get past them.

"You look a little out of sorts," Yuriy says. "I thought I might tell you a story."

Zmiya looks puzzled. There's a brief moment when he might have said, "I'm not interested in any story," but it's gone before he can speak.

"This story," Yuriy says, "takes place in the old country, in a small village. One day a poor man and his wife had so little to eat that after their supper the man was still hungry. He begged his wife to sweep out the flour bin and see if there might be enough flour to make him a nice bun. His wife did as he asked, and set the bun on the windowsill to cool." Yuriy's friends listen and nod at each other and at Zmiya. He shifts on his mattress and nods back.

"But this bun had its own ideas. It began to roll, and it fell onto the bench by the window. It rolled again and landed on the floor. It rolled so well and so fast that soon it was out the door, across the path, through the gate and down the road."

"No!" Ihor says. "What about the poor old lady?"

"She saw the bun getting away and called for it to stop, but it kept on rolling, singing this song: 'I was made from flour and yeast. And I was baked in an oven. And I shall run away from you!'"

"What?" says Tymko. "I've never heard of such a thing!"

"The old woman had never heard of such things either. And then her old man saw the bun and he tried to make it stop too. But the bun only sang, 'I was made from flour and yeast. And I was baked in an oven. I have run away from the old woman, and I shall run away from you.'"

"All this from a bun?" Taras asks, getting into the spirit.

Yuriy nods. "From a simple, fresh, tender bun. Who would have believed it?"

"Then what happened?" Myro asks. He looks like one of the Wise Men, Taras thinks, in the purple-and-silver hat.

"Well, I'll cut it short for you. The bun played the same trick on a rabbit, a wolf and a bear. The bun added a line to the song for each animal. Believe me, they were all getting quite annoyed." Yuriy looks fixedly at Zmiya and pats him on the small bump inside his shirt.

"A thrilling story, isn't it?" Yuriy asks. "I can feel your excitement. The area over your heart is quite warm. But enough of this happy storytelling, we must come to the end. Picture the bun rolling away, followed by an old *baba*, an old *dido*, a rabbit, a wolf and a bear. And no one can catch the bun.

"At last the bun rolls up to the cottage of a vixen, sitting on a bench plucking a chicken for her supper. By the way, it's not that well known, but vixens are very particular about not swallowing any feathers when they eat chicken." The others laugh, but not Zmiya.

"The vixen says, 'Come and let me eat you,' but the bun bargains with her. He offers to sing a fine song if she agrees not to eat him. 'All right,' she says, 'let's hear it, then.' And once more he sings, ending with all the creatures he's escaped from."

Yuriy sings in a very fine tenor, with great feeling: 'I ran away from the old woman. I ran away from the old man. I ran away from the rabbit, the wolf and the bear, and I shall run away from you too!' "Yuriy's friends lean toward him, as if tense with anticipation. Every second there seems less space for Zmiya, less air for him to breathe.

" 'What a fine song,' says the vixen," Yuriy says in a high-pitched vixen voice. 'But I'm a little deaf. Can you sing it again, but this time sit on my tongue so I can hear better.' "

"Oh-oh," Ihor says.

"So the bun jumps on her tongue and begins to sing. It reaches the words, 'I ran away from...' when the vixen's jaws go *snap!* and she eats the bun in a couple of gulps. And everybody else has to go home with nothing."

"Oh," Ihor says, "that's so sad. The poor old man." He moves a little closer to Zmiya.

"And the poor old woman," says Tymko. "She did all the work. Workers should receive some reward, even if it's only gratitude. But preferably a decent wage."

Yuriy bends closer to Zmiya. "What do you think? Wasn't that sad?"

Zmiya gulps. "I suppose... I suppose it was."

"Try not to feel too bad. It's just a story."

"But a very important one," Myro says. "It shows we must be vigilant at all times."

"Or someone might take the food from our mouths," Tymko agrees.

"Never mind," Yuriy says. "It happened far away. The old man and woman are dead and gone." He pats Zmiya again, right on top of the bulge. Zmiya doesn't move a muscle as Yuriy undoes a couple of buttons, reaches under Zmiya's shirt and pulls out a bun with a couple of bites gone – crumbling a bit after being inside the shirt.

"Have some of this nice warm bun," Yuriy says. "That'll cheer you up." He pulls off a good-sized chunk and pushes it into Zmiya's mouth. "Eat. It'll do you good."

Before Zmiya can chew it, he pushes in another piece, and then another. Zmiya can't chew or swallow. The others lean even closer. Zmiya tries to take a deep breath, tries to swallow, starts to cough.

"Oh dear," Tymko says, "the poor man's choking. Give him a little more."

Zmiya holds up a hand to say he's had enough, but Yuriy shoves in the last of the bun. Zmiya can't get a proper breath, just keeps gasping and choking. There's a gurgling noise in his throat. His eyes dart wildly.

"Myro, run and get some water," Yuriy says.

When Myro brings it, Yuriy pours the water on top of Zmiya's head. Myro and Tymko exchange a glance, and Tymko grabs Zmiya and shifts him to the edge of the bed. Pounds the choking man on the back with stupendous blows. Zmiya coughs and sneezes. Tears and snot stream down his face. After a minute or so of pounding and coughing he can breathe again. What looks to be all of the bun and most of the turkey dinner lies on the floor. Myro brings more water and this time they let him drink it. Tymko moves even closer to Zmiya. He glances at Yuriy, raises his eyebrows. Yuriy nods.

"Now," says Tymko, taking Zmiya's face gently in his hands and looking down into the teary eyes, "I hope you liked our friend's story. It's just a village tale, but I think a person can learn from it. I'm sure it holds many lessons, but the one I like best is that a person can be too smart for his own good. Have you ever noticed that?" He waits, brows raised, for an answer. "Hmmm?"

"Maybe."

"So. Listen carefully. We have been patient. That's done with. You have just become a new man. One who doesn't steal another person's food. Or attack a fellow prisoner with an axe handle."

Zmiya nods. The men stand close. They look harsh and unforgiving. Even Myro.

"A thing like that could break a man's legs. Luckily, that didn't happen. Now, no one wants you to find out how that would feel. But it could happen, couldn't it?" Again Zmiya nods. "Always remember, there are many of us. If anything happens to one..."

Shivering, Zmiya swipes at his wet hair and face with his shirt sleeve.

"Well, we've said enough for now. Maybe one day we'll talk again. When you've been a new man long enough that all of this is almost forgotten."

Tymko lays Zmiya gently down and they leave him to his thoughts.

Back at Yuriy's bunk, Tymko says, "Really, it's better if we learn through reason. But maybe some people learn only through fear."

"Is that a scientific conclusion?" Myro asks.

"No," says Tymko. "Just a wild guess."

Taras shares out the remaining bun. Wonders what they've done.

LATE IN DECEMBER he gets a packet of letters tied with twine, all but one from his parents. He tears them open and reads them one after another, though they're smudged with handling and pocked with ink where the censor has crossed something out. He wonders what his parents could possibly have written that would be dangerous to the Canadian government. He reads them out of order, but pieces together a story. The harvest was small but enough for them to buy potatoes, cornmeal and molasses, and a small grindstone to make flour. When cold weather came early, in the middle of October, they bought a load of coal for the stove. Protected by the sod walls, they were warm, but trapped indoors with little to do except worry about him.

In late November his friend from work, Moses, drove out one day in a borrowed wagon and asked them to come and stay with him in town. His parents are more than all right. His mother works three days a week cleaning a lady's house. Mykola helps the local blacksmith when there's more work than he can handle. It's not what was supposed to happen, not the golden wheat sheaf life of the tavern poster. But they're safe and warm and they have good food to eat.

He hasn't felt joy since he left the village and now, for a moment, he's afraid he might faint from the avalanche of feeling. He realizes that his heart has been starved here in this place, not only his body.

The last letter comes from Moses.

"It is a great pleasure to have your parents in my house. They remind me of my Ukrainian father. Already the lady your mother works for says she can't do without her. Your father has made a friend in the blacksmith, William Patterson. Mykola says they are more and more like real Canadians, but I've seen them cry when there were no letters. Since your letters came, they are happier. We look forward to celebrating Christmas.

"Pavlo taught me to sing the church services, but your parents are teaching me folk tales and songs from the old country. Mykola says I have a beautiful voice. I told him it's from my mother. When she sang, I thought the stars must be listening.

"I lost my first family and then I lost Pavlo before I was ready to be on my own. Your parents have taken away that pain.

"Have courage, Taras. You won't be in that awful place forever."

Taras sees a pen stroke, as if someone had started to strike out the word "awful" and then realized how petty that might look.

Taras is unaware of tears on his cheeks until Myro gets up and puts an arm across his shoulder. "They're all right," Taras says. "They're safe."

PART 2

CHAPTER 11

Ukrainian Christmas

January, 1916

CANADIAN NEW YEAR ARRIVES — another holiday for internees and guards — and in a few more days, it will be Ukrainian Christmas — not a holiday. Tymko says the government must think they were lucky to have one Christmas, even if it was the wrong one.

Christmas Eve, many of the men gather in the centre of the bunkhouse and say prayers. Even people who aren't very religious or very political resent being made to work on Christmas Day.

Before they leave the bunkhouse on Ukrainian Christmas morning, Tymko suggests a hunger strike.

"Let's analyze that idea." Yuriy makes his voice sound deep, like Tymko's. "You aren't for religion, but you want to lead a hunger strike so we can have Christmas in peace."

"Certainly," Tymko says. "People must be respected. Every community has its beliefs and customs. That is their right."

"Very interesting," Myro says.

"Besides, protest accustoms people to political action. This undermines dependence on supernatural forces. Teaches people to act to achieve their own goals." Tymko winks at Taras.

Good answer, Taras thinks. He winks back. It makes him smile.

Everyone agrees that a hunger strike is not in the prisoners' interests. It could result in the men not getting fed all day, or even longer, and there's no point in starting anything until they've at least got breakfast in their bellies. What then? In the end Tymko the socialist and Ihor the Hutsul volunteer to lead the men in refusing to work on Christmas. After the usual runny porridge and scorched coffee, they're expected to line up in groups ready to head out for work. Instead the men march in a rapid but orderly manner back to the bunkhouses, before the guards can catch on and lock them out. Tymko and Ihor wait outside to explain what's happening.

In moments the two of them have been locked in the guard-house, as they expected would happen. Each has several candy bars from the prisoners' canteen in his pocket, contributed by men who were saving them for Christmas day. Lying on his bunk, Taras tries to imagine their conversations. First they'd each eat half a candy bar. Then Tymko would analyze, scientifically, how the protest was going so far and predict how long they'd be locked up. He'd probably estimate that it would be only until the middle of the afternoon. Knowing it's their Christmas, how could the commandant be as harsh as usual? After this analysis, Ihor would tell tales about Hutsul life and sing old Christmas songs.

THIS IS PRETTY MUCH what happens, as Taras would hear after it was all over.

When Ihor gets going on the songs, Tymko joins in. The guards must be amazed to hear two-part harmony, baritone and deep bass, coming out of the guardhouse. Somebody bangs on the door with his rifle butt.

"Pipe down in there!" Barkley. Of course. The two men sing louder. He yells again but they drown him out. He gives up.

"Now what'll we do?" Tymko wonders. "I know! Let's fight to keep warm."

Do you think I'm crazy? Ihor's look says.

"Not serious fighting. Just a little wrestling to keep warm. And to keep in shape for the revolution."

"The revolution, is it? Oh, all right. I've nothing else to do. But no damage. Always remember, you don't want to get me mad."

"Certainly not. And we have our coats on to keep us from

getting hurt. *Dobre.* We wrestle."

They circle each other, looking for openings.

"Come on, mountain man, what are you afraid of?"

"Not you, you piece of gristle coughed up by a Russian dog."

Tymko grabs Ihor around his head and shoulders. Struggles to use his greater weight and lower centre of gravity to throw the Hutsul. Doesn't see Ihor's foot snake out and loop around his ankle. Tymko lands with a *whump.* Ihor leaps down to pin him, but Tymko wriggles away and jumps on Ihor's back. Ihor arches his back and Tymko falls to the floor. On their knees, grappling for a hold, each tries for a pin. They yell and grunt, even the hard wooden floor groans under them.

Again and again, one man takes the other down, only to have the victim slide out and appear somewhere else, like a ghost. Sweating and gasping, they peel off their coats.

"Now, sheepman, let's see what you can do."

"More than a moth-eaten Russian bear."

Tymko roars. "Don't call me Russian!"

They're off again. Tymko's stronger, but Ihor's cagier. More agile. Just when Tymko thinks he's got it won, Ihor gets his hip under Tymko's and vaults him through the air, like some heavy bird, a stork maybe, falling out of the sky. He lands in a sprawling heap on the floor, holds up a hand to say he's done.

"You devil. How did you do that?"

"It's a Hutsul thing. We don't talk about it." Ihor flops down beside Tymko, who starts to laugh.

"It was marvellous. I thought I was flying. It was almost a mystical experience." They pull on their coats. "Christ, I wish we had a drink!"

"A glass of plum brandy sure wouldn't hurt. You know, you look like a sheep that slipped on some ice and is afraid to get up."

"I do, don't I?" Tymko says. "Oh, I wish I was drunk!"

"Me too. Really drunk. Stupid drunk."

They're still laughing, arms around each other's shoulders, when someone pounds the door again.

"Hey! Settle down! Don't make me come in there!" Barkley again.

This sends them into volleys – no, cannonades – of laughter. Or maybe it's like thunder, or ice breaking up in spring. They figure Barkley's going to have to come in, now he's made the threat.

The key turns in the lock and he opens the door, rifle in one hand. Coming from bright sun, he obviously can't see them lying on the floor. Where the hell can they be? He feints with the bayonet, trying to look dangerous. Tymko and Ihor laugh so hard they're afraid they'll choke. Barkley, pale as a snowman in the dim light, is threatening them!

"Look out," Tymko says in Ukrainian. "He's got a gun!"

"Just shut up in here!" Barkley snarls. "Or I'll make you shut up."

"Oh dear God, we better be quiet," Ihor says. "He's so scary."

They become instantly quiet, but Barkley can easily see that it won't last and beats a quick retreat. Before he's turned the key in the lock, laughter roars out at him.

"Goddamn hunkie socialists!" he screams back.

Ihor and Tymko laugh until tears stream down their faces. They stagger to the bunks along the walls.

"You're a good man, Ihor," Tymko says.

"Oh, go on," the Hutsul answers, "you must be drunk."

BY THE TIME it's sorted out – the internees agree to work for the rest of the afternoon, all the men will be given supper, including Tymko and Ihor, and that'll be the end of the matter – there's not much afternoon left. Good thing, because everybody's hungry already.

The men are marched out in their usual work gangs, as far as the town centre. The guards make them clear a bit of snow off the streets, but nobody takes it seriously, including the guards. And then, much earlier than usual, they're marched back and allowed to rest until supper. Tymko's right. The brass aren't going to take away supper on a religious holiday. Even if it's one they don't admit exists.

As Taras and his friends line up for the mess hall, Ihor and

Tymko walk up looking surprisingly relaxed. The meal is not as good as the one on English Christmas, of course, but somebody's found a little cream to go in the coffee. The internees who work in the kitchen must have talked the officer in charge into it. The men have had so little fat for so long that it goes to their heads like whiskey.

"Cream is the opiate of the people," Tymko says, raising his cup in a sort of toast.

In the bunkhouse afterwards men gather to hear what it was like in the guardhouse. Soon there's laughter and then a few tentative voices begin a carol. In moments the bunkhouse rings with men's voices. Christ is born and the day is theirs.

ON JANUARY 8th a miracle happens: a mild day.

That's not all. After lunch the internees are taken for baths and then for a visit to the hot springs pool, a short distance up the hill from the bunkhouses. For "swimming," the guards call it. They go in small groups of a dozen or so, taking turns putting on the small assortment of plain black bathing trunks which have somehow turned up in camp.

At first Taras can't believe they have to go outside on a winter day wearing nothing else – is it some bizarre new form of punishment? – but moments later he stands on the edge of the pool and climbs down the steps, and then he understands. To say he likes it is completely inadequate. He has never imagined there could be this much hot water in one place. He smiles at Yuriy and Ihor, who look equally amazed, and wades out toward the centre of the pool. He crouches low until the water reaches his chin, and lets heat enter his body and warm his brain. He never wants to leave this pool, despite its strong · sulphur odour.

Maybe hot water could be the opiate of the people.

The wonder of it is, they're doing something any person might do on a visit to Banff. A tourist, for example, maybe even a tourist from Europe. The Austrian emperor, if he happened to be visiting. It's something people pay to do.

Heat penetrates every part of his body. Tingling, saturating heat — soaking away pain and almost dissolving thought. His arms and legs feel light, his genitals float in the mineral water. If he could come here every day for a week, or a month, he could start to live again. When you're always cold, there's no point worrying when you had your last bath, but now that he's clean and warm he wonders how long it's been.

Who consented to give the internees something so wonderful? Won't the commandant hear what's going on and order them out? Until he does, Taras will let his mind cease its endless working. Let peace lap at his brain.

Is it possible the commandant knows? After all Taras has been through, it's hard to imagine. But the commandant and his ways are a mystery he never expects to solve, so maybe he does know.

Standing near the steps, Zmiya watches him still. Taras looks away. He's not having this time spoiled.

THEY LOOK ALMOST like any group of men discovering the hot pool, except for a certain defensiveness, or vulnerability, in the way they stand, arms crossed or hands touching their chests. Well, who would want to bathe, almost naked, with armed guards standing over them? Even so, a couple of prisoners smile, sun glancing off their faces and pale shoulders.

One man crouches low in the water, arms outstretched, as though in a moment he'll swim to freedom.

The Stoney people say these hot mineral springs have healing powers. Arthur Lake hopes this is true for the prisoners.

On the terrace above the pool, a guard slouches, coat open. Another looks more posed, standing on the stone steps that lead down to the pool, a hand on the wooden railing. Perhaps this separation into two levels, guards and prisoners, makes a fitting image.

His wife, Winnie, has asked whether there are never any happy times in camp. This comes close: for once the prisoners are at least having a pleasanter time than their warders. Arthur Lake, Sergeant Lake, takes the picture.

On January 10th, even the commandant thinks it's too cold – 38 below – for the men to work. It stays that way for a whole week. Men go out only to get firewood.

Barkley comes in to check on them, just in case a drunken brawl may be taking place, and sneers that they're getting a free holiday in the mountains. He launches into the usual lecture on gratitude. It's odd, Taras thinks, that some guards cling to the possibility of gratitude, since they haven't seen a single example of it so far. He closes his ears to the rest of it, just seeing Barkley's red lips flapping in the all-white head.

During this week of "sitting around," as Barkley calls it, escape talk seeps through the bunkhouse like meltwater. Everybody knows men have escaped and not been brought back. Men from the coal towns, for instance.

It's also impossible not to think of women. If only they could see women, talk to women. Touch them.

One day, shovelling snow off Banff streets, Taras notices a young woman watching him. Her face has a lively, curious expression, not the disapproving look he usually sees from the town women. She might almost be ready to smile. For a second she's his Halya.

Some days the picture of Halya he carries in his mind begins to slip and he's afraid he'll forget how she looks. Other times memory surges back — the cool way her eyes take in everything around her, the warmth of her lips, the touch of her body against his — until he thinks he'll go crazy. Most of the time he's aware of sexual feeling as something locked away deep inside him, but there are also times when he wants to yell and scream. Wants to know why everybody isn't yelling and screaming. But keeping quiet when you need to yell and scream seems to be one of the secrets of waiting out imprisonment.

Sometimes he goes to the latrine where he can be alone and relieve that tension, but he feels miserable afterwards, humiliated. He wonders if the others ever do the same, but nobody talks about it. One night, he asks Tymko if it's normal. He says not to worry, that everybody does it sometimes. It's a scientific fact.

AFTER A WEEK of being stuck in the bunkhouse, everyone — except Bohdan the carver, who always has work to do — feels unusually restless. Not that they want to be out felling trees or chopping kindling, they just don't want to be *here*. People try their best to keep the card games and the political discussions going, but every activity, every thought, seems exhausted.

After an unusually lousy supper of fried noodles and sausage shrapnel, Taras sits, with Tymko, Yuriy, Myro and Ihor, around a table in the bunkhouse. Hands have been dealt and each man has a pile of matchsticks to bet with. Yuriy's is the biggest. You'd think Myro the arithmetic teacher would have the most, but Yuriy just has a gift.

They were going to play poker, but couldn't decide on what kind. Tymko suggested hearts and dealt the cards, but nothing's happened since. The only person doing anything at all is Yuriy, who keeps flicking through his cards and nodding wisely.

"For God's sake," Tymko grumbles, "how can your hand be that bloody interesting?" Yuriy shrugs. It's interesting to him.

Taras sits by Tymko, so he should lead, but he just stares into the air, his cigarette slowly consuming itself in the tobacco tin ashtray. Four pairs of eyes drill into him. He doesn't notice; sees only that he's got terrible cards. As usual. Tymko clears his throat loudly.

Yuriy nudges Taras's foot. Ihor whistles through his teeth. Myro pretends to scowl. Taras looks up. Tymko leans toward him and moves the eyebrows up and down.

Taras sighs and lays his cards, face up, on the table. After a moment the others do the same. Time passes.

Suddenly Tymko smacks his fist against the table. "I have it!" he says. "We'll take turns, and each of you will explain why he doesn't at least try to escape."

"What about you?" Ihor asks. "Aren't you in on this too?"

"I thought that might be unnecessary," Tymko says. True. They've all seen the scar on his chest.

Yuriy has an answer ready. He has a better farm than anyone he knew in the old country. Soon he'll be able to make a good living for himself, his wife, Nadia, and her mother. He figures they'll have to let him go some day, as Tymko has said so many times.

"But if I run away... They might send me to prison. Take my farm. Everything we've worked for."

"*Dobre,*" Tymko says, "I can see you've thought it through. Myro?"

"That's easy. I want to be a teacher again some day. A teacher can't have any kind of criminal background."

"Won't it be just the same having been interned?" Tymko asks.

"No. Things won't always be the way they are now. In time, people will realize a wrong has been committed. There will be an apology, and restitution of what has been taken away. I will be a teacher of arithmetic, history or whatever is needed."

The others listen, hoping he knows what he's talking about. It sounds convincing, at this moment, anyway.

"Hey Myro," Yuriy asks, "how *does* an arithmetic teacher get sent to an internment camp, anyway?"

Myro smiles. "Not because of arithmetic. It was my other passion."

"What's your other passion?" Tymko asks suggestively.

"I write articles about interesting people. Interesting Ukrainian people. I wrote a perfectly reasonable article for *The People's Voice* about Ivan Franko."

"Ah, the author of novels and poems," Tymko says. "The great democratic socialist."

"That's him. My article was about his novels and how they helped develop Ukrainians' political and cultural consciousness."

"Subversive, you mean."

"I can hardly think how. But that was what they said. That I favoured a free and independent Ukraine."

"That's a crime now, is it?" Tymko shakes his head. "Well, boys, I've changed my mind. I'll tell you why I'm still here. Other than that I now know what a bayonet feels like.

"You see, the camp is likely the safest place for me right now. Wartime isn't a good time to be a socialist union leader. The government doesn't like them any better than it likes Ukrainians, and I'm both. So I might as well stay here, imprisoned for being Ukrainian." He grins. "There are more Ukrainians in Canada than socialists, so I've got more people to sympathize with me."

"That sounds *scientific*," Yuriy says.

"Also," Tymko winks, "if they did want to kill someone who's escaping, to make an example, who do you think it would be? That's right. The socialist."

"Or one of his radical friends," Myro says.

"That's possible too. Anyway, I'll stay put. Where I can talk to other men, I mean consort with other men, about how the world could be run better. And you, Taras?"

Taras considers. "I don't want to get my parents in trouble. They didn't want to come to Canada, but I had to leave, so they came too." What he wants most is to find Halya, but he doesn't know how. "If I knew how to find Halya..." He leaves the rest unsaid, but everyone understands: he'd escape in a moment. But would he really?

"When we get out of this place," Tymko says, "you might find this woman you love. Don't give up."

If a scientific, revolutionary socialist thinks he shouldn't give up, maybe he shouldn't. In fact, Taras sees that he never has given up. His hopes are like a river: frozen on top, with a cold, silent flow under ice.

The story helps keep him going. In the telling, he understands it better himself.

"Time to get on with your story," Tymko says, as if reading his mind.

Taras hesitates. "You understand, there are parts I don't really know."

"Make it up then. Isn't that what you did before?"

"*Tak.* Anyway, I know some parts because I was there, others because Natalka's friend Maryna told my mother – how Viktor sold his land, the day he left the village. For some other parts...Yes, I make things up. But I know these people."

"Taras, it's all right," Tymko says. "Nobody cares. Just give us some more story. *Proshu.*"

So he does, beginning with Halya and her grandmother Natalka sitting in the kitchen the day before they will leave Shevchana.

CHAPTER 12

A square of linen

HALYA WAS IN the kitchen, breathing in the warmth of newly baked bread. Everything else that spoke of daily life was gone – embroidered linen scarves on walls and benches, herbs and flowers hung from rafters, plain pottery dishes. All of these, all of the icons, clothing, pots and tools and utensils, and Halya's few books, except for one she'd kept out to read on the journey, had been packed in a carved wooden trunk sitting in the middle of the room. A length of cream-coloured linen lay unfinished on the loom. Natalka ran her fingers over the tightly woven square. She'd probably never weave linen again. Only now could she admit how much her hands ached.

Halya paced around the trunk.

"Can't you sit, Halychka? You make me dizzy."

"We're going to Kanady tomorrow. I'm afraid I'll never see Taras again."

"Now, now, Halya. He'll come to Kanady and find you."

"What if he's caught? The government doesn't want young men to leave!" Halya shakes her head and her long hair, in waves from her braids, whips across her face. "War's coming! Everyone says so now."

"Maybe it won't come. Anyway, even if it does, not everyone dies in a war. Maybe he'll –"

"*Maybe?* Maybe's no good to me!"

MEANWHILE, Viktor had decided not to wait for Kondarenko to raise the money to buy his land. Or for Mykola's friend Yarema. Let them find other places to buy. Viktor Dubrovsky couldn't wait around forever. So he'd driven over to see the *pahn,* and they were sitting in a small office off the *pahn's* kitchen. Radoski placed banknotes in Viktor's hand, looking all the while as if he'd like to snatch them back.

Viktor counted the money carefully.

"It's all there, damn it. You don't need to count every crown."

"Certainly not, *Pahn,* but mistakes happen. I know you wouldn't want that. You are respected by everyone as a man of honour."

Radoski rifled through the papers Viktor had given him. "It wasn't easy putting my hands on the cash," he said. "I've had many expenses lately. Had to pay young Kuzyk for training my horse." He threw this last bit in just to irk Viktor.

"That's not my problem, is it, Pahn?" Viktor had no stake in annoying the landlord, but it felt good all the same.

Radoski puffed up with spite. "Of course, you know why he needs money."

Viktor's head started to boil. He'd have liked to wipe the leer off the *pahn's* face.

"He wants to marry your daughter." Radoski barely concealed his glee.

Be calm, Viktor told himself. Soon this posturing lump will be a distant memory. "Wanting is not doing. My daughter will be far away in Kanady."

"Of course, he might follow her. After he gets out of the army." Radoski enjoyed the horrified look on Viktor's face. His lips formed the fat smirk everyone in the village had learned to hate.

"*If* he gets out of the army." Viktor put his purse away, heavy with the *pahn's* crowns. He could barely stuff it in his pocket.

AT THE SAME MOMENT, Halya stared at the loaves of bread cooling on the table. She heard the door open, and her friend Larysa crept in the door, glancing back over her shoulder, as if she were afraid someone was following, or watching.

"Larysa, what is it? What's happened?"

"You mustn't tell anyone."

Halya shakes her head.

"I'm going to have a baby." Larysa's eyes, a little bit blue and a little bit green, filled with tears.

Halya held Larysa close, patting her hand, and they both started to cry.

Natalka came in, bristling with energy. "There now, Halya, it's not the end of the world." Halya and Larysa broke into fresh gusts of tears. Natalka looked more closely at Larysa's red-splotched face and at her belly, and saw that it was rounder than it used to be.

"Dear God."

"That's why Ruslan came to the meeting at the reading hall. We were going to get married. Now his father said he's sleeping in the guardhouse and doing hard labour."

"Ruslan must get leave and come home to marry her," Halya said. She patted Larysa's head, her coiled braids.

"Oh, they won't let him do that. Soldiers can't get married. Not without special permission," Natalka said.

"They could give him permission. Surely the Austrians understand such matters."

"No, I don't think they do."

"They think we're barbarians," Larysa cried. "Who cares what happens to peasants?"

"Do your parents know?" Natalka asked.

Larysa covered her face and wailed. "No, but they soon will. My father will beat me and my mother will push me out the door."

Natalka put her arm around Larysa's shoulders, thinking hard. "If they make you leave, go to Maryna. She'll look after you."

"I want Ruslan!" Larysa shrieked, although Natalka had made a truly generous offer. Too generous, really, to be made on another person's behalf. A person who hadn't even been consulted.

"I know, I know." Natalka kissed her cheek. "And maybe he'll get leave. Maybe it'll work out all right." She clucked like a hen with a hurt chick. "But if there's trouble, go to Maryna."

"What can *she* do?" Larysa said in a shrill voice. "She's just a poor old woman."

"Just go," Natalka said fiercely. "Will you do that?"

Choking on tears, Larysa managed a nod. "I'd better leave now."

The young women embraced. Natalka lifted the skirt of her long apron and wiped Larysa's face. Held her tightly and kissed both her cheeks. Larysa left without another word.

"This is terrible," Natalka said. "That poor child."

"Will Maryna help her?" Halya looked uncertain.

"I think so. Someone must."

Halya picked up the twig broom and swiped at the already clean floor, but Natalka took the broom away and put it in the storeroom.

"Sit," she said. "Read your book."

Viktor complained all the way home. The old horse pulled the cart ever more slowly. She was twenty years old and couldn't be expected to work as she used to, but he cursed and ranted anyway. I'll have a better horse in Kanady, he thought. I'll have many horses. A matched team with harness trimmed in brass. Or silver. Yes, silver! Why not? Halya can keep it bright and shiny. I'll have a good house. Everyone will know who I am.

At home, he stabled the horse, gave her water and hay, rubbed her sweaty back with an old blanket. Natalka always said he treated the horse better than he did his daughter.

"The horse does what I want," he always answered.

This was the last day he'd own this animal. So what if Radoski didn't want her, he'd foist her onto somebody or other. Lubomyr Heshka – he could use an old horse. Maybe he'd even give Lubo a really good deal. Then somebody in the village would remember him fondly. Well, maybe not fondly. Anyway, who cared? He'd never see any of them again.

He went into the house and found Halya on the bench, her back to him, reading. Without even thinking, he grabbed the book and threw it to the floor.

"Poetry! That's not a woman's business."

Halya turned and he saw her tears and fierce anger. Wished he could turn around, go back out and come in again. But he couldn't back down.

"What good is any of this? How does Shevchenko help me? Flowers, pretty words, that's all that poet cares about. Does any of that make me a rich man?"

Halya picked up her book. "This book belonged to Mama."

"You should be doing your work!" Viktor blustered but looked abashed.

"What work should I do? The bread is baked. The floor is swept."

Her face hardened, and it scared him. Didn't she know he was doing this for her, too? There might be pain now, but later would come great happiness. Or that was what he'd been telling himself. Maybe he should have been gentler. A woman will always hate to leave her home.

"Halya, please. You can have books in Kanady. Poetry, stories. Books bound in fine leather."

"All you want is to stop me from marrying Taras."

"You're wrong, Halychka. I want much more than that." He kissed her cheek but she turned away.

"You'll do anything to keep us apart. You'll take me away from everyone I know. And you'll be happy if they take Taras for the army."

Viktor tried not to look happy, but he couldn't wipe away the look, at least not quickly enough, that said he wasn't sorry to get her away from Taras Kuzyk.

"You're glad, aren't you?" Halya looked ferocious. This must be how tigers looked. "I know you are."

"Halya, listen –"

"I hate you!" she screamed.

Viktor wanted to slap her, but he felt a jolt of terror in his belly. He'd sold his land, bought the tickets. What if the new country wasn't what the posters promised?

He couldn't lose heart. "It's for the best. You'll see." He went outside to look over what used to be his land one last time. For a moment he imagined shells bursting and soldiers trampling his fields to dust. Then he shook his head: he'd be long gone before that happened.

NATALKA HAD GONE out a little earlier, to Maryna's house, where her friend sat mending a torn *sorochka*. "Ah, it's the new *pahna*. You'll be off to your estate in Kanady tomorrow."

"Don't joke." Natalka pulled a necklace of amber beads from her pocket. The beads glowed against her lined and sunbrowned hand. "I was going to give this to Halya. Now it's yours." She tried to place it in Maryna's hand, but Maryna pulled her hand away.

"Are you crazy?" she said in a shocked voice. "I can't take that. It's too valuable. You keep it for Halya."

Natalka met Maryna's gaze without flinching. "Halya won't need it. You will."

"Now, just a minute. I'm no *pahna*, but I'm not a beggar yet." Maryna looked so insulted, Natalka wanted to laugh, but she didn't give in to it.

"I didn't say you were. I said you'll need it."

"You are crazy!" Maryna said. But something in Natalka's determined manner – her apparent belief that her friend *would* take the necklace – had her curious.

Natalka placed the necklace on the *peech*. "When Viktor asked for my daughter, I thought he was only interested in her dowry. So I kept something back."

"But Natalka –"

"This is the last thing of value I have left from my own parents. My last chance to make something go better around here. And don't worry about Halya and me. Do you think the wild boar will let us starve? Big, important man like him?"

"Natalka, please –"

"Anyway, it's not just for you." Natalka told her about Larysa. "If there's anything left upon your death, will you leave it to her?"

Maryna took a few more stitches to absorb what she'd heard. "I thought you said I wouldn't die for a long time," she said slyly.

"Well, you won't. But I have to consider everything. So. Your son and his wife are dead and never had children. It's time you were someone's *baba*."

"Hah!" said Maryna, not ready to agree yet. "What do you know?"

"Hah! yourself, old woman."

"Me, old? I'm younger than you!" Outrage turned to laughter.

"Face it, we're both old as the hills," Natalka said.

"Old as a couple of prunes," Maryna agreed.

"Old as Viktor's horse."

They laughed until Maryna got hiccups. Natalka had to pound her back and bring her a cup of water.

"I'll miss you, Natalka." Now they were crying, these two tough old birds.

"I'll send letters. Halya will write for me, and Larysa can read them to you." They wiped their eyes on their long apron skirts.

Maryna sighed. "So that's my life taken care of? You just whirl in here and tell me what I'll be doing till I die?"

"So it seems," Natalka said.

"Oh. Well, I like Larysa. She's a good girl." Maryna gave a slight nod.

"*Dobre.* It's settled. I'll see you one more time...tomorrow." Natalka fought tears.

"If you're lucky," Maryna said tartly.

"Nonsense. You're sure to live that long." And then Natalka was out the door.

THE NEXT MORNING, Viktor Dubrovsky closed the door to his house for the last time. He and Natalka climbed into the wagon. Viktor flapped the reins and they started down the lane. Halya walked beside the wagon. At each house, people waited outside to say goodbye.

Natalka got down to embrace Maryna, tears on her face. Maryna wasn't crying, she refused to. "It'll be better. You'll see. Go."

At these brave words her chest shook, and she thought that if Natalka let go of her she might burst apart, arms and legs and head flying into the morning sky. Natalka hugged her hard and then let go with a great hiccupping sob, and Maryna was still there, in one piece. Halya took her *baba's* arm and helped her catch up to the wagon and climb back in. Of course Viktor didn't stop. He drove neither faster nor slower. That was understandable. He wouldn't want to be seen to let anything or anyone influence him, and certainly not a woman.

The wagon approached Daria and Mykola's house. Taras and Halya had already agreed that he wouldn't come outside to see the Dubrovskys off.

But as the wagon passed the Kuzyk house, Mykola and Daria came out. Halya embraced each in turn. Viktor looked back for a moment and his daily look of antagonism and contempt slipped, changed for a moment to one of pain, and longing. As if he suddenly realized he'd never see these people or this place again. For a moment it seemed he'd speak to them, some word of peace or goodwill, but he quickly gave the reins a shake and the horse plodded on.

When the wagon reached the Heshka house, Lubomyr came out and followed behind. He would go to the station with them and bring his new-old horse and wagon back to the village. Viktor *had* given him a good deal. He'd had no choice; no one else wanted them.

Maryna followed the wagon to the edge of the village and watched it climb the long hill outside Shevchana, growing smaller and smaller until it disappeared, as if it had driven into a hole in the sky.

CHAPTER 13

The new people

April, 1914

MYKOLA AND TARAS spent the rest of the day doing what everyone in Shevchana was doing, sowing their fields. At sunset they walked home through the lane and smelled Daria's newly baked bread before they came in the door. They sat down to a supper of cabbage rolls keeping warm in the *peech*.

Without having talked about it, they had all three felt something changing since Daria had agreed that Taras should go to Kanady. Now when Daria looked across the table into Mykola's grey eyes, she knew the life they'd had was gone. Or maybe it had been gone for a while and they'd only just noticed.

She passed bread to Mykola and Taras and waited to see whether one of them would put the change into words. When neither did, she simply said, "We can go with him."

The idea seemed to echo in the small room; or it sent ripples out into the air the way a stone does in water. It settled. There wasn't much to say, because what must be done was so clear.

After their meal, Mykola walked along the dark lane to Yarema's house. Savelia, Yarema's wife, looked surprised when Mykola handed her the mended bridle he'd brought with him to explain his errand if anyone asked.

Savelia brought tea and bread with *mak* – poppyseed – to the table.

"You wanted to buy Viktor's land," Mykola began. "Supposing you could get some other land, also good, at a fair price..." And Mykola gave them a brief history of how the Kuzyks had decided to leave the village.

"Your price is better than Viktor's," Yarema said when he was done. "And I'll have more land than I do now, so that'll be good. But I'll be sorry to see you go." He didn't say, I'll be losing my best friend, but Mykola understood. Yarema wasn't a man who made close friends easily. Not because he was unpleasant, like Viktor, but there was something almost shy about him. He didn't tell many people about himself.

"I need the money tomorrow." Mykola gazed steadily at his old friend.

"Tomorrow..." Yarema plainly hoped for an explanation.

"Or the day after. It's only a week until Taras is supposed to report," Mykola said. "Can you do it?"

Yarema nodded. "I got the money ready to offer Viktor. You can have it now."

Mykola wrote his old friend a bill of sale. Yarema handed him the money, and a step in a journey of no return was taken. I never even wanted to leave the village, he thought.

"I borrowed this money," Yarema said, "so I'll need to sell my place quickly in order to pay it back. Do you think Kondarenko will want it?"

"Maybe. Or Radoski. Your land joins up to Viktor's land."

"I'll only do that if I have to. I don't like to see land going back to the *pahns*."

"No," Mykola said, "little enough has changed for us as it is." He rose to leave. "Say nothing of this for three days. Everyone knows we plan to drive Taras into Chernowitz to report to the army. They'll think we've stayed over with my cousin." His friends nodded.

Mykola embraced and kissed each one in turn, and felt their tears mingle with his own. He stepped out into the night.

Back at home, he and Daria packed a few things in a linen bag. She pointed to the icons and the portrait of Shevchenko. At first

Mykola shook his head. Then an idea struck him, and he took them down and removed them from the frames, along with the sheets of paper backing that protected them.

"Wait," Taras said and showed them the money he'd hidden in the backing papers. At first he wanted to take the money out, but Daria thought the backing papers might be the safest place to keep it. Mykola laid the images and backing flat on a linen scarf and rolled them into a cylinder, which he bound with a bit of cord and fit vertically into one side of the bag.

They wouldn't have to protect the money for long. Most of it would be gone before they left Chernowitz.

THE NEXT MORNING the Kuzyks tried not to look at anything in particular as they drove down the lane. If they gazed at the houses, the tavern, the stave church, as if trying to remember every detail, it would look wrong. People don't do that if they're planning on coming back. They took it slowly in their old wagon, drawn by their old white horse, Losha. For the first time they thought it was strange to have called a horse "colt" for seventeen years.

Maryna would milk the cow while they were away, and make herself butter. They'd told her they might stay in the city a few nights with Mykola's cousin.

On the way they passed other villages, other houses, churches and taverns, until they all seemed to roll together in their minds into something called the *selo;* the village. There might be villages in Kanady, but they would probably never see a Ukrainian *selo* again.

In a couple of hours they saw the city in the distance, a sight that always gave them feelings of excitement and dread. Mykola spent three years there as a young man, during his army service and afterwards working on horses, but he hardly ever went back after his marriage. Still, he knew where to find things; he knew where he had to go.

The city was still part of him. He only had to take the memories out of his pocket and dust them off a bit.

They stopped to eat the food they'd brought along. Plain

roasted potatoes tasting of the earth. Dark rye bread. Slices of crisply cooked pork. They felt hunger in a new way, and the plain but ample feast couldn't take it away. Taras thought they would feel hungry until they found some new place to be their home.

TODOR'S HOUSE in a workingman's neighbourhood was just as Taras remembered it from a childhood visit. A house made of wood, with more rooms than a village house. It had Ukrainian country things in it and also things of the city, including a sofa upholstered in material printed with flowers. Before Taras first saw this house, if a piece of cloth had flowers on it, that was because a woman had embroidered them there.

Mykola knocked and a wiry man in his forties with greying black hair and and strong cheekbones opened the door. Todor's dark eyes drilled into them as if he sought to extract all that had happened to them since their last visit. He seemed both amazed to see them, and also to realize at once that his old friend would need something from him.

Todor was not Mykola's cousin, because Mykola didn't have a cousin in Chernowitz.

He did have a friend who'd worked at the garrison looking after horses most of his life. Now he trained horses for well-off people.

Todor embraced them in turn: Mykola, Daria, Taras.

"Come in," he said. Inside they met Todor's *baba* Liuba, who kept house for him now.

BY EVENING, many important things had been done. Todor had been to see a friend who knew a man who made passports. They would be ready the next day. The Kuzyks didn't ask how Todor knew who to ask about forged papers. Chernowitz was a big city, and many people passed through it every day, from all over Europe. Perhaps not all of them wanted to remember who they used to be.

Todor and Baba Liuba had also been to an outdoor market where you could get good used clothing. They had bought a second-hand suit and hat for Mykola, and a plain dark dress and a hat with a black feather on top for Daria. Taras had a suit whose jacket and pants didn't quite match, with a woollen peak cap. When they put the clothes on, after Baba Liuba sponged off a few spots, they looked like city people. Not well-off city people; more like a tradesman and his wife, and their grown son.

"*Douzhe dobre,*" Baba Liuba said. She looked rather severe, with the same challenging eyes as her grandson, but when she smiled, the dimples in her cheeks softened her face.

She studied them for a while, then fetched a pair of scissors. She gave Mykola a much shorter haircut, so that no hair stuck out from under the hat, and did the same for Taras. She showed Daria how to wind her hair into a sort of bun that could fit under the hat.

Todor and Liuba had also found one other useful thing: a small wooden chest to hold all the things their friends were taking with them.

When they fell asleep that night, in the unfamiliar world of the city, the Kuzyks were exhausted beyond anything they'd ever known. Taras felt as if he'd been beaten with planks.

THE FOLLOWING AFTERNOON, Todor brought home an envelope with passports for Mykola, Daria and Taras Kalyna, which although false, seemed to exhale the scent of Austrian law and order. Lubomyr Heshka had talked about going to Kanady and becoming a new man. Now, without ever intending it, the Kuzyks had become new people.

"I thought it would be safest if I gave you a new name," Todor said. "May you wear it well." He had named them for the beloved *kalyna* with its green leaves and red berries.

Daria and Mykola handled the passports with amazement. They'd never wanted to travel, never even seen a passport before, but now they had the means and the papers. Of course, they no longer had a home. Or a name.

THE NEXT MORNING, the Kalynas prepared to leave. Todor had gone out earlier and bought the tickets. He hadn't seen any soldiers at the railway station, and everyone hoped it would stay that way.

Todor drove them down to the station in their own cart. There was a bad moment when Colonel Krentz rode down the Stationstrasse on Imperator. He saw them, because he was a man who looked at everything around him, but he never *saw* them. Never saw Taras.

It was decided that Taras would stay in the cart with Todor while Mykola and Daria went inside to make sure there were no soldiers on the platform. They picked up the small chest and their cloth bag and walked up to the main doors.

From the outside, Taras thought the station seemed almost like a church, with its huge dome and the tall arched windows over the doors, front and back, that let you see through to the sky on the other side. From this domed centre, the station stretched out in two wide wings roofed in copper aged to soft green. The uncounted tons of pale stone, the heavy dome, inspired respect, even fear. They spoke of wealth, authority, empire. Taras had now defied the empire, and he couldn't wait to see the last of its grandeur.

Taras saw his parents pass through the far doors onto the platform.

MYKOLA WATCHED the train pull into the station, brakes squealing, hissing steam. The conductor dropped his stepping box, hopped down and began helping passengers off.

Other people stood around the platform waiting to board. Some, dressed in homespun, carrying cloth bags. A man in a business suit and soft felt hat, with a flat leather case under his arm. Two older ladies in long black dresses and neat but faded coats. Their hovering servant, also old, a long white beard trailing down his chest. An old priest sitting on a wooden bench.

And two soldiers paced the platform, glancing about with sharp blue eyes. They never looked twice at Daria and Mykola.

Inside, new arrivals streamed into the station. Mykola went back out to the street to let Taras know about the soldiers. Told him to wait until the last possible moment to board. But how could he get by the soldiers?

Mykola went back out to the platform to stand with Daria. She raised a hand as if to adjust her headscarf, but it was no longer there. Without it, she had to act as though she was someone else, and he could see it was making her tired. She reached up again and changed the angle of the hat so that it shaded her face more.

TARAS CAME INSIDE the station and made his way to a shadowy corner, just as a man stepped through the front doors — a man with a well-fed look and a confident military bearing. A man used to getting his way. Taras shrank against the wall as Krentz strode smartly through the station and onto the platform.

The colonel went over to the soldiers. They shook their heads — no young men trying to avoid the army. Krentz looked up and down the platform, shrugged. Stood near the station wall.

The conductor nodded. People drifted toward him, gripping bags, tickets ready, and began to board. Soon only the Kalynas were left. The conductor's look said, *What's keeping you? Have you never been on a train before?* They hadn't, but things like that didn't bother them any more. They boarded the train.

Krentz strained to see into the carriages. Ordered the two soldiers to search the cars. The conductor looked annoyed at this but said nothing, only looking at his watch meaningfully. Trains must keep to a schedule and he didn't want to get in trouble.

Taras watched through the station windows. He heard a hiss and a chuff; the train was starting up. Krentz was still on the platform. If Taras didn't get on that train, he'd be finished. His parents were on their way to Kanady. They'd given up everything for him.

Looking out to the street, he saw Imperator tied to a lamppost. He went outside, as quickly as he could without attracting attention, giving a little wave to Todor. He stroked the stallion's neck. Untied him and leapt into the saddle, and took off down Stationstrasse. As he rode, he made a loose knot in one of the reins, hoping it would look as if they weren't tied properly.

He heard the approaching engine and the clack of wheels. When he thought he must be well ahead of the train, he pulled up, jumped off the horse and sent him back down the street with a light slap to his rump. He ran between two buildings and sprinted for the track. The train was passing now, starting to pick up speed. He dashed for the door of the last carriage. In a moment he was raising a foot to the first of two steel steps in front of the door and reaching for the railing beside it.

Todor drove slowly away from the station. Mykola's horse and cart now belonged to him.

KRENTZ CAME OUT of the station and looked around for his horse. Imperator had found a grassy strip in the middle of the cobbled street. When he reached the stallion, Krentz saw the apparently slipped knot and shrugged. He mounted and rode off, heard the train's whistle in the distance. He felt annoyed, although not as much as he would have expected. There had been a deserter, and General Loder wanted him caught. Wanted to make an example of him.

As he passed the Seminarska church on his way to the garrison, he pulled up and let his mind review everything he'd seen. Imperator had slipped his tether, tempted by some green grass and a loose knot. But Reinhard Krentz didn't tie loose knots. It wasn't the way he did things. Nor would it be easy for a stranger to untie the horse. He was used to being handled only by Krentz and whoever was looking after him in the garrison.

Or perhaps the person who trained him.

He remembered four people travelling in a wagon. Tradespeople by the look of them; the youngest surely the son of the woman and one of the men.

There'd been something familiar about them, he realized.

He could send a telegram and everything would be taken care of. Guards would board the train and arrest Taras, send him back to join the army. Krentz could have him sent to the guardhouse for a while. He'd be company for that other one from the same village.

So he could have Taras brought right back. But he found himself wondering – did the fact that he *could* mean that he could also refrain?

Taras schooled this wonderful horse. Watched him take Imperator out from under the nose of the seedy old *pahn*. And there probably would be war, and many young men would die. He, Krentz, might die himself.

The comic side of it struck him, the audacity of the young man who'd once replaced a shoe on his horse. And once this rush of fellow feeling was there, it was too late. Krentz burst out laughing. He decided to take Imperator for a good run in the hills.

The conductor worked his way down the aisle. Daria tried to look calm.

"Where is he?" She adjusted the hat, distressed by the unfamiliar structure of twisted black taffeta on her head. The dress felt hot and prickly against her skin, not at all like soft linen. The train was moving. They'd sold their land and left the village, got on a train for God knew where, put on the clothing of strangers...

"Shhh." Mykola pretended to search in the cloth bag for something, his ticket, perhaps, although it was already clamped between his icy fingers. He tried to relax the fingers a little, to let the blood circulate. The conductor edged closer. Only two more passengers until he'd reach them — an old *dido* and a *baba* with her belongings tied up in a *babushka*.

At the far end of the car, Taras entered. Seeing him, Daria felt as if a heavy, wet fog swirled in her head and was afraid she'd faint. But she couldn't do that; she had to keep the conductor from noticing Taras, who was making his way down the aisle.

She caught the conductor's eye. "*Proshu*, how long is the journey to Lemberg?" She used the German name for the conductor, but in Ukrainian the city was Lviv.

The conductor's glance told her it was rude to speak to him without being spoken to first. He was taking care of another passenger, after all. He was an important railway official.

She thought he might even be taking in their rather worn clothing and a certain unease in the way they carried themselves.

"It takes as long as it takes." *Don't bother me,* his eyes said.

Taras edged past the conductor's back and took a seat opposite his parents. The conductor finished with the old couple and moved on to Mykola.

"Here are our tickets – for my wife and I." Mykola handed them over. "And for our son." Now he glanced at Taras.

The conductor turned and almost jumped. "Where the devil did he come from?"

Mykola lowered his voice. "He had to use the toilet."

They could see the conductor thinking, Did I see that one get on the train?

"And where might you be going?" the conductor asked suspiciously.

"To Lemberg," Taras said. He tried to look like an innocent young man excited by his first train journey.

"We're going to attend a wedding," Daria said. "My husband's cousin's daughter is getting married."

"Your husband's cousin's daughter?" The conductor asked skeptically.

"That's right," Mykola said. "She's the same age as my son, and I must say that we had hoped the two of them might... But they live so far away, and we just don't see each other that often. But it will be a good chance to see his family."

"Oh yes, and what does your cousin do in Lemberg?"

"He runs a livery stable, with a smithy attached," Mykola lied. "He's actually done quite well."

Taras was proud. His father was like an actor in a play. Not that Taras had seen a play, but he'd lived in Chernowitz and knew about such things.

The conductor nodded to himself for some time. Something jogged his brain. "Back there at the station...there were soldiers. Looking for someone. I wonder who that could have been."

"I don't know," Mykola said. "They were speaking German." Mykola spoke German quite well himself, but he wasn't going to say that.

The conductor examined their tickets. Considered what to do. Have the train crawling with soldiers and getting off schedule? Or...

"Now that I look more closely, I see these tickets aren't quite correct. They won't take you all the way you're going." The conductor's voice had a sharp edge to it.

Mykola looked at the tickets, "Chernowitz to Lemberg" printed clearly on them. Did the man think they couldn't read? It didn't matter. He wanted a bribe. Mykola pulled out his purse. Hoped the conductor wouldn't sell them out anyway.

LATER, MYKOLA LOOKED OUT THE WINDOW, eyes losing focus. Daria dozed with her head on his shoulder. Taras slept slumped across the seat opposite. Time to wake Daria so she could keep watch. They'd agreed they shouldn't all sleep at once. He touched her arm and she was instantly awake, checking to see that Taras was still there. She listened to the *tik-tik, tik-tik,* as the train ran along the rails. If the conductor put them off the train, what could they do? They must be over a hundred miles from home. No going back.

Nothing to go back to.

Inside Mykola's bag was the last loaf of bread she would ever bake in Bukovyna. She realized how hungry she was. She found it and tore off a chunk.

"Tonight," she said, "I've travelled further than I ever did in my life. I know I will never see our village again." But Mykola was already asleep.

THIRTY OR SO MEN exhale as one. The rail car fades and they're back in the cold, gloomy bunkhouse. But for the moment at least, Taras has escaped and taken them along.

"Yeah," Tymko says after a while, "but did Krentz really let him go? I mean, this big important officer suddenly cares what happens to a common foot soldier? Maybe he's just stupider than you think."

"Tymko, shut up." With slight variations this bursts out of Yuriy, Ihor, Myro and about a dozen others. Tymko grins and shuts up. They know it won't be for long.

CHAPTER 14

A world of grass

TARAS RUNS through towering beeches that grow so close together it's hard to see where to step. The beeches turn into a thick stand of pine with no path through it; and still he runs, and every tree is exactly like the last. There is no place to hide. A single thundering shot echoes in his skull. Something grazes his scalp.

His heart pounds and he begins to be aware of the feeling of dreaming. A bugle sounds, clear and surprisingly loud, and he leaps to his feet. It's the dark of night, icy cold. He thinks he sees a hunched shadow creeping away from him, but the image is gone in a moment.

Guards burst into the bunkhouse, scruffy and bleary-eyed, coats unbuttoned and carrying lanterns, and begin counting prisoners. Most of the men, drugged with sleep, don't even know they're there. When you fall asleep in this place, cold and weary, it's not always easy to wake up.

No one missing. Taras runs his hand through his hair. Did someone touch him as he slept? He shivers. He'll never get back to sleep now. He watches for a long time, but no one moves.

At breakfast a story trickles through the mess hall. In the night a guard thought he saw a prisoner outside the compound, and fired. The bugle sounded, it was no dream. In the morning when soldiers went out to look, they found deer tracks.

Taras has no plans for escape.

BEFORE THEY LEAVE the mess hall, each man is given a pair of woollen pants. Fingering the coarse material, Taras considers its warmth over long underwear. On the worst days he can add his old overalls on top of the new pants.

Then for nearly a week, it's too cold to go outside at all. Taras wears his woollen pants in the bunkhouse. They are the best thing about the week.

ONE EVENING the carver begins work on a fresh piece of pine. Taras and his friends watch with a glimmer of interest, wondering who his next subject will be. Maybe that's what catches the attention of the new guard who's on duty because Andrews is sick. Too late the carver looks up, and in a half second the guard takes away the knife. He also captures the piece of wood – just in case Bohdan Koroluk might try to carve it with his bare hands.

He sits on the edge of his bunk. Taras watches him, wondering what'll happen now. Bohdan working was a constant presence; something they could depend on. He was carving things that made them feel better. Tymko and Myroslav exchange glances. Something has to be done. A cold, heavy mist seems to be settling on the bunkhouse.

"Taras," Myro says, "it's time we heard more of your story. It was like a good book I didn't want to put down."

"Oh, I don't know –" Taras begins. He doesn't really feel like it. The guard's stupid action has depressed him. The guards have so much power over them, and he hates the moments when that becomes too obvious. When his nose gets rubbed in it.

He's decided that the guards can't help being slightly insane, as he defines insanity. He figures they know two contradictory things at once. One, that the men in the camp are here for good reasons, and that the rest of Canada must be protected from them. And two, that the men aren't dangerous and are being punished for no reason at all.

"Now where did he leave off?" Tymko is asking, as though

Taras hadn't spoken.

"Something about his mother," Yuriy says. "How she'd travelled so far..."

"I've travelled further than I ever did in my life," Myro quotes from memory. What storyteller could resist the flattery of a listener's remembering his favourite moments?

They're waiting. Myro beckons Bohdan to come and listen. He comes. He's never done that before. That tips the balance. Taras tries to think where he left off. Ah, the train out of the old country.

Taras makes short work of the voyage, on a ship like a swaying wooden tower — or maybe like the stave church in the village — set in the middle of more water than he ever wanted to see or even know about. At night deep in the ship's belly the air reeks of sweat, vomit, urine, shit. Storms drive waves across the deck. The hold is a wild, rocking cradle.

Water tastes rank. There isn't enough of it for washing.

The long journey west on the Colonist train is an improvement in many ways. He remembers things he thinks his friends might enjoy. And he's thought of something Bohdan will like.

So FAR the train feels safer than the one that rolled them out of Bukovyna. The conductor has not asked for bribes. No soldiers watch the station platforms. The Kalynas no longer keep watch at night. There's a stove at the end of the car if people want to cook. The Kalynas don't want to. They eat bread and hunks of cheese wrapped in brown paper that Batko bought at the last stop. If and when they reach a new place that might some day be home, that will be time enough to resume the business of daily life.

The swaying and the click of the rails is soothing. It asks nothing of them.

The newly created Kalynas struggle to understand their lives. Mykola wanted to make things better in the village, but has become an immigrant. Taras wanted to marry Halya. Daria wanted to keep doing the things that helped her family. She hasn't talked much since the days on the ship. Maybe she can't see any point in it. They're here now, what is there to say?

Before he had to leave, his parents had a place they knew, that felt right and good to them. They sheltered in a house, a village, a landscape. Now they're naked, or good as. They eat bread baked by strangers.

But their eyes never accuse him. It's done, that's all.

He can't hold this country in his mind, there's too much of it. Outside the window, rocks and pines and lakes crawl by, soon to be replaced by prairie. Even further west – if that's possible, and their tickets say it is – a farm awaits them. But he doesn't really believe in it, especially at night. Who gives away land, anyway?

At night a gentle rocking lulls them to sleep on a landlocked ship. They dream. They let time slip through their fingers. For now. That will have to change soon.

As they near the city of Winnipeg, the people and things in the car, which they'd been too detached to notice, become clearer. Last night a baby started to cry and now it cries all the time. The parents and some of the other passengers have tried to soothe the baby. Walking it up and down the car, singing songs in Ukrainian, German, Romanian. By now everyone understands that the mother hasn't got enough milk.

Daria fears the baby will die. She hadn't wanted to know about the other people, but this fear ties her to them.

Older children run up and down the car and sometimes into adjoining cars until the conductor chases them back. An old man carves small objects of wood – square blocks, rough shapes of dolls, tops that spin in the aisle then fall drunkenly on their sides. He gives them to the children, who play with them for hours at a time.

At Winnipeg a man gets on who seems to have more energy, more colour to him, than the train people. Marko Kupiak talks to everyone, learns all the children's names, seems to know all the languages of eastern Europe. He has black hair and sparkling dark eyes. He knows songs beyond counting, sings them to whoever will listen. And he has a talent even more wonderful than his singing.

"KUPIAK!" says Ihor. "I know people with that name. In the village next to mine."

"That's right," Taras says. "Kupiak is a Hutsul."

"I don't know a Marko. But he must be related."

"Yes, he must be. So as I was saying, Marko Kupiak has a talent even more wonderful than singing. The baby starts to cry. He walks up to the mother and offers to hold him. The mother is worn out with all the crying. She hands the baby over and Kupiak holds him with great care. He asks the baby's name: Oleksandr. He sings a song about a baby called Oleksandr, and the baby still cries. And then... He whistles the songs of birds. Real bird songs and ones he's made up himself." Taras feels them warming to the story, senses the slight pause he needs to leave to increase their interest.

"Soon all the children gather close and the adults, too. Some of the birds sing soft and low, some scrap and chirp like old men arguing. Others sound like a *baba* scolding you for something. All the time he cradles the baby in his strong arms. The baby stops crying. Smiles and laughs at the new sounds."

Taras's listeners also smile. The simple story reminds them who they are. Kupiak isn't a rich man, but he has gifts. Taras builds the picture. Kupiak's been visiting his brother Panas in Winnipeg. He's travelling to Moose Jaw, Saskatchewan, and then going home to a sheep ranch in the hills south of town, owned by a man named McLean. McLean is letting Kupiak buy the place bit by bit out of his share of lambs. In ten or fifteen years he'll own it. Everyone sighs. This is how it should go. Work hard, life will be good.

BEFORE THEY REACH the Saskatchewan border, Kupiak hears the stories of everyone in the car. He listens to what the Kalynas tell him and understands that some things have been left untold. He might even guess, considering their son's age, that Taras has run from the army. He tells them the place they're headed, Spring Creek, isn't far from Moose Jaw.

"You'll visit my house," he says. "Enjoy some mountain hospitality." For Kupiak, like Ihor, is from the Carpathians. They've never met a Hutsul before, but they're charmed. When he whistles, their spirits lift. Maybe the baby won't die. Maybe a farm is really waiting.

Kupiak pulls a small package out of his pocket and offers each of them a dried fruit, shaped, or so Taras thinks, like a testicle. When he bites into it he finds masses of seeds – nearly as small as poppyseeds – with unexpected sweetness. After the fig, he offers them dates, so sweet their teeth ache; but their stomachs feel fuller than before.

The baby starts to cry again. Plaintively, desperately. Kupiak talks to the conductor. Both of them head to the next car. Ten minutes later they return with a woman holding a very young baby. Kupiak speaks in a low voice to the woman who hasn't enough milk. After a moment, the two women share a smile and the babies are temporarily exchanged. The men in that part of the train move off a little, and the woman from the other car, Marusia is her name, nurses Oleksandr.

THEY REACH SPRING CREEK the next morning. It's small, a town of maybe a thousand people, with different kinds of stores clustered on a few streets near the train station. They step down onto a packed dirt main street, clutching the wooden chest and the homespun bag. A couple of women walk past them, holding children by the hand. A man drives by in a wagon loaded with lumber. Another in a suit and hat disappears into a door marked "Royal Bank."

No one seems to notice them. They might as well be invisible.

Kupiak has taught them some English words and phrases. They ask several people, "Please, where land office?" but no one seems to recognize this as English. A man carrying a sack of flour works it out, finally, and points the way. Afterwards, watching him disappear down the street, they wish they'd also asked, "Where I buy sack of flour?"

The land agent talks too quickly. "Youmust buildahouse. Break thirtyacres. After threeyears landisyours. Gimme tendollars." Kupiak has told them what the man would say, but the only part they actually catch is "tendollars." They have tendollars ready. They exchanged their Austrian money when the ship docked.

"Ask him about trees," Daria says.

"Land. Trees," Mykola says, as firmly as he can muster.

The agent shakes his head. "Oh no. Not around here. Trees... all...gone." This is clear even to a person who doesn't know the words. He glances at the paper in his hand and tells them that there's a house on the land. They won't have to build a house.

"House," they understand. Good, they hadn't expected a house.

Mykola pays ten dollars and the agent gives him a paper with coordinates for their land. The Kalynas have just bought 160 acres of land.

The agent is good at sign language. He points to a livery stable, mimes hiring a horse and wagon. Shows them where to buy flour, potatoes, a barrel of drinking water. Gives them an encouraging smile as they go out the door. Taras turns back and sees him shaking his head.

An old man at the livery stable, Geordie McIntosh, looks at the coordinates, nods, and loads them and their belongings into a wagon. He drives them down a rough, narrow road into what he calls the south country – dry, grassy hills where hardly a bush can be seen, never mind trees. They know at a glance that no one has ever farmed this land. Wonder if it *can* be farmed. When it rained last. When Geordie talks, it sounds even stranger than the land agent's speech – though pleasant to their ears, with its rolled r's.

A half-hour passes. The view hardly changes. Taras takes in the rhythm of the land, ridge upon ridge melting to a smoky blue at the horizon. Sky so wide and high it makes him dizzy. Geordie points at a small pond with cattail and willow growing around it. "That's what we call a slough." One word sticks: *sloo.*

Mykola wants to ask why they've passed no houses.

Ten minutes later they climb a slightly steeper hill and then roll slowly down the other side, rocked almost to sleep by the swaying wagon. At the bottom of the hill, without any warning, the Scotsman stops and begins to unload. Startled, Mykola and Taras jump down to help. They see a weathered grey shack perched on a more or less flat farmyard. It has two windows, one on the south side and one on the east facing the road. Surely this isn't the house? Behind it to the west, a small *sloo* glitters in the sun. Beyond that, hills roll away for what looks like forever.

It seems that it is the house. Not far away is a very small structure which must be the toilet.

In a couple of minutes, they have laid on the bare grass sacks of flour and cornmeal and a small bag of brown sugar Mykola bought when he realized how hard things might be. The water barrel, the linen bag from the old country, the small chest. A brand-new spade.

Mykola wants to ask a hundred questions but has no words. Geordie accepts his payment and turns back to town. "Good luck to ye," he says, taking his battered tweed cap off to them. He begins his long, slow ride, fades from sight so gradually it's hard to tell he's moving. Later it's even harder to believe he was ever there.

Daria cries softly. This is their *farm*. No village, no neighbours, no garden, no trees. No house. She follows Mykola and Taras to the shack.

The main room, maybe twelve feet square, is filled with a stranger's belongings. A cast-iron stove, a tin coffee pot and a coal scuttle. An old wooden dresser with an oil lamp on top. A galvanized tin pail. A washtub. The small wooden table has a single chair. A tall cupboard has a work counter at waist height, and above that, shelves of common supplies: yeast, baking powder, vanilla extract. Cadbury's cocoa powder.

On the west side, with a small window overlooking the hills, is a second, smaller room, holding a narrow bed with a faded quilt and a chest beside the bed, curtained off by a blanket hung over a rope. Worn clothing hangs from the rope – overalls, shirts, socks. Scuffed boots nestle under the bed beside a chamber pot.

There are other useful things. Chipped dishes and a pottery bowl for mixing bread sit on a shelf. In a corner, a spade, saw, hoe and pickaxe lean against the wall. They can almost see the man who lived here, obviously a bachelor. All his things must now be theirs.

Who leaves their clothes behind? Their boots? Quilt? Kettle

and dishes? No one wants to say it: the bachelor died here.

Mykola and Taras see Daria's thoughts in her face: I can't stay in here.

There is no money to buy the materials to build a house.

That afternoon they consider building a *burdei*. This way of building homes out of and partly in the earth was explained to them by Kupiak. Apparently many others have done it on first arriving in Kanady. Or Canada, as people say here.

To build a *burdei* they will have to dig a hole, probably about half the size of their main room back in the village, two or three feet deep. Then they'll cut squares of sod, which they'll lay around the edges of the hole, like bricks, to make walls. *Then* they'll gather willow wands from the slough, weave them together to frame a roof, then lay more sods on top of it. *Then* if they can find some good quality clay on their land, they'll mix it with grass to form a thick plaster to insulate the *burdei*.

They could do all this, but it sounds like a lot of work just to live in a hole in the ground. A lot of time which they need for breaking land and planting a garden. Mykola takes the one chair from the shack outside, and sits down and thinks.

Daria meanwhile gathers dried twigs and grass and fetches some of the settler's coal. Makes a fire between the shack and the slough and lets it die to a low, steady flame. She sets up stones around it and balances an iron pan over the fire. Puts *salo* in the pan and hears it sizzle; thinks how strange it was to bring a clay pot of pig fat all this way. She mixes flour and water and makes a rough pancake. When she has enough of these, she fries them and sprinkles them with brown sugar. Adds a couple of dates from Kupiak for each person. The dates are a promise that while they've lost a lot, they might also gain something here. Kupiak is proof that it's possible to feel at home.

Eating the plain but delicious supper, Mykola understands what to do.

As the light fades, Taras looks up and sees on top of the hill above their yard a horse dark as charcoal. It turns and gallops down the other side out of sight. He climbs the hill, but it's long gone.

In the distance, in the folds of other hills, he sees bluffs of stunted poplar.

He's safe from the Austrian army, or hopes he is. The *pahn*, Radoski, is thousands of miles away. They'll never see his smirking face again. Surely that's worth something?

Halya is near, somewhere not far from Spring Creek. He can find her.

He see his parents looking all around them and thinks that if Shevchana might be regained without having to retrace their steps, they'd do it in a moment. But no. All that's gone – the old place and its ways. Shevchana before the rumours of war no longer exists.

His parents are small figures in a world of grass.

Stars appear in the darkening sky. A cool breeze touches his face. Below, his parents set out blankets for them to sleep on – on the bare prairie. A shooting star streaks across the night and is swallowed by a hill. A single voice, clear as a flute, seems to answer its brief fire.

No one said there would be wolves.

TARAS WAKENS to see his father headed for the bachelor shack. Mykola comes out a few minutes later with the pail, the washtub, the hoe and the spade they bought in town. He walks over to the north side of their yard and takes a few steps up the slope of the big hill they drove down when they arrived here. He picks up the spade and digs. Taras thinks he must be dreaming, and a moment later he is. Dreaming of Halya, her steady blue-grey eyes. This must be what he likes about her, that steadiness. Some men like pale blonde hair, some like shining black hair. He likes brassy gold hair and that look she gets that says she's not going to back down.

When he turns over an hour later, he sees Mykola dumping something from the pail into the washtub. Sees him walk down to the slough and pick up lengths of dried grass he's cut with the hoe, and toss them into the tub. Normally he'd get up and help, but today he doesn't move.

Batko is doing something secret and magical. Something with

grass and...what? Clay! That's something you could dig out of the side of a hill. And he's doing it early in the morning, so Mama won't know. If he wanted help, he'd have asked by now.

When Taras and his mother wake up, Mykola is nowhere to be seen. In a moment he comes out of the shack and helps get the fire going. Daria doesn't ask what he was doing. This is some kind of husband and wife secret, Taras thinks. If anyone asks what Mykola's doing, there'll be a big argument, but no one's going to ask. Daria makes pancakes again and spreads brown sugar on top. Mykola's seem to disappear in seconds.

After their meal, Taras walks out past the slough and finds a rabbit in a snare he set the night before. Setting snares is something else Kupiak taught them. He skins and guts it and takes it to his mother, who rinses out the cavity, cuts it up and puts it in a pot of water over the fire. Later, he'll go to the poplar bluffs he saw from the hilltop and bring back fallen branches for cooking fires. But there won't be enough for winter. They'll need more coal.

The next task is breaking land. The bachelor did have a garden plot near the slough, about fifty feet square, now covered with weeds. Taras and Daria get busy hoeing and digging the soil for planting. Mykola keeps doing what he's doing and they don't look at him.

By noon, Daria nods to Taras: time for lunch. As she makes more small pancakes, they hear a wagon and see a black-haired man driving a pair of workhorses, and Kupiak shouts out their names. Drives up to their fire and jumps down, laughing. Hugs and kisses them all, full of energy and smiles. Just seeing him, they start to feel better.

Kupiak soon realizes there's something going on, but that things are more or less all right. And nobody's talking about it. Fine. He can do that too.

He unloads good things from the wagon. Loaves of new bread. A jug of milk. A small foil package of tea. A cream can filled with good well water. That's welcome, because the slough water isn't fit to drink and the water from town will be gone before long. They'll have to dig a well.

Everyone gathers around the fire for pancakes and milky tea. The Kalynas may not have any close neighbours, but Kupiak is a village all by himself. He admires the cleanup of the garden plot, walks over the hill with Taras to set new snares and entertains them by playing Hutsul music on a small wooden flute. Before they know it, the sun drops low in the sky and everyone is hungry again.

At the same moment, Daria and Mykola realize it's Sunday. They all sit down to eat on a blanket spread on the grass. Mykola gives thanks to God for friendship and good bread.

Daria serves the stew, offers Kupiak dark bread with a small bowl of salt. He dips the bread in the salt and eats.

Light fades from the clear sky. The strip of air near the horizon turns pale orange and coolness comes up from the earth. Bread and salt is a piece of the old land, eaten under strange stars. Yet here is Kupiak, quite at home. Maybe this will happen to them too, one day. When it's time for sleep, Kupiak gets a bedroll from the wagon and curls up beside them on the grass. Smells of sage and earth mingle.

When the wolves begin their nightly howl, Kupiak explains that they're really coyotes, smaller than wolves and no danger to them. Only then does Taras hear the cries as the new world singing.

THE NEXT DAY Kupiak helps Mykola with his mysterious task. Right after breakfast, they walk away into the hills and come back an hour or so later cradling stacks of something in their arms, something that gets mixed into the clay and grass in the washtub, along with pails of water from the slough. In the meantime, Taras and Daria weed and dig.

Late in the afternoon, Mykola takes Daria's hand and leads her to the shack. On the grass, she sees the bachelor's clothes and bedding rolled into a ball, beside the bedstead and mattress and a few other personal things.

Mykola opens the door. Coaxes her inside.

The walls are now plastered in the Ukrainian style. The icon hangs in a corner, the Shevchenko portrait across from it. The tabletop and the small counter are clean, empty spaces. Daria's embroidered scarves are draped around the pictures and the window frames. From the inside at least, it looks something like a Ukrainian house. A very small one.

Daria doesn't speak at first. She looks at the walls for a long time, thinking of the fact that winter is coming and they must have shelter.

"*Dobre*," she says at last. "I will be able to use this place, but I still need to sleep outside for a while."

Mykola nods. "I'll change the way it looks outside too. Kupiak and I will lay sods along the walls from the ground to the roof, and I'll plaster them too. And we'll put sods on the roof. We'll be warm in the winter."

"I'll be able to cook on this stove," Daria says. "It's not as nice as a *peech*. But it's a good stove."

The men's bodies relax.

"What was it you gathered on the prairie?" Taras asks.

"Buffalo chips," Kupiak says. "In the old country, we used cow dung to hold the plaster together. Here we have buffalo chips."

CHAPTER 15

The Orphan Boy

TARAS COMES SLOWLY AWAKE in the early morning light and realizes the ground has sucked the heat out of him. Yesterday was warm, but the night was cold enough that he can see his breath. His back aches like hell. At home he never had reason to sleep on bare ground. It's interesting in an unpleasant way.

He crawls out from under his blanket, tries to stretch the aches out of his body. Sees one black eye watching him. Kupiak gets up and they walk off a way, blankets knotted around their shoulders, to take a leak. Afterwards they go up the hill to the place where Taras saw a horse. He wonders if he's always going see things like that. Horses made of half-remembered dreams, they must be. Or do horses run wild in this land?

They gaze out over the lines of hills. The sight overpowers Taras with something like loneliness, yet better. He's come to such a different place and seen things he could never have seen in the village. The sun over the hills must be the same one as back home, but it looks different. Everything here seems stripped to its basic nature. He knows they've lost many things, but in spite of this loss, something inside him is struggling to be said. *I'm not sorry.*

Kupiak watches him, pats his arm. Talks about what comes next. By the time they come down, they have a plan. Daria has a pot of kasha simmering. She holds the sugar bag, weighing it in her hand, weighing today against future days. She shrugs and throws a handful into the pot.

"I'm going to town today with Mr. Kupiak," Taras says.

Daria looks puzzled. "Mis-ter?"

"It's how Canadians speak," Kupiak says. "Like *'pahn'* in the old country, only everyone is mister, not just rich people. Mykola, you are Mr. Kalyna."

"And me?" Daria asks. "Am I Mr. Kalyna too?"

Kupiak laughs. "Mister means a man. A woman is Miss if she's unmarried and Missus if she's married. You're Mrs. Kalyna. *Mis*-sus."

"Mis-sus Kalyna. *Dobre.* So why, Mis-ter Taras, are you going to town today?"

"So I can look for work." Daria starts to protest, so he hurries on. "Winter's coming sooner than we think. We need money for supplies."

Her face admits this is true. "And Halya? Are you going to look for her too?"

"Not yet. Later, when I can speak some English."

THEY SET OUT at seven o'clock by Kupiak's pocket watch. Taras finds it strange to see the town again; while he was busy digging the garden, it vanished from his consciousness. Now Kupiak points out places he needs to know about. Coaches him on what to say. First they go to the livery stable, where the owner grooms a horse with a stiff brush.

"You have work, please?" Taras asks.

The owner shakes his head. "Nothing here. You can try the hotel." Taras is amazed. The man said *hotel,* he's sure of it. Hotel is the same word in Ukrainian.

The hotel desk clerk, barely older than Taras, also shakes his head. "Not enough business. You might try the brick plant."

"*Proshu.* Brick...plant?"

"Just south of town." He points the way. "Give them a try."

"*Douzhe dyakuyiu.* Thank...you." Outside Kupiak waits. He'll take Taras as far as the brick plant.

THE PLANT HAS MANY BUILDINGS, some square, some round, in front of a range of rugged hills tall enough that Taras sees them almost as mountains. Near the entrance gate a large brick building stands, where he must ask for work. As Kupiak drives away he walks through the gates alongside twenty or thirty men on their way to work. He's almost at the door of the building when a scowling red-faced man steps in his path.

"What the hell do you want?"

"You have work?"

"If we did, we wouldn't be lookin for no bohunk." Taras doesn't understand the words, but knows he's being insulted.

A man in a black suit and matching felt hat rides up on a Thoroughbred stallion. At a hitching rail near the door, one hand on the pommel, he shifts his weight to his left foot and starts to dismount. A steam whistle shrieks to signal the start of the workday.

The horse shies, throwing the man to the ground, his boot caught in the stirrup. An iron-shod hoof grazes his head. The horse rears again, trying to dislodge the weight, and the man jerks into the air, then slams to the ground. The stallion rears again. Taras runs to him, grabs the bridle and pulls the bay down, lets it feel his strength and hear his voice, soothing. The Ukrainian words mean *good boy, good boy, it's all right all right all right.* As soon as he can safely do so, he reaches back and releases the man's boot. Tethers the horse to the rail.

The man who insulted him hasn't moved.

Taras goes to the fallen man. His suit is dusty and torn, his forehead scraped where the horseshoe struck him. He gasps for breath, tries to move his arms and legs. Nothing seems to be broken. Taras offers his arm and the man tries to get up. His right knee buckles, but he readjusts his weight and is able to rise slowly. When he goes to brush the dust from his clothes, though, he cries out and clutches his collarbone on the left side. Taras supports him until the pain eases a little.

"Thanks." Thanks is *dyakuyiu,* Taras learned it on the train. The man offers his right hand. Says something about horses. Taras hears him say "Brigadier." That seems to be the stallion's name.

Taras takes the hand gently. "Taras Kalyna," he says. This must be the owner. The *pahn*. Fancy clothes, good horse, who else would he be?

The man sees that Taras knows little English. "That was good work," he says slowly. He goes on. Seems to be admitting he was in real danger. Well, it's true. He could have been injured. Or killed. But even when he's thanking someone, he can't help acting like he's better than other people. He almost falls again but Taras steadies him. "Well, if there's ever anything I can do..." The words mean nothing, but their tone says, Bye-bye, then.

"Please...you have work?"

"Uh no, I don't." He doesn't need anyone. Wait, though, he's hesitating. He says a lot of other stuff that Taras hopes could mean, "Looks like I owe you a favour."

Taras understands the man is thinking about it.

The red-faced man pipes up. "We don't need anybody, Mr. Shawcross."

Mister Shawcross, that's the *pahn's* name. A sneer settles on his face. His next words probably mean, "Yes, thanks for helping me when the horse tried to take my head off," because the guy's face looks even redder than before.

Shawcross looks Taras over, nods. Is he thinking of a job Taras could do? He turns to the red-faced man and gives directions. Points to the round buildings in the distance. *Kilns,* he calls them.

The red-faced man hesitates. Shawcross says, *"Now,* Stover." So, Stover is the man's name.

Taras notices that the *pahn* didn't say *Mis-ter* Stover. And that he has not made a friend.

Shawcross holds up a hand and says something more to Stover. He takes Taras's arm and limps inside, past an older man at a desk looking at columns of numbers on a sheet of paper – who looks startled to see his boss with a stranger – and through to a larger room. Oak desk and bookcase. Pen sitting in a marble base. Shawcross looks stunned, but manages to take a sheet of paper from a desk drawer, scrawl something on it and hand it to Taras.

"Thank you," Taras says, but he doesn't know what to do next. Stover hovers at the door. "Take him to Moses," Shawcross says.

"Come on, bohunk," Stover says. As they go out, Shawcross reaches into his desk and takes out a bottle of liquor and a small glass. Taras hears him pour a drink.

Stover leads Taras through an iron door into the noisy plant. A worker grabs bricks off a press, two at a time, at great speed. Others take wheelbarrows stacked with the unfired bricks out the back door to the kilns.

Stover leads Taras into one of the round brick kilns. A tall, powerfully built man in his late twenties loads bricks for firing. A man with dark brown skin and curly black hair. Taras tries not to stare. Stover greets the man as "Moses." The name Shawcross said.

"Dan," the man says. "What can I do for you?"

Stover says something Taras can't understand except for the word "work." He grabs the note from Taras and hands it to Moses.

Moses asks a question. "Work at what?" maybe.

Stover shrugs. He's obviously against Taras doing any work for Shawcross at all. He tells Moses something about "bohunk" and "horse." Telling what Taras did. Sneering as if it's nothing. As if he'd have done it himself if Taras hadn't been in the way.

Moses reads the note and nods. He looks Taras over. *"Dobre dehn."* Good day.

"You know my language?" Taras is amazed.

"Speak white!" Stover kicks the dirt.

"Why should I? I'm black. Haven't you noticed?" Moses says this in Ukrainian, and winks at Taras.

Stover starts to walk away. "Blackie and a bohunk," he says under his breath but Taras hears. "What bloody next?"

"Ignore him," Moses says, still in Ukrainian, "the guy's got his head up his ass. When he can get it out of the boss's ass, that is." Out of the *bossovi sratsi* is how he puts it.

Taras smiles but is careful not to look toward Stover.

Moses leads Taras to the back entrance of the yard and Taras helps him harness a couple of horses to a wagon. As they drive away, Taras burns with questions. How is it you speak Ukrainian?

Where do you come from? Are there other people like you?

Moses gets right down to business. Has Taras built anything before? *Yes, wattle fences and storage sheds. Thatched roofs.* Nice, but can he work with wood? *Yes, he makes carvings.* What about larger jobs? Carpentry? *Yes, he's made benches and tables and helped repair the wooden church.* Bricklaying? *No.*

Moses looks disappointed. Taras sees this will make it harder for Moses to find him something to do. But he's thinking, weighing Taras's skills.

"What did Stover mean, you did something fancy with the boss's horse?"

"His horse bucked him off. I just calmed him down."

Moses nods again. "So you're good with horses?"

"Yeah, I know how to look after them. I learned in my father's blacksmith shop."

Moses smiles. "Can you shoe a horse? Mend harness? Drive horses?"

"Of course." Finally, he's said something that makes Moses happy.

Moses drives toward the centre of town, where, he explains, Shawcross Construction is building a school with bricks from the brick plant. On the way, he points out his house, which Taras realizes is just over a hill from the brick plant.

"Come to my place after work. I'll tell you about Spring Creek."

The construction site swarms with men framing walls, hauling bricks, laying bricks. The hauling is done by enormous Clydesdales. Moses takes Taras to Rudy Brandt, the foreman, who speaks some Ukrainian. Within half an hour, Taras is busy in the site's small smithy with the biggest horses he's ever seen. Taking off shoes, trimming hooves, reshaping and reattaching shoes. The great horses stand calmly the whole time, so strong, so amazing they bring tears to his eyes. Rudy says Taras can make new shoes for them another day.

Later there's a bricklaying lesson. By the end of the day Taras can see it'll be a while before the foreman lets him do anything but practise. But there's work he can do on the inside of the building and they'll start him on that the next day.

After another whistle from the brickyard signals the end of work, Taras walks up to a whitewashed house built in the Ukrainian style, sitting well apart from the Canadian houses of wood or brick, as if a piece of Shevchana has blown across the ocean and planted itself in the prairie. At the back, there's a vegetable garden and a small stable. The hill he noticed earlier, crowned by a thick aspen bluff, separates the yard from the brick plant.

Moses greets him at the door. Inside there's a *peech* and an icon on the wall. Wooden benches around a wooden table. Embroidered scarves draped around the icon and a picture of Shevchenko.

His new friend pours glasses of chokecherry wine. Chokecherry is a berry that grows on the prairies, he says. Taras smiles. *"Tse smachniy."*

As Moses cooks, he asks Taras many questions but reveals nothing more about himself. Soon he dishes up supper, a simple meal but more than Taras has seen in several weeks. Scrambled eggs with slices of sausage. Potatoes fried with onions. It all tastes marvellous. *Smachniy.* He can't help wolfing it down. All he's had since breakfast is a chunk of bread he brought along. Moses gives him second helpings. Finally all the food is eaten, the wine replenished.

"Now," Moses says. "Ask me anything you want."

Taras knows Stover doesn't like Moses and thinks it has something to do with the colour of his skin. *"Proshu,"* he says, "I never saw a man like you before."

"Black, you mean? Lots like me where I come from."

"But why do you have Ukrainian things? How is it you speak my language?"

"I live my life as a Ukrainian. This house belonged to Pavlo Panko, my adopted father. From Halychyna. He left me the house when he died."

"I see," Taras says. *"Dobre.* How did you come to know him?" He should get back to his parents, but nothing can tear him away until he hears this man's story.

"My family lived in Pennsylvania. In the United States. See their pictures?"

He points to two photographs in oval frames hanging on the wall above an old pump organ with music open on its stand. One shows a man and a woman – his parents – and the other his whole family, with a younger Moses kneeling in front of his mother and father. They look a little stiff in their best clothes, hair carefully brushed or, in the case of his mother and sisters, swept up on top of their heads, and proud.

"My father worked in the coal mines. That's how he knew Pavlo. We'd all heard things were better in Canada, and Pavlo thought we should give it a try. At first, it was just something to talk about on a winter night."

Like men in the tavern back home talking about Kanady.

"After a while there was less work in the mine and we all decided to come here. But no one told us how cold it would be. We barely had time to build shacks before the snow fell. All we had to eat was flour and salt pork. Near Christmas, my family got sick with a fever.

"I don't know why I never got sick. Soon I was the only one walking around. First Jessie, my older sister, got it, then Rebecca, then Mama. Then Albert, my little brother. Mama told Papa and I what to do, but after a while she could barely talk. Then Papa got it." The words catch in his throat. He takes a drink of his wine and goes on in a quiet, even tone.

"I was ten years old. I knew how to make pancakes from flour and water. How to fry up salt pork. After a while nobody but me was hungry. I tried to keep the shack warm, but the frost kept creeping up the walls and windows. Even so, they were all burning up with fever. I put damp cloths on their foreheads, I talked to them. One morning I didn't think Mama and Papa could hear me any more.

"But Jessie was starting to get better. She looked at me and said, 'Go for help, Moses.'

"I think that was what I was waiting for. Someone else to take charge. So I put a bridle on Billie, our plough horse, and rode to Pavlo's homestead. It started to blizzard. I made it to the house before it hit."

Moses seems to be looking at something far away. Taras wants to ask what a blizzard is like but doesn't want to interrupt.

"I yelled at Panko, told him he had to come, but he said we wouldn't get a hundred yards. Wouldn't even know what direction we were going. He told me afterwards that I kept hitting his chest and arms and screaming. Once I ran out into the storm to get the horse and head home, and he had to drag me back. The blizzard lasted three days."

Taras is almost afraid to breathe.

"When the storm ended, we made it to the shack. All my family were dead. Jessie, too. Frost on their hands and faces. Eyes frozen over like they were made of glass. There was a story about it in the paper. They called me the Orphan Boy."

Taras can see it as if the people were in the room with them. No one has told the Kalynas, either, how cold it will be here, and now he wonders. Surely it can't be colder than in the old country? What if it is?

"I thought it was my fault."

"How could it be? You were a child."

Moses shakes his head. "You don't think that way. It was up to me, and I failed. Pavlo helped me bury them. We had to wait till spring. He took me in and raised me as his son."

"Why did he build his house in town?"

"When he adopted me, he got a job at the brick plant. He'd decided that neither of us were meant to be farmers, and he wanted me to go to school. So he built us a little piece of *Ukraïna*. People in Spring Creek thought it was odd, but they didn't want to fight with the man who looked after the Orphan Boy."

"Did they call you the Orphan Boy in school?"

"Some did. Some called me the black hunkie. Some just called me Blackie. 'Hey, Blackie! Whatcha doin'?' I heard that a lot." Moses gets up to make coffee.

"I only went for six years, enough to read and write and work with numbers. Then I got a job at the plant. I always worked hard to be the best. At work I'm not the Orphan Boy. I'm the one who keeps things moving. All the stuff Shawcross has no idea how to do."

Taras smiles. It's not hard to believe that Shawcross is a bit useless. "What happened to Pavlo?"

"He died a few years back. He had a disease in his lungs. Years of mining coal causes it. I looked after him and he taught me everything he could." He pauses a moment, as if not sure Taras is ready to hear the rest.

"I didn't only learn his language. He taught me to sing the church services."

"You're a *cantor?*" Taras tries not to sound too amazed.

"Sometimes – when they bring in a priest from the city. At first, the few Ukrainians scattered around here didn't want me. Didn't think a black man could be a cantor. But they got to know me. Now... Anyway, there's nobody else."

"But are you Ukrainian, then?"

Moses raises his eyebrows at Taras. "You tell me."

Taras doesn't know the answer. It's time he got back to his parents. They could never guess that he's got work and met a black man who is somehow Ukrainian. Now they'll be able to buy supplies for winter. He has a friend who speaks his language and Moses says there are some other Ukrainians on farms not too far away.

Other bohunks. Moses has explained the word to him.

He asks Moses if he's seen anyone who resembles Viktor. A short, stocky, arrogant man with a smart, lovely daughter, Halya, and her *baba,* a tall, hardy old woman with a sharp tongue. Moses hasn't seen them.

"Most likely he'll be on a farm working for someone, or maybe he's got a place of his own."

"He'll have a place of his own, all right. Viktor could never work for anyone else."

"If he's here. I'm sure you'll find him. Halya and her *baba,* too."

Moses lends Taras his horse to ride to and from work. She's a bony old white mare, but she's good natured and she can get him there and back. Moses pretends Taras will be doing him a favour. Molly can eat the Kalynas' grass, save him money on feed. Taras knows the benefit is all on his side. The walk home would take over an hour. He promises to bring Moses some of his mother's bread.

THE INTERNEES LIKE THIS STORY. Most have seen a black person at one time or another but not up close. Not to talk to. Tymko explains that black people originally came from Africa. Some people know exactly where Africa is. Others have only a hazy idea. Bohdan asks whether, if he could touch such a person, the colour would come off on his hands. Taras assures him it would not. He sees Bohdan thinking about what wood he might choose to carve the likeness of Moses.

Myro takes on what Taras has come to think of as his teacher look. "This is not the first time a black man and a Ukrainian have been friends," he says. People look up, amazed. They're going to get two stories in one night. Both apparently filled with marvels.

"You see, Taras Shevchenko wasn't only a painter and a writer. He was also a fine singer and actor, and he loved the theatre. One night in St. Petersburg he went to hear a great American actor – a black man called Ira Aldridge – perform in *Othello*. He was so moved it made him weep and he went backstage afterwards to thank Aldridge. He hugged the actor, he kissed him."

Taras wants to say, "What's *Othello?*" but he doesn't want to stop Myro in full spate. His friend's face seems to glow as he warms to his topic.

"They couldn't understand each other's languages, but they became friends, united by an unbreakable bond. And what was that bond? The knowledge that neither of their peoples were free." Taras sees that he's not the only person who doesn't understand this.

"You see, black people were brought from Africa to North America as slaves. Kidnapped, to tell the truth. They worked on plantations and as servants. It was worse than serfdom." His listeners look skeptical. They've always believed serfdom was the worst thing.

"Now, only a small number of black people in America were free at this time, and Ira Aldridge was one of them. While he was in St. Petersburg, he and Taras went everywhere together, to the best houses, the liveliest parties; and everywhere they went arm in arm. It was the most amazing friendship. A proverbial friendship. A friendship for the ages."

"You say they walked down the street arm in arm?" Yuriy says.

"Certainly. That was very common among gentlemen in that time. No one thought it weak or foolish. Men were not afraid to kiss each other as friends."

"Well, that happens in the village when you meet an old friend or relative," Ihor says. "But afterwards we don't walk around arm in arm like little girls."

"That may be," Myro says, "but they did. And Shevchenko was so moved by his friend's soulful acting that he made a portrait of him."

"I wish I could see that," Yuriy says.

"Moses knows songs his people sang when they were slaves," Taras says. "Did Shevchenko and this actor sing songs?"

"I'm sure they did. No one mentions what songs they sang. But I can guess."

"What do you mean?" Yuriy asks. "Do you know slave songs?"

Without hesitation, Myro sings in a strong baritone:

> Go down, Moses, way down in Egypt land
> And tell old Pharaoh, to let my people go

"That's all very well," Tymko interrupts, "but it sounds like a lot of unnecessary emotionalism. They should've been talking about how to make revolution. How to free their people. Not prancing around St. Petersburg thinking what great artists they were."

"It wasn't like that."

"No? What was it like, then?"

"It was like this," Myro says. "Art feeds the heart and the soul. Without heart and soul, what good would revolution be?

Revolution for what? Theories are fine, but what kind of people do we want to be?" A few people nod. "Until we know that, we can't make anything. Remember the words Taras recited? From the old man in the reading hall? 'Examine everything you see. Then ask yourselves: Now who are we?' "

Momentarily at least, Tymko is silenced.

EARLY IN FEBRUARY, 1916, just when Taras begins to believe the world has contracted to the space of the bunkhouse, the weather turns. The temperature rises to above freezing by mid-afternoon. He and his friends have to return to work and it actually feels good to be outdoors. The next day, Saturday, it's cold again and for all they know could stay that way for a month.

Tymko says everyone should have Saturday off as well as Sunday, anyway. He says some day everyone will take this for granted.

By Monday it's 7° Fahrenheit, and it stays mild all week. Water trickles everywhere. The air is soft and moist from melting snow. Mere breathing is pleasure.

On Wednesday Taras sees a man escape under cover of smoke from burning brush at the buffalo enclosure near town and feels pleased about it the whole afternoon. On Thursday, a soldier dies of heart failure at the Banff hospital, after lying ill with influenza for a week in the soldiers' bunkhouse. The guards mutter among themselves that no one cares about their welfare. Now you know what it feels like, Taras thinks. No, probably they don't. It wouldn't occur to them.

Then it grows bitterly cold. Somebody called Brigadier Cruikshank visits to examine conditions in the camp and finds that both prisoners and soldiers are overcrowded in the bunkhouses and that guards are working eighty-five hours a week. He notes that having the prisoners walk to the worksites is highly inefficient: "The length of the march to and from this place, about thirteen miles, when the snow is deep, as it has been this winter, amounts to practically a day's work in itself."

The prisoners learn about it, as usual, from hearing snippets from the guards. They knew it all along, but this time one of the brass has said it. Surely the government will listen.

"Just don't expect it to make one damn bit of difference," Tymko says bitterly.

It doesn't. Days and weeks pass; nothing changes.

CHAPTER 16

What is it to be Ukrainian?

ONE VERY BITTER NIGHT, Myro and Tymko want to hear more about Moses, while Ihor, Taras, Bohdan and Yuriy want to talk about Shevchenko and Ira Aldridge. Why are people different colours? Yuriy wonders. Why do they have different religions and ideas? Bohdan asks, and Ihor demands to know, "Why do some people think they're better than others?"

As usual Tymko has a lot to say. You could write down the things he says and publish it in a book, Taras sometimes thinks. Then he could send the book back to Shevchana, and the men would talk about it in the reading hall. Tymko says, among many things, that people learn to think of themselves as a group. "Could be a family, could be a small village, or a great big city, or even a whole country." So far so good, but where's it taking him?

"People are always looking at those outside their own group and seeing monsters," he goes on. "Small differences in the shapes of faces, the colour of skins. Partly it's that they want to think their group is the best. And partly it's because they're afraid. If they admit that another group is all right, they wonder if it makes *them* not all right."

"Oh, that's silly, it can't be like that," Yuriy says. "And differences aren't always small. Not if a man has dark brown or black skin. That's very different."

"Yes and no," Myro says. "We must ask what defines a man. He must have eyes, ears, a nose and mouth, and the senses that go along with those parts. He must have a mind to think and a heart to feel, and a soul to long for a good and useful life, and to know God. If he has all those things, then a different colour is a small thing."

"That's true, I guess," Taras says, remembering the brick plant, "but it attracts a lot of attention when you see a black man where everyone else is light-skinned."

"Maybe so," Tymko says, "but I think the ruling class likes to make such distinctions. Because they want others to serve them. The way the slaves did in the United States." He waves his finger in the air to emphasize his points. "So they make themselves believe that black people are very different, and that black people aren't as good as they are."

"Okay," Ihor says, "but something else interests me. And that is, what makes a person Ukrainian or not Ukrainian? Taras's friend Moses is a black man whose family came from the United States. Then he was raised by a Ukrainian, and learned the Ukrainian language and religion. Does that make him Ukrainian?"

"How can it?" asks Yuriy. "He wasn't born Ukrainian."

"So. *Dobre*. None of us can ever be Canadians then," Tymko says, sinking his teeth into the argument.

"Sure we can," Yuriy says. "We can be more than one thing. I can be Canadian *and* Ukrainian."

"So can Moses, then," Taras says.

"Maybe we should ask, what *makes* a Ukrainian?" Myro says.

Yuriy thinks. "Well, we are a group of people with...common ancestors. We speak the same language, we look much the same. We know we're a people."

"Wait a minute," Tymko says. "Where I come from, many Ukrainians speak Russian because lots of Russians live among us and they have a lot of power. Does that mean they're not Ukrainian?"

"I guess not," Yuriy says. "But maybe they're less Ukrainian."

"Less Ukrainian!" Tymko roars. "Are you saying I'm less

Ukrainian than you?"

"No, of course not. Forgive me. I'm just trying to work things out."

Myro holds up a hand. "Let's look at some of the possible things that make us Ukrainian. One is language. Now, if I take a Ukrainian baby to another country, let's say England, will the baby still be Ukrainian?"

No one has a ready answer. "I think," Taras says finally, "that the baby would still be Ukrainian if it was taught about its own country. If it knew where it came from and knew the language. But if it only knew the language and ways of England, then I guess the child wouldn't be Ukrainian."

"So language is a necessary part? And customs and ways of doing things?" Myro asks. People nod, fairly certain this must be the case.

"I hate to tell you this," Myro goes on, "but there are already children of Ukrainians in Canada who don't know the Ukrainian language. I used to have a part-time job teaching kids like that the language."

"So they're not Ukrainian, then?" Taras asks.

"They think they are. But their parents had to learn English when they came here, and at first they thought it would be better for the children to speak only English, in order to be accepted. Later they realized they wanted them to learn."

"Maybe a Ukrainian is someone who comes from Ukraine," Taras suggests.

"What Ukraine?" says Tymko. "We haven't got a country. We're all chopped up and parcelled out to other countries."

"And yet," Ihor says, "I believe we are a country. And I'm a Hutsul, so I don't always think of being Ukrainian, but inside, I am."

"What was it Yuriy said one day?" Myro asks. "Something about Ukraine already being a country. He said, 'I already live in it in my mind.'"

"*Dobre,* so Ukraine is an idea in our minds," Taras says. "And a person is a Ukrainian if he thinks he is." He sees a vision of Halya. "Or if she thinks she is."

"Sounds good to me," Yuriy says. "But then, what about a Jew? Many Jews live in Ukraine — the idea of Ukraine in our minds, I guess you could say — and they work and raise families there."

"Is a Jew a Ukrainian, then?" Tymko asks.

"How can he be? He's a Jew."

"What about Taras's idea?" Tymko persists. "You're a Ukrainian if you think you are. If you're involved in the life of Ukraine. If you speak the language."

"But I've always thought Jews were very different," Yuriy says.

"Different in religion, yes," Tymko says, "but even there, remember that the Jewish religion is the foundation of the Christian."

"Is it?" Yuriy asks, surprised.

"Of course," Ihor says. "Their Bible is our Old Testament."

"How do you know?" Taras asks. He's never heard anything like this.

"I know because near where I lived there's a whole Jewish town and I've talked with their rabbi. We talked about religions and he told me something I really knew myself. We Ukrainians haven't always been Christian."

"Of course not," Yuriy says. "Only since the days of Yaroslav the Wise."

"Before that, we were what they call pagans," Ihor says. "We honoured the earth and the sun and we kept our own festivals." He turns to Myro. "Isn't that right, Professor?"

"It is right."

"So what's our true religion?" Ihor asks. "We Hutsuls have become Christians, but we remember the older times too. If the Christian way doesn't work for us, then we'll try the old ways. Medicines and chants and spells. Old Ukrainian ways."

"Interesting questions," Tymko says, "but where do we end up? Can a man be more than one thing at a time, as Yuriy suggests? We all must think it's possible, because here we are in Canada, and yet we haven't stopped thinking we're Ukrainians."

Myro smiles. "A masterly summing up."

"See," Yuriy says, "I knew I was right. Even the professor and the socialist think so. And what else do they agree on?"

The laughter is good-natured. Taras considers how complicated thinking can be.

Tymko could be reading his mind. "Enough of such hard topics. It's time we heard more of Taras's story. Let's see, where did he leave us last?"

Yuriy thinks. "He was asking Moses if he'd seen Viktor and Halya. And Moses said Taras was sure to find them. So I want to know if he did. I want to know what comes next."

"I didn't find them. I only know Viktor got a farm somewhere near Spring Creek. Halya and Natalka must have been there too, but after that..."

"Tell us what you *think* happened," Ihor says.

"I can't. I don't know any more than you do."

PART 3

CHAPTER 17

The *pahna*

"OH MARYNA." Natalka swipes the broom over the already clean kitchen floor. "If only you were here. If only we could laugh and cry together as we used to. The wild boar will never be at rest until he's a wealthy *pahn* or whatever they call it here. He won't be happy until Halya marries some rich man." She puts away the corn broom Viktor bought her – imagine *buying* a broom! – and goes to the table to knead bread. She loves punching and pummelling it until it's the way she wants. If only her son-in-law could be improved so easily.

"I see him always thinking, scheming. He reads newspapers, trying to understand the language, trying to find out how things are done here. I don't see any rich young *pahns* around here looking for a wife, but I'm not trying the way Viktor is, so maybe there are some. He'll find a rich man if he has to make one out of dust and straw. We have lots of dust and straw, as it happens." She murmurs and frets as she shapes the bread into loaves and puts it into pans.

"And now what? He wants us to have a new name. We are to be the Dobsons. He saw this name in a newspaper. He thinks it will make us English. As if a different name can do that. He will be Victor Dobson and Halya is to be Helen. And what do you think he's cooked up for me? I'm to be Nancy! *Nancy Dobson!* Do

I look like someone called *Nancy Dobson?*" She spots an old newspaper folded and placed high on a shelf.

"Newspapers, everywhere you look. He's driving me crazy." Complaining and raging eases her feelings and has made her almost cheerful.

THE WOODEN FARMHOUSE, about eight miles west of Spring Creek, is plain and solidly built, but there's nothing to tell you the people who live here are Ukrainian. The living room furniture came with the house: a dining table and four chairs, a worn sofa, two upholstered chairs, curtains and a dreamy picture of a stream ordered from something called the Eaton's catalogue. Viktor already has an old copy of this book of everything you could imagine buying. But there are no embroidered cloths, no icons, no table runners to be seen. Viktor's shaking off the old country as fast as he can.

Halya and Natalka sit at the table mending clothes one evening, chatting comfortably in Ukrainian.

Viktor reads a newspaper, straining to wring meaning from the foreign words, the unfamiliar letters. He gets the weekly paper from Mr. Hamilton when he's done with it, and the occasional Moose Jaw paper whenever his employer goes to town. For Viktor *is* working for another man, despite what people in the village would have predicted. He's feeling out the new world on the road to being an important man.

"Give me the white thread, Halychka."

Halya passes the thread. "There you are, *babusya.*" They laugh.

"You should try to speak English," Viktor says, very grumpy.

"I'm old," Natalka says. "Let me speak my own language."

"Yes, you're an old woman. But Halya needs to learn."

"Pah! English hurts my tongue."

"I work for Mr. Hamilton. He helps me learn. So I can help you and Halya." Halya peers at her sewing as if it's the most fascinating thing she's ever seen.

"This is a good place," Viktor says. "The land is good too."

"Oh yes," Natalka says. "That must be why the owner was so

eager to get rid of it." Viktor takes a deep breath to keep from rising to the bait.

"I've explained that to you. He bought a bigger farm closer to town. This is a good place and I've got us this house, bigger than in the old country."

"But not nearly as nice. There's no *peech*. And you won't let us put up the icons."

Viktor tastes hot words in his mouth, but again holds them back. He waves his hand as if to say that he can't be bothered trying. He turns to his daughter.

"Time to look around, Halya. Time to stop mooning over that boy." Halya stares out the window. "He'll be in Bosnia by now and will have forgotten all about you. He could even have been killed."

"He'd never forget me. And he hasn't been killed. I'd know."

Viktor ignores this claim. "There is something in this paper I want you to hear. He reads haltingly, translating as he goes. " 'Lady...desires...companion and...home helper.' You understand? A *pahna* wants someone to come live in her house. Talk to her, help around the house. 'Must be well spoken and clean. Apply by letter to Shawcross Ranch, Spring Creek.' "

He tears out a neat square of typed words framed in an important-looking black box. A happy smile spreads over his face.

Halya looks horrified. "I couldn't do that, Batko. Honestly, I couldn't."

"Nonsense. You would be perfect."

"I don't know their language!"

"You'll learn. In the meantime, I'll write to her. Mr. Hamilton will help me."

Halya continues to protest, but Viktor only smiles. He sees it all in his mind. His girl, in the *pahna's* house.

"Now, I will teach you how to greet these people. They don't say *'dobre dehn'* as we do, they say 'good day.' It means the same thing! Say after me, 'good day.' "

Halya picks up her sewing and runs out of the room. Viktor shrugs. He begins the letter.

WHEN VIKTOR GOES to see his employer, Halya picks up the newspaper. She pays more attention to Viktor's English lessons than she lets on, reads the newspaper when he's not around. She, too, needs to know how this place works. She's learned that the best thing to be is British. Everyone else is judged by how close they come to Britishness. Other peoples who speak their own languages are considered quaint, a bit embarrassing, as if they must be trying to speak English and failing.

From advertisements she's learned what things cost. What a hired girl can earn working long hours in a farmhouse or a house in town. If she had to leave, she could be a hired girl, but how could she leave Natalka? For now she waits, works in the house and yard, and sometimes in the fields. Here luck is with her. English women don't work in the fields, as far as she knows. And Viktor wants them to be as English as possible. Luckily the crop was planted when he bought the place.

She'd never imagined Viktor would consider sending her to a place where he didn't have daily control over her. Only the sweet, succulent promise of a daughter learning to be like an English *pahna* could have tempted him to this.

When Viktor returns from Mr. Hamilton's farm in time for supper, he's still smiling. Back home no one could have imagined Viktor Dubrovsky smiling. Mr. Hamilton will post the letter in town. Halya prays there will never be an answer.

VIKTOR AND HALYA sit on upholstered chairs in the parlour of Louisa Shawcross, a well-dressed, bored-looking *pahna* in her fifties. Halya wears an attractive cotton dress, dark blue printed with white flowers. Wishes she were somewhere else. Viktor puffs himself up in a black suit.

"My daughter very clean, strong. She work hard. No trouble."

Halya sees a slight smile of contempt behind Mrs. Shawcross's *pahna* manners. "I see, Mr., um...Dobson?"

"Yes," Viktor says. "I change name so we more English. I want learn her...to be lady. Like you, madam."

Mrs. Shawcross smiles. "Does Helena speak English, Mr. Dobson?"

Halya shakes her head, but no one notices. She's Helena now, is she?

"She speak a little now. She learn fast, lady. Very smart girl."

"Can she read and write?"

Halya understands the question and feels annoyed by it. "Yes," she says in English. "My language. I read and I write. Read poetry." She straightens her back and holds her head higher.

The *pahna* gives her a closer look. Oh no. Now the woman seems to find her interesting.

"I like to read poetry too. All kinds of literature. Perhaps we might get on."

Halya tries not to look horrified. She'd never have spoken if she'd thought the *pahna* would *approve* of her reading. She sees that Viktor can hardly believe his luck. He's never imagined any good could come of reading poetry. Well, what he thinks of as good.

"We have a woman in twice a week to do all the cleaning and wash clothes. But I assume you are capable of preparing meals." Halya looks puzzled. "You know how to cook?" she asks slowly. Halya nods.

"Well, then, I think Helena might as well begin at once," Louisa Shawcross says. "Then, tomorrow, perhaps, you can bring the rest of her things."

What's she saying? Has the woman hired her? Just like that?

"Thank you, madam." Viktor looks as if he's afraid to say another word in case the *pahna* changes her mind. Afraid of seeming too pleased. Besides, he probably can't think of any more English words.

Don't leave me here, Halya thinks. Please don't. But Viktor is going to. She realizes they don't expect her to say a thing.

HALYA'S ROOM is definitely a lady's room: soft blue walls, a fancy brass bedstead and a polished walnut dresser. White organdy curtains. A framed print of a lady in a tight striped satin dress hangs over the dresser. The lady looks around her nervously, her small mouth pursed. She is outdoors, in a forest or garden, about to slip a folded letter into a crack in the bark of a tree. A note to some forbidden lover? It looks like some things are the same even for English women.

Halya hangs her flower-print dress in the closet. The *pahna* has asked her to put on one of her old dresses. She said it would fit perfectly and it does. It's deep green and beautifully made. Halya knows at a glance that some poor woman spent long days on its cutting and sewing, especially on the vertical pleats across the bodice. She has to take shallower breaths because the waist is so snug. Apparently, though, it should be tighter, because Mrs. Shawcross tried to make her put on a corset that laced up the back. Halya couldn't hold back a small shriek and that made the bossy old crow give up on corsets.

Of course a *pahna* would be bossy. What's the good of servants if you can't make them do things they don't want to do? she probably thinks.

The lady in the picture must be wearing one. Nobody's waist could be that small naturally. Halya wonders how women in such garments are expected to breathe. She wonders why looking so thin is considered attractive.

The *pahna's* given her shoes to wear, too, black leather lace-ups with small, raised heels. They make her carry herself more stiffly. She has to think before she moves.

Halya looks at herself in the mirror. The green dress flatters her, seems to make her brass-coloured hair shinier. "Helena Dobson," she says to her image.

Another reflection appears in the mirror. Mrs. Shawcross watches from the doorway.

A FEW DAYS LATER, her chores done until it's time to make supper, Halya sits in the dining room with pen and paper, bathed in light from the double windows, practising writing. The *pahna* actually *wants* her to do this. In fact she taught Halya the English alphabet herself. Halya still finds this alphabet confusing, because some letters are the same and others totally different. And some are just missing.

She can't believe she lives here now. It's the first time in her life that she's slept anywhere other than in her father's house. She doesn't miss him. She does miss Natalka. Wonders what she'd think of Mrs. Shawcross.

The *pahna* is like no person she's ever met. Interfering. Rich. Thinks other people are here for her entertainment. And she's crazy for reading books; novels, she calls them. And for teaching Halya to read them. In English. Halya has no idea how long she'll be able to stand it, but has to admit it's interesting. She wishes she could tell Natalka all about it. Well, sooner or later the old lady will have to let her go home for a visit. Won't she?

She pulls a paper from her pocket with words written in Ukrainian.

Don't say my love is gone from the earth.
If he were, I would know.
His voice comes to me on the wind.
One day he'll find me, or me him.
Yesterday I saw a swallow burn
a dark shadow on the sun.

As warm rain turns to bitter snow,
oh, swallow, ride the bright sky
across this wide land
and bring him home.

She stares at it, trying then crossing out different combinations of words. She wishes she could talk to Shevchenko. He would help her find the words and rhythms she needs.

Halya hears the *pahna* coming and hides the poem. Mrs. Shawcross enters, a little drunk, a glass of sherry cradled in her long fingers. "Hard at work, I see. Would you like a glass of sherry?"

Halya shakes her head. Louisa gave her a glass yesterday and she thought it was disgusting.

"No, thank you, Mrs. Shawcross." Halya is sure that no reaction of any kind, let alone disapproval, gets into her voice, but the lady must hear something. Her face flushes and she leaves the room.

THAT EVENING, from the kitchen window, Halya sees the *pahna's* son ride up to the barn. Mrs. Shawcross says that he stays in town most of the time, in a room at the hotel, but sleeps at the ranch a couple of nights a week. He dismounts, and a hired hand leads the horse into the barn as Ronald Shawcross walks up to the house. He's a tall man with smoothly brushed brown hair, and he's what people would call handsome, although there's a self-important look about him she doesn't really care for.

Halya hurries to her room. The *pahna* has said that she "must meet Ronnie," so Halya changes into the green dress Mrs. Shawcross likes and goes down the hall toward the parlour and stops in the doorway. Louisa Shawcross and her son are drinking sherry and haven't seen her yet.

"So you've hired one of those Galicians, Mother." Ronnie lights a cigarette from a leather case. "Plenty of English girls who'd love to come here."

"Oh yes, *English* girls. Can't cook anything but roast beef and canned peas. But Helena... Well, you'll see. She's interesting."

"You haven't time to turn bohunks into ladies, you know. Don't see why you'd want to."

"You wouldn't. And don't say bohunks. It's vulgar."

Bohunks. Is that what this man calls Ukrainians? Halya comes in to get the introduction over with. In the green dress she must look a bit like an Englishwoman. Well, she's not an Englishwoman. She looks at the *pahna's* son defiantly.

Mrs. Shawcross smiles at her. "Helena, this is my son, Ronald."

"How do you do, Mr. Shawcross." Halya makes the small gesture between a nod and a bow that Louisa's taught her. "Dinner is ready, madam." Louisa has been drilling her in these phrases for several days now.

"Thank you, Helena. Please set another place for my son."

"Helena..." Ronnie says. "Not a Galician name, I would have thought?"

"In my language, I am Halya." She turns and goes to the kitchen. She can still hear them as she carries roast lamb and vegetables to the dining room.

"You never mentioned she was beautiful," Ronnie says.

Oh shut up, Halya thinks. Stupid calf.

And then the *pahna's* voice. "You're to keep away from her. Do you understand?"

"Mother, what on earth are you on about?"

"And what brings you here tonight? I really wasn't expecting you." Halya has never heard any mother talk to her grown son this way. She wishes she could catch all the words.

"It's that pack of coyotes, Mother. They killed a couple of my lambs."

"*Our* lambs, Ronnie." Halya misses the rest, but they're arguing — something about his father's death and Ronnie running the brick plant.

"Mother!" she hears Ronnie say. "I hadn't realized you had such a poor opinion of my abilities."

"That is because you don't pay attention," Mrs. Shawcross says in a nasty tone.

Ronnie's face turns an ugly purple. Halya thinks he'd like to strangle his mother.

Mrs. Shawcross notices Halya in the doorway. Halya steps forward.

"Dinner is on the table, Mrs. Shawcross." Another of Louisa's little phrases.

"Thank you, dear. Ronnie, will you give me your arm?"

Ronnie lets the question hang, looking at Halya's face — no, gaping — slowly forgetting his anger.

Have you never seen a woman before? Halya wonders.

Finally he offers his mother his arm and leads her into the dining room.

CHAPTER 18

Conspirators

March, 1916

A SMALL PARTY cuts firewood. The temperature is well below zero, but it doesn't feel as cold as it would've in January. The sky is drenched in sun. Ice crystals reflect minute flashes of light. Impossible not to feel that winter's back is broken. Sergeant Lake calls the lunch break and the men scatter to log and rock perches. Taras and the carver happen to sit near Lake in a sheltered corner of the clearing.

They see a black, weasel-like creature high in a tree. It leaps to the next tree. Its long tail works like a sail in the sparkling air.

"What's that?" Bohdan asks. Taras sees he'd like to make a carving of this animal.

"Pine marten," Arthur Lake says. "Almost looks too large to be so agile, doesn't it? Moves like a squirrel. Eats them, too." The marten pounces on some small animal and begins tearing it apart.

Taras raises his arm to take a bite of his sandwich. He hears a sudden squawk, sees a blur of claws and feathers, and the sandwich is no longer there. Until it disappeared, Taras had considered the sandwich barely edible, but now it seems like something precious. Lake can't help laughing.

"What the hell's that?" Taras glares at a handsome grey bird high up on a branch, pecking at the icy blob.

"Whiskey-jack. Also known as a grey jay."

"Grey thief." Taras picks up a spruce cone and flings it at the bird, but it falls short. The bird doesn't shift a feather. He has to laugh.

Bohdan gets up to watch the bird more closely. Follows it as it hops to another tree.

"Look, I've got something I was saving until I was desperate." Lake pulls out a thick slice of frozen fruitcake, takes a jackknife from his pocket, cuts the cake in two and hands one half to Taras. "My wife made it."

"*Dyakuyiu.*" He takes an icy bite and sweetness fills his mouth. Seeing Lake's knife, Taras decides to tell him about Bohdan and his carvings; how his knife has been taken away.

After a moment's thought, Lake hands over the knife. "You give him this. I'll come and see his carvings some time."

Taras puts the knife away in his pocket. No one has seen. "*Dobre.* I'll give it to him." He bites off another chunk of cake and warms it in his mouth, tastes raisins and dates and chopped apricots. *Smachniy.*

Taras has cleared brush at the buffalo paddock under this man's direction and cut trees for roadbeds and fuel. Of all the guards, only this one gives you room to breathe. Only this one seems interested in where he is.

He's learned to refer to the prisoners as Ukrainians.

The marten appears in a much closer tree. Stares at the humans as if he's trying to work out what they're doing there and how this can benefit him.

"He's like us," Arthur Lake says. "Has to find something to eat."

"Working in an internment camp is a damn hard way to find something to eat."

"Bloody hard," Lake agrees. "We're sitting here freezing while the pine marten stays warm and eats fresh meat."

"And the grey bird steals our food." The whiskey-jack still pecks away at the bit of sandwich. "I guess he'll know better next time."

The break is done. They pull themselves up to get on with the work.

THE TEMPERATURE CREEPS above freezing and the men unfasten their mackinaws. By mid-afternoon, Sergeant Lake tells them to stop – they've felled and trimmed as many trees as they can carry. They take the logs back to camp, cut them to fit in the stoves, stack them in the bunkhouses. They line up early at the mess hall, some of them without coats.

Sergeant Lake sets up his camera as the internees climb the steps to go inside. Only a few men notice him. At the last moment, a man called Yars sees him and turns, hands on hips, to the camera. His face, his posture say, "What the hell do you think you're looking at?"

Arthur Lake takes the picture.

BACK IN THE BUNKHOUSE, Yuriy pulls a small sack of potatoes out of his coat and hides them under his bunk. He tells his friends what they'll be buying next time they go to the canteen. Cigarettes and more cigarettes. To pay for the potatoes. He's been collecting them for several days. Also sugar, and raisins.

They look at each other. This can mean only thing.

They borrow Bohdan and his new knife to peel the potatoes.
They borrow Taras's extra shirt, recently washed.

They borrow a clean handkerchief from Myro.

Yuriy has noticed a closet in the prisoners' laundry shack. It contains an old galvanized boiler, leaky if you fill it too full, but usable. No one bothers with it since a new one was bought. To clean their clothes, people heat water on the wood stove and pour it into round wooden washtubs where they rub their garments on scrubbing boards. Then of course they need to rinse them. The whole process takes a fair bit of time.

This means that no one should get too suspicious of how long it's going to take Taras and his friends.

They begin early on Sunday. Six men — Yuriy, Taras, Tymko, Myroslav, Ihor and Bohdan take over the small room. Myro keeps watch at the door. They clean the boiler, set water to boil and begin peeling potatoes.

That is, Bohdan peels potatoes. He doesn't like other people using his knife. Once a little guy called Big Petro took Bohdan's old knife without asking — to cut his toenails. Big Petro's toenails were thick and yellow, like hooves. Of course the knife slipped. It took hours to stop the bleeding.

After the potatoes are peeled and rinsed, Bohdan chops them up and puts them in the boiler with lots of water. Yuriy simmers them on the stove for twenty minutes or so and then takes off the scum with the clean hankie. He adds the sugar and raisins and a small package of yeast and cooks the whole mixture a little longer. They let it cool a bit and carry the boiler to the closet.

"It's going to smell," Tymko says.

Bohdan pokes out a couple of knotholes in the outer wall. "That'll help. Anyway, people bring in smelly laundry. Who's going to notice?"

Myro has to fend off a couple of men who want to wash their clothes.

Taras's shirt makes a good cover to keep dirt out of the boiler while allowing the fermentation gases to get out. The conspirators shut the closet door firmly. Pails of water are hot now, in the new boiler, for their own laundry.

CHAPTER 19

Where is Halya?

EVERY DAY brings a little more sun. Taras feels a pool of warmth inside him, as if the light shines through to his bones.

His friends want more story, but what they most want to know he can't tell them: Where is Halya? He agrees to talk about his time at the school building site, but soon he'd like to stop. He hopes when it's warmer they'll forget all about it.

HE'S IN CHARGE of the horses now. His favourites are Charlie and Bessie, lead horses for the four-horse team. They're so smart, they follow his signals almost before he gives them. At the end of the day he drives the team to the livery stable. He curry combs all four and brushes dirt out of the long feathering over their feet. The time he spends with them is a gift.

He's also a decent bricklayer now. One day he's working on a wall when Dan Stover shows up. He comes every two weeks to pay the men their wages, but today the boss is with him. Shawcross walks around the foundation, observing the progress with the air of a *pahn* back in Bukovyna.

Out of sight of the boss, Stover jabs Taras's arm. "War's coming, hunkie. Saw it in the paper. You wait, they'll send you foreigners back where you belong."

"Get lost, Stover." This is Frank Elder, one of the best workers at the site. "Only people who aren't foreigners here are the Indians."

"That's garbage. This is our country. An English country."

"I imagine the Indians wish we'd all go back where we belong." Elder winks at Taras. "You especially."

"Shut your face. Hunkie lover." Stover swaggers off, trying to act like he doesn't care what Elder said, but he does. People respect Elder. It's the end of July payday. They all gather near the wagon. Shawcross calls each man's name and hands him a pay packet.

He goes down the list of men who have worked there a long time. The foreman, Rudy Brandt, Frank Elder, Jimmy Burns, Arlen Sundstrom, Johnny St. Hilaire, and several others. Taras is always last.

"Taras Kalyna," Shawcross says finally. He pronounces it "Ka-*leen*-uh." Taras takes the envelope and counts his money. Shawcross climbs into the wagon without looking back. As he and Stover drive off, Jimmy Burns, a stocky man in his twenties, stares after them.

"Lord of the bloody manor. Hands us our pay like he's doing us a favour."

"You're complaining? I haven't had a raise in ten years. Not since old man Shawcross died." Frank rubs his hand over the back of his neck, aching from unloading and laying bricks. He's a wiry little guy with foxy red-gold hair. Even in his fifties Frank gets more done than most young guys. He knows how to move. Doesn't waste energy.

"I've lost count how many of little Ronnie's damned buildings I've worked on," Frank says. "But he never understands why we're important. Not like the old man. He had more sense in his little finger —"

"Isn't it time we did something about it?" Rudy Brandt asks. Rudy's also in his fifties. Grey hair grows at his temples and in his beard. He's grown a little stooped working on what Frank calls "Ronnie's damned buildings," and must be wondering how long he can keep working.

"Maybe we can do something," Frank says. "We can talk." Taras can see that Elder's waiting for him to move off before saying anything else, so he goes back to laying brick. But he's curious. What can they do?

TARAS GETS UP and walks around the bunkhouse. This part of the story makes him bitter and he's a little tired of trying to entertain his friends. He doesn't hear any of them telling *their* lives to pass the time.

He can't tell them anything more about Halya, not even guessing. In a little while, his story will come to the one last thing he knows and hasn't yet told.

THE SHERRY BOTTLE sits untouched on the table. Ronnie and Mrs. Shawcross, whom Halya now thinks of as "Louisa," listen to "Helena" read, haltingly, from one of Louisa's novels.

"It is a truth uni...versally ack...now...ledged that a single man in poss...ession of a good fortune must be in want...in want of...a wife."

"A bit difficult, surely, for a beginning reader?" Ronald says, forcing Halya to stop.

"Helena's not exactly a beginning reader, I find. She could already read very well in her language. And now she can read in English. We work on it many hours a day."

"Still...all that prissy old-maid stuff."

"You know nothing about it. Austen is a model of beautiful English. Why should my companion read anything else? Excuse me a moment. Carry on, Helena." Louisa leaves the room.

Halya continues. Sometimes she thinks she actually is Helena, when she reads this strange but fascinating book. Is this how *pahnas* live in the old country? Clean and tidy in comfortable chairs, reading books aloud to their menfolk? She's read every word in this book several times over. One day she began to understand it.

"However little kn...known the feelings of such a man may be on his first entering the neigh...bour...hood..." Ronald approaches and stands over her. Halya freezes.

"Please," he says, "don't stop on my account."

"This truth...is so well fixed in the minds of the surr... ound...ing families that he is considered...the rightful pro...property of some one or other...of their daughters —"

He bends as if to peer at the book and Halya looks up, embarrassed.

Louisa appears in the doorway. "Ronald! Don't bother Helena."

He jumps at the sudden sharp voice and backs, shamefaced, away. Louisa allows herself a little smile.

THE MORNING WHISTLE BLOWS on a hot July day. At the construction site, the sun pounds down on the men's heads as they stand listening to Shawcross.

"I won't mince words, men. The plant faces serious difficulties. Prices are falling and the country's in a depression. I won't let anyone go if I can avoid it. But I must ask every man here to help by working an extra hour a day."

Shawcross looks taken aback by the sudden angry buzz. If anyone's let go, Taras thinks, surely it's going to be him. A couple of men actually glance his way.

Frank Elder steps forward. "For the same pay, Mr. Shawcross?"

Shawcross tries for an understanding smile. "I know it's a sacrifice, but with the situation so difficult... If you can see your way to that, men, I think I can keep the brick plant *and* Shawcross Construction going."

"You want us to work extra for *nothing?*" someone asks, just loud enough to be heard.

Shawcross pretends not to hear. "I have every hope this will be only a temporary measure. Well, that's about it, then. Thank you for your attention."

Shawcross nods and walks back to Stover and the wagon with the air of having managed a difficult task well. The men mutter among themselves, but Stover's watching, and everyone knows he's the boss's toady.

"Say, Stover," the boss says, "I'm going to be at the ranch tomorrow. I'm going to take the dogs and hunt down those coyotes. Want to come?"

He wanted us to hear, Taras thinks. The *pahn's* going hunting and asks his man along. Stover looks foolishly pleased. As if he's the boss's friend.

NEXT MORNING Stover and a couple of Romanian shepherds from the ranch, with a pair of greyhounds, mount up in front of the ranchhouse. Shawcross appears at the top of the hill and gallops down on Brigadier. He wears English riding clothes – bright red jacket, black boots polished to a deep gloss. He looks excited and a bit out of control. As if he's been drinking.

"I've found where they're denning," Shawcross shouts. He doesn't see his mother and Halya at the open kitchen window.

"Idiot!" Louisa says through her teeth. "Thinks he's a bloody Englishman." Louisa gives her head an irritated shake like a pony shaking off a horsefly. "Damn fool can't resist striking poses."

Halya is too amazed to say anything. Louisa turns and goes to her room.

The riders move off, Shawcross and the hounds in the lead.

Three hours later they return with carcases of four coyotes. Shawcross has hacked off one of the tails and tied it to his saddle horn. Halya sees him ride past with the bloody stump. He dismounts, leaving the shepherds to see to the horses and comes into the kitchen, blood on his hands and shirt. As he pumps water from the cistern into a basin, Halya looks at his hands, horrified. Ronnie sees blood swirl in the basin and for a moment he must see the scene through her eyes; his glow of triumph fades.

AFTER SUPPER Ronnie and Louisa sit down to listen to Halya read. Ronnie sees Halya's sun pendant, Taras's gift. She couldn't wear it in front of her father, but here she can.

"That's a lovely pendant. Where on earth did you get it?"

"From the old country, sir." Halya holds her face still; opens a leather-bound book.

"So what are you and Mother reading now? More Austen?"

Halya hears the voice of a man sure he can get past any woman's defences. She hears a very different voice inside herself.

"It's *Mansfield Park,*" Louisa says. "Now hush, Ronnie."

Halya reads, more fluently than before. "And how do you think I mean to amuse myself, Mary, on the days I do not hunt?" She knows she's reading well; of course she's been through it a half-dozen times now. "My plan is to make Fanny Price in love with me. No, I cannot be satisfied without making a small hole in her heart."

Halya almost smiles. This must be what the *pahn's* planning to do to her. While imagining she'd never notice. And before moving on to whoever caught his eye next.

Louisa closes her eyes, focuses on Halya's voice. Ronnie sits up straight, eyes riveted on her face. Halya does her best to ignore him. Or maybe she's even playing with him.

"She is quite a different creature from what she was in the autumn. She was then merely a quiet, modest, not plain-looking girl, but now she is absolutely pretty." Halya looks up with a frown as Ronnie moves his chair a bit closer. "In that soft skin of hers, so frequently tinged with a blush —"

Ronnie leans forward in his chair. Halya stands. "I... My throat is very dry, madam. I may... I mean, *may* I be...excused?"

"Certainly, Helena." Halya hurries to the kitchen, although she still hears their voices. Louisa turns on her son. "Ronnie! I will not have her upset!"

"I was just listening —" He tries to look the injured innocent.

"Ronnie, please. I'm your mother. I've had to dismiss too many hired girls because of you. I won't have Helena bothered."

"Of course not, Mother. It's just, I think I may be getting...interested in her. She's rather impressive, in her way. Though certainly not of our class."

"Ronald! Understand this. Helena is in our house as my companion."

"Of course. I mustn't think of her. And yet..."

"No! Absolutely not. Anyway, I think she may have a sweetheart."

"Then he'd better look out."

Louisa picks up the book and throws it at him. Ronnie laughs. A thoughtful look comes over his face.

Louisa grimaces. "I hate it when you start thinking."

"Thinking? Me?"

"All right, I hate it when you start plotting."

"You're so suspicious, Mother. I can't think why."

Too bad, Halya thinks out in the kitchen, he's getting "interested." He said it right in front of his mother. Louisa will be watching her every minute. She'll have to be very distant around Ronnie. An old bachelor – as he seems to her – isn't of the slightest interest.

Even if she didn't already love someone.

CHAPTER 20

The professor's story

ONE SUNDAY in mid-March, a day well above freezing, the men are again taken to the hot springs. The air feels soft and warm on their faces as the heat works through them, shoulders to toes. But as delightful as all the soaking is, they don't forget they have chores to do.

Afterwards Taras and his friends gather their dirty clothes and walk to the laundry shack. Set water to boil, sort clothing, add soap. Take their first small taste of potato wine. They decide it's coming along nicely. Not nearly as strong as vodka, of course, but that would have required a still. But in a couple of weeks, if no one finds it in the meantime, it'll be finished, or at least as close to finished as they're going to let it get. Tonight is just a teaser, a small cupful each, but the effect is pleasant. Relaxing. Tongue loosening. They agree not to look too pleased when they go back. Not to breathe into anybody's face.

Back in the bunkhouse Ihor wants to hear more about Shevchenko. Wants to know why the poet died relatively young – only forty-seven years old. He turns to Myro the teacher and Shevchenko scholar.

"You should know," Myro says, "that our Taras had something in common with many of us here. He was persecuted because he wouldn't keep quiet about being Ukrainian. Wouldn't stop writing his Ukrainian poems. If he could have been content to be an almost-Russian painter, an almost-Russian writer, he could have lived a comfortable, safe life."

"You told us before that the Russians were always spying on him," Yuriy says. "Always looking for radical ideas in his poems and paintings. But how did they have time to find out what a Ukrainian artist was doing and saying? And why did they bother?"

Myro smiles. He likes a good question. "Again, we must look to history. Russia had long been an empire – with other peoples under its rule. It saw *any* change to that empire as a loss of power. Dangerous, intolerable. If it allowed Ukrainians to think of themselves as a separate people, the empire might begin to crumble. A separate people would want its own government. Ukrainians would want to run their country in their own interests."

"But how did they know what Taras was doing?"

"The tsars have always had secret police and spies and henchman. This is how you keep subject peoples in line."

Tymko nods. "Even the government of Canada has spies," he says. "Looking under rocks for socialists."

"True," says Myro, "but they haven't yet perfected it the way the Russians did. As soon as Taras began to publish poems in Ukrainian, that in itself was a provocation. Or at least a reason to keep watch on him."

"Just to use the language?" Taras asks. "His own language?"

"Yes, just to use the language, never mind his ideas about a free Ukrainian nation. Even to claim that Ukrainian was a separate language was considered highly suspicious. Most Russians thought it was just an inferior form of Russian. The most they would allow was that Ukrainian was a language for peasants and servants and buffoons, suitable, at most, to the production of coarse or bawdy comedy."

"They had a pretty good opinion of themselves," Yuriy says. Everybody laughs.

"Indeed," Myro agrees. "To rule others, it helps to think you're better than they are. That your subjects wouldn't know how to get on without you."

"There's the irony," Tymko says. "The longer a people is ruled by others, the more it turns out to be true. How can you rule yourself well if all your important decisions are made by people far away?"

"Of course, as a radical socialist, you aren't particularly interested in promoting national barriers," Myro says smoothly. He even waggles his dark eyebrows, making Yuriy, Taras and Ihor smile.

"Not in general," Tymko admits, a little embarrassed. "But I think Marx would have come around on this topic. And as long as there *are* countries, I think Ukraine should be one, too."

"Careful, there's a patriot's heart beating somewhere inside you."

"Never mind his heart." Yuriy's getting impatient. "Tell us about the spies."

Taras and the others nod their approval of this request.

"All right. Well then. In 1846, the poet was in Kyiv and joined a group called the Brotherhood of Saints Cyril and Methodius. Scholars, writers; men of high ideals and passionate friendships. Strictly underground, and dedicated to Ukrainian national rights, language and culture. All this to be achieved through democratic means. And at the meetings, Taras read his poetry, especially poetry filled with anti-tsarist ideas."

"I've never heard of any of this!" Ihor exclaims. "You don't hear so much up in the mountains. What happened to them?"

"There was a spy in the next apartment, listening through a hole drilled in the wall."

"You're making that up!" Yuriy says with a goofy grin. "Aren't you?"

"No, I'm not, truly. Ridiculous as it sounds, that's what happened. This spy denounced the Brotherhood, and they were arrested."

"No!" Ihor says, as if he sees it all before him. "Was that the end of them?"

"They were tried in St. Petersburg. Taras received the harshest sentence – because of his poems. Ten years exile in military service, at Orenberg in eastern Russia. 'Forbidden to write or draw' was added to this sentence – in the tsar's own hand."

"The almighty tsar went to all that trouble?" Tymko asks.

So, Taras thinks, something even Tymko didn't know. *Dobre.*

"For ten years he couldn't draw?" This is from Bohdan, who has moved closer. He must be remembering when his knife was taken away.

"Not exactly. You see, Orenberg is a long way from Moscow or St. Petersburg. And Taras was a very engaging fellow. He made friends with the man who ran the camp, visited his family. And after a while, he acquired the things he needed."

A smile creeps over Bohdan's face. It's like Sergeant Lake giving him a knife.

"He still had to live in the barracks," Myro goes on, "and he had to learn to march like any other conscript. He was no good at it, and the sergeant in charge made his life as miserable as possible, because he hated seeing Taras given privileges he didn't have.

"The next year there was a military expedition to the Aral Sea, and they needed an artist to draw maps of the areas they charted. Taras got to be that person, although this fact was carefully kept from the tsar and his officials."

"That doesn't sound too bad," Yuriy says.

"It was better than life in crowded, unclean barracks, but it wasn't a healthy place, either. Travel to the Aral Sea took weeks crossing a desert. Scorpions and huge poisonous spiders could crawl under your blanket at night. And the extreme heat wore him out."

He stops to answer a question about what scorpions are, then continues.

"All told, he spent ten years in exile. He made many friends and painted many pictures. Yes, even though the tsar had forbidden it, he continued to sketch and paint, and to write letters and poems. He was such a spirited, sympathetic fellow. Almost everyone liked him. Many loved him. Even, for a time, the governor general's wife in Orenberg."

The others can't believe it. "How could he spend time with these people?"

"Incredible, isn't it?" Myro says. "But you see, the empire wasn't quite as solid as it looked. New, more liberal ideas were finding their way in from France and elsewhere. And through his friendships and his art, Taras Shevchenko had joined a small but important element of Russian society. Tsarism was starting to come apart. Not fast enough for people who wanted change, but still, it was starting."

"Yes, but what about Shevchenko?" Ihor asks. "Did he die at this Orenberg?"

"No, he was finally released, the last of the Cyril–Methodius group to be freed. But his health was gone. He was like an old man. He died in 1861. He missed seeing the end of serfdom in Russia by months."

"That's a sad thing," Ihor says.

Taras thinks of the poet's humiliation in the army in Orenberg. The army doesn't want a bunch of unruly people, all different, all going their own ways, he thinks. It wants people who can be parts of a machine. The army tells the machine where to go and what to do, and it goes there and does it.

He hopes the poet wasn't hurt too much by the army. Shevchenko is their heart. Ardent, striving, damaged, but in some way still free.

Between the potato wine and the professor's lecture, it's been a good evening.

TARAS WAKES to stunning silence. His body tells him he's overslept, but the light's dimmer than it should be; whiter. The windows must be caked in snow. The bunkhouse feels like the hold of a ship frozen in ice, the air so still he's aware of every breath. What if they're running out of air? Good thing the stoves have long since gone out, or they'd be breathing smoke.

It's not as cold as he'd have expected. It's like someone draped a huge quilt over the building. He has no desire to go outside, not even to find out what kind of thin gruel the kitchen will dish up. If anyone's in the kitchen. He wonders how long they'll be left alone. What if there's no one else out there? What if the rest of the camp suffocated in their beds? They're locked inside this place.

How could they get out?

They've got Bohdan's knife. That would be a start.

He sees Yuriy sit up and look around. *What the hell?* his face says. A few other men start to move.

Shovels scrape outside, thump against the door. After a while this stops and the door opens, spilling fresh air and light into the room. Andrews and Bullard come in, red-faced and panting. Taras tries not to smile. For once guards are doing the peasant work.

They pick Taras and Yuriy to come out and shovel snow. They shouldn't have let on they were awake. Luckily they already have on their sweaters and coats. "The rest of you Sleeping Beauties get moving too," Bullard says. Taras reminds himself to find out what Sleeping Beauties are. It's clearly something every Canadian is supposed to know.

Outside the world is silent except for a peculiar ringing. The snow is broken only by narrow paths the guards have dug to the bunkhouses and the spindly tracings of bird feet. He and Yuriy have to widen the paths so several men can walk abreast. Without any talk they set to it. It's not very cold and the work soon makes them almost hot.

EXCEPT FOR THE SHOVELLING of snow, no prisoners will work today. Many of the guards are leaving to join the Canadian Expeditionary Force in Europe, and until new ones come there won't be enough left to guard work gangs. Maybe these volunteers still see war as a chance for honour and glory, even though everyone, including the prisoners, has heard what it's like – months or years in trenches with very little to show for it.

But the soldiers who guard Taras's bunkhouse and work gang aren't going anywhere. One way or another they're unfit for active service – through limps, bad lungs, age or other difficulties. This saves the internees having to get used to new ones.

In an hour Yuriy and Taras reach the dining hall, along with the diggers from the other bunkhouses. They can actually smell something cooking. Smells like bacon. Impossible. They turn to see guards herding the rest of the men down the paths. Soon they're all sitting at the long wooden tables. With the sloppy corn-meal mush, each man has a piece of bacon. A single rasher of bacon, as one of the guards put it.

How can this be? Maybe it's a reward for shovelling, but every-body's getting it, not just the men who shovelled. In the time it takes to consider such questions, all the bacon has disappeared from the room. Maddened by the aroma, Taras decides to eat his last candy bar when he gets back to the bunkhouse.

THE FEELING OF SNOWY STILLNESS remains and some of them wander up and down the aisle with faraway looks on their faces. Some lie down and look ready to fall asleep. Tymko gives Taras a forceful look from under his eyebrows: *Get on with the story.* But Taras is coming to the moment where he loses his freedom. Worse, he's losing control of the story. He'd like to leave it for a while. Or just leave it.

The carver watches him, waits for an answer. Since he got Sergeant Lake's knife, he's done a bluejay, a whiskey-jack and a chickadee on a branch. He's going to sell them to Lake. Bohdan Koroluk seems prepared to wait until he gets what he wants.

All right. *Dobre.* He'll tell it and be done.

CHAPTER 21

Talking union

August, 1914

THE DAY AFTER Shawcross's coyote hunt, Moses drives to the construction site to deliver bricks. Taras and Frank Elder help him unload.

"Some of the men are talking about starting a union," Frank says quietly.

"Could be dangerous." Moses has heard the talk for a while now but kept out of it. As a black man, he'd find it even harder than the others would to get another job.

Taras and Frank move over a stack of the newly arrived bricks and Taras begins laying them. Frank slips behind the stack to pick up a few fallen bricks.

They hear the jingle of harness and Stover drives up with the boss for the ritual handing out of pay packets. But first Shawcross strolls around the site examining the progress of the work, and Stover saunters by and shoves Taras into the stack. He doesn't see Frank.

Frank screams as the bricks fall on him. Stover runs to the other side where Frank writhes on the ground, clutching his wrist. Shawcross rushes over.

"Bloody bohunk! Watch what you're doing!" Stover says, his face turning redder.

Jimmy Burns has seen everything. "You pushed him, Stover. I

saw you."

Shawcross doesn't seem to hear. "Stover," he says, "take Mr. Elder to the doctor."

Jimmy helps Stover lead Frank outside. Shawcross speaks to all the men but looks particularly at Taras. "We must all work very hard to prevent accidents." As he speaks, he sees the pendant around Taras's neck, like the one Halya wears.

"Where'd you get that thing around your neck?"

"I made it," Taras says, wondering why the boss would care.

Shawcross keeps gazing at the pendant until he realizes the men are watching him, looking puzzled. "All right then, we'll all try to be careful." He actually bends, picks up a few bricks and helps rebuild the stack.

SHAWCROSS WATCHES Halya across the table. When Louisa goes to her room with a headache, he actually dries the dishes for her, although knowing where to put them away is beyond him. Later they sit in the parlour with cups of tea made by Halya, and she takes up a book, Jane Austen's *Persuasion*. She identifies with the heroine, Anne Elliot, whose foolish and vain father reminds her in some ways of Viktor.

After a moment Ronnie goes to the piano and leafs through his songbooks until he finds one he likes. He sings, in quite a pleasant tenor, "A wandering minstrel, I, a thing of rags and patches, of songs and snatches, And lovely lu–ull–abies..." She hears the rhymes, the light and playful tone and forgets to look away.

"What is *minstrel*, Mr. Shawcross?" she asks when he's done.

"Ah well, a minstrel is a man who wanders the countryside singing and hoping to earn a little silver to buy his bread. He doesn't make a lot and so he has to wear rags and patches."

Halya can't believe her ears. *"Kobzar,"* she says. "In my country we have this also."

A COUPLE OF WEEKS LATER, Natalka sees that English *pahn* fellow ride up to the house on his fancy horse. Viktor sees him a moment later, leaps from his chair and twists himself into a poor imitation of a soldier standing to attention. Natalka can't help a snort. Viktor asks her to bring tea and the English biscuits he bought in town. Runs out to shake the fellow's hand. Manages not to salute. By the time Natalka gets back with the tea and biscuits, Viktor sits on the couch, Shawcross on one of the upholstered chairs. Natalka pours tea and Viktor passes the plate of biscuits to Shawcross, his face radiating an almost childlike pride.

Natalka picks up her sewing and sits in the furthest corner, invisible as only a woman can make herself, but watching as hard as she can.

"Yes, Mr. Dobson," the *pahn* begins, "my mother is well pleased with Helena. And I must say that I too...am growing fond of her."

Hah! Natalka thinks. First it's Helen and now it's Helena! My-my-my.

Viktor isn't sure he understands. "Thank you, sir. I happy my daughter with your mother. She fine lady."

"Yes, Mother is certainly a lady."

"My daughter must learn this. To be lady."

Ronnie looks thoughtful. "Yes, you're right. That's very important. But I was wondering...has Helena ever had a sweetheart? Maybe in the old country?"

"Yes...I forbid her to see him."

"You don't think he could be here in Spring Creek?"

"Before we left he is taken for army. I tell her maybe he already dead."

"You're helping her to forget him. Good. You see, Mr. Dobson, I think I would like..." he stops to take a deep breath, "to marry Helena."

Shawcross looks a little surprised, hearing himself say this.

Natalka knows the word "marry." Her eyes shoot poison, but no one notices.

"Marry, sir?"

"Yes, that's right. She has made a strong impression upon me. But first —"

Viktor is losing the thread. "What you say, sir? You don't want marry her?"

"I've been thinking about what you said – that she must learn to be a lady. And I'd like her to learn the best English. Now, there's a very fine school in Edmonton."

"*Shkola?* You want send her to *shkola?*"

"Yes, I think that would be good. And then, next summer, if she agrees, we could be married. If you don't mind, I'll ask Mother to speak to her about the school."

Viktor seems to be having trouble breathing and his face turns pink. This must be beyond even his wildest hopes. Well, maybe in the far corners of his mind...

He manages a deep breath. "Yes, sir. Let your mother speak."

"Excellent. I'm so glad you approve. Well, good to sit down with you, Mr. Dobson." The *pahn* gets up and they shake hands some more.

"Goodbye, Mr. Dobson. We'll speak again."

"Goodbye, sir." Viktor sees him to the door. "Best wishes to your mother."

The second the fellow's out the door, Natalka jumps up.

"All that talk in English. What was that about?"

"Nothing," Viktor says airily. "He's looking for a new horse."

"A horse called Halya? Is that what he's looking for?" She can see by Viktor's face that she's guessed right. Well, it's not going to happen if she can help it.

"Leave it, old woman. Eat an English biscuit. Be glad you have food."

Natalka knocks the fancy biscuits to the floor. Viktor picks one up and nibbles on it, just to annoy her. With a look of injured dignity, he heads outside. But Natalka sees that by the time he reaches the door, his face wears a rapturous smile. This could never have happened in the old country, he must be thinking.

HALYA WALKS in a garden of hardy rosebushes and perennials, as close to an English garden as Louisa could get in these dry grasslands. This English garden is tended by one of the shepherds, who helped look after a rich man's estate in Romania. Halya's talked to him a few times, but she doesn't see the shepherds often because they sleep in a separate bunkhouse and cook their own food. Cornmeal. *Mamaliga*. She'd like that.

As she comes back to the house, Halya hears the Shawcrosses arguing.

"No! I don't want her to go away!" Louisa's voice floats out the kitchen window.

"Come on, Mother. You're always at me to get married."

"I have told you, Helena is *my* companion."

"Don't you want me to be happy?" Ronnie's voice takes on his wheedling tone.

"Not if it makes me unhappy." Louisa sounds furious.

Ronnie tries to sound reasonable. "You can't expect a young woman to spend all her time with an old one. Anyway, you will be happy. You'll have a lovely daughter-in-law."

Halya doesn't even consider not eavesdropping. These people are planning her future, or think they are.

Louisa changes tactics. "She's a Ruthenian. I thought you were concerned about our position in society."

"I've thought about that." Even outside, Halya hears triumph in Ronnie's voice. "Our position means we can do what we like. Mother, we're the *Shawcrosses.*"

"Helena is mine. Find someone else." But she seems to have nothing to threaten him with.

"You know, you've never approved of any of the girls I wanted to marry."

"Ronnie, I warn you —"

"Oh poor, dear Momsie. You'll come round. You always do. For your little Ronnie."

"I cannot believe you're so selfish," Louisa says in a strangled voice.

"I can't think why not, you've known me all my life. And anyway, if I am selfish, whose fault would that be?"

"Oh, do shut up." But it's clear Louisa's given up, at least for the moment.

"Where is the delightful creature, by the way?" Ronnie asks, triumph in his tone.

"Out walking. She wanted some exercise."

"Good. I'll teach her to ride. I can see us galloping through the hills. Mr. Ronald Shawcross and his wife, the admiration of lesser mortals. Yes, she's a Ruthenian, they'll say, but you wouldn't know to talk to her that she wasn't a born Englishwoman."

There's a long pause and Louisa apparently realizes she has a card left to play.

"At any rate," she says, "this may all be quite beside the point. Helena may not want you."

"She will want me, I'm sure. She's starting to like me, or at least tolerate me. And her father would marry me himself if he could."

"Speaking of her father," his mother says peevishly, "perhaps I'll send her home for a visit. Give her time to consider."

"All right, Mommy, whatever you think best."

Louisa gives a snort, and probably hopes she hasn't miscalculated.

HALYA AND VIKTOR quarrel at the parlour table. Natalka listens.

"I don't want to go away." Halya's lips press together, her jaw set.

"You will. Or you can leave my house. And take the old woman with you."

"Batko!" Surely not even he would cast out an old grandmother he'd uprooted from her home.

"This fighting isn't good," Natalka says. "Let me speak with Halya alone."

"You should call her Helena now." Viktor never stops hoping this will happen.

"Tsssh! How can Halya suddenly be Helena? Just let us talk."

"Talk, then. You women are all the same." Viktor stomps outside, slamming the door.

Halya starts to cry.

"Stop that," Natalka says, a little crossly. "It's hard to think when you're crying."

"But Baba —" Halya wails.

"Halya, pay attention to me! Why not go to this school?"

"What?" Halya looks outraged. "You're on his side?"

"Listen, sweetheart, *pampushka,* it's easy to disagree with him, he's such a wild boar." Halya smiles. "But be careful. Every now and then he might have a good idea."

"But Baba!" Halya's wailing again.

"You're still not listening. First, you didn't want to go live with that *pahna,* and now you can leave."

"She's not so bad —"

"Bad, good, that's not the point. It was not your choice. Or mine. Nothing new there. But now they'll let you go, so that's one point. Second, they want you to go to school and learn good English and how to behave around English people."

"That's what you *want* for me?" Halya can't believe it.

"Sure, why not?"

Halya is too outraged to answer.

Natalka charges on. "Only don't think of it the way they do. Don't do it so you can marry the son."

"But that's why they want me to do it! I'm sure of it."

"Darling, we aren't going to get anywhere if you don't pay attention. What they want is one thing. What *you* want is another."

"I don't see how going away will get me what I want."

"Not right away, maybe. But this is our country now and we have to learn how to live in it. So maybe your father is partly right. You need to learn good English."

"You agree with him?"

"I agree you should learn English. I do not agree you should forget Ukrainian."

"But —"

"Then, when you finish school, do what you want. In Canada, I hear, people are free."

"I can't believe you're saying this."

"I may be old, *liuba,* but once in a while I get a new thought." Natalka looks so teasing and shrewd that Halya laughs.

"Good, laugh. It's a big improvement on 'But Baba.' And better than listening to you arguing with the wild boar. And remember, in the old country, you could be somebody's wife and keep his house and have babies. That's it! Here you might make some other kind of life."

"What kind?"

"How do I know? We've only been here a few months. But you better find out before you make any choices."

"How did you figure all this out?"

A sheepish look crosses Natalka's face. "I suppose I didn't, really. But Maryna said some things about coming to Canada. Lately I've been thinking she was right."

"Seriously, though, even if going to school was a good idea, you'd be alone with him all winter. You'd go crazy."

"You think so? I don't go crazy that easy. Maybe it's the boar that's going to go crazy. Anyway, you let me worry about that."

Halya can't believe the way their talk has gone. But at least she's stopped feeling like a horse that can be bought and sold. "All right. I'll do it."

Natalka hugs her, kisses her on both cheeks. "Good. That's my precious girl." She grins. "But don't sound like you want to. Or he'll be suspicious."

They look out the window. Viktor is skulking around the garden, violently pulling up weeds and kicking clods of earth. They burst out laughing.

"*Dobre*. I'll be a good girl obeying my father. But I'll look really miserable about it." She tries to arrange her face into a look of unhappy subjugation.

"I'll tell him. But you go to your room. I don't think I can keep a straight face otherwise." Halya hugs Natalka and runs out of the room.

SHAWCROSS GALLOPS up to the construction site and almost leaps from his horse. Hands shaking, face shiny with sweat, he tethers Brigadier to a rail. Shouts at the men to gather around. Will he ask them to work even more hours without pay? Taras wonders.

"I've come from the telegraph office! England has declared war on Germany!" His voice is hoarse with excitement. A few men cheer. Frank Elder, a cast on his left wrist, stops trying to line up a brick with his right.

"Shawcross Brickworks and Construction will be part of the

fight! We make the best fire-resistant brick there is! Brick to line the boiler rooms of battleships to come!" His eyes dart around the group of men. As if he imagines himself leading them into battle, Taras thinks.

Shawcross looks puzzled. Why aren't the men more responsive? "The mother country needs our help."

What is mother country? Taras wonders. England is the mother of Canada?

"Now I know some of you will want to enlist. Those who are young and single. You have my personal assurance a job will be waiting for you when you come home again. The rest of you are needed here. Some of you may leave the construction side and work at brickmaking. So we can increase production of genuine Spring Creek firebrick!"

A few more cheers come. The boss looks around at the faces. Some men look worried, others cynical. He imagines what they might be thinking: Shawcross is only thirty years old – is *he* planning to enlist? His face turns dark red.

"I will be here to lead this work. I would like nothing better than to see action in Europe myself. But I have a widowed mother to care for. And the plant to keep running. For the war effort. The mother country!" He splutters to a halt, more and more embarrassed.

I see, Taras thinks, you can't go into the army because of your two mothers.

At closing time, Taras runs to the brickyard to find Moses. The workers stand around outside the gates talking about the news of war. He sees Moses and hurries toward him.

"Hey, hunkie," a voice calls, "gonna enlist?" Stover. Of course. Taras can't think what to say. "You're a dirty coward, then. Come to this country for an easy ride."

Moses catches Taras's arm and steers him away from Stover.

"Why do these men want war?" Taras asks. He hasn't thought much about war since he came to Canada. It never occurred to him that he might have to join the army here.

"Because they don't know what it is. They want to be powerful and push people around. They don't think they might be the ones getting pushed."

"Or killed," Taras says.

Moses and Taras walk through the town, past the bank and the grocery store and the blacksmith shop. People wander down the middle of the street, yelling, setting off firecrackers, waving British flags. Tuneless fragments of patriotic songs – "Rule Britannia" and "God Save the King" – surge through the air. A small group of men drinking from a whiskey bottle pushes past, and Taras gets separated from Moses.

"We'll show those bloody Germans!" one of them screams.

Taras looks at them more closely and sees Dan Stover and his friends, cheering wildly. Taras doesn't understand. He didn't think Canadians had anything against Germans. Rudy Brandt's a German. He does his job well. Everybody at work likes him.

Taras happens to look down the street to the railway station and sees a couple of women on the platform, surrounded by excited, milling young men. The older woman has her arm around the other and is trying to pull her through the knot of men and into the station. The young woman, a slim, upright figure in a close-fitting green dress, has hair the colour of brass; it glints in the sun.

"Halya!" Taras screams, but his words are lost in all the noise. He tries to run after her but can't make headway against the surging bodies.

"Halya, wait for me!" But she disappears inside the station. The person who hears his shout is Dan Stover.

"Look at that foreign bastard! Won't fight for the country that took him in." Stover has a look of joy and fury, as if for the first time his life makes sense; as if he finally knows who he is.

For a second Taras sees the sweat-streaked, feral face as Stover's fist crashes into the side of his head. Darkness shadows his brain. As he goes down one man punches him in the gut and another kicks him in the side.

Then Moses comes, bigger and stronger than any of the brawling men. He knocks Stover to the road where he lies still.

One of his pals throws a punch, but he's really drunk. Moses steps aside and his fist connects with the guy's nose. He feels the warmth of blood on his hand. The third guy tries to kick him, but Moses grabs his ankle and he goes down, looking puzzled, and disappointed. Moses waits to see if either of them will try again, but after a moment they bend to help Stover.

Their happy day is ruined. They haven't shown the bloody foreigners anything.

Moses helps Taras to his feet and supports him as they walk slowly away through the crowd. Incredibly, almost no one seems to have noticed any of it. No one follows the Orphan Boy. And his Ukrainian brother.

Days later, will somebody remember seeing a punch thrown and a bright arc of blood, and think, What happened there? Did I really see that?

A rock smashes the window of Schmidt's Grocery. Taras can't understand what's happening. Is war here already? Then he remembers.

"Moses! Halya was here. I saw her."

THE SUN SETS as Moses drives up to the Kalynas' yard, Taras lying in the back of a borrowed wagon. The doctor has seen Taras, cleaned his scratches and bruises. There are no broken bones. His parents watch from the road as the wagon comes down the long hill. This must be the Black Ukrainian. As the wagon stops near the house, they see Taras, and Daria can't stop a small scream. Mykola and Moses carry Taras inside and lay him on one of the newly made grass beds wrapped in woven willow. They cover him with blankets and watch over him as night falls. Mykola lights the coal oil lamp. Daria brushes Taras's hair from his forehead.

Moses tells them what happened and what the doctor's said. Let him rest, give him water when he's fully conscious again. He tells them that Canada has declared war on Germany.

"I wish we'd never come here," Daria says. "I hate this place."

"And yet," Mykola says, "if we hadn't, Taras would be in the army."

Daria nods. This will be a big war now, not some skirmish in Bosnia.

As they grow calmer, they become more aware of Moses – a black man speaking to them in their own language. Already it feels quite natural. Taras has talked about him, of course, but seeing him is another thing. Perhaps Moses is the single greatest wonder of this whole journey. A man who was not born a Ukrainian has become one.

"Taras said he saw Halya. Just before the men came after him."

Taras moans. His fingers worry at the blanket; reaching, seeking. He dreams a summer day of hazy golden light. Hears a laugh and sees Halya walking on a steep hillside. Her hair, in waves from her braid, blows free in the wind. The grass on this hill is the grass here in Canada, thick and pale. And then her hair is grass. He calls to her, but she doesn't hear. He tries to follow, but his legs won't move. Then he's awake, looking up at his parents.

"She's here. I'm going to find her."

HALYA LOOKS OUT the window at a green lawn sheltered by tall trees of a kind she's never seen before. A fence of pointed black iron pickets surrounds it, with a heavy gate that clanged shut when she and Louisa Shawcross came through it. The school is two storeys tall, made of red brick with many windows. They walked up wide stone steps to the double wooden doors. Louisa took her to an office marked "Registrar" and enrolled her in the school. Afterwards Halya was almost afraid to see her go.

They came here, by taxi from the train station, through well-shaded streets with grand houses on them, and Louisa climbed into a taxi again to retrace her path. Halya had nothing to say about it. Baba said to come here, but Baba has no idea what it's like. Halya doesn't know a soul. She has to stay for ten months.

A FEW DAYS LATER Taras rides Moses's horse Molly through town on his way to work. He stops in front of a brick building with a makeshift sign: Recruiting Office. Inside, young men sit on a long bench waiting to be examined. Through an open doorway, he sees the doctor listening to Dan Stover's chest with a stethoscope. The doctor shakes his head. Stover seems to argue; then plead. The doctor shrugs; gets up and calls the next man.

"Hey, Taras!" Jimmy Burns, the young man who spoke up when Stover knocked the bricks onto Frank Elder, calls out. Taras follows the voice to the side of the building where young men are busy digging trenches. Moses says this is being done to help attract more volunteers. Taras wonders what's so attractive about digging. He rides Molly closer to the trenches.

"I passed my medical," Jimmy says, excited. "I'm in!" He seems to have forgotten about unions. He has a look on his face Taras can't understand – fervent, exalted. As if he's heard a voice more powerful than any human one, and doesn't need to hear any other.

Stover stumbles out the door. He doesn't see Jimmy or Taras.

TARAS STABLES MOSES'S HORSE and they walk to work together. Taras is going to work at the brick plant over the fall and winter, along with most of the construction crew. Inside the gates they see men in groups, talking, gesturing. About the war.

Frank Elder joins them. "Did you hear? Jimmy Burns went and enlisted."

"Thought he would," Moses says.

Taras sees Shawcross ride up on his horse and goes up to him.

"Excuse me, Mr. Shawcross. I need to go away...a little while."

Shawcross smiles with an look of sincere good humour. He does this look so well that Taras wonders if he mistakes it for genuine himself. "Certainly. Every man who enlists can have his old job back." What could be fairer than that? his look says. *If* you come back...

"No sir. Not enlist. There is person I must find. From my village."

"Oh, from your village," Shawcross says. "Where do you come from, anyway?"

"I come from Bukovyna," Taras says.

"Bukovyna... Good God, you're not Austrian?"

"No. I am Ukrainian. Austrians ruled us."

"Oh, I see," Shawcross says thoughtfully. He smiles as if a pleasant idea has occurred to him. "Well, I'll think about your request. Carry on now." Shawcross doesn't dismount, but turns Brigadier toward the town's main street.

Moses watches him go. He explains that Taras should never tell the boss anything more than he can help. And that this isn't the time to press for a union. Working at the plant they can be said to be contributing to the war effort and will be probably not be pressured to enlist. Moses doesn't want to enlist, because he's sure he'd be the only black man in a regiment filled with strangers.

So they should stay, and keep their heads down. Winter's coming. Most men have families to provide for and there are almost no other jobs in Spring Creek. Shawcross has even dropped hints about unemployed men in Regina who'd be glad to have their jobs.

CHAPTER 22

The policeman

MYKOLA BREAKS LAND with a horse and plough belonging to Kupiak's neighbour and Daria weeds the small vegetable garden. When the ploughing's done, Mykola will shoe horses for the neighbour. He allows himself a moment to remember Shevchana in April as he began sowing his crop. Work Yarema will have finished.

Daria happens to look up the hill, where occasionally someone goes by on horseback or in a wagon, and at that moment someone does appear. A man in a red jacket rides toward them. She feels almost as if she's summoned him.

Reg Statler, in his forties, gets off his horse and introduces himself as a member of the Royal Northwest Mounted Police. "Mr. and Mrs. Kalyna?" he asks.

Mykola nods. "Yes. Our name Kalyna."

"Mr. Kalyna, we have information that you are Austrian citizens."

Mykola barely understands. "No Austrian. Ukrainian." Daria takes his arm.

"But you're from an Austrian territory, and Canada is now at war with Austria. Do you understand?" The policeman doesn't appear to be enjoying this. "I'm afraid this makes you enemy aliens."

Mykola shakes his head. "Canada our country now." Daria nods.

"Yes, I know, but the government is worried about immigrants from Austria. They're afraid you may be spying for Austria. Or helping them." He can see that this is too much English for them.

And that spying for Austria has to be the last thing on their minds.

"I don't understand," Mykola says. Kupiak taught him these words.

"I'm sorry, but you must report each month to the local police. And surrender any firearms you own."

"What is firearms?" Mykola asks.

"It means guns. Do you have any guns?"

Mykola shakes his head. "No guns."

"We make snares for rabbits," Daria says, as if that will make it clearer.

"Very well. Good. You have no guns. But you must report on the first day of each month until further notice. To the police station in town. A red brick building. Your son, Taras Kalyna, will do the same." He has no idea how much of this they understand. Or if they even own a calendar. He feels stupid. "Well then, I'll be on my way. Good day to you."

"Good day," Mykola says, but it isn't a good day. Not the worst day of their lives, of course, but definitely not good.

"ARE YOU IN CONTACT with the Austrian government?"

"No, sir."

"Do you possess any guns or other weapons?"

"No, sir."

"Were you sent here to spy for the Austrian government?"

"No, sir. I do not spy for them. I'm Ukrainian."

Taras is in an office in the red brick building Statler told Daria and Mykola about. He sits in a hard chair, Reg Statler in a similar one behind a wooden desk.

"Just answer my questions," Statler says. "Don't add anything or leave anything out. Are you quite sure you have no gun?"

Taras could swear the policeman doesn't want to be doing this. That he doesn't believe Taras and his family pose the slightest danger to Canada.

"No sir. But if we had gun, we could hunt for meat —"

233

"Do you support the Austrian emperor and the Austrian government?"

"No! Sir."

Half an hour later, weary and humiliated, Taras leaves the office. As he comes through the door, he passes Viktor on his way in. They stare at each other, astonished, especially Viktor. Taras wants to grab Viktor and make him say where Halya is. Viktor moves toward the desk where Statler sits, knowing Taras can't do anything.

Taras watches through the window as Statler questions Viktor. Finally the door opens. Viktor walks toward a horse and wagon, determined not to see Taras. He tries to stand tall, but shame bows his shoulders. He sees Taras but won't look right at him.

Taras steps toward the wagon. "Viktor. Where's Halya?"

"Gone away," Viktor says with a sullen look. "You'll never find her." Saying the last words seems to revive him. Here is still one power he has – to hurt Taras.

"I must see her!" Taras moves in front of Viktor's horse, ready to grab the harness.

"She's going to school! She's going to be a *pahna*." Viktor manages a small gloat.

"You're crazy! How can Halya be a *pahna?*" Perhaps Viktor really has gone mad.

"She's going to be married. Do you hear? To an Englishman!"

"You're lying!" But Viktor looks too pleased to be lying.

"Am I?" he says. "Wait and see." He climbs into the wagon, flaps the reins.

Taras reaches up and grabs Viktor's arms.

"Tell me where she is! Tell me!"

"You'll never know." Viktor struggles to pull free.

Statler comes to the door and Taras has to let go. Viktor straightens his shirt and drives away. Taras would follow him, but the horse is stabled at Moses's place.

THE FOLLOWING SUNDAY afternoon, Moses drives Taras and his parents into town to his house. Even though Daria and Mykola have been told what to expect, they can't stop staring. Taras knows what they must be thinking: they've been transported home without the trouble of train journeys or being rocked and shaken in the stinking hold of a ship. Daria runs her hand along an embroidered shawl.

But they haven't come to admire Ukrainian embroidery. On the table Moses has laid out some clothing. He picks up a lady's suit jacket of lightweight wool, hip length with gathered sleeves and neat pockets, and helps Daria try it on. It fits very well and its royal blue sets off her dark hair and eyes.

"You're sure your mother wouldn't have minded?" Daria asks, running her had over the soft material.

"She'd have been happy for you to wear it." Moses holds up the matching skirt, which also looks like a good fit. "She didn't wear this suit often, that's why it's hardly worn. I suppose it's a bit old-fashioned..." He remembers it was purchased over twenty years ago.

"No," Daria says. "Ukrainian things are beautiful, but so are these."

He hands her a cream cotton shirtwaist with sewn-down pleats across the front. Black leather shoes with a small velvet bow on each toe. A black felt hat with a blue feather.

Daria takes off her flower-print headscarf, knotted under her chin in lifelong custom, and tries on the hat, amazed at the feel of it on her hair. And the way she looks in the mirror Moses hands her. She likes this hat, even though she hated the one she wore on the train leaving Chernowitz.

For Mykola, Moses has a black wool jacket and pants and a brown felt hat from his stepfather, Pavlo. A pair of sturdy work boots. Two dark blue work shirts.

He has one more gift. He's filled an enamelled tin washtub with hot water and set out towels and soap. There's bread and butter for them to eat afterwards and tea keeping hot on the cast-iron stove he uses in summer. He and Taras leave them alone to bathe.

They walk around the town, past the new school Taras is work-ing on, past the brick plant with its great kilns, and slowly back to

Moses's house. Daria is outside, wearing the new clothes, her dark hair still damp. She braids it and winds it around her head, and as it catches the light, she looks for a moment like a much younger woman. Mykola sets the hat on her head and they laugh. She folds her old scarf and puts it in a cotton bag with their other things.

"Who is that beautiful Canadian woman?" Moses asks as he and Taras reach the house. They all laugh, as if it's a special occasion: Christmas, or maybe Drenched Monday.

On the ride home Daria and Mykola sit very straight on the wagon's backless wooden bench, along the main street, past shops and the hotel. About a block ahead, Taras notices a stocky man in a black suit. Something familiar about him. Why does he keep staring?

The man turns and walks down the side street. They're halfway home before Taras understands that the man he saw was Viktor, out for a Sunday stroll. A new man in a black suit. It was the suit that fooled him.

A FEW DAYS later Natalka sits mending Viktor's socks when she hears the sound of the wagon. He comes in the door carrying packages. What could this be? He opens one and takes out a large piece of cloth. Lays it out on the table, gently smoothes its folds. Its design is red, white and blue, with a large red cross in the centre. This must be the flag of Canada.

He hands her a second package. She wonders if the grimace on his face is an attempt at a friendly smile.

"A present for you." She looks at the paper wrappings but makes no move. What if he changes his mind and starts yelling?

"Open it." He nods, first at her and then at the package.

Oh yes, and what if it's a trick? No, probably it isn't. And the way he's stretching his lips probably is a smile. But Viktor being nice, or at least trying to be, is a disturbing sight. He hasn't got the knack, due to a lifelong lack of practice.

But she opens the package. Inside is an attractive Canadian-style dress. She holds it up so the skirt skims the floor. Viktor has chosen black. What else for an old lady, he must think. She considers throwing it back at him, but all in all, she'd hate to fight with him on such a momentous occasion. The wild boar has smiled, or as close to it as he can manage, and has bought her a dress. A dress she could actually imagine wearing.

Still, don't make it easy for him, her inner wisdom suggests. "You think this will make me English?" she asks tartly.

"No," he says with a look of resignation. "But it couldn't hurt."

He's so comical she wants to laugh. "Soon you won't remember what it's like to be Ukrainian," she chides.

"Good. I can't wait for the day."

Well, at least this is still the same Viktor, not some shape-shifting demon.

Natalka takes a very deep breath and forces herself to speak. *"Dyakuyiu,"* she says. "In this dress I can go to town with you some time."

Viktor feels his face go red. He hadn't imagined she'd ever thank him. Now he too must struggle for words. *"Bud laska."* Be well. He picks up the flag and goes outside.

CHAPTER 23

Speak white

SHAWCROSS RUNS two shifts a day, turning out a seemingly endless stream of bricks through fall and early winter. When the weather's bad, Taras stays in town with Moses. His parents are safe. The bachelor's shack is now a tiny but warm house. She and Mykola have plenty of food. Mykola dug a root cellar for carrots and potatoes and squash. Moses, who does have a gun, shot a deer and Mykola butchered it for him. Mykola's share is smoked and stored in the root cellar.

At the beginning of each month they report to the police.

Taras learns more English. Most of the workers like him although they find him a little too serious. He's known for his strength and his willingness to learn.

On Sundays, he rides around the countryside on Moses's horse, stopping at farmhouses to inquire after Viktor. No one seems to know him, although Taras does meet a couple of other Ukrainian families, from Halychyna. One day, at a farm west of Spring Creek, someone thinks there might be a Ukrainian family living "out past the Hamilton place." Taras follows their directions, through a long stretch of flatter land that looks good for farming, and stops at the Hamilton farm, but no one is home. He takes a close look at several nearby farms, but sees only Canadian farmers with young families out in the yards.

He rides further west to one more farmstead. But the white frame house has lace curtains and a British flag hangs from the front gate. Discouraged, he turns for home.

Why would Viktor send Halya away? Where could she be?

JOHN MADISON, a fortyish man with sharp features and a sharper tongue, teaches Halya geography and history. He walks the aisles, gripping a wooden ruler. Stops at Halya's desk, slaps the ruler into his hand. "Helena. Primary exports of Brazil." He points the ruler at her.

Confused, she answers in Ukrainian. "I don't know."

"Speak English, girl, not gibberish."

"Speak white!" a girl called Bella says. She and her friends laugh. They're several years younger than Halya and because she's older they think she must be stupid.

Without even stopping to think, Halya turns on Bella. "You're an ignorant, nasty fool!" she says in Ukrainian. "Your brain is smaller than a pig's!"

"Helena! That's enough!" Madison points the ruler at her. "You really must speak English. Your employer is paying good money for you to learn."

"You don't know your ass from your elbow!" This last bit she manages in English except for the "ass" part. He seems to guess the Ukrainian word without translation.

"Helena, that will do!" Madison grasps her hand, palm up, and hits it hard with his ruler. Everyone falls silent.

Halya stares at him with pure hatred.

ENGLISH CLASS IS BETTER. One day Miss Greeley, a grey-haired lady in her fifties, who wears what she calls "good, stout shoes" for her long walks, asks if anyone has read a novel by Jane Austen. Halya raises her hand. Frowning, Miss Greeley asks which one.

"Pride and Prejudice," Halya says. The teacher still looks skeptical, as if a Ukrainian-speaking student coming up with a Jane Austen title is something which might happen by chance every now and then, but nothing more. Halya wants to take that look off her face.

"*Pride and Prejudice* is one of the greatest novels in the English language," she says. "Its opening lines are often quoted." Of course, Miss Greeley doesn't know that she's imitating Louisa Shawcross. "It is a truth universally acknowledged, that a single man in possession of a good fortune, must be in want of a wife."

"Oh! That's rather amazing. Do you know what it means?"

"I think so," Halya says. "People want their daughters to be...provided for. So they look around and...and see if there are any rich men for them to marry. So when Mr. Bingley rents a house near the Bennet family, everyone rushes to meet him."

"Very good, Helena." A smile breaks over the teacher's face. As far as Halya can see, none of the other girls has shown evidence of having read any novels at all. They haven't heard of Jane Austen, either, to judge by their faces. They must be wondering how a bohunk girl has memorized the opening of *Pride and Prejudice,* whatever that is.

Miss Greeley begins to talk about eighteenth-century England. She still has the smile.

She asks more questions as she goes along and Halya answers whatever she's asked. But she doesn't offer any more comments because she sees how angry she's made the other girls. The bohunk's not supposed to know anything. Especially about English novels.

Yet how could she not understand it? She might as well be one of the Bennet girls herself, with Ronnie Shawcross a third-rate Mr. Darcy. Mr. Bingley in the book was nice, though. She could almost fall in love with him herself.

Soon Miss Greeley is lending books to Halya and helping her if she has difficulty reading them. She corrects Halya's pronunciation and grammar gently and praises her essays. She arranges for Halya to learn typing from the school secretary in the late afternoons after classes end. Halya works hard at it, understanding that it's something a person can be paid for doing. Maybe the school secretary will retire some day and she can have the job. Not only that, typing's fun.

Halya asks if there are typewriters somewhere in the world that use the Ukrainian alphabet. Miss Greeley doesn't know.

IN THE DORM ROOM one night, a few weeks after the Jane Austen episode, Halya sits in her room writing at the desk, the door ajar. Bella darts in and grabs the piece of paper. Halya runs after her, but three other girls hold her to keep her from getting it back. Well, she could get it back if she was willing to have a fight. But she doesn't want to get thrown out of the school. Now that she's actually learning things.

"Oh look, girls," Bella says. "The bohunk can write English." She looks the sheet of paper over. "Would you believe it, the bohunk is writing a poem! But she doesn't seem to have heard it's supposed to rhyme." The others giggle. Bella reads aloud.

> *In this prison no one knows my name.*
> *These walls are hard and cold,*
> *the air thick with strange words*
> *flung against my ears like stones.*

The girls laugh loudly, then fall silent. They see that there's really nothing very funny about it. They let go of her arms. Halya finishes the poem, reciting from memory.

> *At night I hear my father's voice:*
> *Forget your love. He is gone.*
> *But rage keeps my courage strong*
> *And he turns to ice. Heart, blood, bone.*

With Halya staring them in the eyes, the girls can find nothing to mock. Bella drops the poem to the floor and walks away. "Stupid bohunk," she mutters.

One night Halya wakens from a dream, her face wet with tears. In the dream she was speaking English and had forgotten how to speak Ukrainian.

I can't live here, she thinks. I'm losing my language.

She sits on the edge of her bed. She hadn't realized how lonely she would be in this place. But she can't let the Ukrainian words for everything she knows be lost. She begins to speak, quietly, in Ukrainian. *"Ya* Halya Dubrovsky... My name is Halya Dubrovsky. I come from Shevchana in Bukovyna and my grandmother is Natalka. I'm here in this school because I want to know how to live in this country. I don't think I will be going back to Shevchana." She touches the pendant on her night table.

"I love a man named Taras. He loves me. I will find him again or he'll find me. Some day we'll be together." As she speaks, her voice grows stronger. "I won't ever forget him or my darling *baba.* I won't forget our food or the soft linen *sorochka* or the warm *peech* or the great poems. My mother's books. I have all these things inside me."

Someone pounds on the wall. One of Bella's friends. Halya stifles a snort of laughter. Oh well, she can stop for now. It's enough.

A LETTER COMES from Louisa Shawcross. Halya imagines her at her dining room table, sipping tea or sherry, writing. Choosing each word with care. Imagining Halya back at the ranch, once more under her gaze. Her power. Halya knows how Louisa sees her — as an experiment. She once heard Louisa say, "It will still be such fun to see how she turns out."

"I hear such good reports of your work as make me very proud," the letter says. "You have succeeded beyond our hopes. In fact, I hear that you are even learning to use a typewriting machine. That is commendable, but surely not necessary to someone who will have a superior education. Ronnie and I have been talking about you often. I must admit, he speaks of you in a way I've never heard him speak about any other girl. I will leave that until he can speak for himself, but I begin to think you will one day be more than just my companion. I can hardly wait until spring to see you again." Halya stops reading, dismayed.

It's not that she hasn't worked it out. "Ronnie" wants to marry her. Or at least he likes to imagine he does. Really, he just thinks it's a bit of a challenge, so he's determined to get her. They've sent her here to learn to be an English lady. Then she'll be good enough to marry Ronnie. But is he good enough for her? She smiles. Decides to list his good points.

So. He sings well and sometimes he acts charming. There must be some other good points, but she can't think of a single one. Most of the time his own mother can't stand him.

All right, then. Bad points. This part's easy. Ronnie expects his mother to give him everything he wants. He's vain and greedy and his hands look like an English lady's. He'd be useless at any real work. His wife would have to be a second mother.

Anyway, she's going to marry Taras. So she can't marry Ronnie. For a moment she feels guilty for fooling the Shawcrosses. Letting them pay for her education when she never meant to marry Ronnie. Yes, but what else could she do? Viktor was prepared to kick her out of the house if she didn't. Oh well, she'll think of what to say by the end of the school term when she goes back to Spring Creek.

But she can't settle into sleep that night. The end of term isn't all that far off. None of the Bennet girls had to deal with anything like this. Of course Lizzy refused Mr. Collins, so it can be done. Mr. Collins didn't take it well, though.

By Christmas Halya can read novels with ease and write very correct essays and letters. Not even Bella can find much to tease her about any more. Miss Greeley suggests she look at the novels of Charles Dickens and she reads *Oliver Twist* in a blaze of excitement, hardly able to stop for classes or meals. She thinks about all these English books and how they've become part of her. Is she becoming English? Yes, some part of her is, although her Ukrainian self is always there watching, comparing, criticizing. She wishes she could also read Ukrainian novels; wonders if there are very many. She knows there's a writer called Yvan Franko, but she's never seen any of his books.

Viktor thinks they're no good. This makes her long to read them, but she has no idea how she could get hold of them.

Halya is the only girl to stay in school over the Christmas holidays. For some reason, Louisa thinks this will be for the best.

Probably so that when she gets home she'll be so starved for the sight of people she knows that Ronnie will look good to her. Halya thinks this isn't too likely. As it happens, Miss Greeley stays as well; she lives in a small suite in the school. They sometimes go for afternoon walks or talk about novels in the teachers' Common Room. All day Halya has access to the library and she reads everything she can, starting with the rest of Dickens. The more she reads, the more she asks herself who this English-Ukrainian Helena-Halya person is. Miss Greeley is puzzled about her too; Halya hears it in her questions. Halya has obviously shattered her notion of the not-too-bright peasant. Maybe you're learning from me, too, Halya thinks.

She's been living without any news of the war. Now she asks Miss Greeley for the old newspapers from the Common Room and learns about trench warfare on the Western Front. She looks for articles about what's happening in Bukovyna, but can't find a thing. People in Canada must not be interested in Ukrainian places. But there's more than enough to read about mud and rats and lice in the trenches; and terrible weapons that kill people in staggering numbers.

Louisa's letters never mention the war, let alone trenches.

On Christmas Day Halya is all alone. She eats leftovers the school cook has set out for her. This isn't her Christmas, but still it feels lonely to be by herself. Natalka must be lonely too, cooped up on the farm with Viktor. Halya writes to them, but says very little. Nothing Viktor won't like. She always throws in something in English, so Viktor can see her education is taking. She makes the wording difficult so he'll really have to sweat.

When Miss Greeley comes back from dinner with her sister's family, she invites Halya to her sitting room for tea and Christmas cake. There's something touching about seeing the place her teacher emerges from and retreats to each day. Her big walnut desk and bookcases filled with books Halya's never heard of. Miss Greeley sees her looking at them; she hesitates and then reaches up for what must be a favourite. She hands Halya a copy of

George Eliot's *Middlemarch*.

Halya holds the book as though it's a delicate child, strokes the black leather cover. Opens it to see the handwritten words, "This book is the property of Miss Letitia Greeley, M.A." She doesn't know if she's trying to thank Miss Greeley, but Halya finds herself talking about her life in the old country and after a while she tells her about the Shawcrosses. Not too much, because she doesn't want to worry her teacher. She sees her teacher is already worried.

As if that wasn't enough, she tells about Taras.

JUST BEFORE SCHOOL starts again, she and Miss Greeley read about an event on the Western Front. Up to their knees in mud, English and German soldiers, with the consent of a few officers, arranged a truce for Christmas. The rain that had fallen for weeks stopped, and men began singing carols across the lines. Then soldiers left the trenches and met in the battered ground between. Exchanged gifts: cigarettes; sweets; whiskey. There was singing, laughter. Somehow they found a piece of ground level enough for a soccer match. They all knew it had to end, and as daylight faded their officers ordered them back to the trenches.

As they read, the young and the older woman see each other's tears.

THE WINTER TERM moves along too quickly. Halya's learning more than she could ever have imagined. Her reading and writing skills are the best in her class. She knows she won't be coming back next year and wants to store up all the knowledge she can. She lives each day in a frenzy of reading and writing that never seems enough. Bella and her friends think she's sucking up to the teachers. Why else would anyone work so hard?

In early April, 1915, another letter comes from Louisa. Once again, she praises the reports on Halya's work. Hints at the bright future she sees for her. Mentions Ronnie in terms of great affection, as though Halya must feel the same way.

The end of the letter makes her heart race. "My dear girl," Louisa says, "we simply can't wait until the summer to see you.

We plan to take the train to Edmonton on the last Friday of April. On Saturday I plan to catch up on some shopping, and in the evening we shall take you out to dinner. Wear your best frock, my dear, as it will be very special."

Baba, Halya thinks, how did I let you talk me into this? Did we think this day would never come? She tries to throw the letter down, but it might as well be welded to her palm.

Lately she's had trouble seeing their faces in her mind. Now they're as good as standing right beside her.

They're coming! What am I going to do?

HALYA SITS in the dining room of the best hotel in Edmonton, the Macdonald, with the Shawcrosses. She knows she looks beautiful in a deep blue gown Louisa had sent to the school that afternoon. Ronnie can't keep his eyes off her. Louisa is happy to be with her favourite again. She touches Halya's arm, almost like a lover herself.

"Truly, it's been so dull without you. Ronnie and I missed you every day."

"Every day and every night," Ronnie says with a slightly knowing look. But nothing too overt. He actually seems a bit in awe of Halya. Or of whatever story he's made up about her. Either way, she's clearly no longer a plum he expects to fall in his lap.

Dinner has been splendid. Ronnie says so. Oyster soup. Filet of sole with wine and mushrooms. Roast partridge and something called bread sauce. Asparagus dressed with lemon butter. Chocolate cake, four layers tall, smothered in whipped cream.

Halya is worn out from the effort of eating all these things and behaving like a lady, and trying to ignore hints from Louisa and amorous glances from Ronnie. Why, why, did she agree to go to school? As she thinks this, another voice in her head says, So I could read George Eliot. And all the other ones. She has finally got to read books. Nothing can make her renounce them now.

A waiter sets down a coffee service: pale rose china cups and a silver pot, sugar bowl and creamer. He pours steaming coffee and departs with a bow.

"It'll be lovely to have you home again," Louisa says. "You can read to us. And Ronnie'll play for you."

Ronnie sings softly, "A wandering minstrel, I..."

Halya can't help but smile. Ronnie gives his mother a significant look. She beams and rises from the table. His eyes flash to a small royal blue velvet case on the table. The case itself has exhausted Halya during the meal. Trying not to look at it, trying to see only the starched white tablecloth, elegant china, gleaming silverware.

"Will you excuse me a moment? I must wash my hands." Louisa walks away from the table. Halya wishes she could go with her, but she doesn't think of it in time, and once Louisa's gone she doesn't have the strength to say anything. Her hands must remain unwashed. Ronnie is suddenly nervous and tries to cover it with talk.

"Winter's been simply dreadful. So much snow, so many men gone to war. I had to hire a bunch of foreigners at the plant." He doesn't notice Halya freeze when he says *foreigners*. "Jabbering away, not a word of English, except somehow they picked up the word *union*. Damned radicals should be sent back where they came from."

He takes Halya's silence for boredom. "But enough of misery. Spring's almost here. Trouble and ill humour are forgotten." He opens the velvet case to show her a pearl necklace, touches her hand gently. "Helena, this is for you."

Halya draws her hand away. "It's beautiful, Mr. Shawcross, but —"

"Please don't say no. I want you to have it." Halya can't think what to say to stop him. "You must know I care for you. You're everything I've ever wanted —"

"Mr. Shawcross, don't —"

"Please let me say it. I want you to marry me. I know you may not be ready, not yet. But just say you will...one day...not too far away. Helena?" Halya is almost touched that he really seems to care for her. But the word *foreigners* rings in her ears. She makes herself see the selfish boy behind the words.

"Halya. My name is Halya."

Shawcross loses his thread. "What?"

"My name is Halya Dubrovsky. I'm Ukrainian. What you call a foreigner."

Aghast, Shawcross sees his mistake. "No, you're more than that... And I can give you even more. Wealth, social position. I love you, Helena."

"My name is Halya Dubrovsky."

"What does it matter what your name is? I'd love you whatever it was."

But she sees Ronnie's trying to keep panic from his voice.

"It matters." Amazingly, she is finding words to say to him.

"You speak English beautifully. You'd never have to speak Ukrainian again."

"I need to speak it."

"You're right, I don't understand. It's just words. What difference does it make? Why do you need Ukrainian?"

"I need it, that's all."

He takes her hand. She sees him thinking: *All I have to do is reason with her. She'll come around.* "Surely," he says, "you can see that English is more...well, cultivated, more —"

She jerks her hand away. "No! I don't see. My language is as real as yours. Do you think English didn't sound strange to me at first?"

At the tables around them people turn to stare. Eyebrows rise. Lips curl. Ronnie tries to keep things quiet.

"Halya," he pleads, "I wasn't thinking. Of course your language is just fine."

"Mr. Shawcross, I can't marry you." Ronnie sees she means it, moves in an instant from disbelief to anger. He leaps to his feet. The other diners don't matter now.

"I don't understand. After all we've done for you. Sending you to school —"

"I'll pay you back. I don't know how, but I will."

"Pay us back with what?" he sneers. "It's that damned peasant, isn't it?"

Halya looks astounded. "What? What did you say?"

Ronnie is taken aback. He's almost revealed that he knows Taras. But Halya doesn't even know he's in Canada.

"That peasant. Your father told me about him. Always hanging around you."

"What do you know about Taras?" Does this spoiled brat know where he is?

"Viktor told me about him, but I couldn't believe you'd prefer someone like that. His family didn't even have a proper house, just some peasant shack." Ronnie's dredging up every ignorant comment he's ever heard about Ukrainians. "They barely had clothes to cover their backs or potatoes to put in the pot. That's what you want, is it?"

Halya sees everyone in the room is either watching them or pretending not to. A pair of waiters huddles, clearly trying to think of something, anything, they can do to stop it.

"You'd turn me down for some buffoon...some *nobody?*"

"Don't call him that, you skunk! He's a better man than you!" The words pour out before Halya knows they're coming. She feels like an actor on a very large stage.

In some part of her mind, she hears Lizzy Bennet's reply to Mr. Darcy: "In such cases as this, it is, I believe, the established mode to express a sense of obligation for the sentiments avowed, however unequally they may be returned." She wishes she could have said something more like that. Oh well, *skunk* was good too.

For a few seconds Ronnie looks devastated by the ruin of his fairy tale, but then the self-satisfied smirk he carries with him like a talisman comes creeping back. A piece of his heart may be breaking, but that leaves the rest of it to carry on life. After all, he's still the richest man in the district. He can have any woman he wants. Well, except Halya.

The waiters move toward them, determined to do something, when Louisa returns, hair smoothed, lip and cheek rouge renewed, her smile just beginning to fade.

"Helena? Ronnie? What's happened?"

"I'm sorry. I must go." Halya gets up from the table and moves toward the door.

"Ronnie, what have you done?"

"What have *I* done?" He tosses the necklace to the floor. The string breaks and Halya, turning, sees glowing pearls stream across the dark carpet.

The waiters leap to pick them up.

"I'll go after her. Shall I do that, Ronnie?"

"I never want to see the bitch again." Halya hears this, along with everyone else. "I'm going to my room." She moves behind a pillar as he marches to the elevators and stabs the button. As if he's forgotten his mother exists. He steps into the elevator and is gone.

A moment later their waiter helps Louisa out of the dining room into the foyer. The second waiter wraps the loose pearls in a linen napkin and hands them to her as she reaches the elevator. As soon the elevator door closes on her, they hurry back to the dining room.

Halya gets her coat from the cloakroom and sets out for the school. She loses her way a couple of times, curses the flimsy dress, but eventually makes it back, cheeks red, and panting from exercise and fury. She feels sorry for Louisa, but that's her only regret.

THE NEXT MORNING, she packs her clothes. At first she keeps only her own things and folds everything Louisa gave her in neat piles on the bed, but a voice in her head says, You don't think she's going to want them now, do you? Halya realizes she can't afford such high-flown ideas. They're for ladies in novels. And she actually said she'd pay them back!

She can't go back to the farm. Viktor will never speak to her again, anyway. Then how can she see Natalka? What if Natalka's sick? How would she even hear about it?

But she's free. She never has to spend another minute with Ronnie or Louisa. But she does have to leave school, just when she's learning so much. What's she going to do?

Find work, find a place to live. The voice in her head again. She knows nothing about how to do either of those things.

Yes she does. She grabs a newspaper, a few days old. Searches the advertisements. What on earth can she do that anyone would pay her for? Women in Jane Austen novels don't have jobs, except for servants and governesses. Oh. She's been a companion. Is that a job? Well, it's one she never wants to do again.

You know typing, the voice says. Maybe you could work in an office. Or in a restaurant. The voice doesn't seem to know how you go about this, though. Maybe you just go in the door and ask. No, she can't do that! She sees a heavy door slamming in her face.

Yes she can, if she has to. *She does have to.*

My name is Halya Dubrovsky. I can speak Ukrainian and English. I can work hard.

She spots a notice about a place for rent. "Light housekeeping room near train station. Very clean." She tries to remember where the station is. My God, she'll get lost, she'll have to sleep on the street. How can she rent a light housekeeping room when she has no money? She has to find a job really fast. And what? Sleep on the street till they start to pay her?

She reads the notices for jobs. A couple of dozen of them are in offices. Most of them ask for several years of experience. She starts to cry.

The voice: Quit blubbering. Make some plans. She remembers walking past a small café with Miss Greeley. A sign in the window said: "Help wanted. Apply within." Ah...you do just go in and ask.

Halya realizes she can't just run away. She has to say goodbye to Miss Greeley. And ask for some advice. It will be hard. The teacher will try to give her money, she knows that. To help the only student in decades of teaching who's ever quoted Jane Austen.

Miss Greeley notices Halya in the corridor by the Common Room and comes out to see her. She sees there's something wrong and asks Halya up to her suite. Halya sits on a chair with a rose-coloured needlepoint cover and looks at the bookcases for what she knows is the last time. She explains that she's leaving school. And why.

"Surely your fees have been paid until the end of June," Miss Greeley says. "Why not stay and finish your year?"

"I can't. Not now. Maybe they can get some of their money back."

Nothing the teacher can say will keep Halya from leaving, but the older woman does convince her to accept a loan of twenty dollars and to take a slip of paper with her name on it: "Letitia Greeley, The Briarwood Academy, Edmonton." She writes down the phone number. Halya promises to call if she gets in trouble.

Halya also refuses to leave until Miss Greeley agrees to keep her brass pendant until she can come and pay her back.

EVERYTHING in the rented room is shabby. Grime lurks in all the corners. Lighting is a low wattage bulb hanging from the ceiling. The soiled bedspread would probably fall to pieces if it were ever washed. The linoleum, worn through to the backing in places, smells sour. On the lumpy bed, the newspaper is open to the employment section. Halya has circled the possible jobs. Almost all have a pencilled line drawn through to show she's already been turned down.

She reads a letter from her father, hears his angry voice. "You ask for money to come home, but I have no money for you. You could have married Shawcross. You could have been one of them. I suppose you were thinking of that bastard Kuzyk's son. You can stop worrying about him. I have heard from Lubomyr Heshka from our old village. He emigrated just before the war. He assures me that Taras Kuzyk died in a skirmish in Bosnia in the summer of 1914. You wasted your chance for nothing. You are no longer my daughter."

Halya weeps in the filthy room. Sees Taras lying in the dirt, a bullet deep in his chest. All winter long, thoughts of him have sustained her. Now that's over.

She wonders for a second if her father's lying – just to hurt her. He couldn't be that cruel, could he? And yet, she's given him his worst disappointment, just as he saw the road to his dreams open before him. But the name of Lubomyr Heshka convinces her. She heard before they left Shevchana that he was talking of coming to Canada.

She can't know that Viktor *has* heard from Lubomyr, but that the man who died in Bosnia was Taras's friend Ruslan.

She closes the newspaper and sees the headline: "FRENCH SOLDIERS GASSED AT YPRES." She reads it before she can stop herself. The Germans opened canisters of chlorine gas and let the wind blow yellow-green clouds to the opposing trenches. The French commanders thought it must be a smokescreen, and that, hidden in mist, the Germans would suddenly attack. As the gas entered the trenches, the soldiers remarked on the smell of pineapple and pepper, a not unpleasant mixture. In moments they felt sharp chest pains; their throats burned. Someone realized it was gas and everyone fled. Afterwards, the chlorine slowly destroyed their respiratory organs and they suffocated, often over days or weeks.

How can this be happening? Surely not even the worst person in the old village could have imagined something like this.

Why keep trying? There's nothing here for her, nothing anywhere. After a long time, head aching from weeping, she remembers Miss Greeley. Letitia Greeley wants her to be safe. And Natalka, her darling *baba,* will be thinking of her, hoping she's all right. Unless she's ready to die and disappoint these people, she has to keep knocking on doors.

She picks up the loaf of bread she bought earlier; tears off a chunk and eats it. It tastes like dust but she chews until it's moist enough to swallow. Keeps going until her stomach feels not full but less empty.

Miss Greeley's money is almost gone. The room is paid up for a month, but in a few days she won't be able to buy bread.

CHAPTER 24

Hope

April, 1916

BY THE END OF APRIL, there's more sunshine and Taras feels something warm slip inside him. It takes him a while to name it, but at last he realizes it's hope. He sees it in the others as well, Yuriy especially, but he'd expect that. Tymko shows it by a desire to wash his clothes. Taras, Myro, Bohdan, Yuriy and Ihor also believe they'll feel better with clean clothes.

In the wash house they sort garments, light a fire in the stove and set water to boil. Bohdan has carved a wooden shim, and he wedges it under the door to make sure no one comes in unexpectedly. Definitely a prohibited use of the knife Sergeant Lake gave him. And over several weeks, each man has stolen a cup from the dining hall. Each dips into the potato wine and drinks.

"Dobre," Taras says, his throat burning. "It's not that bad."

"Well, it is," Yuriy says, eyes watering. "But it's better than you'd expect."

Taras sips again. Feels the alcohol hit his brain, his muscles. He hasn't had a drink for such a long time. He wants to laugh. Everyone drinks.

Myro and Yuriy dump the clothes in the tubs and pour in soap, humming to themselves. They drink and wait. The room is getting warm. The water bubbles and they pour it on the clothes and set more to heat.

The first cups of wine are gone. These are their first real drinks, beyond quick tastes to see how it was developing. Now that it's not too bad, Taras thinks it would be foolish not to drink it down before someone else finds it. He looks at the others.

Tymko's eyebrows rise to their highest peaks. One by one each man nods. Yuriy grins and leads the way to the closet. Each fills his cup again.

"A toast to the humble potato, boys." Tymko raises his cup.

"*Barabolya!*" Yuriy cries. "You'll always have a place on my farm."

"*Kartopliya!*" Bohdan says. "Oh, if we only had some *varenyky*. Then we'd be set." He tosses back half his drink and so do the others.

"If only we had some beautiful women to make them for us," Tymko says. "Warm, shapely women with breasts like soft pillows, and hips —"

"Beautiful women with black eyes and curly black hair, yes," Ihor says. "But with breasts a little smaller than pillows..." He stops when he sees the longing on the faces of the other men.

They go back and stir the clothes around. Throw in the rest of the water. Myro rubs his shirt against the washboard, trying to get out stains. Singing a little song.

"So it's spring," Tymko says. "Time to clean everything out and start fresh. Not just clothes, either. We can clear out old ideas that aren't helping us. We can analyze our lives and figure out what to do when we leave here."

Yuriy throws a wet snotrag at him. Tymko grabs somebody's shirt and wraps it around Yuriy's head. Bohdan protests. It's his shirt. Socks fly around the room. A couple land on the stove and start to sizzle.

Taras leaps to rescue what he believes to be his own socks and catches a sopping shirt in the back of the head. Suds stream down his sweater. Soap bubbles fly past him, flashing small rainbows.

Tymko ties a hankie on his head like a woman's headscarf and stuffs a pair of wet socks under his shirt for breasts. He starts to hum, deep in his belly. He begins to dance, light on his feet as a young woman, weaving between the other men. They clap their hands and shout. Stamp their feet. They pinch Tymko's sock breasts as he passes. The melody spins around the room. The cups are empty.

Whuuump! Suddenly there's pounding on the door. "Quiet down in there!"

This sets them laughing. They know that voice. It's Jackie Bullard, now dubbed Bullshit by most of the men. He never learns, never knows when to walk away from trouble. Any moment now he'll be calling them slackers.

He tries to open the door, finds it won't budge. It can't be locked from the inside, so what's keeping it shut?

"Open this door at once! Or I'll get an axe and break it down!"

Again they laugh, but not as much. Bullshit is spoiling their mood. If they let him in now, he's going to find the boiler. They were going to keep the rest for another day. At least they're almost sure they were going to keep it.

"Open the door! Don't make me tell you again." He thumps until their ears ring unpleasantly. Or is that the wine?

"Oh shit, boys," Tymko says, "I guess that's it." He takes the socks out of his shirt, leaving two big wet spots, and removes the hankie from his head.

The thought of Bullshit dumping out their wine after all their work and scheming is too cruel. Only one thing to do.

There's a little left after each man fills his cup. The first man to knock his back – Bohdan, surprisingly – gets that. Myro takes the boiler to the washtubs and sloshes water around inside it, then dumps the rinse water in the drain. Tymko carries the boiler, cradling the six cups, back to the closet and shuts the door on it. Taras is grateful to them, because it's taking all his concentration to stay standing up.

The thumping is now like artillery fire.

Bohdan gets ready to open the door. Myro resumes rubbing his shirt against the washboard. Taras splashes warm water on his face and rubs it with his shirt sleeve.

Tymko breathes into his hand, sniffs and shakes his head:

Don't breathe in Bullshit's face. They nod.

Bohdan removes the shim and slowly opens the door. Jackie Bullard rushes in, red in the face, his bayonet thrust out in front of him, and almost trips in the puddles of water and clothes strewn on the floor. He sees Myro's black hair dripping water, Ihor's curling moustache flecked with foam.

"Clean this up at once! It's disgraceful. We don't give you this wash house just to make a mess, you know."

Taras almost chokes from the need to laugh. Who knew Bullshit could scold like an angry *baba*? He hears a strangled noise in his throat.

"You think it's funny, do you?" Bullshit's face is getting dangerously scarlet.

Now the others, even Myro, stagger around laughing.

"You're drunk! Aren't you? All of you, drunk!" Bullshit sounds outraged.

Tymko is immediately calm and serious. "Certainly not," he says. "We just like to let off a little steam while our clothes soak."

"We were practising a Ukrainian dance," Yuriy says. Bohdan nods.

"Don't worry," Tymko says. "It'll be clean and tidy when we leave." But he can't suppress a small snort of laughter.

The guard tries to smell Tymko's breath. Tymko smiles but doesn't exhale.

"See that it is. Or there's going to be trouble."

"Absolutely. It'll be clean as wissel." Bullard stares. "Clean... as...a...whistle."

Bullard heaves a great sigh. They can guess what he's thinking. The men are plastered. He could get them all in big trouble. And yet, they've obviously drunk the evidence. And they'd have the mess tidied before he could be back with reinforcements. The look crosses his face that he's tired of being mad and making people do things. And then there'd be a huge stink as the brass tried to find out where the raw materials came from. It's most likely potatoes from prisoners working in the kitchen and they'd all be punished, and it's all so bloody boring, and wearying.

"All right, get the mess cleaned up, and I'll forget all about this. And stay here until you can walk straight. And shut up about it with the other men." *Or I'll make you pay later,* he doesn't say, but it's understood. Still, for Bullshit, this is pretty decent.

The moment he's gone, Bohdan shuts the door and replaces the shim. They all collapse onto the floor. It's warm in the shack. There are no guards making them grub roots or chop wood. They'll have to finish their laundry in a bit, but for now they sit smiling. They've created something, Taras realizes. Yes, it was only something to get pleasantly drunk on, but achievement can be measured by the difficulty of the task as well as by the end product. Sometimes getting pleasantly drunk among good friends is a noble goal.

THE HOPE Taras has begun to feel continues, but he doesn't think the guards feel very hopeful. As the weather warms and the number of escapes goes up, they get testier, hold their bayonets more grimly at the ready. Even Bud Andrews, the most affable of them, looks ready to take someone's head off. Like all the guards, he hates being sent after escapees. Taras thinks this is because it's most likely to end in failure. And if it doesn't, there's a good chance he might have to shoot someone.

Often so many soldiers are out searching that there aren't enough left to guard the internees. So one day Taras's bunkhouse is assigned to tidying up around the camp. They work up to the woods above the bunkhouses. In the trees the snow's still deep, but meltwater trickles through the cleared areas, an image in miniature of the great river system it feeds.

AFTERWARDS no one knows who started it. The prisoners are warm from the work but not as tired as usual. Guards stand around in groups talking. The first snowball hits Yuriy, then Bud Andrews catches one in the head. Each looks ready to punch somebody. In seconds, Taras, Bullshit, Ihor, Bohdan and Barkley have wet snowy circles on their clothes. Taras lobs a big sloppy one. Tymko catches it in the forehead and goes down as if shot. He gets up laughing and runs into the trees, where he makes beautiful, hard snowballs and wings them at everyone, with no discrimination between prisoner and guard.

Some are small and deadly accurate. The bigger ones, almost cannonball size, have a shorter range but usually hit something. It's a blizzard of snowballs. War without death or wounds. Everyone's panting. Yelling. Snow fills boot tops, slides down collars, soaks every coat, sweater and pair of trousers, right through to long underwear.

Andrews laughs so hard he has to be pounded on the back. Even Bullshit isn't mad.

Tymko looks around and nods. He brushes off what snow he can and flops to the ground. As if it's a signal of surrender, soldiers and prisoners fling themselves into the snow, gasping. Those who have cigarettes pass them around. Tobacco smoke and the aroma of wet wool fills the air.

Taras is warmed through, almost as warm as in the hot pool.

ON MAY 10 two men, known as the *dvi Wasyls* – the two Wasyls – because they have the same first name, escape on the way to the Spray Bridge worksite. Sadly, they're recaptured the next day, putting an end to the song Taras and Yuriy were making up about their heroic deeds.

A few days later a clutch of well-fed men in suits turns up to see the commandant. Who are they? Men from the government? The American consul, who's supposed to make sure the internees are being treated correctly? The Red Cross, who also monitor the camps?

No. They're from the Canmore Coal Company. The reason for their visit spreads through camp like an outbreak of dysentery. It seems that so many men have enlisted in the armed forces that many industries are now short of workers. Industries like the Canmore Coal Company. They want to talk to some of the prisoners about working for them. They ask for five men, former employees, and are willing to guarantee their good behaviour.

For a week or two nothing happens – the government must be mulling it over – but everyone knows coal is once more in demand, for the navy and for industry.

MAY 13 is a bathing day, followed by a glorious soak in the pool. Taras can still hardly believe it. Back home, anything this good would be reserved for *pahns*. Here they're allowing in peasants, agitators, foreign scum. An hour's small reparation for unjust imprisonment.

Or at least, to use Tymko's words, it's a contradiction.

The next day, the American Consul does appear, to check on conditions in camp. But no one Taras knows even sees him. Later, they hear that he found everything satisfactory.

"Let him try it if he thinks it's so satisfactory," Taras says.

"It is satisfactory," Tymko says. "For him. He gets to inspect things, ask nosy questions, annoy the commandant – a good thing in itself, let us remember – and then take the train back to Calgary for a good dinner." Is that all there is to it? Taras wonders.

The miracle of the snowballs persists in the prisoners' memories. Then on May 20, one of the guards, Private Brearly, walks into the woods near his house in Banff and cuts his throat. The news spreads through camp, and Taras can see that the death shakes the other soldiers. It seems to Taras that escape is also difficult for guards.

The men in suits from the Canmore Coal Company return.

The five men they asked for are "paroled" to work in the mines. Taras is even more outraged than Tymko. Apparently the internees are all too dangerous to be on the streets. Spies. Saboteurs. Revolutionaries. Isn't that what the government thinks? Suddenly it doesn't matter, because now the country needs more workers. Before it didn't need them, in fact there were too many.

Taras will not forget this lesson. It's the closest he's felt to the socialists, who at least have theories about why there are concentration camps in a supposedly free country.

Concentration camps for people who were invited to come to Canada.

Could Taras one day be offered the same chance as these men who walk quietly out of camp to a waiting truck? He doesn't believe it will happen.

In the meantime, escape is possible if you want it badly enough. Yuriy and Ihor have kept track of the number of prisoners who have freed themselves since the camp opened. Sixty-one men have run — or more likely walked — away. Almost two thirds of them — thirty-nine — are still out there. Free. And it's nearly time for the camp to move back to Castle Mountain for the summer. Its wire fence is tall, but tents are more porous than wooden bunkhouses. Anyway, at least it'll be warm.

The guards tell tales of sudden snowfalls in July.

CHAPTER 25

Back to Castle Mountain

June 27, 1916

ONCE AGAIN Taras rides a train to Castle Mountain, windows raised to warm breeze, to sky a hard deep blue. He and fifty others are going to get the camp ready. He plans to take it as slow as possible and hopes the guards get the point: *Let's everybody not get excited. It's too tiring.* It's a reasonable hope. The soldiers are usually more relaxed when there aren't so many prisoners to guard.

Prisoner. Enemy alien. Internee. That's what he's been for almost a year; back then another train brought him this way.

He lets the swaying motion open up memory: wind knifing rain into his face, lightning searing his eyes, mud running like a river. The storm a reckless giant stalking the valley. A spirit, his own, howling like wind.

That night three men escaped. So, he'd thought, it can be done. Over the year he kept track of the ways people got away. He found no real pattern, just that you had to get into the trees. After that, rain, smoke or fog could help a man hide there.

In his favourite escape story, three men helping carry the prisoners' lunches took off in the opposite direction from the work gangs, along with the lunches. He imagines having all he wanted to eat for a day or two. Even it was only the *pokydky* the government feeds them.

He wonders what happened to the ones who got away. He

imagines lives for them, pleasant, comfortable lives. Warm, clean beds. Delicious, wholesome food and, yes, an occasional drink. Church on Sunday.

The train pulls into the siding, and the immensity of Castle Mountain asserts itself once more. It's some kind of change, but he's also back where it all began.

Their first job is to unload a freight car full of tents and equipment and clean up the site. But they don't even reach camp before a new guard, Private Edwards, takes Taras, Yuriy, and a couple of other men, Tony Rapustka and Panko Marchuk, on a mission to carry baggage to the Parks foreman's camp west of the internment camp. The foreman himself comes along to direct them.

What kind of trouble can four prisoners, an armed guard and a foreman get into, especially when the four prisoners are carrying heavy burdens?

Foreman Wilson also needs trees cut and trimmed to make poles for *tipis*. No one explains why he needs *tipis*, but then no one ever explains anything to internees. Wilson leads them into shade-dappled woods and they fell the trees he points out – tall, slender trees with very straight trunks. The guard is calm and quiet, just the way Taras imagined it, and he works at his own pace and lets time pass.

As he trims branches from one more lodgepole pine, he hears a small, strangled sound and looks up. A tree plummets toward earth – or rather toward Tony Rapustka. Straight for his head and shoulders. A moment earlier Rapustka might easily have been daydreaming or imagining there would somehow be a good dinner back in camp, but now he suddenly realizes the enormous importance of his head and shoulders – if only to himself. He leaps out of the way of the tumbling, plunging trunk; and having leapt and found it pleasant, he leaps again; and yet again. Finding himself now in the shelter of the forest, he begins to run, and it must be that he finds that good also. He moves deeper into the trees.

"Halt!" screams Private Edwards as Rapustka crashes through the trees. He raises his rifle and fires. Rapustka stumbles. He must have hit the man.

"You got him! I'm sure of it," the foreman yells.

Edwards tears into the trees. No sign of Rapustka anywhere. He makes a half-hearted search, but he has to keep an eye on the other prisoners. Edwards has the only weapon, and even if Wilson did have a gun, a Parks foreman has no authorization to go around shooting people. So they'll all have to go back so Edwards can talk to his captain. The captain will send soldiers to cover the places a man might be most likely to come out of the trees.

Taras and Yuriy flash each other happy grins. Rapustka is their hero for the day. They can still see him leaping: once, twice, three times. He's flown like a bird. And he's got a nice head start. A squirrel high up in a tree makes a chattering noise as if warning them all to leave, and the internees start to laugh. Until then they wouldn't have dared. Wilson laughs too, but Edwards merely tightens his grip on his rifle.

Next morning the guards look really unhappy. The prisoners think there must have been another escape, but they haven't heard anything and nobody seems to be missing. Unhappy guards are a common enough thing, but this is a different, hard-to-define unhappiness. For once it doesn't seem to be connected to the prisoners.

A week later, back in Banff, Taras and his friends return to the bunkhouse after supper. Tymko has found a discarded copy of the local newspaper, the *Crag and Canyon,* and it has a story about the camp. Reading it, they finally learn what happened the night of Rapustka's flight. One of the guards, Henri Martin, was posted at the bridge across the Bow River at Johnson Creek to keep an eye out for him. At the same time, a local game warden, W. H. Fyfe, armed himself with a revolver and also set out to look for Rapustka.

"Well, that's sensible," Tymko says. "He was probably afraid Rapustka would strangle some game with his bare hands. And eat it. Absolutely against the law." He thinks for a moment. "Okay. Here's how I think it went." The others give him the floor.

"So. Henri Martin sees a shadow moving through the trees along the water. Could be a bear or an elk, but he's almost sure it's a man." Tymko mimes a man skulking through the trees, arms raised like antlers.

" 'Who's there?' Martin yells. 'Halt, or I'll fire!'

"But the shadow man keeps walking. Who but a fleeing prisoner would do that? So Martin creeps toward him, bayonet fixed. The unknown man draws his gun, yells, 'Stop!'

"Martin sees the gun raised toward him and a second later a shot echoes across the valley. The shadow man writhes on the ground, holding his wrist. Martin fires a second shot that grazes the man's shoulder. Martin hurries over. *He has Rapustka.*

"'You asshole!' screams the wounded man. 'I'm the goddamn game warden! Why'd you shoot?' The soldier doesn't say a word.

"'You got my wrist! I'll probably be crippled for life!' The guard tries to offer his hand and the game warden kicks it away. 'I hope they send you to goddamn jail for this!' "

Taras and his friends applaud. But there's more to the story in the paper. Myro reads it aloud. "This is the first time one of the guards has shot a man since the internees were stationed at Banff, and it is the irony of fate that a white man should be chosen as the target."

The first part is strangely comforting. The guards have never before managed to hit anybody with their rifles. Not for lack of trying, of course.

But the men are puzzled by the "white man" part. "What are we, then?" Yuriy asks.

Tymko explains. "To the townspeople, well, most of them, whiteness is what sets them apart from what they consider lesser peoples. Whiteness means intelligence, resourcefulness, hard work, superior organization. We internees are believed to lack these qualities, and so they believe we aren't white."

"What?" Ihor says. "That's crazy."

"Being white also means speaking good English," Tymko goes on, "and this is taken as further proof that eastern Europeans belong to some other race – because otherwise they'd have been *born* speaking English."

There's laughter when Tymko jeers at such ignorance, but it still hurts.

"But really," Yuriy says, "what is a white man, then? We don't look any different from them."

"No," Tymko says, "we don't. Well, they have better clothes."

On June 30, all the internees, 312 men, make the move to Castle Mountain. They spend the day putting up tents and settling in. Except there is no settling; everything changes from moment to moment. Within days, twenty-six more prisoners are paroled. On July 4, Wasyl Pujniak and John Kushniruk escape. Two days later, four men are sent away because of illness and four more are sent to the Canmore coal mines. On July 7, nine more leave to work for individual farmers. That leaves 267.

Taras feels angrier each time he sees a group of men moved out of camp. Why these men and not others? How can the government explain why some men who were dangerous before are not dangerous any more? Were these men never as dangerous as the ones who remain? Is he himself more dangerous than he thinks?

Next day, fifty prisoners are paroled to the Canadian Pacific Railway. Tymko feels bad about it: he worked for the CPR years ago, but they didn't ask for him. "My politics," he says. But he admits it could be because the men they took worked for the company more recently. Either way, it takes the heart out of them to see so many leaving while they must stay. The 312 men have become 217.

Tymko offers his usual analysis. Once, workers were needed for Canadian industries, so Ukrainians were welcomed. Then there was a depression and fewer workers were needed. Ukrainians became unwelcome. Now many young men are in Europe fighting and Canada needs workers again. Especially for the industries that keep the war going.

This still makes sense, but it doesn't seem to help – and just when Taras had started to believe the most important thing a man could have was a good analysis.

Since the release of so many internees, Taras and his friends have heard no reports of sudden spates of murder, sabotage or spitting in the streets. No outbreaks of subversion. Of course, they don't get the newspaper every day. Tymko says that must explain it. In reality, there must be a constant parade of death and carnage.

TARAS SITS IN THE TENT one night smoking a hand-rolled cigarette Tymko gave him. Smoking still makes him dizzy, but it's one of the few things you can choose to do in this place. He imagines his father, who never smokes: "So, you want to be dizzy, is that it?" Apparently he does. Yuriy, Tymko, Ihor smoke every evening. Even Myro sometimes puffs away, a distant look on his face, thinking important professor thoughts.

"I see you've decided to give up on your story," Tymko says. The others turn from staring at canvas walls to staring at Taras.

"I never said I was giving up."

"No. Not in words." Tymko lights a cigarette, watches Taras through the smoke.

"I didn't like how it was going." Taras blows a wobbly smoke ring. "Too miserable."

"Even more reason to tell it, then. Don't you think, Myro? It'll make him feel better."

"It might. What do you say, Taras? You've taken us this far. Why not tell us how you came to be here? I know I've been wondering."

"Me too," Yuriy says.

"And me," Ihor adds.

"Oh, all right. Just to keep you quiet."

He begins the part he couldn't tell back in the bunkhouse when he could imagine Zmiya in the corner listening. But Zmiya's not with them now, he's in a tent near the back of the camp.

"Well," Taras says, "in spring, 1915, all us workers who were building the school the summer before were still at the brick plant making bricks for the war. Shawcross was even taking on a few more men, including some from Regina. Many of them were what Shawcross called 'foreigners.' They'd been in unions before and they wanted to be again. So by June people were talking about it a lot." He stops for a breath.

"So Moses and Frank Elder went to Moose Jaw one Sunday. They met some union people to learn more about how to organize.

And then they talked to every man in the plant about what they'd learned. Everyone but Stover."

"Because Stover was the boss's man?" Tymko asks.

"Yeah, and because it was the last thing he'd want. He already had what he wanted. He could bully people because we knew Shawcross wouldn't stop it. And he had enough money to go the saloon when he wanted. So they never asked him, but I think he knew something was up.

"I admit I was never interested and I just forgot about it. But Frank and Moses made plans for a meeting. By early August, they were ready. One day I was loading bricks into the kiln for firing, and Moses came in. 'Meeting tonight,' he said. 'To talk about a union.'

"I didn't want to go. I said, 'I don't even know what that is.' "

" 'Never mind,' Moses said. 'Just come.' "

We all sat on wooden chairs in a meeting room Frank Elder arranged in the Anglican church. Frank was standing in front of a table at the front, leading the meeting. Moses sat behind it.

"So the guy from Moose Jaw is willing to come down and help us organize," Frank said. "And I think we're going to be in a strong bargaining position."

Angus McLean, red-haired and strong as a blacksmith, stood up. "Why's that?" he asked. Angus's job was hauling clay from pits in the hills near the plant. I think it was the only job he'd ever had.

"It's like Shawcross told us," Frank said. "The government needs brick for warships. So the money's there. Shawcross is gonna do just fine out of the war."

"Profit *and* patriotism," Moses added. "He's got them both."

"I'm not saying it'll be easy," Frank went on. "But if we stick together, if we don't let Shawcross break us...I think we have a chance."

"Och, that's good," Angus said, "and I hate to even say this, but what if it doesnae work out?" There was a long silence.

Finally Moses stood up. "If it doesn't work out, they'll fire whoever they think started it all. I guess that'd be me and Frank."

"I can't afford to get fired," Angus said. "I'm running a few head of cattle in the hills, but I'm not making much."

Moses agreed. "Nobody can afford to get fired." He looked around the room. "Taras? Are you in favour of the union?"

I was startled. I'd only come to listen, and because Moses wanted me to. But they all seemed to be waiting, and I took my time, but I stood up too.

"I don't know," I said. "In the old country, you can't have anything like this. But here in Canada... Maybe a union is good."

Just then the door burst open and three Mounties, led by Reg Statler, came in, moving fast. And they came right for *me*, and Statler grabbed my arm.

"Taras Kalyna," he said, "you are under arrest for seditious behaviour under the War Measures Act." He spoke in a loud voice, but I didn't think he believed what he was saying.

"And for suspicion of being an Austrian spy," he added.

I told him, "I'm not a spy! You know I'm not." I'd been reporting to this Mountie Statler once a month since the last fall. I was sure he'd never suspected me of anything at all.

When I spoke, he hesitated a moment and I thought he looked ashamed.

"Officer, this is a peaceful meeting," Moses said. "Nothing to do with sedition or spies."

"This man is an Austrian citizen. He's spreading seditious propaganda." Statler said this in a loud voice. I thought he was trying to convince himself.

"Mr. Kalyna was invited to the meeting —" Frank Elder said, but the policemen ignored him. "He came to listen!"

"Take him away," Statler said. He looked like he'd rather be anywhere else.

"No! Wait!" Moses shouted.

"I'm not a spy!" I yelled, but they dragged and shoved me out the door.

"All right," Tymko says, "I see why you didn't want to tell us. It's miserable, all right. Do you feel any better yet?"

"Not that I can notice. I'll let you know if that changes."

"That was rotten luck," Yuriy says. "You weren't even trying to start a union."

"Doesn't matter," Tymko says. "When the boss wants to get rid of you, he can always come up with something."

"But why would he want to get rid of me? He liked me at first. He could have been killed or crippled by that horse if I hadn't helped him."

"Bosses don't feel gratitude," Tymko says.

"He did at first. He gave me a job. Even though Stover didn't want him to."

Taras thinks about that day, and the few other times he talked with the boss. The day he asked for time off to look for someone. An odd question from Shawcross.

"One day he noticed the pendant I was wearing. He asked me where I got it. I never thought about it till now, but why would he care?"

"The one you made?" Myro asks.

"That's right. And I made Halya one just like it."

"Did he see hers somehow?" Yuriy wonders. "Did he meet Halya somewhere?"

"How could he?" And yet, why would Shawcross ask about the pendant? Why would he get that look on his face like he was hatching something?

A scene unfolds in his mind. Shawcross talking to Reg Statler. Kalyna's an Austrian, he says. I know, Statler says, he reports to me every month. And Shawcross says, Why hasn't the fellow been arrested? And Statler says, There's no reason to. He hasn't done anything.

Taras imagines the boss thinking: So Taras hasn't done anything. If he does, though, look out. Shawcross will make sure Statler does his duty. More than his duty. And then he somehow finds out about the union meeting.

He remembers something else. "The day the war broke out, I saw Halya going into the train station with an older lady. An English lady."

"Going somewhere on the train," Myro says. "I wonder why."

Taras remembers Viktor's gloating face outside the police building. "Viktor said Halya had gone some place I'd never find her. He said she was going to school and she was going to marry an Englishman."

"Could the English lady be your boss's mother?" Myro asks. "And Shawcross the Englishman she was supposed to marry?"

"How could they have even met?" Taras asks. It seems too fantastic to be true.

"But why would they send her away to school?" Yuriy wonders. "I know! To make her more English. More *white*, eh?"

"Where would boss people find an English lady school?" Tymko asks. "That's what we need to figure out."

"A school like that would have to be in a big city," Yuriy says. "I don't think they have *pahna* schools in every little town."

"The most likely places are Winnipeg or Edmonton," Myro says. "I don't know Winnipeg, but I'm from Edmonton and there's a school for young ladies there. Private school. People pay to send their daughters there."

"Sounds like boss business to me." Tymko's eyebrows rise into his thoughtful owl look. "I bet Halya's in Edmonton."

"That's in Alberta, right?" Taras says. "It can't be so far away."

"Ten, twelve hours on the train," Myro says. "They make a lot of stops."

"I could write her a letter." Taras feels his heart pounding.

"Would she do well in school, do you think?" Tymko asks.

"Oh yes. Halya loves to read. She's very smart."

CHAPTER 26

The People's Voice

May, 1915

HALYA CLIMBS a steep, dark staircase one slow step at time. She's out of chances, having already failed to get every job in the newspaper advertisements that she could possibly pretend to be qualified for. The people at the top of the stairs haven't even advertised. But they are the people she'd like to work for. She's only just realized that. She'd been standing outside, head down, and feeling she'd reached some kind of end. She'd happened to look up and seen a sign on a door she hadn't noticed was there.

In a moment she's reached the landing and stands before an office door. On its glass panel, a sign reads: *The People's Voice,* Western Canada's Ukrainian Newspaper. Below, it says, "Nestor Mintenko, Editor. Zenon Andrychuk, Reporter." Hunger and fear knot her stomach, and she hopes the sponge bath in her room this morning has done its job. She hesitates a moment, then knocks and goes inside.

Two men sit typing. The older one, a stocky guy of about fifty, looks as if he's seen it all. He must be Nestor Mintenko. The second is a thinner, scholarly looking man in his early thirties: Zenon. Halya sees him looking at her with interest. She's wearing a plain navy blue dress; yes, one of Louisa's, but she can't worry about that now. Her hair is neatly braided around her head. She tries to make her face look both interested and hopeful, but she's afraid they'll see the desperation underneath.

"*Dobre dehn. Ya Halya Dubrovsky.*"

Zenon smiles encouragingly.

"I wondered if you had any work." There, she's said it.

"Sorry, kid, we can barely pay ourselves," Nestor says. He looks like a person of natural kindness and compassion who feels he must appear firm, even brusque.

"I can read and write Ukrainian...also English." I'm one of you, a Ukrainian, she wants to say. How can you just turn away?

"I'm afraid —" Zenon says.

She doesn't have to search for the words, they come out like rapid gunfire. "I can type sixty-five words a minute, and I'm very accurate. I can write clear, grammatical letters in both languages." They look unmoved. What else can she tell them? "I've studied the poetry of Taras Shevchenko and the novels of Jane Austen." That's better. Having mentioned these two touchstones, she feels on firmer ground.

Nestor, unfortunately, looks like he's trying not to laugh, but Zenon...she thinks he may be intrigued.

"It *would* be helpful..." he says with a slight smile.

Nestor shakes his head. "We can't afford —"

There's no turning back. Miss Greeley's money's gone. "I'm very interested in writing."

"We do all the writing here," Nestor says.

"I can spell very well... My typing is extremely..." Oh, she's told them that.

"My handwriting, did I mention? My handwriting is clear and legible. I received a prize in my class for Composition. My essay... about the novels of Charles Dickens..."

The men exchange a look. Shevchenko, Austen *and* Dickens? they must be thinking. How often does a person with those qualifications walk up their dank stairway? Hope makes her heart race. She sees Nestor's brief shrug. A real smile breaks over Zenon's face.

"Look," Nestor says, "I can't afford to hire you full time. But I have an uncle who runs a café. I think he needs someone. You could work there maybe four nights a week. And, say, three afternoons a week for us. How does that sound?"

Like heaven, she wants to say. "It sounds very good. When may I begin?"

Nestor telephones his uncle and Halya can see that everything is being agreed to. He gives her a piece of paper with the address she should go to and settles the details of hours and pay at the paper. It's not much, but with evenings at the café, it will keep her. And she'll be working on a newspaper. A Ukrainian newspaper.

For the first time she admits that coming to Canada has allowed her to have a new life. She is a woman with employment. Moments ago she was adrift on dangerous, open seas. Now she's landed on a small, dry island with kind people. Her father wouldn't like them, but that only speaks in their favour. And every day she'll be able to speak her language. Maybe some time they'll let her write for the paper. Sooner or later they'll need help with something or one of them will be sick, not that she wants them to be sick, but that'll be her chance.

Nestor tells her she'll be starting at the café this very evening. Suppers will be provided in addition to her pay. She hopes they won't see how hungry she is. She hopes they'll feed her before she has to start. After that, she can work as long as she has to.

CHAPTER 27

Absolutely splendid

July, 1916

ONE DAY hikers from the Alpine Club of Canada arrive at Castle Mountain camp on their way up to a place called Ptarmigan Lake. The commandant assigns Yuriy and another man to help them clear trails. Yuriy comes back afterwards with a strange smile on his face.

"I have seen beyond this place," he says. "These fellows, they think there's nothing better than climbing mountains. They're in love with mountains. They kept saying, 'Smell that air. Everything's so fresh.' One of them gave me a drink of whiskey from a silver flask."

The others pretend not to believe him.

"No, really, and they shared their lunch with me when they saw the stuff I had. Roast beef sandwiches! And little fishes out of a jar."

His face glows as if he'd partaken of the loaves and fishes in the Bible.

"You were like a man lost in the desert," Tymko says. "Such men see illusions. No doubt you had the same gristle and onion sandwiches we did. It only seemed like roast beef."

"*Gristle* and *onions?* That's a new low."

"Well, I *say* gristle, but who knows what it was. The onions were real, though."

Yuriy smiles, then turns quiet. "I could see so far. I felt like I could walk right out of here if I wanted. It was so beautiful it made the backs of my knees ache."

"That was fear of heights," Ihor says. "All you flatlanders have it."

"Believe what you like. When this is all over, I'm going to come back one day and climb that son of a bitch." Yuriy jerks his head toward Castle's summit.

This statement creates complete belief about the little fishes among the other men. Until now each has vowed that once free he will never set foot anywhere near here again.

A WEEK LATER it's sunny but not too hot and the hikers are back, this time to climb Castle. Sergeant Lake is going too, and has asked for Yuriy and Taras to come along. The plan is to climb as far as the treeline, tidying the trail as they go. Of course it's the internees who'll be doing the work, Taras thinks bitterly. All right, maybe Sergeant Lake also wanted to give them a day away from camp, but Taras resents the idea that they can be lent out to the commandant's cronies. He does want a break, though, so he keeps his resentment to himself.

As they climb, they're able to keep mainly in the shade. Taras finds himself looking at trees and all the small green plants at their bases, not as things which will give him more work, but as marvellous examples of the variety of nature. He notices how fresh the air really is. Feels his legs grow heavier from the climb and the altitude. After a couple of hours they see some well-shaded boulders to sit on and stop for lunch.

The hikers are a jolly pair with their well-stocked rucksacks and jaunty hats and alpenstocks of polished wood. Some of their exuberance starts to rub off on Taras, although it doesn't entirely dispel the feeling of being treated like a servant. Still, it's hard to dislike them. He makes himself think of the man who tends the garden at Radoski's house.

Lunch has been prepared by the officers' cook. Arthur Lake opens the wicker hamper Yuriy has been carrying and hands each man a linen napkin, a small white plate with a Canadian army crest and an oblong packet of waxed paper. Taras and Yuriy too. Taras peels his paper back and finds a glorious sandwich made with thick slices of ham and cheese spread with mustard. From a glass jar, Lake distributes slabs of pickle and salty green olives stuffed with pimento. Another glass jar marked "Gaston Monac" contains fancy sardines in olive oil. These must be Yuriy's "little fishes." When the sandwiches disappear, Lake finds a second one for each man and when these are also gone, brings out fluffy scones, split in half and thickly spread in the middle with butter and something the climbers call greengage jam. Also available is a jar of "Goodwillies Currant Syrup." Lake serves cups of tea from steel Thermos bottles.

Nobody here has a gun.

Taras and Yuriy exchange a look. How is it they are receiving this food? It's much too fine. They really should keep quiet about it when they go back to camp. Except, what if they already smell like ham and cheese and sardines and olive oil?

Taras realizes the climbers are settling in for a good rest and a gab.

"Did I mention my granny's a hiker?" asks Arthur Lake. Looking at Lake, Taras imagines a tall, slightly gaunt old lady toting a tent and camera tripod.

"No, I don't believe you did," says Norman Sutton, a young lawyer from Calgary who wears knee-length tweed pants – Arthur Lake called them knickerbockers – over socks knit in a diamond pattern. "Where does she hike?"

"I believe anywhere she takes a mind to. Last time she was up on Sulphur, sleeping in her tent, working her way slowly up. Got altitude sickness at about 7,000 feet and had to come down. 'Bloody hell,' she said, 'I wanted that summit.' "

Taras looks out at the Bow Valley, sees the railway track and the road they're building. It actually looks more like a road from this height than it does when you're working on it. Beyond, the river sparkles in the sun.

Gazing at the snow-topped mountains across the valley makes him almost dizzy. The Alpine Club people know all their names but reel them off too quickly for him to remember any. They live in a world he can barely imagine, come to the park only to climb. They like to reach summits, which they describe as "magnificent" or "splendid." The new road will take them to more distant summits they want to conquer. They already have the railroad, of course, but they want to be able to drive their cars right up to the mountains. They tell tales of ascents they've made, of perilous trips over giant icefields and visits to glowing ice caves formed in "seracs" at the mouths of glaciers. Norman Sutton describes the inside of one of them.

"At first it seems pitch dark. The cave mouth is filled with dazzling white light, like a misshapen sun hovering in the darkness. After a bit, your eyes grow accustomed to the dark. You see the roof and arching walls of the cave, like the inside of a giant belly — let's say, the belly of Jonah's whale. This belly is ringed by parallel ridges of ice, roughly hewn as if by a giant chisel. Its surfaces gleam like crudely cut jewels. Deep blue, azure, sea green."

Nobody says anything for a few minutes. Taras can almost imagine coming back too, if it meant he could see such a wonder.

THE NEXT DAY there's a big to-do over the arrival of a steam shovel to help with the road-building work. As a prisoner in a place that makes no sense to start with, Taras has found that he can't predict which events will make him crazy, but the steam shovel turns out to be one of them. Last summer the internees were forced to grub roots and shift rubble with picks, shovels and bare hands. Now the Parks authorities have decided to speed things up with modern equipment. He thinks of all the ground they cleared, working in the most primitive way, when all along machines could have made it so much easier. Maybe they thought Ukrainians wouldn't mind. Wouldn't know any better.

Twenty-one prisoners are sent to the nearby railway siding to unload the thing from a flatcar. The operation is so delicate that even the Parks foreman and some of the guards help.

Only two prisoners escape during the general confusion. Taras, Tymko and Yuriy catch sight of the commandant storming across the compound to yell at Sergeant Andrews, who was in charge of the operation. Andrews, not a tall man to begin with, shrinks before the tirade. Taras and Yuriy laugh so hard they have to bend over. Tymko just shakes his head.

"Now there's an example of lousy boss technique," he says. "The top brass walks across a lot of dirt to bawl somebody out? No! The soldier crawls on his belly to the commandant's tent. Even I know that, and I have no plans to be a boss."

Still, the past couple of days have been more entertaining than usual.

And on the third day, just when Taras decides things couldn't get more exciting, Jackie Bullard bounces into the tent before breakfast to tell them that not only will they not work today, but there will be a *royal visit*. The Duke of Connaught and his wife, and their daughter, Princess Patricia. A rare and unexpected treat! The duke, who is "the king's younger brother," will inspect soldiers, prisoners and the camp itself. The men have to clean up, shave, tidy their hair. Make the tents as neat as they can.

Bullshit seems to expect them to be happy.

Should he act grateful? Taras wonders. "Sounds magnificent," he might say. "A *real* British princess. Absolutely splendid." No, better not. Bullshit hates sarcasm because he's never sure he understands it.

"Make sure nobody farts when the duke goes by," Tymko says in Ukrainian. As usual, Bullshit thinks the internees are laughing at him. He'd probably like to tell them off, but they'd all pretend not to understand and he'd end up looking stupid. Stupider.

When these royal people finally arrive, Taras thinks they make a pretty poor showing. The Duke of Connaught is dressed in an ordinary suit and some kind of outdoor cap. His wife, who doesn't even step down from their railway car, wears a plain dress with only a many-pointed lace collar by way of decoration. Neither of them has a crown or costly jewellery. Their daughter, Princess Patricia, hasn't even appeared, so there's no way of telling if she's the beautiful princess you expect from folk tales.

The duke walks stiffly up and down the ranks of soldiers.

Occasionally speaks to someone or nods with good-humoured condescension. He does the same with the lined-up prisoners, although he doesn't look too closely. A scruffy bunch, he must find them. They don't even have uniforms. Taras thinks about not farting. As Tymko says, around this place you swallow a lot of air. It's the only thing they have an endless supply of.

"Very good. Carry on, then." The duke reaches the last man and is joined by the commandant, who takes him on a tour of the tents. That'll be delightful, Taras thinks.

At last everything has been reviewed or inspected or commented upon and the guests return to the train. The soldiers cheer loudly and the duke and duchess wave graciously from the platform at the end of the car. Taras watches as they turn and go inside. He imagines a servant appearing instantly with glasses of champagne, perhaps the very kind served at the soirées Shevchenko attended in St. Petersburg, and soft, fine-textured *pampushkas* drenched in butter and thickly spread with greengage jam.

TWO DAYS LATER Taras watches fifty more prisoners – leaving 167 behind – march out of the stockade bound for the Crow's Nest Pass Coal Company. He knows several: John Dobija, Andrew Rypka, and a Romanian, Constantine Bota, who complained to the American Consul last fall. The brass must have forgotten, or they'd have made sure he was the last man to leave the camp on the last day it operated, assuming there will ever be a last day.

No, come to think of it, that'll be Tymko. The Revolutionary.

PART 4

CHAPTER 28

Gut shot

July-August-September, 1916

TARAS PESTERS anyone, prisoner or guard, who might possibly know about a girls' boarding school in Edmonton. No one's heard of it, including Bullard, who's from there. When Taras asked him about it, he actually seemed sorry he didn't know. Maybe it was the idea of a mystery to solve. No, Taras has to admit it, Bullshit wanted to help.

Andrews remembers that a guard called McIntyre lived in Edmonton and goes to ask him. He comes back and reports that McIntyre is gone. That afternoon another soldier accidentally shot him in the leg and the doctor sent him to the hospital in Calgary.

"Maybe the wrong people have the guns," Taras says. Andrews gives a half-smile. He looks so tired of being in this place, although maybe not as tired as Taras, who has lately decided that he doesn't believe there'll ever be a real road. Only an ugly scar in the forest.

JULY CRAWLS to an end. Taras watches other men leave the camp: fourteen more are paroled. At the end of the month, 103 new prisoners arrive from the Brandon camp, which is being shut down. Does this mean their own camp will also close one day? Tymko says yes, but it's just one more thing Taras is afraid to believe in.

One evening in early August, Taras's gang comes back to camp a bit late to find guards and prisoners swarming everywhere. The

Banff doctor watches two guards carry a bleeding man on a stretcher to a waiting truck. Who is it? What happened?

Taras spots Tymko and Yuriy near the truck. "It's John Konowalczuk," Tymko says. "He ran away with a couple of other guys after a smoke break."

"They shot him from behind," Yuriy says, his face white.

"Through the hip bone," Tymko adds. "The bullet passed through his belly on the way out." He looks sick too. "They're taking him to Calgary on the train."

"Gut shot." Yuriy's hands shake.

Taras can't believe it. But why not, he's always known it could happen. Hoped it wouldn't.

"They had their pockets stuffed with bread." Yuriy is close to tears.

"Where's the other two guys?"

"Gave up when they saw John was shot," Tymko says. "They're wandering around the camp. Telling people what John said."

"What did he say?"

"He said, 'I thought the soldiers would not shoot at us. I thought it was only to scare the prisoners,'" Tymko says. "Shit, I would never have made that mistake." Not after being stabbed, he means.

At first Taras wants to weep. Then he wants to hurt somebody back. Who? The commandant? The people in Ottawa who dreamed all this up? He's watched the commandant drilling the soldiers and has decided that he compares very badly with Colonel Krentz. And this is the man the people in Ottawa picked to have power of life and death over them.

This is the man who decrees what shall be done with their days. The man who wastes their time, their bodies, their spirits.

TARAS STARTS to keep a tally in his head of men paroled. On August 24, fourteen men are paroled to the Canmore Coal Company. Two days later, nine men are sent, *all by themselves,* to the Canada Cement Company in Exshaw. Up until now, departing parolees had to be supervised by soldiers or company officials during the move. What can this mean? Is it more evidence that at least some of the internees have been discovered *not* to be dangerous? Three days later, fifteen men are sent to Canmore. Two days after that, ten more go to Exshaw. That's forty-eight prisoners who are no longer terrifying.

That night, huddled in the tent, Taras, Tymko, Yuriy, Myro, Ihor and Bohdan continue to feel like dangerous men.

The light fades and September begins, and at supper one night Taras meets Nick Boyko, who says he used to live in Edmonton. He asks about a fancy schools for girls. Nick grins. He used to be the janitor at Briarwood Academy. He even remembers the address.

Taras composes a letter. It's hard to know what to say. Maybe Halya's not there at all. It was just a guess, after all. But he makes himself concentrate. Tells Halya how much he misses her. Asks if she's all right. Whether it's true that she's marrying an Englishman. He waits.

One evening Myro comes back from the canteen with the latest *Crag and Canyon*. He traded a soldier some cigarettes for it. It has an article by a Banff man who visited the camp. Taras never imagined any one would come here on purpose, but it seems the doctor sometimes invites people. Myro reads the article to his friends.

"Of the many beautiful motor trails radiating out from Banff the one par excellence is that leading to the internment camp at Castle Mountain, and the person who makes the trip with Dr. Harry Brett misses none of the delights of the trail. The road winds, twists and turns in a bewildering manner, each turn disclosing some new scenic beauty until the brain grows dizzy in the endeavour to retain an impress of each."

"I see it at last. We *are* lucky to be here," Tymko says. "Look how happy this idiot is after just one visit."

"Skirting the Vermilion lakes," Myro continues, "which can only be likened to azure jewels in settings of emerald, crossing innumerable mountain streams which babble stories of the hills from which they flow, passing mountain sheep and lambs which look with inquisitive eyes upon the car and its occupants —"

"Those aren't sheep and lambs!" Yuriy breaks in. "Those are innocent Ukrainians."

"The road winds on until Castle station is reached…" Myro skips a paragraph or so to the spot where the writer arrives at the camp, "a veritable white city…ideally located beneath the shadows of Castle Mountain, laid out with all due attention to the laws of hygiene, and cleanliness is one of the watchwords. Pure water is piped down from a stream up the side of Castle Mountain and every attention is given to the health and well-being of the inmates of the camp." Laughter and shouts of disbelief. Myro skips ahead.

"The officers, from the Commandant down to the non-coms, have a true conception of the meaning of the word hospitality, which they dispense with lavish hands, and a dinner in the officers' mess tent leaves nothing to be desired by the most fastidious epicurean.

"To reach the limit of enjoyment the night should be spent at the camp, if one is fortunate enough to receive an invitation from the officers. The evening can be most pleasantly spent in watching the fantastic shadows which play over the heights of Castle Mountain." He skips ahead again. "And to be awakened in the morning and introduced to a plate of hot buttered toast and a huge cup of steaming coffee with the request or command to partake of it before arising is the acme of hospitality. A substantial breakfast in the officers' mess, followed by the run to Banff in the fresh, cool air of the morning, makes one think that this old world is a mighty pleasant place to live in."

They look at their shabby clothing, their coarse, reddened hands. Finally Yuriy asks, "What's an acme?"

"I'd like to introduce this guy to my fist," Ihor says. "That's my idea of mountain hospitality."

"Maybe he could join us in our dining tent," Yuriy says. "I'll give him hot buttered toast right up the *sraku.*"

"Never mind him," Tymko says. "He's not even part of the actual ruling class. Just one of its toadies."

"No," Myro says, "let's be honest. He's an asshole."

TARAS WONDERS if he should try to escape before the winter snows arrive. One chilly day he grubs roots. They look exactly like all the others although he's better at digging them now. He's sweating, but he's also cold, with only a button-front sweater over his shirt and pants.

He blows on his bare hands to warm them, looks to the mountain side of the road. Mike Pendziwiater, a man he knows only to say hello to, walks slowly, looking neither right nor left, into the trees! Slowly, that's the key. As Ihor says, if you want to escape, don't look like you're trying to. Taras goes back to digging. He feels a little warmer, or so it seems.

Mike is missed when they return to camp. Taras tries not to laugh at how outraged the guards look about this latest example of ingratitude. A search party gets ready to go out, but a man hails the soldiers at the sentry post. It's Mike, reporting in. Men lined up at the mess tent rush over to him. Guards yell. Mike doesn't say anything. Taras watches the guards consider putting Mike in the hoosegow or denying him supper, but after they've hollered at him for a while they let him join the others for supper. Mike still doesn't say a word.

Six days later, he walks out again. This time the guards are ready. Bullets fly all around him, but Mike keeps going, untouched, and disappears into the trees. Again the guards can't find him. Again he walks back to camp in time for supper. They send him to the guardhouse overnight.

"Is he crazy?" Tymko rails. "The man was free!"

"I hear they might send him to an insane asylum," Yuriy says.

"Then he wouldn't have to work outside," Ihor says. "They probably have better food too. Maybe that was his plan."

Plan? Taras thinks. The most likely outcome would be getting shot by the guards.

"Anyway, what's insane about wanting out of this place?" Ihor says, as they walk back to their tent. "Maybe he just needed a long walk in the forest."

As he speaks of forest, Ihor's eyes soften and he's back home, warm in a sheepskin coat, a curved pipe clenched between his teeth.

After supper he and Taras stop to smoke, looking up at Castle in the fading light. Sometimes Ihor will stare at it for half an hour. Coming from mountains more rounded and worn, he strives to understand the Rockies. His conclusion pains him.

"I can't find this mountain's spirit."

THAT EVENING, Yuriy sits on his pallet, holding a letter from his wife Nadia, his mind far away, tears in his eyes. Taras approaches quietly so as not to startle him and pats his shoulder, knowing that it doesn't help. Or maybe it does, but not enough.

Next morning it's very cold. Yuriy puts on his woollen pants under his serge overalls and his outdoor sweater over his shirt. Looks like a good idea, Taras thinks, and does the same. At breakfast, he misses Yuriy for a moment, then sees him, quick as a weasel, duck out of the cooking area, where a guy he knows works, pockets bulging. Later, on the march to the road bed, he watches Yuriy without seeming to and so notices the moment when Yuriy looks calmly around him, then drifts slightly off course until he's in the forest. He doesn't run, he lies on his belly until the work gang passes. Taras gazes straight ahead.

Yuriy is missed at lunch break. The guards look suspiciously at Taras. He manages to look as puzzled as the rest of them really are. Andrews and Bullard are sent to look for Yuriy, but have no idea where to start. With them gone, there aren't enough guards to supervise the work gang and they're marched back to camp.

Two weeks pass and Yuriy hasn't been caught. Two and a half weeks. The men in the tent are surprised Yuriy didn't tell them what he was planning. Finally Taras tells Tymko, Ihor and Myroslav about the day Yuriy calmly walked away on the road to the work site.

The next evening they hear rough voices outside the tent and Yuriy staggers in after being shoved by a guard. For a moment no one speaks. Then Tymko gives him a huge hug.

"It's our Yuriy back!" he says. "Our favourite son of the soil! Where in hell have you been?" He looks Yuriy over, sees rounded cheeks and a look of well-fed contentment. Definitely not the Yuriy they last saw.

Yuriy grins. "If that Mike guy could do it twice, I figured I could do it once. I went to see my wife."

"And how is Nadia?" Myro says.

"Nadia's beautiful. The harvest is beautiful. Thirty bushels to the acre."

"Was she glad to see you?" Tymko asks, waggling his eyebrows.

"Very glad." Yuriy grins.

"Did you walk the whole way?" Taras asks.

"Walked, got rides with farmers. Sometimes they took me home for a meal. I even stopped once and worked on a threshing crew so I could buy more food."

"Did you walk back too?" Myro asks.

"No need. My neighbour – a good man, not the one who got me sent here – lent me some money until Nadia can sell the crop. I took the train back. Got off at the Castle siding and walked in."

"Why'd you come back?" Tymko asks. "You must be as crazy as that other guy."

"I didn't want to get Nadia and her mother in trouble. Or give that other bugger a chance to run to the police again. I did what I had to. Now I'm back. Also, I couldn't desert all you guys. You'd be lost without me."

"That's true," Ihor says. "We'd be really short of bullshit."

"Anyway, I feel like a man again."

Tymko winks. Yuriy's got his swagger back.

"They're not going to punish me. I guess coming back cancels out leaving."

THE LAST WEEK in September Taras's letter to Halya is returned. Someone has scrawled on it "No longer a student here." *No longer.* So she was there. Now she could be anywhere. Is she married? Does she still think of him? He can't answer those questions. A crumb of hope has kept him going, but now it's gone, or nearly gone. Snow covers everything and temperatures have dropped below freezing; the camp is truly a white city. Soon they'll go back to Banff for another winter of aching cold, poor food and clothing and lost freedom. Who said serfdom was abolished?

CHAPTER 29

Ways of leaving

THANKSGIVING is a holiday, with a not bad meal. But at night the temperature falls to ten below. Taras's sweater is worn thin. They all need winter clothing but no one can say when it will come. That's the thing about this place. No way to learn anything about your own imprisonment. When it might end. What your crime was.

The last day of October heavy snow falls. The commandant's tent is given to the prisoners for a dining tent. The prisoners' dining tent, which has a stove, is turned into sleeping quarters. Two of the smaller tents are still needed to accommodate all the men, and small stoves are found for each of them. One of them is the commandant's stove, a guard tells Taras and Yuriy.

"The commandant's *own stove*," he says in wonder. He must expect joy and gratitude. Maybe tears. That's the acme of hospitality, Taras doesn't say.

He and his friends end up in the former dining tent. Oleksa and Kyrylo and their group are there too, still playing cards and denouncing the government.

They find that having a stove doesn't quite make up for their boots and socks falling apart. But in the evening, lying with their feet toward it, it's an improvement.

They'll move to Banff in another week. In a couple of days

they'll start dismantling the camp. Already it gives off a faint odour of abandonment. By the last night only the tents are left to strike. For next year, no doubt. And the year after that? Taras can't let himself think about it.

A week into November, the prisoners huddle in the tent after supper. In one corner, Oleksa and Kyrylo and Toma play cards in the dying light. The deck is grubbier than ever.

"They can't keep us here forever," Kyrylo says, chewing on his droopy moustache.

Oleksa snorts, continues arranging his cards. His red-brown moustache seems to glow in the lamplight. As usual, there's the impression that it doesn't match his white-flecked dark hair. He spits a stream of tobacco juice into the dirt.

"No, really, people will start to question this. You'll see."

"Maybe when the road to Laggan is finished." Oleksa throws a card into the middle of their circle and takes the trick.

Kyrylo picks up the filthy cards and shuffles.

Taras becomes aware of a sound like a giant breathing. Maybe it's Castle Mountain, finally showing its spirit. Seconds later he smells smoke.

Outside someone shouts. "Christ! It's the hoosegow!"

"Fire! Fire!"

The noise grows to a roar as Taras and his friends run to the tent door, sure the fire is upon them. They come back when they see that the hoosegow sits far enough outside the fence to be no danger to the camp.

Taras feels a bit of warmth in his belly. For once a hand goes to the prisoners.

In the tent Oleksa and his friends, looking bored to death, play one more trick. Then Oleksa looks at Kyrylo and nods. They throw down their cards and go out to look, along with their buddies. Taras and his friends follow.

The smoke thickens and the fire roars. Outside the fence guards run around the fire, blankets flapping, but after a while they just watch. There's not a lot left to burn and snow cover will contain the fire.

Internees stand along the fence. Already the jail has lost the look of a building. Logs wrapped in fire sag at new angles. A plume of smoke rises high overhead and sparks spit at the guards. It must be warm by the fire.

Thank God there was no one in the hoosegow.

At last the roaring fades and the fire dies to glowing stumps. Prisoners drift to their tents. Leaving sentries to watch overnight, guards straggle back to their tents, as the commandant slips out of the compound for a look.

"Son of a bitch burned real hot. Like a big goddamn bonfire."

"Good way to say goodbye to this stinking place."

"Goddamn stinking place."

"God, I need a drink."

The guards probably have whiskey. Whiskey would be nice now. Or potato wine.

Taras and his friends go back to the tent. The cards are still on the ground. Oleksa and his friends haven't come back. Their blankets are gone. Taras remembers Oleksa nodding to Kyrylo.

"What in hell?" Yuriy says. "Nobody asked us."

"Didn't trust us," Ihor says.

"Maybe they thought we weren't ready to go," Tymko says.

"And maybe they're right," Yuriy says. "I'm not, anyway."

"Me either." Taras has known this for a long time.

"If I ever try to escape," Ihor says, "I don't want it to be this cold."

This would be a good time to be asleep. To have missed the whole thing.

Next day the guards stop by the tent and discover men are missing. They get nothing out of Taras and his friends, who are apparently not even awake. Once awake, they swear they got bored watching the fire and came back to sleep. The guards tear across the camp like demented squirrels, looking for the captain in charge. They'll have to go out and search, but there really aren't enough of them and the escapees have about a ten-hour start.

The hoosegow smoulders as the prisoners take down the tents. Taras still feels pleased. Someone's managed to strike back. He likes the fire even if it happened because of someone's carelessness and the escaping men only took advantage of the situation.

No, it had to be Oleksa and the others. They were waiting for it. Since the prisoners have been eating in the commandant's tent, they've been outside the fence in the evenings, with more chances to hide and start a fire. More stoves with live coals a man might conceal somehow. Oleksa knew as he played that last card game that it was just a matter of time until he heard the shouting and the flames.

THAT AFTERNOON they make the short train ride to Banff and are marched to the Cave and Basin camp. On the way through town Taras picks up a *Crag and Canyon* lying in the road. He and Tymko take turns looking at it as they walk. In an article about the "diminished number" of internees, he learns that the town of Banff no longer likes having the camp on its doorstep. Apparently the town no longer "derives any pecuniary benefit from the interns." Tymko reminds him that everything seems to come down to profit. The story says that "the great majority of our citizens are of the opinion that the scenic outlook is not vastly improved by the presence of the slouching, bovine-faced foreigners."

Taras is surprised such words still hurt. "You'd think we asked to come here."

"Pah! Never mind," Tymko says. "They think they're being sarcastic, but I could be way more sarcastic than that. They're just a bunch of spoiled kids trying to be clever."

This winter Taras and his friends find themselves in a different bunkhouse. Most of the men are different than the ones from last winter, and there's one big change for the better. Zmiya won't be with them, watching Taras and his friends. Realizing this, Taras finds himself taking a deep breath, feels his shoulders relaxing.

CLEARING SNOW off the Banff streets a week later, Tymko finds another newspaper someone dropped. It says the "alien curs" have been making catcalls at local women while being marched through the town. The commandant must take "strenuous measures," it says, "otherwise some muscular Canadian will wade into the gang of foul-mouthed, leering Austrians and, armed with a club or some other persuasive weapon, teach the brutes a lesson they will not soon forget."

Even Tymko has little to say. They decide not to show the story to anyone else.

"Why do they hate us?" Taras asks.

"Why does one people ever hate another?" For the first time since Taras has known him, Tymko shows no interest in analysis.

JUST BEFORE CHRISTMAS, Myro grabs a copy of the *Crag and Canyon* that a guard left in the canteen. A General Cruikshank has recently inspected the camp and some prisoners brought grievances to him. "A number of the interns took advantage of the occasion to complain to the general that the guards were ungentle in handling the prisoners," the newspaper says, and adds, "the majority of the foreign scum should be 'gentled' with a pick-axe handle." Taras begins to wonder if people are leaving newspapers around on purpose for them to find.

THE FIRST WEEKS of December are warmer than last year, which is good because winter coats haven't come. Daytime temperatures are above freezing and water still runs in the Bow. But on Canadian Christmas Eve, it turns much colder. The men are brought back from work early and allowed to visit the canteen after supper.

Ihor stumbles into the bunkhouse that evening, his face a pasty grey. Taras missed him at supper and wondered where he could be. He sits down on his bunk, shaking. Myro wraps a blanket around him and brings him a glass of water, all they have to offer.

Tymko gets the story out of him. He manages only a few words at a time, his body convulsed by dry retching. A Romanian, George Luka Budak, thirty-five years old, was found under his bunk in the guardhouse in the middle of the afternoon. His throat was cut through the larynx and his stomach so badly slashed that his bowels spilled out. For once the guards managed to get a doctor quickly.

Private Bernie Woolf, a Jewish guard who speaks Romanian, was called to see if he could find out what happened. There was blood all over the floor and all over Budak. A straight razor covered in blood lay on the floor. Budak couldn't talk, but he could nod a little. Woolf was supposed to find out what happened – ask Budak if he'd done it himself. Woolf thought maybe Budak had agreed with this, but he couldn't be sure the man even knew what he was being asked. Woolf knew that was what the brass wanted to hear, though. He said he thought Budak was probably saying it was suicide. By 4:20, Budak had gone into shock and died. Woolf had fled the building.

He ran into Ihor before supper. He needed to talk to somebody else who spoke Romanian. He told Ihor everything he'd seen. They both threw up in the trees near the bunkhouse. Melted snow in their mouths, swirled the water around and spat. Melted more and swallowed it. They weren't interested in supper.

Budak hadn't been in the guardhouse as a punishment, though. He'd been staying there because he was afraid of some of the other prisoners. "I never talked to him." Ihor says. "Maybe he'd still be alive."

Taras knew who Budak was, like everybody else. He knew the man was pushed around sometimes. Not by anybody in Taras's bunkhouse, but sometimes you'd see a sudden movement in a clump of men, or hear a harsh shout. Now the man's dead.

Why didn't people like him? Because he was Romanian? Or because he always said there was no reason for him to be there? Because he wasn't an Austrian citizen and so could not have been an "enemy alien."

Of course, the Ukrainians never thought there was any reason for them to be there either.

Taras has asked Tymko why people in Banff would hate the Ukrainians. Now he wonders if anyone hated the Romanian enough to kill him.

He remembers passing the guardhouse in the afternoon. Did he see someone outside the building? Someone who slipped back among the trees when he knew he'd been seen? Or is he imagining things because he knows the man is dead?

The official story is suicide, but suddenly no one feels safe.

ON DECEMBER 28, a fine day just two degrees below freezing, six guards, caps in hand, carry the coffin of the Romanian Budak. Some walk very upright, others with heads slightly bowed. There is almost no snow on the ground, an oddity so late in December. Arthur Lake frames the scene in his camera's lens.

He's heard the stories about Budak's death. Murder by guards. Murder by another prisoner. Suicide brought on by terror or insanity. Budak was beaten up by somebody a few weeks before he died, that much is certain. Spent his last days in the guardhouse because he was afraid that person – or those persons – would get to him again. Was last seen shaving with a straight razor, apparently upset and agitated. And found moments later tucked under his bed, gushing blood, stomach cut open, guts spilling onto the floor. If he was going to do that to himself, why did he bother to cut his own throat? For that matter, how could he do it?

No one will ever know the answer, unless the person or persons who may have attacked him talk about it. If he did it himself – and Arthur has his doubts about this – they will never know what went through the man's mind.

George Luka Budak is to be buried in the Banff cemetery. Well away from the ordinary law-abiding citizens of Banff, the ones whose internal organs will remain in their cold bodies for all the years it takes for them to become dust.

The guards pass without noticing the camera.

THAT EVENING in the soldiers' mess, the guards talk about a new weapon in the war, the armoured fighting vehicle. Also called a landship, it runs on caterpillar tracks and has a heavy gun that can fire in many directions. The British Navy developed it after the Army wrote off the idea. It has the capacity to cross No Man's Land and make it to the German trenches. It could mark a turning point in the wretched warfare that keeps men pinned in trenches, only to be slaughtered in their thousands – for little or no gain – every time an offensive is ordered. Sergeant Lake refrains from the obvious comment: there are worse places to be in this war than the Rocky Mountains.

Except if you were George Luka Budak.

CHAPTER 30

The violin

January, 1917

JANUARY CONTINUES to be quite mild. On Ukrainian Christmas, January 7, the thermometer reads one degree above freezing. The prisoners don't have to work, a change from last year. The dining hall has a tinselled Christmas tree. Green and red streamers loop across walls and dangle from the ceiling. The commandant approved the purchase of the streamers but this year the prisoners had to hang them. Not even Tymko can explain this, since it clearly takes away recreational pleasures from the guards. Still, Taras and his friends are glad not to be expected to work on what, for some unknown reason, the brass call Greek Christmas.

The dinner is better than average and the prisoners get their mail after the meal. Taras has a letter from his parents. So does Myro. Tymko gets a card from someone he knew in the mine, Ihor from a friend in Pincher Creek.

Yuriy gets one from his wife. Taras happens to turn toward him as he opens it. A huge grin pulls at Yuriy's face. He begins to cry – still grinning like a madman.

"Yuriy?" Taras asks. "Is everything all right?"

Yuriy sobs harder. His shirt collar is getting wet but he doesn't notice. "Nadia..." he manages to say, but he chokes on the next words.

"Nadia..." he tries again. "Nadia..." He gives up on words, and with both hands makes a rounded shape over his belly.

"She's...?"

Yuriy nods, sobbing so hard Taras is afraid he'll choke. Tymko gives him a couple of hard whacks to the back.

"Tymko," Yuriy says when he can speak, "we should make some home brew. You could all drink to my beautiful Nadia."

AFTER SUPPER they lounge around the bunkhouse. Andrews and Bullard, who have been on leave, walk through and come up to Taras and Tymko.

"So it's Christmas for you guys today," Andrews says.

"What's it to you?" Tymko takes a half step toward Andrews.

Andrews holds his ground. "Just wanted to say Happy Christmas."

"We're sorry you're not with your families," Bullard adds.

Tymko looks hard at Bullard, decides he probably means it. Actually, Bullshit has improved a lot. They'll have to stop calling him that.

LATER TARAS watches Bohdan, who has almost finished carving a Madonna in a Ukrainian headdress.

"Did you...know someone like that?" Taras asks.

"No, she's just a face that comes into my dreams. Pretty, isn't she?"

Taras nods. Like the woman Bohdan carved before, she looks like Halya.

Somehow the bunkhouse feels peaceful. A single voice – Myroslav's – begins a *kolyiadka,* an old Ukrainian carol. "Sleep, Jesus, Sleep."

Others join in, find harmonies, until the building hums. It sounds stronger, more confident, than last year. Suddenly a deep bass anchors the song. Taras looks at Tymko, eyebrows raised. Tymko the radical. Tymko the big atheist. Tymko smiles a bit sheepishly and shrugs. Christmas is Christmas.

When the *kolyiadka* comes to the end, they hear men singing in the next bunkhouse, and then the others take it up, until the whole camp is singing. When they've all reached the end, Myro uses the moment of silence to begin a new carol: *"Khrystos naro-dyvsia"* – "Christ is born."

JACKIE BULLARD stops by Taras's table at breakfast the next morning. Says he was walking around the camp the night before and was amazed to hear the singing

"They probably heard you in Banff," he says, and adds after a moment, "you Austrians really can sing."

For once Taras doesn't bother correcting him.

SERGEANT LAKE often comes in the evening to see Bohdan. The carver has been working on something new, hollowing short, straight pieces of poplar into tubes, designed to fit together using notches and grooves. One evening he asks Arthur Lake to take these tubes home and glue them together into a single long tube. He has marked places where he wants Lake to drill holes and given him a carved mouthpiece to fit into the end of the tube.

Near the end of January, Arthur brings back the result.

The carver holds the object as though it might shatter in his hands. Lifts it to his lips and blows a note. It sounds to Lake like a clarinet, or some other kind of flute. Bohdan moves his hands over the holes and produces a series of notes that gradually resolve themselves into a scale. He couldn't have been sure until he tried it whether the holes were in exactly the right place, but they are. The men realize it too, and a sigh wafts through the bunkhouse.

Bohdan begins to play a mournful tune that seems to have ridden the wind down from mountains, although not these mountains. The men gather round and in moments most are in tears. Although at first Arthur Lake thinks the song is sad, he soon realizes it has an underlying joy to it. He can almost see those ancient mountains, hear the streams flinging themselves against the rocks that line their beds. It gives him an idea.

THE VIOLIN BELONGED to Minnie's brother Edwin, who was killed in the Boer War. She kept it, thinking a child of hers might one day want to play. Their daughter was never interested, and it sits in its worn case, on a shelf at the top of their closet. When he takes it in his hands, Arthur thinks the finish looks too dark and feels tacky to the touch. He moistens a cloth with linseed oil and gives the deeply scored wood a polish, which brings up a depth of grain he couldn't see before. Minnie says the bottom and sides are made of maple and the top of something called Cremona spruce. These woods must have some peculiar affinity for assisting the creation of music. The same for the "solid rosewood pegs" which he supposes must keep the strings from slipping out of tune more efficiently than lesser woods. He picks up the bow and draws it across the strings with an awful wail. No wonder people compare violins to cats screeching.

Minnie smiles at the look on Arthur's face — as if someone was sticking needles in his bones, she says. She tells him he can have the violin. He puts it down and throws his arms around her; gives her a long, warm kiss on the lips. She laughs and squirms a bit, but kisses him back. He's always liked to hug and kiss her, but he's noticed himself doing it more since he's worked in the camp. Probably a result of seeing all those men without women. Thinking how they'd like to have someone like Minnie with them. He's only managed to marry the perfect woman. That means she can do things well, practical, useful things; she likes him under the covers; and she doesn't take any bollocks from anybody. Including him.

After his two-day leave is up and Arthur is back in the soldiers' quarters, he goes one evening to the carver's bunkhouse. He strides down the central aisle. Stops at a table and chairs roughly in the middle of the room. Sets the case on the table and sees many pairs of eyes watching. He takes out the fiddle and bow, waits for someone to approach. Several do, but the man who comes closest is Ihor the Hutsul. His eyes glitter in the soft light. His hands tremble and his lips move without sound. Arthur hands him the fiddle.

Ihor draws the bow across the strings. Although they're still out of tune, they already sound better than when Arthur did it. Ihor begins to tune the violin. The carver grabs his flute and gives

Ihor notes, and he tunes the fiddle to the clarinet. At last Ihor's satisfied. He picks up the fiddle, tucks it under his chin and plays.

Oh, Arthur's never heard anything like it. Back home it was music halls and prom concerts and gramophone recordings of famous singers – everything from opera songs to saucy ditties he'd heard at the London Hippodrome. This music gets right down to it, no introduction, it just flows. Dead serious, kind of melancholy, he thinks, imagining how he'll describe it to Minnie. Before he can come up with any other adjectives, the music has him around the throat and doesn't let go. Plunging rivers, dark forests, remote mountains, deep snow, fierce sunshine. People who've lived hundreds of generations in the same place.

The carver joins in with the flute, a descant Arthur thinks you'd call it, another melody that wanders around the strong line of the Hutsul's song. Already Arthur has lost track of how long they've been playing. He doesn't want it to end. Maybe it won't, maybe it'll go on and on like a river. He's wind-driven snow, a fish deep in a river, a star wheeling across the sky.

Just when Arthur thinks it never will end, it does, suddenly. The bunkhouse is so quiet he hears himself breathing. The men have drawn closer during the song. It seems they all inhale as one. He's always loved wondrous, magical things. Other people don't always see what he sees, but maybe they don't have the desire to see them. Or is it a knack?

Ihor nods to the carver and begins again, a much livelier piece with a bounding, dancing rhythm that has Arthur's head bobbing in time. After a moment, Yuriy moves toward the musicians and begins to dance. The others move away until there's a circle around Yuriy as he whirls, leaps, kicks his legs high in the air. Someone shouts and then many others, and Arthur sees this is part of the music. As if they said, "Oh, well done! Yes! Yes! Yes!"

Others form a circle, hands joined, and dance around him – similar patterns to Yuriy's but not so difficult. The music speeds up and another man joins Yuriy in the middle. Tymko, who must be nearly fifty, dances up to Yuriy in a way that even Arthur sees is the throwing of a challenge. Tymko leaps higher and Yuriy has to copy him. He whirls longer and faster, and Yuriy must try to better him. And then he drops out of sight so that Arthur has to climb on the end of a bunk to see him. Tymko squats on his heels. One leg shoots forward and comes back, then the other follows, faster and faster, until it's almost a blur. Yuriy tries to keep up with him, but looks stiff and slow in comparison. Tymko throws his hands behind him, fingers touching the floor, and again kicks out his right leg, his left, and so on, and makes his way around the circle in the centre of the room. The men shout wildly. Clearly this is a test of a man's skill and heart. Arthur shouts too and sees the young man Taras break into a grin.

In a flash, Yuriy holds out his hand to Tymko and they dance together a moment to even louder cheers, then melt back into the circle of men. Two others take their place in the middle, then two others, and so on; but none matches Tymko or even Yuriy. Tymko is king of the dance. But it's all exciting to Arthur. He sees that no two men do things quite the same. The dances must vary between regions. Together they make a new dance and all the while they shout until finally the music stops and the room fills with cheers. Tymko collapses, gasping, on a bunk.

Time to go. Arthur Lake makes his way to the door. Ihor nods, then the carver. As he reaches the door, another cheer bursts from the men and follows him out into the night.

A moment later the music begins again.

CHAPTER 31

Simple justice

January, 1917

THE NEWSPAPER OFFICE is still decorated from Christmas. Halya is working with Zenon on an article called "Simple Justice, An Independent Ukraine." She sits at the typewriter; he leans over her, dictating. It's the most exciting work she's done since she came to the paper almost a year ago.

"Can't wait to see this in print. Nestor's putting it on the front page." Zenon's eyes blaze, he digs his hands through his hair from forehead to nape as if pulling out invisible tangles. He can hardly keep still. Halya's never seen him like this. It's how some men look if they've had a drink or two.

"Just the last paragraph to go," she says. "Starting from 'Ukrainians have waited too long to be free...'"

"Right." He takes a deep breath. "Ukrainians have waited too long to be free..." he nods his head a couple of times and the next phrase comes to him: "always confined and deprived of liberty by foreign empires. We are a nation, and we know...we know..."

Halya types the words. Zenon begins to pace, but Halya has an idea and she can't wait. "We know that no people is born to be ruled by another."

He smiles. "Good." She types the words and he continues. "When this terrible war ends, we will find a way to build our future. The time must soon come when...when we will cast off our… No, that's no good. When we will…"

"The time must soon come when Ukrainians will be together in their own country," Halya says. Zenon nods and grins. She types.

"A free and independent Ukraine," he adds, and she types the last few words.

"It's going to be splendid!" Halya says. Her eyes meet his and she can't help a little clap of her hands.

"Couldn't have done it without you." For a moment it looks like he'll kiss her, but he doesn't quite.

Nestor watches them, enjoying their camaraderie, wondering if it's going to move into something more.

When the story comes out at the end of the week, Halya and Zenon are thrilled, although Nestor suddenly feels a nagging worry.

A WEEK LATER Halya comes to work and sees the glass in the door broken, the door ajar. The office has been ransacked. Zenon sits at his desk, stunned.

"What happened?" she asks.

Zenon hands her the local newspaper, displaying the front-page headline, and she reads, "Ruthenians Preach Treason." Her brain tries to take in the words, the strange reasoning that says wanting a free Ukraine is a crime.

A policeman enters and comes over to the desk. "Are you Zenon Andrychuk?"

Zenon turns to face him. "How may I help you?"

"We want to ask you some questions about your recent newspaper article, which we have reason to believe constitutes an act of treason."

"For saying Ukraine should be free?" Zenon asks, still in shock.

"Canada is at war. You advocate taking territory away from our ally, Russia," the policeman says.

"Only by peaceful means!" Zenon says. "As an act of common decency and justice."

Nestor has appeared in the doorway. "An independent Ukraine would also take territory from Austria, Canada's enemy," he says. "Is that also treason?"

"Just come with me, please, Mr. Andrychuk." Zenon gets his hat and coat and goes with the policeman, who manages to look both triumphant and bored.

"Can't you do something?" Halya asks Nestor. He looks almost as panicky as she feels.

"I better go along," he says, and rushes out the door.

Halya starts tidying the office – sweeping up glass, picking up and sorting the papers strewn about the room. Placing a piece of cardboard over the cracked window. By quitting time, Nestor hasn't returned, so she closes up – she has her own key now – and goes home.

That night she sits in her furnished room trying to read when there's a knock at the door. It's Nestor, and she's never seen him so upset.

"Zenon...?" she asks.

"They've charged him and taken him to jail."

"My God! What can we do?"

Nestor shakes his head. Usually things bounce off him pretty quickly, but not this.

"And the paper? Are they shutting us down?"

"Not at the moment. But they can do it any time they want."

Halya looks scared. She should ask him in. Give him a cup of tea. But he's still hovering in the doorway.

"So I guess you just became my star reporter."

"Nestor, I'm afraid for him."

"Me too." Nestor looks haggard. "But we'll do everything we can for him. Right? Now I'm gonna get him a lawyer." In a moment his footsteps echo on the stairs.

NEXT MORNING Nestor is in the hall replacing the glass in the office window when a tall, middle-aged person in a long overcoat and fur hat appears at the top of the stairs and nods to him, then goes into the office and introduces himself to Halya. Zenon's lawyer is Joel Greenberg, a Jewish man whose parents came from Chernowitz and whose grandparents came from various points in eastern Europe. He speaks Yiddish, Ukrainian, German and

English, all with an edge of long-suffering humour. Joel Greenberg knows what it's like to wish you had your own country, although his expectations are lower than Zenon's. He makes his living working for some big companies but also donates time to helping immigrants and their families. Everyone in his family has been an immigrant at one time or another.

The hat and coat go on the wooden coat tree. Greenberg sits at Nestor's desk. Nestor proceeds to pound a nail in the wall and Halya pulls up a chair.

"So," Greenberg says. "I've seen him. He says to tell you he's fine."

"Is he fine?" Halya asks.

"He says to tell you he is."

"I feel responsible," Halya says. "Some of those words were mine. The very ones the police got upset about. I suggested them."

"This is the last time I want to hear you say that. Ever. I've already got a client, I don't need another one. And I'm sure Mr. Andrychuk has a better idea than you do about what upsets the police. So does Nestor here."

"That's true." Nestor sighs and puts down the hammer. "Halya and Zenon are such idealists. I should have known better."

"Of course. We should all know you can't say what you want in this country. We should only say nice, inoffensive things. Keep pictures of the king on the wall." He looks up to where Nestor is putting up just such a picture, beside the one of Shevchenko. Halya can't help laughing.

"Now Zenon is, of course, from Galicia," Greenberg goes on. "So when he said he wanted Ukraine to be free, he was referring to freedom from the Austrian Empire."

"No," Halya says, "he wanted all Ukrainians to be free, as far east as Kharkiv and south to Odessa."

"That's the last time I want to hear you say that, too. And by the way, there are more Jews in Odessa than there are Ukrainians."

"How do you know that?"

"My mother's father came from there, that's how."

"Was he Ukrainian, then?" Halya asks.

Greenberg laughs. "People from Odessa didn't think that way.

They thought of themselves as citizens of the city. My grandfather was a Jew of Odessa."

The picture is up. Nestor straightens it and gives it a mock salute. "Good thing I never let him put *The Communist Manifesto* on the bookshelf. Of course, he was only interested in it as a historical document."

"Not even funny, Nestor," Greenberg says. "If you'd had that up when the police came, I'd never get your boy off. It's going to be hard enough as it is."

"You mean you're going to get him off?" Halya's been too consumed with guilt and worry to consider the possibility.

"I'm going to put up one helluva fight. If I can't do it, I don't know who can."

Nestor looks worried. Maybe nobody can. And until the preliminary hearing, which won't be for another month, Zenon will sit in jail.

Halya feels an icy stab of guilt. She *is* responsible. If only she hadn't egged him on. If only she'd shut up.

IN THE END, after a quick trial in which a bored judge seems deaf to all his arguments, Greenberg loses, but does win Zenon a shorter sentence than he expected. Three months hard labour. The newspaper is put on notice: watch what you write. We can close you any time we want.

A FEW DAYS LATER, Halya sits at her desk, scanning long lists of names of internees in concentration camps that Nestor obtained from the Canadian government. Lately she's been wondering again if her father lied about Taras's death. What if he really did follow her to Canada, only to be interned? She's been through the lists of men in the Brandon camp in Manitoba and the Spirit Lake and Kapuskasing camps in Ontario, and is now working her way through the many camps in British Columbia and Alberta.

Looking through the list from the Banff camp, she sees the name Taras first and then the initial "K" and can't hold back a small shriek. Nestor rushes over to look, in time to see her disappointment. Kalyna, not Kuzyk. He pats her on the arm and it's too much. She starts to cry, and Nestor puts his arm around her.

"I'm sorry," she says. "You shouldn't have patted my arm. Sometimes sympathy is harder to take than indifference." She manages a small smile and goes on searching.

CHAPTER 32

They're not like us

January, 1917

THE DAYS are viciously cold. Taras is tired before work even begins. The chill clutches at his heart, his gut.

One morning he's felling and trimming trees when all at once he feels he can't do it any more. Just can't do it. He throws down the axe. Let them send him to the guardhouse.

Close by, a prisoner shoves someone who got in his way. The second man shoves back, and they fight. So cold and hungry they can barely stand, still they thump each other. A couple of scarecrows, thrashing around in the snow. There are bloody noses before Andrews and Bullard can stop it. Barkley fires his rifle in the air. Just what an asshole like Barkley *would* do. What good is a gun if you can't scare people with it?

The two men sit stunned, their blood a scarlet code written on the snow. The other prisoners watch them. Some flop down on the ground. The man who started it begins to weep. The other one crawls over and pats his back.

After a while the guards decide to call it a day, and the prisoners carry the tree trunks back to camp.

THAT EVENING an officer they've never seen before comes into the bunkhouse with Andrews and Bullard. He looks briskly around and glares at the men. What the hell do *you* want here? their faces give back. We have done our day's work. Eaten food that leaves our stomachs aching with hunger. Food so poor and sparse that our muscles have shrunk and the cheap, worn clothing hangs on our bodies. Our gums bleed.

"I'm Captain Workman," says the tall, angular young man with close-clipped black hair and moustache and a back held unnaturally straight. "I am in charge of camp arrangements now, and I'm going to run a very tight ship. Captain Roderick Workman. Remember that name."

Why? Taras wonders. *We aren't going to be friends.*

He tries to understand what lies behind the harsh manner. What this man believes or guesses about the people he's in charge of. And who he thinks *he* is. That part's easy: he appears to think of himself as a very important kind of person; skilled, intelligent, upright. Part of the natural ruling class.

"You people have had it pretty good here." The men stare in disbelief. "Your maintenance is costing the Canadian government a great deal of money. From now on things will be different. There will be an end to all waste and unnecessary expense."

So. He seems to think they've all come here for a holiday in the mountains. It's an Austrian custom, isn't it? See the beautiful scenery and bathe in the mineral waters? And they've actually been expecting the government to pay for this. How selfish.

Andrews and Bullard watch uneasily.

At first Workman doesn't notice their discomfort, so intent is he on his message. He looks more closely at the prisoners and sees hatred in their eyes.

"Very well," he says crisply, "that's all." Taras thinks he meant to say much more, that he'd had a long speech prepared. But he turns and walks out, followed by the guards. Angry voices rise like a sudden gale. Yesterday Taras wouldn't have dreamt he could want to kill a man five minutes after first seeing him.

Hating's not worth the trouble, he knows that, but for a moment it feels good.

Still, he wonders what in hell goes on in the man's mind. Workman reminds Taras of some Austrian officers he crossed paths with when he was looking after horses for the army. Their posture, their way of speaking, made it clear that they came from the better class of people, and he didn't.

Here in the camp Taras has seen hostile and surly guards before, but Workman has something extra. He must come from a very well-off family. You can hear it in the way he speaks – his words clipped and ringing with authority. Almost as if he speaks for the Canadian government and the king and the Duke of Connaught all rolled into one.

Something must be keeping him in Canada, something that would have made it impossible for him to fight. Like the bad lungs or consumptive limps of some of the soldiers in this camp.

Or is just that the well-off family has pulled some strings to keep him out of the war?

Or is he not the top product of the well-off family? Maybe the older, smarter sons are already off in the trenches. Maybe Roderick has just failed at something else, and is here to make his name in an unexciting posting in an internment camp. If ordinary soldiers hate it here, how must this fancy captain feel?

THE NEXT MORNING Taras wakes chilled, from his belly to his toenails. His cheeks feel frostbitten. His brain, however, seems to have been working briskly all night, reviewing everything he's learned since he came here, and the moment it thinks he's awake enough to take it in, it starts telling him what it's figured out.

He is an Austrian. Austrians are not as good or intelligent as people who originated in Britain. They don't think or plan as well. They don't feel pain or cold as much; or hunger. They are suited to hard, physical work. There is a good reason why they're here.

They're Austrians. The enemy.

Dobre. He can almost believe it himself, despite a lifetime of thinking he's Ukrainian. Except that he's actually seen *real* Austrians. Colonel Krentz, for example, but he's just one of many. And aside from the German Prisoners of War who were around when the camp first began, Taras never sees anything like real Austrians *here.*

Haven't any *real* Austrians ever come to Canada as immigrants? Why aren't any of *them* interned? They'd be even more dangerous. More Austrian.

So where are they? There seems to be only one possible answer: they must be out blowing up bridges. He wonders how many bridges it's been so far during the war. If only the government realized that there are people in Canada who are *more* Austrian than the internees, they would probably do something about it. Save lots of bridges.

Taras is completely certain, and has been for some time, that there haven't actually been any bridges blown up since the war started. By Austrians or anybody else. Despite the withholding of newspapers and other sources of information, he thinks they'd have heard about it if bridges were exploding at regular intervals.

He himself would have had a hard time blowing up bridges around Spring Creek, for the simple reason that there aren't any.

"CHRIST, IT'S FREEZING," Yuriy says from his bunk.

"There's frost all over the goddamn walls!" Myro doesn't swear, or didn't till now.

"Fuel has been found to be an unnecessary luxury," Tymko says.

"What's next?" Myro wonders.

"Food," says Tymko. "Then clothing." He pauses. "Then dirty jokes."

"Then clean jokes," Myro says, and for a moment there's a rustle of laughter. They aren't sent to work that day. They spend the time huddled around stoves, going out in one-hour shifts to cut firewood.

This allows Taras to continue his philosophical rants and musings.

ALL RIGHT, he may as well think about this matter of being white or not white. Apparently Ukrainians are not white; this has been made clear by the Banff newspaper. Given that Austrians and Ukrainians seem to be roughly interchangeable, does that mean that Austrians are also not white? He wonders if anyone's told them.

Can Austrians also only be gentled with the handle of a pickaxe?

Damn, he should be writing this down. But he can't write that fast. Or he should be telling it to Tymko. It's his kind of subject. There's just one problem; even Tymko has lost interest in talking politics the last few days. Taras hopes he's not getting sick.

So, back to thinking about whiteness. And also Austrian-ness. He tries to imagine the thoughts in the mind of the commandant. "Oh," he might say to himself, "I'm in charge of all these dangerous Austrians. I'll have to watch my step... Oh, say, I learned German in school, perhaps I could talk to some of these chaps and trick them into telling me their plans for espionage and sabotage. Yes indeed, if I could prevent one bridge or building from being blown up, I would surely be promoted. I could forget about this dull, boring assignment."

He wouldn't think or do this, of course. Because when they really consider it, the commandant, and all the guards, know perfectly well that the prisoners are, with a few exceptions, Ukrainians who speak Ukrainian.

And that no man in this camp has ever imagined, let alone planned, how to spy on Canada and report his findings to somebody in the Austrian military; or how to blow up bridges or railroads. They have to know this.

But there's another way of thinking – if it can even be called thinking – that can divert their attention whenever they get too close to admitting to themselves that the prisoners are here for no good reason at all. It can be summed up in the phrase Taras heard early in his imprisonment: "They're not like us." That was Taveley, a soldier who was sent away because he was too nasty, too prejudiced to fit in, even in this place.

Racial superiority is a way of thinking that helps reinforce all the selfish and all the stupid reasons why the internees have been put here. How soothing it must be to have, always ready to hand, that feeling of comfortable superiority toward the people you exploit. They're used to it, in fact they're suited to it. They don't mind it; it's all they know.

Taras thinks that the commandant probably also agrees that it's important for Ukrainians to be imprisoned because their labour competes with the British-born and northern European workers who came here first. Yes, the Ukrainians were invited to come, when they were needed, but now they're unwelcome. If they can't be shipped right back, they must be imprisoned. And while they're hanging around eating free food, there is, as luck would have it, a highway that needs to be built. And in summer, nine holes of a golf course.

And after all, as they're not *white,* they really shouldn't mind too much.

Or maybe he doesn't think about any of it. Maybe Taras is giving him credit for more brains than he's got. As far as he can tell, even the soldiers think the commandant is a bit stupid. So maybe he just sits in his office during the day and goes to the officers' mess in the evening. From what the *Crag and Canyon* writer said, the food and drink are good and just what a senior officer requires. The commandant doesn't have to know why he's here and why there's a camp here. He just has to keep it going and keep order.

Maybe Workman's trying to make a name for himself so *he* can be a commandant some day.

Workman. Now, that's an odd name. Shouldn't it belong to a man who works with his hands? Maybe he's trying to run away from his name. Trying to rise above it.

Taras's theorizing carries him through the afternoon. As a topic for serious thought, Workman has been of some use. Just not in the way he aspires to.

THE NEXT DAY it's apparently a few degrees warmer, because the men are sent out once more to work in their flimsy clothing, guarded by Andrews and Bullard. They've been promised new jackets and pants, but nothing comes when it's needed. By noon everyone's dead on their feet, shaking with cold, including the guards.

"They're freezing, for Christ's sake. Let's call it a day," Bullard mutters to Andrews.

Andrews thinks for about six seconds. "Hey, everybody, let's get the hell out of here." Neither of them care that the prisoners heard.

The men nod at the guards in some kind of acknowledgement. Not that they're suddenly comrades, but still, they did something. Even Bullshit, in fact it was his idea. They stumble off through the trees. When they reach the bunkhouse, they're too tired to do anything but slump on their bunks. Even Tymko, usually sustained by political analysis and sarcasm, looks defeated.

"It's thirty below out there," Myro says. "Our coats are shit."

"Food's shit," Yuriy says.

"The new captain's crazy," Tymko says sadly.

"Even the *guards* think so," Yuriy says.

"We have to do something," Tymko says.

Taras hears a new tone in his voice. Or maybe an old tone — the way Tymko sounded the night they met him.

"What *can* we do?" he asks.

"Yeah, Tymko," Yuriy says, "don't you socialists have the answer to everything?" Tymko gives him a dirty look. "No offence."

Yuriy's only voicing the question many of them have been thinking: If your political analysis is so goddamn great, why can't you think of something we can do?

"I was in a hunger strike when I first arrived at Castle Mountain," Taras says. "And once, we refused to work when it was too cold. But now we need something more."

"Like what?" Yuriy asks.

A man called Nick Melnychuk starts coughing. He's been coughing for a couple of weeks, but now it's getting worse. He didn't get out of bed this morning.

Taras realizes Nick must be really ill. He has a vision of the old man in the village reading hall reciting from memory.

"We can remember who we are."

"What?" Myro asks.

"We're not Ruthenians or Galicians or bohunks, or any of their words for us. We're Ukrainians." Taras wonders where his words are coming from. "And if we stick together, we might get somewhere."

"So what do you want us to do?" Tymko asks quietly. No sarcasm, no anything.

Taras looks around at his friends. Surely it's not for him to say. Isn't that up to Tymko the socialist and Myroslav the teacher, the ones with the quick minds and tongues? They're looking at him. What can he suggest? Maybe it doesn't have to be anything new. Maybe they just have to decide how far they're prepared to go with it.

Next morning Andrews and Bullard come into the bunkhouse. The men sit on their bunks wearing their outdoor clothes with their blankets wrapped around them. Even with all three stoves going, the bunkhouse is below the freezing point. Melnychuk lies in his bunk, extra blankets piled on top of him.

"All right, men, let's get a move on." Andrews sounds unsure of himself. The prisoners don't move. Don't even look at the guards.

"What's going on here?" There's an edge in Bullard's voice. "Line up, men."

Still nobody moves. Melnychuk cries out in Ukrainian, in some dream of long ago.

Taras steps forward. "We can't work in this weather if we don't have warm coats." His voice is calm but very firm.

"It's not up to us, you know that." Andrews looks uncomfortable, maybe even scared. "You have to come."

"Or they'll cut your rations," Bullard says half-heartedly.

"So we'll only get half as much slop?" Tymko asks. "What was it we got last night? I've chucked up better looking stuff than that. Better tasting, too."

"You know we don't cook the food," Andrews says. "Look, you really have to come."

"Could you work on what they feed us?" Tymko asks.

"You think we enjoy it out there all day?" Bullard asks, getting a little chippy. "Least you guys keep warm working."

"No," Taras says. "We don't keep warm. The government takes our freedom. The government makes us work. So the government should take better care of us."

"And that includes a doctor for Mr. Melnychuk," Myro says, nodding toward Nick, who is lost to the world.

"Line up, men," Andrews is almost pleading. "We gotta go now."

The prisoners don't move or speak. They barely blink. They've all heard that Canadians think Ukrainians are stoic. If so, they'd rather be stoic somewhere out of the wind.

"I'm sorry. We got no choice," Andrews says. "We have to report you." He says this as if he really doesn't want to.

Another figure appears in the doorway. "Why aren't these men moving yet?" Captain Workman. He spots Melnychuk. "Who's that malingerer?" He strides toward the sick man.

"Sir, I believe that man is not well," Andrews begins. His arm goes out as if to hold Workman back, but stops in mid-air.

"He's here to work, not lounge around." Workman reaches Melnychuk and pulls away the blankets for a better look. "Get up, you lazy bloody bohunk!"

He grabs Melnychuk's arm and pulls. Melnychuk groans.

A howl echoes through the vast room like some ferocious choir. Myroslav leaps forward, eyes burning, face white. But before he can get to Workman, Taras is on the captain's back, dragging him away and Tymko nails him with a solid punch to the forehead. Workman goes down like a felled pine.

That's not all. Just as Taras grabbed Workman, Andrews made a move as if to stop him and Myro punched him in the jaw. Andrews and Workman don't move. Everyone is still. There's no going back.

Myro tries to shake pain from his hand. "Goddamn it," he mutters. "I hit Andrews."

At first Bullard can't even move. He bends over Andrews, totally vulnerable if anyone else wanted to hit a guard, but it seems no one does.

After a minute or so Andrews can stand. Bullard tries to get the captain to his feet, with Tymko's help, but he's not fully conscious. Bullard picks him up like he's a sack of potatoes.

"Christ," Tymko says as Bullard carries Workman out, "that's done it."

TARAS AND TYMKO are marched into the commandant's office. Bullard and Andrews stand at attention behind them. A fire roars in the Quebec heater and the room is almost stiflingly warm. The commandant, his forehead and cheeks splotched with red, pushes away a tray with a hearty breakfast of eggs and bacon and stands to confront them.

This is the first time Taras or Tymko has seen him up close. They see that he's really rather small, and the whites of his eyes are threaded with red veins. For someone not seen outdoors very often, his hands look severely chapped. His lips are pale and tight.

"What the hell do you think you're doing?" he says. "You assaulted an officer!"

"Captain Workman attacked a sick man," Tymko says. "A man delirious with fever."

"That's beside the point!" The commandant is now several degrees more furious. He mustn't have expected them to answer back.

"Not to me." Tymko stands his ground. Nothing to be gained by being timid now.

"You do not attack a military officer!" The commandant shouts these words, his voice rising in pitch. Says them as if even a prisoner must recognize the sacredness of rank.

"I never attack anyone before," Taras says. "It never happens if Captain Workman behaved right." He can't believe it, but he sounds like Tymko. Strong.

"Proper behaviour of my officers is not for prisoners to decide! Furthermore, you had already disobeyed your guards." He nods at Andrews and Bullard, who look sick. "All of you will return to work at once!"

There's a long moment of silence, then, "Too cold," Taras says. "See this jacket." He grasps a fold of threadbare fabric and holds it out for inspection.

The commandant barely looks at the jacket. "Nothing wrong with it. Thousands of Canadians wear jackets like that." For a moment he falters and seems almost to doubt his own words, but he soon whips up his moral outrage again. "*Just* like that!"

Amazing. He can deny the evidence of his own eyes. That's what his work is doing to him. Still, Taras carries on.

"We need better food to work in this cold."

"And Mr. Melnychuk is seriously ill," Tymko says. "He must have a doctor."

"Mr. Melnychuk will be seen to in due course. But you're here to work, damn it, not be mollycoddled." The commandant is still angry, but he seems to be losing force.

"We commit no crimes," Taras says. "We are prisoners because we are Ukrainian."

"You're here for good reason! And I'll not stand for any of your radical agitation."

Taras hopes his own face doesn't look that purple. He makes himself stay calm.

"I am no radical. I want to be treated right."

"You will all go back to work. Now!" The commandant's fury has escalated again, but it seems to take a terrific effort.

"Not without food. Not without better clothing." Taras can't believe the way words keep flying out of his mouth. He's always tried to avoid trouble in the camp, but something in him has crossed a line and isn't going back. Not today, anyway.

"We'll see about that!" the commandant shouts hoarsely, and they know what's going to happen.

They're going to be punished with the worst this guy can think of.

THE INTERNEES, the entire camp, guarded by about fifty soldiers – but not by Andrews and Bullard – are lined up along the river below Bow Falls. Sergeant Lake is also absent, in the guardhouse with the other two for protesting against the punishment about to take place.

Where in summer Bow Falls pounds the rocks, the water now has frozen in the act of falling and formed a wall of ice, delicate as lace, yet heavy. Surely it will come crashing down any moment. A thought drifts through Taras's stunned mind. The men from the Alpine Club would love to see this. It looks rather splendid.

A narrow channel of water still flows. Taras and Tymko are hauled forward to have their arms bound to heavy wooden yokes.

The guards' hands shake as they tie the ropes. They don't look at the prisoners. The commandant watches with a righteous expression on his face. Roderick Workman, standing further back, looks shocked at the way his new regime has worked out. Perhaps he didn't expect anything like this to happen.

The guards find a place where the bank rises above the river and the water is chest deep. It takes a half-dozen of them to throw Taras and Tymko into the water and drag them, by other ropes attached to the yokes, through a river more ice than water.

The shock is beyond Taras's understanding. The cold goes straight to his heart and entrails. His chest and belly cavities seem to fill with ice. Time slows, pictures crowd into his head. Viktor raising his arm to strike Halya. Reaching for the railing by the steps to the last car on the train out of Chernowitz. Stover and his friends beating him the day the war began.

The guards drag them for ten, twenty, thirty seconds.

Taras sees an image that is not a memory: Budak bleeding out his life, guts splashed on the guardhouse floor. Someone watches from the doorway. Who? The man runs away.

"That's enough. Pull them out," the commandant barks.

Tymko is hauled unconscious from the river, his lips blue, ice clinging to the black hair. Taras stumbles onto the bank. Prisoners rush forward, struggle to undo the wet, already freezing knots binding the men to the yokes. A guard slices through them with his bayonet. Their workmates wrap Taras and Tymko in blankets and carry them at a quick jog the half mile to the bunkhouse.

The scarecrow, Zmiya, follows behind.

The prisoners disappear from sight, followed by dispirited looking guards. The commandant stands alone. He looks puzzled, as if this wasn't quite what he'd imagined.

CHAPTER 33

The soul

THE NEXT MORNING Taras and Tymko lie still in their bunks. Taras is awake, Tymko in a deep stupor, his breathing shallow. Around them, prisoners who slept with their coats on over their work clothes are slowly getting up to face the day.

Somehow dry clothes were found for Taras and Tymko last night and some people even lent them extra blankets. Some stayed up all night with them. Ihor. Yuriy. Bohdan. Myro. Taras will always remember Myro's pale face, his dark eyes watching over them.

Taras feels warm for the first time in months. The last blanket did the trick. That and some heated stones Sergeant Lake and another guard brought in and placed at their feet. Oh, and the brandy they dribbled down his throat.

They've achieved one thing, at any rate. Melnychuk has been taken away to the Banff hospital.

In the water he thought his heart would stop. Maybe it did stop and he was dead for a while. It felt like it. When they dragged him onto the shore, dripping and freezing, it seemed as if his soul floated in the air a few feet above his body. That one looks miserable, it thought. Doubt if he's going to make it. Too bad, he's young.

While the prisoners carried his body to the barracks, the soul wandered along behind. Watched the men settle him on his bunk, gentle as mothers, and pile blankets on him and Tymko, forming the rough lengths of grey wool into body-shaped mounds tucked close around their throats and shoulders. As Taras's body slowly warmed, the soul began to reconsider its position. Maybe it wasn't all over. The soul thought of summer and hot sun, remembered steaming *borshch* and warm *chorny* bread. It saw his mother's face and then his father's. They smiled encouragingly, as if the Taras on the bed was a baby they were urging to walk. The soul began to think of the lump under the blankets as itself and drew closer. He is me, it thought, or I am him. Little by little it came closer, until it let itself become one again with the man. Instantly the calm, distant wisdom the soul had possessed moments before was gone and he was aware of pain and bitterness. But also of growing warmth.

Andrews and Bullard enter and the men rise to their feet, as if a gust of wind blows through the room. Their eyes drill into the guards, accusing.

"We didn't do it," Andrews says. "We refused to take part."

"They docked us a month's pay," Bullard says. "We have families, too, you know."

"The commandant wants everyone else back at work," Andrews says. He looks very calm, beyond pleading or coaxing or hectoring. He'll report their answer, whatever it is. If the commandant wants some other answer, he can come and ask himself.

Andrews never reported that Myroslav punched him.

Nobody moves. The guards leave and the prisoners take deep breaths. They pace slowly around the room, looking grey and a little blurred, as if walking in water. Pale shadows move beside them. Visions of themselves before they came here. Wraiths of wives, sweethearts, children, parents they once lived among. Ihor takes up the violin and plays for them, especially for Taras and Tymko. The music is slow and sad but not despairing. Another way of saying, "Remember who we are."

On the third day the cold snap breaks and the commandant sends word that new coats are on the way. Everyone knows this is as close to victory as they'll get. The men go to work, everyone but Taras and Tymko. In the evening, Ihor sits at the foot of Taras's bed and plays.

For days Taras is too ill to move except to squat over a chamber pot. Tymko is mostly unconscious, moaning in his sleep and calling out names.

One afternoon Tymko sits partway up, supports himself on an elbow and looks around with comprehension in his eyes. He takes in the bunkhouse. Taras on the next bunk. The fact that it's warmer than he remembers. Taras brings his pillow over and places it behind Tymko's neck and shoulders.

"Holy shit, how long has this been going on?" Tymko coughs a wet, hacking cough, until Taras pounds him on the back with big, panicked whacks.

"Stop!" Tymko croaks, "you're killing me." He takes deep, wheezing breaths until he can quiet his breathing. He tries moving his arms and legs, fingers and toes.

"It seems I'm not used to talking."

"No," Taras says. "Not for over a week. I think it scared the commandant a bit. It's all right if someone gets killed trying to escape. But I don't think it looks good if you die from a punishment. He actually sent over some coal for the stoves."

"Jesus. Coal."

"*Tak*. I know."

"My clothes feel stiff enough to walk around on their own. I must be filthy."

"When you feel up to it, Andrews says we can go for a bath and then into the hot pool."

"I feel up to it right now. I want to feel hot from my eyeballs to my toenails."

"Take it easy. You have to be able to walk. And eat."

A puzzled look settles on Tymko's face of a person trying to decipher the meaning of "eat." Taras offers him the half sandwich he saved from the lunch the cooks brought over. Tymko holds it as you would a frog that might jump out of your fingers.

Or a bun that might run away.

"My dear little sandwich," Tymko says. "You're not much, but you're all I've got." He takes an exploratory bite. Chews. Nods wisely. Swallows.

"I'm alive, then. *Dobre.*" Encouraged by his success, he eats more. Soon the scrap of food is gone. Tymko drinks eagerly from the cup of water Taras offers, then belches softly. "Got anything else?"

Taras reaches into a pocket. Offers a small bag of chocolate-covered sweets. Sergeant Lake brought them. Tymko takes one and lets it melt in his mouth. Sinks back against the pillows and lets his mind wander. For several minutes neither man speaks.

"Tymko," Taras says after a while, "when you were out of your mind —" He reconsiders. "No, I mean when you were unconscious, you did a lot of moaning."

"I was in pain, I suppose. Who wouldn't moan?"

"You called out a name. I wondered...did you have a wife? Or a sweetheart?"

Tymko pulls himself all the way to a sitting position. "What name?"

"Oksana."

Tears fill Tymko's eyes. His chest shakes and he coughs until Taras has to pound his back again. The tears flow down his cheeks into his stubbly beard.

"I shouldn't have asked." Taras sits on the bunk and puts an arm around Tymko's shoulders. "I'm sorry."

"Oksana was my daughter." Tymko's words come out haltingly. "My little girl." He clutches his hands to his belly and a strangled scream escapes his lips.

"She drowned." It comes out so garbled that Taras wants to ask him to repeat it, but doesn't dare.

"She drowned!" Tymko says, loudly, forcefully, as if he has to get it right. He grabs Taras's shoulders and shakes him. "I couldn't swim. My child drowned!"

He collapses against the pillows and weeps until he passes back into sleep.

When Tymko wakens the next day, Taras can see he's doing better. His face has more colour and his eyes look brighter. Arthur Lake comes by and takes them, along with some other prisoners who missed their last bath, to the bathhouse and then into the hot pool. Tymko stays by himself at the edge of the pool. Taras watches him lean against the side wall, soaking up enough heat to keep him warm the rest of the day. Enough to let him creep back into life.

TYMKO SLEEPS most of the afternoon. When he wakens, he speaks to Taras of a daughter full of daring and mischief, with dark eyes and near-black hair worn in long braids. In the old country she'd have been considered wilful and unfeminine, but Tymko was determined not to hold back her spirit, even if the first grade teacher said Oksana asked too many questions. He was determined that she should be able to try for any sort of future she could imagine.

At the miners' union picnic, she ran off to be with her friends. He wasn't worried until he heard the other girls screaming. When he reached the swiftly flowing creek, before the other adults realized a child was in danger, she was already being carried away. He ran along the bank and when he had her in sight he leapt into the water. It reached only to his chest, he was sure he could catch hold of her, but she was tossed out of his reach and sucked under. He dived deep to look for her, scraped his hands over rocks where her clothes might have snagged. He knew she was gone but kept searching. She washed up on shore a half mile away where the river took a sharp turn. Friends from the mine found her and carried her home.

It was the first time since he'd become a socialist and an atheist that Tymko seriously considered God might exist after all and was punishing him for leaving the church.

That night he sat by his daughter's bed, her face warmed by lamplight. His wife's photograph, framed in carved wood, watched from the wall over the bed. Friends and neighbours came quietly in and left again just as quietly. His friend Anton the Czech sat for many hours, offered him whiskey from a pocket flask. Tymko could sense him there in a wooden chair, his warmth radiating into the room, but inside he found only the chill of water that has not travelled far from a glacier.

He could not imagine allowing people to lay Oksana in the earth. He knew it was crazy, but he kept thinking she might not be truly dead. Maybe if he watched faithfully she would come back.

When Anton returned the next morning, he touched Tymko's hand and Tymko knew what was going to happen. It seemed his heart tore in his chest and he fell on the planked floor and knew nothing more for a long time. He awoke in his bed the next day after the people from the union had seen to her funeral and burial.

Here in the almost empty bunkhouse, Taras can't think how to help, but he takes Tymko's hands in his and holds them.

THAT NIGHT Tymko has a coughing fit, bringing up ugly green sputum. Friends bring him their handkerchiefs. "I tell you, boys," he says, "I'll never go down a goddamn mine again in this life. Not by the holy saints Cyril and Methodius." He winks at Myro. "Whoever they were.

"You can't imagine what it was like in the mines," he goes on without waiting for encouragement. "It was quite the life, even if it did rot your lungs. I never met so many different kinds of people. And we got along pretty good. Mostly, anyway. Nobody gets along all the time." Taras looks at him, wondering if it's good for a sick man to talk so much.

"We were union men. Full of hope. I wish you could have seen those coal towns. People built houses as soon as they could afford it. Their kids went to school and had warm clothes and took music lessons. Music lessons! Violin. Piano. *Bandura.*

"We built labour temples. Churches, even. We dressed up in suits and went to the photographer to have our pictures taken. Why, I wonder? So we could see how well we were doing? Or we dressed up in old country clothes, the women practically glowing with embroidery. Miners swaggered as Cossacks. We had more Cossacks than ever were in all of Ukraine. We even had a Ukrainian theatre group." He grins. "I took the part of a *hetman.*"

"You, Tymko, a Cossack?" Myro shakes his head.

"It was a good part. I pretended he was a socialist, and after that it was easy."

Other men come to listen. Tymko coughs for a couple of minutes and goes on.

"I wish I could show you the picture of Rainey and me, taken in Mr. Gushul's studio."

"Rainey?" Yuriy says. "That doesn't sound like an old country name."

"She came from Scotland. She had the loveliest accent. I could listen to her for hours."

"Not all men like to listen that much to their wives," Ihor says.

"Maybe not, but my Rainey had this way of rolling her r's, and when she spoke, I listened. I'd have listened even if I hadn't known what she was saying. And she was a big supporter for the union."

"Scottish wife," someone breathes. "Who would have guessed?"

"Anyway, to continue about the picture. We looked really smart, Rainey said. None of you have seen me with tidy hair and a well-trimmed moustache, but you could almost have called me a handsome devil. And now the proof's gone."

"Gone where?"

"Government took it off me when I came here. You never know what secret, subversive meaning it might have."

"You've never mentioned a wife before," Bohdan says.

"No. That's because she died. About six months before I lost my daughter."

"I was afraid you'd say that. What was the matter?"

"Well, the odd part is she died of tuberculosis." Tymko's matter-of-factness stuns them. Surely a man can't talk this easily about such hard things. "Now, you'd think it would be a miner who got the TB, but Rainey must have had it even before we met. One day a neighbour found her lying on the ground in front of our house. She'd had a sudden hemorrhage – bleeding from her lungs – and by the time a doctor came..."

No one dares speak. "The union did everything for the funeral. There was a band with trumpets and bugles and a long procession through the streets. Snow was very deep that winter. The men worked in shifts to dig the grave. Burned coal, let the embers warm the ground. Because I wasn't in the Ukrainian church, we had a ceremony in the English church."

He stops and it seems he's done. Yuriy is longing to know what comes next, but like the others, he doesn't want to make Tymko tell more painful things. Tymko sees the look.

"When I lost my daughter, everything was gone and I had to decide whether to keep on with my life. Finally I thought, well, if I don't have my family, I've still got socialism. And my friends in the union and my work in the mine. Of course I didn't know that in 1913 Canada would fall into an economic depression. Factories didn't need so much coal. It took a while to catch up to our mine, but by the spring of 1914 I was laid off. Nothing to do but sit in my snug new house and wonder how to buy food."

"That's why I lost my job too," someone says. "No demand, the boss said."

"That's right," Tymko says. "There was no longer any demand for Ukrainians. Before, there was, so they wanted us to come. Then there wasn't, but we were still here. That's a big reason why we're all in this hole."

"Not for me," Yuriy says. "We had this neighbour who didn't like me and he told lies about me to the police."

"Me too," Taras says. "My boss wanted me out of the way."

Tymko's face tightens. "I told you we got along mostly. But when the war broke out, some people said us Ukrainians should be let go. They said Austrians were taking jobs away from Canadians."

"Well, we know what some people can be like," Yuriy says. "They want everything to be for the English."

"Yes," Tymko says, "but these were other Ukrainians. From the provinces in the Russian empire. I thought they were my friends." For a while no one can speak.

"We must not give up hope," Ihor says finally. "One day we'll leave here. We'll go on with our lives. This terrible time will be forgotten."

"No," Myroslav says. "It will never be forgotten."

AT BREAKFAST a story goes around the prisoners' mess hall. Private Amberly — the kid who told Taras to hand over the pocket watch — has left the camp. Private Amberly who helped two men escape. Andrews says it's true. Some time in the night Amberly walked into the woods and wasn't missed until morning roll call. A search party found him in a clearing not far from camp, sitting on a log, an empty whiskey bottle propped in the snow. His hands and feet were frostbitten and some of his toes will have to be amputated. He's in hospital in Calgary and won't be coming back. He has been declared unfit for service.

CHAPTER 34

Edward Bellamy

A WEEK LATER the temperature hovers around freezing. Taras is dressed but still lies on top of his bunk. Tymko is asleep. They have refused to work until they see a doctor. The door opens and Bullard and Andrews enter. Andrews fidgets with his collar.

"Attention, everyone. The American consul's coming to inspect the bunkhouse. Everyone stand to attention!" Something in his voice convinces them to stand up in a semblance of order. Although he hasn't said please, he's somehow implied it.

The guards walk through the bunkhouse and stop near Tymko's bunk. He's awake now, but making no move to get up. Taras sits on the side of the bunk.

Myro is close by. "Who is this American consul?" he asks.

"New man. Name of Bellamy," Andrews says. "Somehow he heard there'd been a strike. Maybe he came to find out why you prisoners wouldn't work."

"So the commandant asked him to come?" Yuriy asks.

"You kidding?" Bullard says. Yuriy grins. "But consuls from non-combatant countries have the right to come, under the Geneva Convention, and I guess this one takes it seriously."

Andrews goes outside for a moment and brings in Edward Bellamy, a man of maybe fifty years, very neat and compact, with a serious expression and a look of authority.

Bellamy looks at the internees. "Please, there's no need to stand." The internees sit on their bunks. He turns to Bullard. "Is the bunkhouse always this cold?"

Bullard looks confused. "No, sir...I mean...uh, lately —" He doesn't say it's usually colder, but maybe Bellamy figures it out.

The consul strolls over to Tymko's bunk. The guards follow.

"What's wrong with this man?" He stares right at Andrews.

"He's, uh, not well," says Andrews. "Neither of these men is well enough to work."

"They...took a severe chill," Bullard says. Taras almost wonders if they're trying to get the consul suspicious.

"Took a *chill?* I'm asking what's wrong with this man." You'd have to be a tougher man than either Bullard or Andrews not to answer the consul.

"He was punished, sir," Bullard says.

"Punished how?"

Bullard squirms. "They were dragged through the river."

"Extraordinary. What were they punished for?"

Taras sees Bullard getting more and more nervous, his forehead sweaty. "They refused to work," he explains. "Said their clothes weren't warm enough.

"Said the food was bad," he adds.

"Commandant says they're socialists," Andrews says, as if they might as well get everything off their chests at once. "Radicals."

Bellamy studies Tymko, who meets his eyes squarely, and then Taras, who decides it's his moment to speak.

"We protest our continued imprisonment. We have committed no crimes. We want only to live and work in our new country."

The consul watches Taras for what must be a full minute.

"Are you a socialist? A revolutionary?"

Taras looks right back at Bellamy. "If a revolutionary is someone who wants freedom, then I guess I am."

A ghost of a smile touches the consul's lips. He turns to Andrews. "Have these men been seen by a doctor?"

"No, sir. Medical officer's on leave."

"There must be a doctor in town. Am I right?"

"Yes," Andrews says.

"I want to see the commandant now. I'd like this man to come with me." He nods at Taras. He leaves the bunkhouse, followed by Andrews, Bullard and, more slowly, by Taras, who can't even guess what kind of trouble he's going to be in. He's scared but can't make himself regret that he spoke out. That'll come later, he supposes.

They stop inside the door of the administrative building and Bellamy dismisses Bullard and continues down the linoleum-floored hallway to the commandant's office with Andrews and Taras. He asks Andrews to wait outside with Taras, knocks and goes into the warm, bright office.

As the consul enters, the commandant stands. Once again Taras sees the person who rules his days, much closer than he'd have wished. The man is calmer today, not so red in the face, and Taras can't believe how utterly bland he looks. Sandy hair and moustache, pale blue eyes, but uniform pressed and boots polished fit to be seen by the king if he happened to drop in.

"Good morning to you, sir." Bellamy steps up and shakes hands. "I believe you were expecting me."

"Good morning, Mr. Bellamy. Sir." The commandant makes a slight bow and gestures at a small side table with a pair of upholstered chairs on either side. A tray of tea and biscuits on a china plate sits on the table. They sit. "Will you take tea? And some biscuits?"

"Thank you, commandant. I've completed my inspection and spoken with some of the men."

"I trust you found everything in order?"

Bellamy regards the commandant thoughtfully. "I cannot say that I did."

The commandant gives a little start.

"The internees complained of being poorly fed and clothed —"

The commandant makes a small strangled noise as he tries to interrupt, but Bellamy waves it off. "I was inclined to believe it when I saw their shabby outerwear. And the bunkhouse was not particularly well-heated."

"Sir, we have been instructed to keep costs down. We do the best we can —"

"Has it occurred to you," Bellamy rolls on as if the commandant hasn't spoken, "that the Canadian government, having taken these men from their homes and families, has a serious responsibility toward them?" There's a strong enough edge to his voice now that even the commandant hears it.

"We have always —"

"They must be treated correctly."

"Certainly. No question."

Taras can't believe the man's ability to lie. Or is there some way he's convinced himself that things really are good for the men? In which case he has learned well how to lie, first and foremost, to himself.

"Now." Bellamy leans across the desk. "I understand two men were punished."

"Two radicals, sir. I felt I must make an example."

"Entirely unacceptable. You had them dragged through icy water. That's barbaric! You could not treat an actual prisoner of war in that manner. You could have killed them. It was your own idea, I suppose?"

Taras begins to shake. He can't believe he's hearing this.

"They were completely insubordinate. Attacked a guard."

"Indeed? And what were the circumstances of the attack?" Andrews has inadvertently drawn further into the room and Bellamy turns to him. The commandant must wish Andrews wasn't there but now can't get rid of him.

"Speak up, Sergeant," Bellamy says.

"Well, sir, they were concerned about another prisoner. A fellow who was ill... Captain Workman..." Andrews is obviously looking for some way out of this.

"Please continue," Bellamy says. "What did Captain Workman do?"

"He...attempted to, uh, rouse the sick man. Tried to pull him to his feet, you see." He stops but the consul nods, as if to say there must be more. "He called him... He called him...a lazy bohunk.

The internees are very sensitive to –"

"Yes, quite." The commandant glares. "That will be all, Andrews." His look says that if ever there were a soldier who could forget about any kind of promotion, Andrews has shown himself to be that man. Andrews withdraws just beyond the door.

Bellamy makes the commandant wait a few moments, then speaks with unconcealed contempt. "Sir. Has it occurred to you to think of these men as a resource?"

"Certainly, sir. They have built a number of roads and a bridge and an extra nine holes on the golf course –"

"Ah, the golf course. Yes, I see. Not exactly essential to the war effort, but I suppose a golf course is always a delight in and of itself."

"I suppose so…Tea, Mr. Bellamy?" The commandant pours tea, offers biscuits, cream and sugar, all of this completely ignored by his guest.

"I must consider what report I am to make," the consul says. He watches the sweat break out on the commandant's brow.

"Now. I am aware of the change in Canada's labour situation. A great many of your young men are away fighting the war and Canada is now short of labour."

"An unfortunate corollary of war, if I may say –"

"My government is also aware that a great many of the prisoners in this camp have been released to work in mines, on the railroad and indeed on farms and ranches."

"That is correct. We have been able to supply a number of mines and a cement plant in the area. A thoroughly satisfactory arrangement for everyone."

"Except for the remaining prisoners, I would suppose. And except for the complete outrage of logic their release implies."

"Er?" The commandant stirs his tea vigorously. "Don't quite follow."

"I mean, sir, that if these men were previously far too dangerous to be allowed their freedom, what must now be the consequence of their release?"

"Sorry? Still don't quite –"

"I would assume that when these alarming fellows were allowed to leave, there must have been an outbreak of violence, lawbreaking, perhaps even sabotage?"

"I'm not aware of any." The commandant picks up an iced biscuit but obviously doesn't realize the force he's putting into it. It bursts into tiny shards and sprays the table and the front of his uniform. He tries, furtively, to brush them away but only manages to stain the cloth.

"No factories blown up or bridges bombed? No attacks on government buildings? No murder and mayhem in the streets?" At last the consul takes a sip of tea.

"Perhaps you understand me? I don't believe these men are any danger to Canada's peace. If any of them have committed crimes, they should be dealt with according to the law. The rest should be released and, I would suggest, compensated for their imprisonment."

Taras takes a deep breath and feels his chest and belly relax. He realizes he's barely been breathing all this time.

The consul has confirmed Taras's own ideas. The consul is telling off the commandant. Taras will never forget this. He has his own analysis. It's not so different from Tymko's, but he's pieced it together himself.

"Released? Compensated?" the commandant is saying, as if he can't believe his ears. "Now look here, that's the business of the Canadian government." He looks happy to have thought of this objection and it invigorates him for a moment. He takes another cookie.

"It *should* be. And don't mistake me, I'm under no illusions about what's likely to happen. However, be assured that if there is any repetition of such scandalous acts of inhumanity here, I will raise holy hell with your government, and the world press will know of it! And that is *my* business."

"You can't mean —" The commandant tries not to choke on the cookie.

"I'm only sorry I can't do more. Now, I understand from our ambassador in Ottawa that there are plans to close this camp down in the near future."

"Do you indeed?" The commandant looks vexed. "I was not aware that was being discussed beyond Canadian government circles."

"I expect your prime minister knew of our interest in the camps. He no doubt wished to remind us that we will need to be vigilant about our borders as more of these internees are freed."

"Oh, I wouldn't worry about that. The great majority are going to companies where they have previously worked. And I really believe most of the prisoners have learned their lesson."

Bellamy takes a long sip of his tea. "What lesson might that be? Is it that they somehow made a mistake in being born Ukrainians?" Again the commandant looks baffled. "Never mind that. You confirm this camp will not exist much longer?"

"I believe that is a real possibility, perhaps by midsummer."

Bellamy eats a biscuit and follows it with more tea. The commandant breathes a sigh of relief. The interview has been most unpleasant, he must think, but it's almost over.

"I'd like one of the prisoners to come in for a moment," Bellamy says.

"Now, do you mean?" The commandant looks horrified.

"Yes, I think that would be best." Bellamy turns to Andrews, still lurking in the hall. "Sergeant Andrews, please bring in the man who spoke up in the bunkhouse."

"You mean Taras Kalyna, sir?"

"Yes, Sergeant, if that is the name of the man who spoke up." Andrews goes back into the hall and waits a moment. Taras nods; Andrews doesn't want the commandant to think he's been right there listening all this time. He tries to smooth his hair. Andrews pulls a comb from his pocket and hands it to Taras. Helps him button the front of the mackinaw. Then they enter the room. Not sure what to do, Taras stands quietly to attention.

"Thank you for coming, Mr. Kalyna." The commandant almost jumps out of his chair when he hears Taras being addressed politely. "I thought the internees might like to know that the Canadian government is making plans to dismantle the work camps within the next few months. How does that sound to you?"

The commandant looks aghast, and Taras is totally startled to be asked about anything. "You mean, they'll send us home?" he manages to say.

"I'm afraid not right away. The plan is, you'd work for various industries for six months of what your government calls parole. It is likely that work can be found for all of you – in mines, on the railroad or in the forest industry. You'd sign a contract to stay six months. After that, you'd be free to go home."

"All the men would be free to go home? We would work only six months?"

"That's my understanding. A regular job, and you'd agree to stay six months."

"We would be paid same as other workers?"

Bellamy glances at the commandant, who nods. "Yes, that's right. The same rates."

Taras struggles to take it in. Nothing in the last half hour is like anything in the last year and a half. The cold that works to the bone, the threadbare clothing, the sparse food and misery of spirit threaten to overwhelm him. To stay alive in this place he's been forced not to dwell on when or even if he'll ever leave. Now he stands in a warm room and hears a fairy tale.

"I don't understand. Why does the government do this?"

"It's simple – there's a shortage of workers. Because so many men are away at war." Well, isn't that what Tymko always says? "And I think they realize by now that your people are not their enemies."

Taras almost breaks down in tears. He doesn't think the government will ever say what Bellamy just said, but it feels good that somebody said it. "We are not enemies. We should be free." Taras wants to feel joy but can't forget his lost days.

"Apparently this is the best that can be hoped for. I thought you would like to know there will be a limit to this incarceration. You might explain it to the other men."

Taras is suddenly tired to the bone. "*Dobre.* I will tell them. Thank you."

"Thank you, Mr. Kalyna. Andrews will accompany you back to the bunkhouse. I will speak to the commandant about the possibility of obtaining a doctor for yourself and the other man who was punished."

As they leave, Taras sees the commandant stir his tea with unusual concentration.

CHAPTER 35

Kvitka

THE DOCTOR has come, several times. One day near the end of February, as the mountain snowpack begins to thaw, he declares Taras fit for work and Tymko nearly so. That evening they walk to the bunkhouse after supper in their new woollen mackinaws, a sleet-filled wind at their backs. Out of nowhere, it seems, they hear boots pounding and hoarse, raspy breathing. Taras turns to see a stocky man with an angry, red face. Sees his arm rise.

The knife slices through Taras's coat and into his chest. Blood gushes out in time with his heartbeat. On his own he would fall but the screaming man holds him tight. Twists the knife free and then Taras falls. The man raises his arm again. Taras sees the arc the knife will take.

Tymko catches the man's wrist and snaps it with an audible crack. The knife floats to the ground. The man sinks to the snow, clutching his wrist, lips stretched in a howl so wild and hoarse his throat will surely tear. Face wet with snot and tears. And so close Taras sees right into his eyes.

How can Viktor be here?

Tymko tears off his jacket, folds it and presses it against the wound, but blood still spurts out. Taras is intrigued by the dark puddle in the snow. *Kalyna, kalyna.* Sleet drenches his hair and coat.

Guards come running. Andrews sends a private for the truck they use to fetch supplies. Bullard picks up the knife and puts it in a pocket. He and Andrews lift Taras into the truck box still bleeding. Tymko keeps pressure on the wound all the way to the hospital.

TARAS WAKES SLOWLY. An hour drifts past, and he understands he must be in the Banff hospital. A private room with a soldier sitting by the door. Why? Ah... He's too dangerous to be near other patients. The guard will keep him from escaping. Good. He feels the wound in his chest in a distant way. They must be giving him medicine for the pain. Best not to move if you can help it, a voice inside him says. It's quiet in the hospital.

And warm, deliciously warm. He sleeps.

Wakes to see a nurse looking down at him. Tall and pleasant looking, with red-gold hair, she's the first woman he's been near since he came to the camp. He's amazed by how strong she looks; by the colour and texture of her skin, the warmth in her eyes. He wishes he could touch her just to know what that feels like.

"That's better. Sleeping Beauty's finally waking up." She has a strong Scots accent – like Tymko's Rainey had. It takes Taras a few moments to get an idea of what she said. *What's Sleeping Beauty?* He has a feeling he's heard those words before. One of the guards...

"You must be hungry. Can I get you something to eat?"

This can't be heaven, but it will do for the present. *"Proshu,"* he says, and sees she doesn't understand. "Please."

"You haven't eaten for two days. I'll bring you something easy to digest." She swishes out of the room. The guard looks sad to see her go.

Looking at the nurse is easy to digest. She looks so healthy. So good. So smart. Taras can't believe his luck.

Now that he's more awake, though, pain rakes his chest, pulses with each heartbeat. He tries to take slow, shallow breaths. The throbbing subsides a little. His head goes fuzzy.

He awakens again when Miss MacQuarrie, which she tells him is her name, comes back with a bowl of oatmeal, brown sugar and warm milk. She cranks up the head of his bed and it feels as if barbed wire is being dragged through his chest. Once he gets his breath back she feeds him lovely warm porridge.

"You're lucky, you know. The knife missed your heart and lungs and a major artery. Of course, you'd have been luckier not to get stabbed in the first place." She spoons up more porridge and holds it out like a robin offering its baby a worm. The whole bowl seems to disappear in seconds.

When he tries to puzzle out her name, wanting to thank her, she says he can just call her Flora. *Kvitka,* he says. Flower.

Kvitka offers him a muffin with butter and marmalade. Taras shakes his head. She gives it to the guard.

"You know," she tells him, "this boy's going nowhere for quite a few days. You could give yourself the occasional break."

The guard nods with a foolish grin. After she leaves, he does step out for a while.

NEXT DAY Tymko is allowed to visit, accompanied by Bullard. The relief on Tymko's face seems to say he believes Taras will live and that it's not what he was expecting.

"I wrote to your parents. I said you'll be all right soon. Nice to see I wasn't lying."

Taras feels a smile tugging at his face. He'd forgotten smiling, lying here all day. Like the rest of his body, the face has been taking advantage of the time off.

"They sent that guy to the crazy house," Bullard is saying. "He wouldn't stop yelling. And crying. Who was he, anyway? Did you know him?"

"I knew him...once. He was always...a bit crazy." Taras turns to Tymko. "Like Yuriy says, there's one crazy bastard in every village."

"He's only been here in camp for a few weeks," Bullard says. "He was helping out in the kitchen. They say that's all he was good for. They say he never talked to the other men. Stole the knife that night. Why do you think —"

"I don't know." Taras doesn't want to say too much with Bullard there. "Maybe he didn't like being locked up."

"Must've been it," Bullard says. "Well, who would?" Was that

Bullshit talking?

Bullard nods at the other guard and suggests a quick break. He's actually figured out on his own that Taras isn't going anywhere. Even if Tymko could carry him, the pain would probably kill him.

"I broke his wrist," Tymko says. "That should slow him down a bit."

"Poor Viktor."

"Poor Viktor? He tried to kill you!"

"I know," Taras says. "Poor Viktor."

"So who is he?"

"Halya's father."

Tymko slaps his forehead. "Should have guessed."

"He's always hated me. I don't know how he got here."

"Maybe the cops decided he was a spy."

Taras starts to laugh at the idea of Viktor spying, but stops before he can hurt himself more.

"He'd be really bad at it. Trust me, nobody would ever tell him anything."

"Maybe it was like with Yuriy – somebody complained about him."

"Maybe." Taras doesn't want to think about Viktor. "How is everybody? How's the professor?"

"Professor's good. He's teaching the men arithmetic. All the ones who couldn't go to school. Or didn't go long enough."

"Damn, I would have liked to do that." Myro will probably tell them who invented arithmetic and all sorts of interesting things.

"We had to think of something, now that we don't have you to tell us stories."

"I need to know more about arithmetic." Taras's eyes close and in a moment he doesn't remember what arithmetic is, but it doesn't matter.

"All in good time," Tymko says. Taras is already asleep.

ONE MORNING Flora cranks up the head of Taras's bed and he manages not to yelp. She no longer has to help him with the oatmeal. What's he going to do when it's time to go back to the camp and there's no oatmeal, and no Kvitka? She's also brought two muffins and hands one to the guard, who on this day happens to be Bullard, without comment, and he wanders off to eat it. She performs her usual chores – writing things on a chart, filling his water glass – then pulls the room's plain wooden chair near the bed and sits. Taras can see she wants to say something, but can't imagine saying anything back. Since he was stabbed everything happens far too quickly. Before he can take in one thing, another thing happens.

"I've seen you before, you know." Undaunted by his blank stare, Flora continues. "One day they were marching you men through town. On your way to clear snow from the streets. I saw all the people watching. Clucking and disapproving."

She waits for him to decode the words, and continues.

"I wanted to speak up, but I was afraid. I wanted to say that it's not right, the way you're treated. The government just wants someone to blame."

Taras can only gape. He's seen women around the town staring at the internees as they pass, their lips pressed firmly together. For some unknown reason Flora is not like this.

"I knew Ukrainians in Blairmore," Flora says. "They were wonderful people, I'll never forget them. They were really strong for the union."

"The union?" Taras says. "You're for unions?"

"Oh my, yes. My father is president of the union. Alexander MacQuarrie. He helped to organize the men. 'Without it,' he says, 'it's every man for himself.'"

"I almost joined a union," Taras says. "Before they arrested me."

"Well, maybe some day you will. It's grand, you know. You're never quite so alone as you were before."

Taras can't grab hold of all her words but he understands that she likes him and she likes unions. She beams at him like a human sun. Something of her radiant health and sturdy good will steals into him.

"Thank you, Flora. *Dyakuyiu.*"

"You'll thank me by resting and getting better." She cranks

down his bed and tucks his covers up under his chin. And then she's headed for the door, squeezing past Bullard, who has come back in. He winks at Taras.

"Wish she'd look at me like that."

"Be happy you got the muffin."

Bullard laughs. Taras feels his lips stretch in a small smile. He can't believe they spoke to each other almost like friends.

CHAPTER 36

When I die, who will care?

Tymko leads Taras into a corridor of ice that gleams deep blue and flashes splinters of sun in their eyes. In the middle of town, by the Brewster Company residence hall, the internees have built an ice palace for the winter carnival. It looks like a military stockade, or maybe the wall around a castle, with corner turrets and the entrance in a central tower. Inside the wall the prisoners have built a maze from great blocks of river ice.

Taras wonders what an ice castle has to do with the war effort. No, that's the wrong question. The real question is, if you have serfs, what can you get them to do for you? He wasn't a serf in the old country, but now he is. But who actually owns him?

The single corridor branches into two. Taras has no idea which way to go, but Tymko leads him to the right and around a sudden doubling back in the path. Chill comes off the ice in waves. His breath makes thin clouds that vanish an instant later. He stares into the heart of an enormous block, trying to find meaning in the things that have happened to him. He feels Tymko watching, like a mother alert for signs her child is tiring.

"Leave me alone here a moment."

Tymko almost protests, but changes his mind and walks off. Taras goes slowly forward until he comes to a dead end, which forces him to backtrack to another branching place. He decides that since before he went right, now he should go left. This soon leads to another dead end. He turns back a second time and sees a passage at right angles to the one he's in. He follows it to a square space in the middle of the maze.

The maze reminds him of his recent life. Wandering down closed passages, taking right or left turns without knowing where they lead. He runs mittened hands over the ice and feels a stab of panic. What if he's lost?

He knows he only feels fear because he's been ill. They wouldn't make a maze people could get lost in for long. He slows the taking in and letting go of his breath.

Who would enjoy this? People for whom life's major questions have already been answered? Being safe, do they like to play at being lost? Taras considers his life in camp as a maze. Is the way out a doorway to something better? Or will it lead to a place where he'll still be lost?

The cold saturates his bones. He needs Tymko to get him out of here. The thought is no sooner formed than his friend's hand touches his arm. At the entrance they find Sergeant Lake, who has arranged this strange treat. Supported by Lake and Tymko, Taras thinks he has enough strength to make it to the bunkhouse.

On Banff Avenue, Indian people called Stoneys have set up *tipis* along the main street. Tymko says the citizens of Banff enjoy having the Stoney people – *Nakodah,* he calls them – on display in the middle of town. For a little while. It makes their own lives more interesting in some way. More colourful. Taras wonders if the *Nakodah* enjoy it.

Lake stops to speak to a family: a man and woman in their early thirties, with their daughter, about fourteen. They wear coats made from white woollen blankets, with wide stripes – bright green, red, yellow and black – along the cuffs and the bottom hem. Their deerskin mittens are decorated with colourful beadwork that reminds Taras of Ukrainian embroidery. Their hair hangs in long braids. They look so neat, so tidy, in their dress and in their way of doing things. Their *tipi*, which the woman and daughter have just finished putting up, has painted animal figures on the outside.

The man has an open, pleasant look. A curious look. His wife smiles a friendly smile, and their daughter has an expression that says she understands her own worth. He thinks of Halya, when they both attended the village school and Halya was best at every subject.

Arthur Lake introduces the family as Sampson and Leah Beaver and their daughter, Frances Louise. Tymko can't seem to take his eyes off the girl. She must remind him of Oksana. Somehow Lake understands that Tymko wishes he had a gift to give her. He reaches into his pocket and pulls out one of Bohdan's carvings, a chickadee perched on a bit of tree branch. He hands it to Tymko, who gives it to the girl. She examines it and smiles. Thanks him. Her parents watch, letting the girl handle things. When it's time for everyone to move on, the woman takes something from the pocket of her blanket coat and gives it to Tymko. It's a beaded flower, a wild rose, worked on a piece of deerhide.

"You sew that on your coat," she says.

"Thank you," Tymko says, "I will." Taras knows he'll do that only when he leaves the camp. In the meantime he'll keep it hidden. Too many things can be taken away in this place.

As he watches the pleasant and friendly Beaver family, Taras feels a sudden certainty that he and Halya will never be together. She has been taken away to a school and married to an Englishman. He will never find her, and even if he did, what would be the use? He takes off the one thing he's managed to keep from his old life, the sun pendant he made in the smithy in Shevchana. He hands it to the girl who reminds him of Halya. She looks worried, not sure if she should take it. He smiles and makes a gesture to say she should put it around her neck.

Leah Beaver looks at Taras. When he nods at her she tells Frances Louise in *Nakodah* that she may put on the pendant. The girl flips back the hood of her coat and places it around her neck. "Thank you," she says in a serious voice.

He nods. He hopes she'll have a happy life.

Taras feels much lighter without the pendant, and calm.

AT THE BEGINNING of April, they start Taras working half days. He doesn't feel ready, but it does help him push away the picture of Viktor in what he imagines as an all-white room, in a white-covered bed, staring out the window at snow. Or the vision of George Luka Budak's bloody death.

He'll be leaving soon, but he doesn't think about it much. He can't stand to feel anything too strongly. He keeps an image in his mind of thick grass in the hills near Spring Creek, touched only by the trails of wild animals.

ONE AFTERNOON near the end of April, Taras is sent back to full-time work with a new gang, cutting brush and trying to dig roots in the Banff recreation grounds. Damn stupid thing to be doing when the ground's still frozen, but he's stopped expecting his orders to make sense. Luckily they're close to camp, so he won't have a long march to and from the work site.

He thinks the guards are going to go easy on him. He sees them talking together, can almost hear their words: "That's the one who got stabbed."

He doesn't know the men in this gang, except for one. God knows why they had to end up together. After an hour or so he finds himself working near Zmiya the snake. He tries to widen the distance between them, although he can't believe even Zmiya would attack a recently wounded man. Yet why does he now move closer again? Taras stops digging.

"Your wound," Zmiya says. "Has it healed?"

Taras has a mind to ignore the question but after a time he says, "It's mainly healed. I can't do heavy work."

He's answered. Some kind of conversation has begun.

"I couldn't believe it when that guy stabbed you."

Being watched by Zmiya is like being watched by a wolf, or a fox. There's always something in the eyes you can't understand.

"Why not?" Taras asks, suddenly angry. "Isn't that what you wanted to do?" He pulls at the root but it won't come out.

"Yes. It is what I wanted to do." Zmiya moves closer, takes hold of the root and pulls with steady force until it comes out of the cold earth.

"You're happy, then." Taras starts in on another root.

"At first I was mad," Zmiya says calmly. "He took away my chance."

"At first." Taras isn't sure why he's bothering to keep this going.

"I thought you were going to die. After a while I saw that wasn't what I wanted." Zmiya's pale, unevenly coloured eyes never waver.

"What did you want?" Now Taras really needs to know. This whole stupid thing has gone on too long.

"To hurt you." The eyes glitter.

"I see. A noble goal." Taras tries to keep his voice even, but he can't disguise his contempt. He goes on digging. But he can tell the snake isn't finished.

"I was afraid you'd die and that I'd made it happen."

"It wasn't you. How could you have made it happen?"

"I hated you," Zmiya says, as if his words are totally reasonable. "I thought he might have caught that from me."

"Oh, for God's sake. Viktor hated me from before. From the old country."

"So did I."

So. This must be what he's been wanting to say. It makes no sense. Taras takes a step toward Zmiya. "You're crazy. I never knew you."

It's loud enough to make a guard look up.

Taras makes several quick jabs in the dirt. Zmiya grabs hold of the root and pulls. Surprisingly, it comes out easily.

The guard has already lost interest.

"I knew you. You took my job." Taras hears anger growing in the man's voice.

"How could I do that? I only had one job outside the village. I got it because I looked after the colonel's horse."

"*Tak,* I heard you tell the story. To your friends."

Taras smells a sourness on the man's breath as if acid works away in his belly.

"Before it was your job, it was mine. I looked after horses in the garrison." Zmiya cuts a root off below the ground and pulls it out. Goes on to the next. "Then they fired me."

"Fired you. Why?"

"One day a horse kicked me while I was braiding her tail. I grabbed a chunk of wood and hit her." He goes on digging. "Krentz saw me."

"He fired you for good reason, then. And you blamed *me?*" Now Taras is angry.

"Normally, I'm very good with horses." Zmiya speaks in a matter-of-fact tone. "But I used to see my father beat our horse at home, and when she kicked me, I didn't think."

"It had nothing to do with me."

"But listen. My job meant everything to me. It got me out of our shithole of a farm. When I lost it, I had to go back. Had to obey my father. And wait for him to die and leave the shithole to me. I couldn't afford to get married. Finally I couldn't stand it, so I left."

Taras tries not to, but he can see it all in front of him. He knows about cruel and bitter men because, again, there's somebody like that in every village.

"And here in Canada?"

"I worked on the railroad. I was doing all right until I got laid off. I had nothing to live on, so they sent me here."

"That's too bad." Taras speaks without much sympathy.

"When I saw you, it was too much. You took my job." Zmiya stands still, one foot on his spade. "Krentz liked you."

Taras remembers a night shortly after he came to camp. "That night at Castle the Germans and the Ukrainians got fighting? I suppose it was you who hit me." He sees from Zmiya's face that he's guessed right.

"Do you still hate me?" Might as well know where things stand.

"Not any more. None of it was your fault."

Fine, Zmiya admits the truth. It doesn't make up for what he's done. "You don't think this makes us friends all of a sudden?"

"Oh no. Just thought I could clear the air a bit. So I can stop carrying this around."

He pulls out a kitchen knife sharpened to a wicked point. Never mind how he got it or how he sharpened it. Being a prisoner can bring out that sort of ingenuity in a person.

Taras remembers the ride in the icy water. Zmiya could stab him right now.

Zmiya makes sure the guard isn't looking, then hurls the knife in a high arc, twisting end to end. It plummets into the trees, flicks against branches, sinks harmlessly into snow.

"I won't bother you again." He waits for some kind of answer, but none comes. "I wish I was more like you. I wish I was a better man."

Taras makes himself answer. "Maybe when you get out of here."

Zmiya shrugs. "Maybe."

Still the snake waits. What does he want now?

Taras plants his spade, raises his right foot. A thought flares in his brain like lightning, and before his foot touches the spade it resolves into certainty.

"It was you, wasn't it?"

"What?" But he knows.

"You killed Budak." Taras sees the shadowy figure, the sudden movement into the trees. He looks into Zmiya's marled eyes. "I saw you by the guardhouse."

Zmiya's eyes blur with tears. "I only wanted to scare him. I wanted him to know, wherever he went I could find him."

"You killed him with that knife." The knife lying in the trees maybe thirty feet away.

"No! The guardhouse door was open. He saw me and he thought I'd come to kill him. He tore his guts out with the straight razor." Pain twists Zmiya's gaunt face. This must be what he sees when he tries to sleep.

"I never planned to kill him."

"You never went for help." Taras feels as if he's stumbled back into the icy maze. This is what he's been trying not to know. "You cut his throat."

"He was going to die anyway. I couldn't let him talk." Zmiya's eyes gleam in the late afternoon light. He seems to want Taras to believe him. "I get sick when I think of it."

Budak is dead and buried, and nothing can help him. He should never have been here. But Zmiya should never have been here either. Is it possible Zmiya wouldn't have hurt anybody if he hadn't been in this place? There's no answer to that question.

Another memory presses itself into Taras's thoughts. "Once, in the bunkhouse, when the heavy snow fell and we couldn't get out...you touched me."

Zmiya seems to grow smaller, to wither in his shell of bone and flesh.

"I could have killed you, but you would never have known why. I saw that was no good."

Taras can't stop the shudder that shakes his body. The air feels colder. He knows he hasn't yet recovered from his wound.

"Don't ever come near me again," he says.

Zmiya shakes his head. "Are you going to say anything?" He doesn't speak in a threatening way, but more as if he just wondered.

"No. It wouldn't help. But when you get out of here..."

"I know." The cat's eyes watching Taras still hold some spark of light. "I suppose it's the last time we'll talk."

Taras nods. The light fades. Zmiya turns away.

"When I die, who will care?"

"I don't know." Taras tries to force his spade into the cold ground. In a moment Zmiya goes back to work. Soon it's dark and the guard calls them to march back to camp.

PART 5

CHAPTER 37

Goodbye Bullshit

May, 1917

THE BUNKHOUSE already looks deserted, bunks stripped to their frames, stoves sitting cold along the central aisle. Men gather their things and stuff them into knapsacks. They wear new summer jackets and tweed caps and have recent haircuts. They look like a bunch of Ukrainian Englishmen, Taras thinks. He and Tymko grab their knapsacks and head for the door. Tymko sings in his deep bass: "Oh, I'll be working on the railroad, all the livelong day..." They're going to Edmonton, where Halya might be, to work as trainmen for the Canadian Pacific Railway. Tymko's done this before, walking the tops of the cars as they're shunted around the yards. He says Taras will learn how to do it in no time.

Outside, the sun seems uncommonly bright. All at once they see what people who aren't prisoners see: a magnificent mountain valley. They have lived in the midst of unfathomable beauty – too cold, too hungry, too sad to notice. Too angry.

Taras remembers Ihor looking for Castle Mountain's spirit. He thinks the mountains are too remote, too pitiless, to notice the troubles of a few hundred men. Maybe they've simply been waiting for the prisoners to go. He used to think that if he got out of this place he'd never go near it again, but maybe he'll come back one day and climb to the clouds.

Myro's pale, serious face glows in the sun. Yuriy counts the hours until he can go back to his farm. Ihor's going to work for his friend, a rancher near Pincher Creek. The fiddle makes a bulge in his knapsack, its neck and scroll sticking out the top.

Sergeant Lake steps forward and takes Taras's hand in his own with sudden, rough warmth. He's been standing near the bunkhouse door, shaking hands with each man as he leaves. He gives Taras an envelope with a small photograph inside: Taras and a group of other prisoners sitting on a ledge in the snow.

Men climb into the back of large trucks with canvas tarpaulins on metal frames over the boxes. They'll be driven to Calgary and sent on trains to their various destinations. The trucks take Taras back to the day the Austrians came to Shevchana. A seed of war planted in every heart. He escaped that war and became a prisoner in Canada. But he's alive.

Tymko pulls him toward the trucks. "Let's get out of here."

Taras takes a last look at the camp. "Goodbye, stinking prison."

Tymko grips his arm. "Not just prison. *Shkola*. Here you became a man, a leader. Like Myroslav, you have now been to university."

"Leader?" says Taras. "Why would I be a leader when we've got you?" Laughing, they climb into the truck.

Andrews, Bullard and a couple of other guards stand watching. "Good luck to you," Andrews calls out and others echo him.

The guards have been in a better mood for weeks as news has come back from the Battle of Vimy Ridge, near Arras in northern France, where Canadian troops have won a tremendous victory. Where before they were parcelled out among the British divisions, the Canadians fought together for the first time at Vimy, under Canadian command. The guards talk of sound battle plans, excellent scouting and effective use of artillery fire to support the infantry. They believe the Canadians have shown up British military thinking as antiquated and inflexible. For the first time they're happy to talk about the progress of the war.

They seem to have found a pride they didn't have before. Life is moving forward. The camp is closing, and many of them now seem to believe internment was a stupid idea.

The prisoners have earned twenty-five cents a day. Taras has spent every cent of his. He imagines all the cigarettes he smoked lined up side by side, covering every inch of the bunkhouse floor. Or a model of Castle Mountain made of piled-up candy bars. Nobody's been able to tell the internees anything about the things the government took from them when they came to camp. Well, he knew from the beginning he'd never see Moses's watch again. He's not sure how he knew; he was so much more innocent then.

The trucks roar to life and some of the guards wave. At first none of the men raises an arm. Then, what the hell, Taras and a few others raise their arms. Someone shouts, "Goodbye, Bullshit!" Moments later the guards are out of sight. As they drive out the camp gate, the men cheer wildly. It's uncomfortable in the back of the trucks, but no one cares. They sing songs about harvest and village maidens.

Taras doesn't join in. It was hard to learn not to hope. He can't start again until he's sure he won't have to come back here. And if there's ever another war, will it all begin again?

ALONE IN THE NEWSPAPER OFFICE over the lunch hour, Halya sits at her desk working on an article about a group of Ukrainian men she discovered almost under her nose in Edmonton. They live in caves dug into the riverbank below the Macdonald Hotel. They take any hourly work that comes along, but there isn't much of that around. Somehow they have survived there through the terrible winter. People in downtown Edmonton call the caves the Galician hotel.

She has no trouble writing articles for the paper. It's what she likes best, and although her style is more personal than Zenon's, Nestor has admitted that she is now Zenon's equal.

A man enters, stooped, unkempt, in dark work clothes. Halya looks puzzled for a second or two, then runs to him.

"Zenon! Thank God!" She holds him close. Feels how his arms and chest have contracted. As if muscles and flesh have fallen toward the bone.

"Halya! My dear, sweet Halya!" His voice is hoarse. He begins to cough and can't stop for a couple of minutes. She pats his back until he's able to bring it under control.

She sees his gaunt face, the shadows under his eyes. She also sees something she couldn't acknowledge before. Zenon loves her. Not just as friend and colleague. He clings to her as if she represents all beauty, all light, all goodness.

She also feels a great affection for him. He's so like her, with his passion for learning, and for reading and writing.

He's known all the time they've worked together that there was someone she loved in the old country and was searching for. That must be why he hasn't spoken before.

What will happen if she tells him that she's finally accepted her father's word that Taras died in the service of the Austrian army?

CHAPTER 38

What good is that to me?

THEIR RENTED ROOM near Edmonton's Strathcona rail yards is big enough for two beds, a small table, a dresser and a couple of chairs. A sink and a small cupboard with cups and plates. Toilet down the hall. The boarding-house grub is plain but there's lots of it. Peas are still overcooked, but you can usually tell what the food you're eating is. And there's more of it. Taras and Tymko spend extra money to buy things the landlady doesn't serve. Apples. Loaves of bread and honey to spread on it.

They've found a fancy store that sells the things the Alpine Club members ate. Their favourites are greengage jam and jars of sardines in olive oil. Gaston Monac sardines. They keep an empty jar on the table to remind them – they're making up for almost two years of eating *pokydky*. The food soothes and strengthens them, takes away a little of the pain. Now and then Taras catches himself laughing and it's like a sudden break in the weather.

They came to Edmonton in early May, and now, in late July, Taras has learned to be a trainman. He moves along the tops of the railcars, sure-footed as a mountain sheep. Almost back to his old strength. What he needs is a few months at the forge, making iron do what he wants.

This Saturday afternoon Taras writes a letter to his parents. His parole will be finished by the end of October and then he can come home. Tymko is out buying newspapers. He buys them constantly, hungry for news of the revolution in Russia, and struggles to keep it all straight in his mind. The Petrograd strike in February, over 200,000 people. The tsar's attempt to break the strike. Mutiny in the Petrograd garrison, and the sailors of Kronstadt.

He should be happy but can't quite settle into it.

He keeps waiting for an unmistakable sign that his dream has come to pass. Power seems to flow to the Bolsheviks: Stalin has been released from prison; Lenin has returned and taken control of the Bolshevik party. They have support from the army, from the workers. Yet the provisional government, with its liberal outlook, clings to power.

Some nights he can barely sleep.

The outside door slams and somebody pelts up the stairs. Tymko bursts in, sets down a couple of bottles of beer and flings a newspaper on the table. *The People's Voice.*

"There! Something Ukrainian!" He sets to opening the beer.

"Government Closing Internment Camps," the headline says. And beneath that: "by Halya Dubrovsky."

"Tymko!" Taras yells. He tries to understand what he's read, but his thoughts spin out of control. It says Halya. His Halya? She works for a newspaper? How is that possible?

It's Saturday. Will the newspaper office be open? What if it's not his Halya?

Tymko gives Taras a small shake to get his attention. Taras shows him Halya's name.

THEY ARRIVE at the newspaper office as Nestor is locking the door. He wears what must be his best suit and a brown felt hat. Looks as if he's in a great hurry.

"Please," Taras says, "I must speak to Halya Dubrovsky."

"Won't be in today." He looks at his watch. "She's getting married." He rushes past them down the steep stairs. "She'll be back on Monday. Try again." And he's gone.

They follow him to a domed church and watch as Nestor runs up the steps.

They wait in the shade of an elm tree. Taras barely breathes. Halya is a popular name among Ukrainians. He tries to imagine a bride who is not *his* Halya.

After what seems a very long time the doors open and it is his Halya, plainly dressed but beautiful in a light grey suit. Her husband looks worn and thin, but his face glows. Halya wears a flowered headdress with long ribbons catching the breeze. At the church door, a few people embrace them. Nestor and his wife. People from the church. A grey-haired lady in a tweed suit and sturdy walking shoes. She wears a necklace that flashes a moment in the sun.

For some reason he can't guess, Halya has given her pendant to this old woman. She was marrying another man and so she gave away the pendant. How could she do it?

And yet, didn't he give his away?

Halya and her husband lead the way to the church hall; they don't notice two men in work clothes under an elm tree.

"She didn't even see me."

Tymko shakes his head. "It must be that her father told her you were dead."

"That's what he'd do, all right." Viktor's nowhere to be seen. Is he still in the asylum? Is this the *Englishman* he said Halya would marry?

"I'm sorry," Tymko says. "But listen. In a few months our contracts will be up. We'll be free."

"Free!" Taras turns on him. "What good is that to me now?" He stares at the tall domes. After a while Tymko takes his arm and leads him away.

For the first time Taras wonders if Halya even knows where Viktor is. If she's here in Edmonton, where's Natalka? What's happening to Viktor's farm?

CHAPTER 39

A place by a lake

November, 1917

THE LONG two-storey frame building sits among poplar trees by a tranquil lake. A tall fence runs around it. A sign points to the boardwalk that leads to the asylum office. This place reminds Taras in some way of the old country. Tall trees; blue sky; high, fleecy clouds running with the wind. Bird calls and the scents of late autumn. A moment of balance between seasons; before winter forces its way in. It has an air of village peace, of nothing too much happening. That peace was an illusion. Maybe this is too.

At the office he asks to see Viktor. A nurse takes him to a sunroom where patients look out large windows to the lawns and the lake. Viktor is there but he doesn't seem to notice the view. The nurse calls his name twice before he turns. He sees Taras, and his face and shoulders slump onto his chest. Tears runnel his cheeks, his body shakes.

The nurse looks worried. Taras is afraid he'll be asked to leave. "Please. He hasn't seen me for some time. Can you leave us alone a little while?" The nurse hesitates, then nods and withdraws to the doorway.

He's told them Viktor is his father. Tymko didn't think he'd be allowed to visit if he told the truth.

Taras sits down beside what has become an old man. When Viktor starts to choke on his tears, Taras reaches forward and touches his hand and Viktor becomes calmer. Reassured, the nurse leaves.

"If you're here about Halya..." he begins in a dull monotone.

"I know, she's married."

"Married?" Viktor looks stunned.

He didn't know?

"Yes. I saw her at the church."

"Did you speak to her?" Viktor looks a little more animated. But still confused.

"No, of course I didn't speak to her." Taras pulls his chair closer. "Didn't you know? You told me she was getting married."

"She didn't marry that one."

There are so many questions, but Taras holds to his purpose in coming. "I want to know now, why do you hate me? What have I ever done to you?"

Viktor looks at Taras with a kind of puzzled longing.

"Why couldn't you let me be with Halya?" Taras says.

"Don't say her name." Viktor weeps again. "I no longer have a daughter."

"Has something happened?" Taras hasn't seen her since her wedding. "She's not dead, is she? Viktor! Is she dead?"

"We don't...speak any more. She doesn't write."

Halya is alive and his heart can beat again. "Why not?"

"She wasn't a good daughter." He doesn't want to continue, but Taras's eyes drill into him. "She wouldn't marry him...that rich fellow. That brick man."

"*Shawcross?* She wouldn't marry Shawcross?"

"She would have had everything she needed. I would have been welcome in their house. It would have been so easy for her." He could have been a big man.

"He wasn't worthy of her. Don't you know that yet?"

Viktor is suddenly angry. "She was still thinking of you!" The anger dies away to bewilderment.

"She's married. How can she be thinking of me?"

Taras sees that Viktor is about to tell the truth. It's as though the words are already formed and working their way, like barbed wire, through his throat. Across his tongue.

"I told her you died." His voice cracks. "In Bosnia."

"Viktor, we loved each other. How could you hurt her that way?"

"I wanted her to marry the Englishman. I thought if she believed you were dead..." Viktor's lips purse. He looks so childish. "Nothing has gone as it should."

Taras makes himself stay patient. "Tell me why you hate me."

Viktor sighs. "Your father stole from me...everything I ever wanted."

"You're crazy. My father doesn't steal."

"I wanted her, but she chose him."

"You wanted to marry my mother?" Is this the big secret no one would tell him?

"Mykola stole my woman and he stole my son. You should have been my son." He speaks as though Taras must see the justice of this. Taras wants to weep at the madness of it.

They sit for a quarter hour or so, companionable almost. Or so it must appear to the nurse, who looks in for a moment. You stupid, stupid man, Taras thinks.

"I'm sorry... Sorry I tried to kill... I was...a crazy man." Viktor takes deep sobs of breath and eventually grows quiet. As if a demon has left him.

"I don't understand why you were sent to the camp."

"That bastard Shawcross. Told the police I was a socialist." He looks amazed that such a thing could happen to him. But resigned, somehow. Or just tired of it all.

"Would you like to go home?"

CHAPTER 40

Such food

ON THE TRAIN RIDE, Viktor doesn't talk. He stares out the window as if wondering where he is. What country. Does he see the rolling hills of grass or some old country scene? Taras takes it a mile at a time, glad for the train's slow, steady movement. He rode a train to flee a country and cross a continent. A train took him to prison. Now a train rocks him home. He hardly dares think "home," but hopes that's what it is. At last Spring Creek comes into sight. He'd forgotten how small it was during the six months he lived in Edmonton, how isolated and undefended. He imagines an invading army bearing down on Spring Creek.

There's no snow, but he sees the quiet, waning look to the land and sky. The hills drawing into themselves, for now, as the light fades. The train pulls into the station and Taras wishes he could have a few more minutes before he has to move into this world.

His friend waits on the platform. As Taras steps down, Moses folds him tightly in his arms. "Thank God," he says. Taras feels a change in Moses and finally takes time to think of what his life might have been in the last two years. Up until now Moses has been someone who helps him, as a family member might. Now they can just be friends.

Viktor has crept down the iron steps and stares at Moses in utter wonder. Taras has told him that his friend will drive him home, and he's told him Moses is a black man, but the reality is more than Viktor can take in. As if he wasn't paying attention one day and life left him behind. Of course, it's been much more than a day.

Taras's parents wait at the farm while he does this last thing for Viktor. All three men are silent as they drive down the main street, everything so different from the day war broke out. They pass the police building where Taras and Viktor once had to report. Viktor doesn't even notice. He seems half asleep.

Schmidt's grocery store is gone. The building is there but it's called McGregor's now. The old green door and the window trim have been painted red.

A grey-faced old man goes down the boardwalk with careful steps and stops by a store window where prices of beef and lamb are displayed. Something familiar about him.

"Jimmy Burns," Moses says. "Gassed at Ypres. By the time they sent him home, he looked like that." The young-old man walks away without going into the store. Taras remembers him standing hip-deep in a hole in the ground, grinning.

"Look over there." Moses points to the brick front of the black-smith shop. The sign reads: "Patterson & Kalyna, Blacksmiths." Torn unwillingly from the old village, his father is once more doing well. He feels the same pride he felt when Mykola stood and talked to the men in the reading hall.

Maybe he will spend some time working at the forge.

An open car approaches on the other side of the street, driven by Ronnie Shawcross. A young woman sits beside him, wearing a navy blue suit and a hat trimmed with ostrich plumes. Ronnie doesn't see them, and that's good. Taras and Moses exchange a glance.

"Poor woman," Taras says. "She must have been desperate." He tries to smile. Thinks of the village jokes about Radoski's wife.

"Taras, listen. I think we're going to get the union. We're meeting Sunday afternoon. Why don't you come?"

"I don't think so. I'm tired. I need to forget all that."

Moses looks disappointed but doesn't press him.

They pass out of town and continue west down a dirt road. Stubble shines red–gold in the late afternoon sun. The air feels so benign and clear that breathing is like drinking spring water. Taras feels himself drawn to this land, even to the loneliness he feels when he looks across the hills or at occasional farmyards sitting along the road or hidden in valleys. This sparseness feels good, though it goes against everything he knew in the old country, with its fields and forests, the compact villages with houses set along a grassy lane.

After about ten miles, Viktor points and Moses stops at a two-storey frame house with a British flag and lace curtains at the windows. Taras remembers searching for Halya and thinking this place couldn't be Viktor's. He helps Viktor out, walks with him to the door. Moses waits in the wagon.

Viktor opens the door. "You see. Things have gone well for me. Very well." He looks miserable, and immensely tired. Taras sees the portrait of the king, the lace tablecloth and a china tea service on the table. Viktor looks at these things with pride, and then bewilderment.

The lace tablecloth now has a linen runner down the centre embroidered with cross–stitch flowers and other Ukrainian motifs. Similar cloths adorn the chairs and the icon in one corner and the portrait of Shevchenko in another. All these things come from their old house in Shevchana, and none of them were on display when he was sent away.

The portrait of the king is almost completely hidden by a hand-worked scarf draped around it. Without a word, Viktor looks to all corners of the room, trying to take it all in.

After a few moments, he nods to himself. He pulls the scarf off the king's portrait and drapes it over a chair. He takes down the portrait and places it on the table. He also takes down a small British flag which he folds and lays on top of the portrait, where he also puts the china tea service. He picks up the portrait, weighted with these objects, and walks out the open front door. Tosses everything into the autumn grass and comes back inside.

Viktor takes down the icon, a gilded likeness of the Madonna, and holds it against his heart. He sobs like a child. "I shouldn't have told her you were dead."

"Stop hating me, Viktor. It's killing you."

Viktor struggles to speak. "I don't hate you any more."

They hear the back door open. Natalka, wearing the English-style dress Viktor bought her, comes in from the garden carrying a sack of cabbages. She stops in the parlour doorway and the sack slips from her fingers. Cabbages roll across the floor like big green heads.

"Taras? Viktor? What's wrong?"

"Don't worry," Taras says. "It's all right with me and Viktor." He should go to her, hold her, but he thinks Viktor needs him to stay close.

At first Natalka doesn't talk. She looks from Taras to Viktor, sees the scarf on the chair, the missing place where the king's portrait hung.

"A letter came," she says. "I got the neighbours to read it for me. They said he was sick and he had to stay in this hospital place. Nobody knew how long." She pauses. "It's been almost a year." She seems amazed, as if this is the first time she's put this fact into words.

"He's better now," Taras says. "He's come home."

Finally Viktor finds his voice. *"Dobre dehn,* Natalka. I hope you've been all right on your own."

She looks a little amazed but then decides it's not too strange: she's seen something like this fellow before; he's similar to the Viktor who sometimes gives people presents.

"Oh, I was afraid at first," she says. "Then, you know, I just went on with my work."

"Dobre. Thank you for looking after the house. And the garden. *Dyakuyiu."*

"Bud laska."

The air between them changes. Viktor's power is gone. He's just a man.

"Of course I couldn't plant all the land."

"You planted a crop?"

"Only about ten acres. But it was a very good crop. Took me many weeks to harvest. The neighbour's been grinding some of it for me. I give him bread. Oh, and the garden was good." She begins picking up the scattered cabbages.

"You did well."

Natalka looks pleased that Viktor has acknowledged her work. Taras sees she's trying to find courage to ask about Halya.

"I saw Halya," he tells her. "I was in Edmonton the day of her wedding. She looked very well."

Natalka cries as she hasn't cried since Halya left. Since the old boar was taken away. Or even on her own in the long winter nights. Taras holds her close and feels a connection to Halya through her.

"If only I could see her. I wanted to write to her but I didn't know how."

"I'll write to her," Viktor says as he falls into an armchair. "At that newspaper."

Taras realizes he can't leave Viktor there. "Come, you need to lie down."

Natalka leads the way to Viktor's room, smoothes the bedcover, closes the window that's been letting the wind in. Taras takes the icon from Viktor's hands and sets it on the dresser. He picks up a woollen blanket draped over a chair and covers Viktor's shoulders.

"Perhaps some water?" Taras asks, and Natalka goes to fetch it.

Viktor sits heavily on the bed. "Can you forgive me?"

"Yes," Taras says, and is amazed to find it's true. He's been through too much to hold onto this any more. "Now rest. We'll talk again." Viktor nods.

"Don't tell Halya I'm alive," Taras goes on. "She's married now. It won't help her to know."

"That's right." Viktor stretches out on the bed. By the time Natalka returns with water, he's asleep. Taras realizes he's desperately thirsty and drinks the water himself.

ON THE RIDE to the farm, Taras answers a few questions for Moses and then grows quiet. The sweep of the land and the golden haze that outlines every blade of grass seem to make human talk unnecessary. He realizes his friend has been lonely without him. From a distance Taras sees his parents' new frame house — only two rooms so far — and a small barn.

Daria and Mykola hold him tight, all of them woven together like the patch of linen left behind on Natalka's loom. Daria pats his cheeks, his hair, his arms. Kisses his face. His father hugs him with a blacksmith's strength. When they let him go, Taras looks at Daria more closely. His mother no longer wears a headscarf. Her dress looks like what women in town wear. Would he even have recognized her on a busy street? His father looks older, but fit.

The house is warmed by a clay *peech* and the Shevchenko portrait hangs on the wall. Also the icon. Daria's embroidered scarves decorate the walls. Two upholstered second-hand chairs finish off the room. A fine meal is keeping warm on the *peech*. Soon they gather at the table and Mykola speaks a prayer of thanks.

Taras hasn't eaten such food for more than two years. *Borshch, kutya,* potato dumplings, garlicky beans, carrots with dill and roasted pork. As his body warms from the familiar foods, he thinks of the knife thrust so close to his heart and lets some of the terror float away. It's not forgotten, just not as close as it was.

He tells Daria and Mykola that he saw Halya marry another man. Knew that she must have believed he was dead. He tells them everything that's happened with Viktor. That Viktor asks their forgiveness. That he loved Daria.

"I should have told you before," Mykola says.

"Never mind," Taras says. "It's all over. I can never see Halya again."

Later, Moses, Mykola and Taras go to the barn. A smokey grey colt stamps its feet in a stall.

"I got him from a man on a ranch near Lillestrom. He traded me for working on his horses' feet." Mykola watches Taras appraise the colt's slender build, the cloud of pale blue-grey spots on his rump. "They call these horses Appaloosas. Indian horses." Taras nods.

"I thought you'd need a horse. He's pretty raw for a three-year-old and he won't be an easy one to train, but maybe you can do something with him."

Taras strokes the horse's neck and feels his face and body relax. He talks to the colt in the easy way he has and picks up a home-made bridle of braided leather with a leather thong for a bit. With more touching and talking, he gets the colt to accept the bridle, although he thinks for a moment it's going to bite him. Taras lifts a worn saddle Mykola got from Kupiak and sets it on the colt's back. The colt snorts and kicks at the stall.

"Easy boy, easy Smoke." He doesn't know what they've been calling the horse, but Smoke feels right. He pats the horse's neck and flanks and calmly tightens the cinch. Leads him outside and mounts. The colt rears and sidesteps, almost throws him. Taras keeps talking and urges him forward. Lets the horse feel the pressure of his legs. "It's okay, Smoke. We're going to have a ride, that's all. Well, I'll be the one riding, but you'll be all right."

Taras takes Smoke up the big hill behind the house and away across the hills, every step a conversation about whether the ride will continue and on whose terms. Taras decides to go where the horse wants to go, at the speed the horse wants to go – a roaring gallop. Smoke takes him into hills covered in woolly tufts of grass. Wind slips past, smelling of grass and sage. He's never had a ride like this.

After a while Smoke slows to a walk and Taras is able to turn him for home and coax him into an easy trot.

At the top of the hill above the house, he dismounts. Smoke is still restless, pulling against the reins. Again, Taras examines his colour and conformation. Smoke is like the horse he saw that day in the old country when he went to deliver the *pahn's* stallion. It must have been a waking dream, because there were no wild horses near Shevchana. No Appaloosas.

He thinks he and the horse have things to learn from one another.

CHAPTER 41

The union man

WALKING TO MOSES'S place on Sunday, after all, Taras sees men from the brick plant headed the same way. They meet at the door as if instinct has carried them to this house upon a signal no one else can hear. Taras thinks of soldiers marching in formation. These men come from many directions, each on his own path.

Taras reaches the open door at the same moment as Frank Elder and Frank shakes his hand as they go in. In a few minutes about thirty men have crowded into the room. They sit on benches, the floor and even the *peech*. Taras knows at least half of them. Some of the new men from Regina talk to Moses in Ukrainian. So does Rudy Brandt, his old foreman.

Moses stands under Shevchenko's portrait and waits for quiet. "We tried this a few years ago and the boss broke us. We're stronger now."

He turns to a man leaning against the wall. "Like I promised, I went to Moose Jaw to ask the union people to find us an organizer. This is Cecil Coulter, and he wants to help us."

Coulter is a tall, brown-haired man in his forties, wearing a worn grey suit and old but superbly polished black shoes. The men look unsure. This guy might be too old to stand up for them in a hard fight.

"Isn't he a little old?" Taras mutters to Frank Elder.

"Don't underestimate him," Frank says softly.

Coulter gets up and stands near the *peech*. "I'm happy to be here," he says. "And proud to meet a group of men who want to work together. Who want to exercise their rights. Because, yes, we are all taking part in a lawful meeting. In this province you have the right to form a union and no boss can prevent it." When he speaks, he doesn't look all that old.

There's a collective drawing in of breath. Everybody knows. This is it.

"I think we're all resolved here," Frank says, "but we're not sure what we have to do next. We're afraid Shawcross will show up with the cops again." A few people look at Taras. "We need to know how we can make ourselves stronger."

Cecil nods. "There are rules for starting a union and there's no question you can satisfy those rules. The economy's strong, the plant's in great shape. Shawcross can't pull something like that again. For one thing, too many people would know. I can promise you that."

Cecil speaks with feeling, with no empty posturing, no false bravado. The men like what he says. They look tense but determined, in this Ukrainian room under a poet's gaze.

"This is like our first meeting in some ways, though," Frank Elder says. "Taras was here then too. What do you say, Taras?"

Taras thinks of his days at Shawcross Construction. Rudy Brandt teaching him to lay bricks. Looking after the most amazing horses he'd ever seen. Jimmy Burns, who'll never get to join a union. And Dan Stover.

"That first meeting, I was a boy, I didn't know anything. You all know what happened to me after that meeting. Two years in a stinking internment camp. And what have I learned? It's no use to say you have freedom if you can't live it."

"Hear, hear," says Frank.

"You have to stick up for yourself. It's natural to be afraid, but you don't have to stand alone." *Dobre*. This time he got to say something sensible.

The men give him a cheer. Ask what they have to do to set up a union, how it can be managed. And then, "All in favour of the union?" Moses asks. Every man raises his hand.

They pour outside, shaking each other's hands.

Taras doesn't know why he looks up the hill at that moment. He sees Shawcross on Brigadier waving his arm in a signal to advance. Then over the hill's crest, egged on but not led by Stover, a bunch of toughs, about forty of them, come running.

Well, they always knew there could be trouble. Just not this soon.

"This is it, boys!" Cecil Coulter peels off his suit coat and unbuttons his shirt cuffs. "They're drunk!" he shouts. "The bastards are drunk! See that red-faced hooligan at the front? That one's mine."

A diamond willow staff Moses has been working on is propped up against his house. He picks it up and holds it out in front of him, a barrier that says, They shall not pass.

Cecil steps forward to meet the hooligan, who's well over six feet tall and must weigh at least 250 pounds. He can't lay a finger on Cecil. He can't even *find* Cecil, who dances around a half step ahead of him, peppering the goon with punches to the nose until he goes down spurting blood and barely conscious. A cheer goes up from the workers who see it. Who'd have guessed the union guy was a trained boxer?

As the goon lies on the ground, Cecil spots the brass knuckles he was wearing and calmly steps on the fellow's fingers.

Taras strikes out at the pack as if he's getting even for all the rotten things that have happened to him. Six months of good eating have given him back his strength; he's light on his feet from walking the rail cars; and he's never been so angry. A short, stocky bruiser with black hair that sticks out like porcupine quills is suddenly in front of him.

"Come on, you bastard," he yells. "Come on and fight."

He lurches forward and swings as hard as he can, but Taras steps sideways. He only hits the guy once, in the jaw, but it's enough.

Moses wields his staff against the surging bodies. One of them might have a broken arm, the way he's squealing.

And then really close, almost in Taras's ear, a voice screams, "Hunkie bastard!"

It's Stover with a poplar branch he must have found on the hill and before Taras can move, Stover whacks him across the back.

Moses knocks it out of his hand with the staff and, while Stover's off balance, Taras lands a heavy punch to the jaw and knocks him unconscious.

"Hunkie bastard yourself!" he says. He catches Moses's eye. It sounds so ridiculous he almost laughs.

Moses wades into the fight, the willow staff whirling.

The moment Shawcross sees his stooge fall, he digs his heels into Brigadier's sides and gallops straight at Taras.

At the last moment Taras dodges. As the horse passes, he grabs Shawcross's leg and jerks him from the saddle. His old boss shoots into the air and floats toward the ground. Lands with a thump that knocks the air out of his lungs and stares at the sky, mouth agape.

Brigadier keeps going.

The fight boils on around them. Taras sees flashes of Cecil Coulter bouncing around, picking his victims. A guy the size of a small tree falls. Frank Elder yells furiously as he kicks a thug in the ankle, and Rudy Brandt gives another one a knee to the stomach. The plant workers are normally peaceable men who wouldn't hit anybody, but now they feel no guilt about fighting dirty. They didn't start this and they're outnumbered.

Shawcross staggers to his feet. Yells, "Goddamned foreigner!" He picks up Stover's branch and swings it at Taras's head.

Taras grabs the branch, wrests it away and breaks it over his knee. Shawcross throws himself at Taras, but he really shouldn't try it, because Taras hasn't just fallen from a horse and had the wind knocked out of him.

Shawcross's right fist flies at him, but Taras moves back and the blow meets only air. Before he can set up again, Taras hits him twice, three times, and sees Ronnie's surprise, and then his fury. He throws punch after punch, but Taras ducks some and blocks the rest with his forearm. More or less at will, Taras lands solid punches, until Ronnie's gasping for breath. Spit dribbles down his chin, blood seeps from a cut on his forehead.

Taras knocks him down onto the dry grass. Sits on his chest, pinning his arms.

"Never get in a fist fight with a blacksmith," he says as Shawcross struggles. "Stop all this right now."

Shawcross sees he can't do anything more and lets his body go limp. Taras gets off him and helps him to his feet. The fight now has the feeling of a mechanism unwinding.

"Get out of here! All of you!" Taras yells at the toughs. He keeps a hand on Shawcross's arm.

The toughs see Shawcross and step back from the brawl; wait for some signal. Shawcross nods.

Taras turns to the workers.

"Mr. Shawcross agrees to the union," he calls out. Again the boss manages a slight nod and the workers cheer. The rowdies go back the way they came, helping their wounded.

"You can have your union. But you'll never have Halya." Something of the spoiled, sulky boy creeps back into Shawcross's face. "She thinks you're dead."

"Yeah, I know all about it. Save your breath for the walk home." Brigadier is nowhere to be seen. The horse has better sense than its owner.

"Viktor will never tell you where she is." Nothing wrong with Ronnie that a little spite won't set right.

"Look, try to get it straight. I don't care what you think about anything." Taras feels a growing willingness to hit Ronnie some more and Ronnie sees it.

Shawcross turns to Stover, lying flat on the ground trying to work out what's happened. Shawcross helps his man to his feet and they walk away. Now they'll have to drive the rowdies back to Regina or wherever Stover found them.

The workers cheer.

Cecil Coulter, his white shirt torn but his face untouched, grins as he pumps Taras's hand. "Well done, brother."

Moses embraces Taras. Nobody's fooled. Life doesn't usually work like this. A black man and a hunkie know how seldom things go their way, but it's a sweet victory.

Taras goes into the house and sits by the *peech*. Waits for the excitement outside to fade and the men from the plant to leave. At last it's quiet and Moses comes in and puts the kettle on for tea.

Taras's right hand aches; the skin over the knuckles is torn. But he's done what had to be done. He can go back to breaking land for his parents and maybe he'll help at the smithy. Some day he'll want to do other things, but for now this is enough.

He knows he won't be able to stop thinking about Halya, but he won't try to see her. She has a new life, one he hopes makes her happy.

PART 6

CHAPTER 42

The bear or the monkey

October, 1918

TARAS AND MOSES walk up the hill behind the Kalyna house after Sunday supper. Smoke grazes beside Batko's gelding in a new paddock behind the barn. It's almost a year since Taras came home after his parole in Edmonton, and there's no snow; but the air has the bite of winter.

"I've helped Batko break enough land to prove up," Taras says. "I'm going back to Edmonton for a while."

"Edmonton. Where Halya is."

"I won't try to see her." But he avoids looking at Moses. "Tymko's written. He's not well."

"So you'll go, then."

Taras knows that Moses wants him to stay. That there's nobody else he feels so at ease with.

"Yeah. In a week or so. I'll see Tymko first. If I decide to stay for a while, I think the railroad will take me back."

"Your parents —?"

"I've told them. Can you come out here sometimes? Take Smoke for a run?"

"Sure. I'll come." Moses smiles a little. "I'll take Smoke out *if* he'll let me."

"Thanks."

"I better get home before it's dark, get an early night." There's a trace of sadness in his voice. He missed Taras during the two and a half years he was away. "I always have more trouble waking up in the morning when the light starts to go."

"I'll come back, you know," Taras says. "I just have to do this first." They walk down the hill, stopping at the paddock so Moses can give Smoke some oats.

"I'm thinking of making a trip myself," Moses says. "We get a week's holiday now, and Shawcross is letting me take an extra week without pay, so I wrote to my aunt and uncle in Pennsylvania, and they asked me to come."

Taras remembers Tymko telling them that some day everyone would have holidays.

"How will you go? It's a long way."

"Not so long on the train. I can get on at Moose Jaw and it'll take me most of the way. I can sleep a lot." He almost leaves it at that but decides to go on. "I don't know if they'll recognize me after such a long time. But I need to see some people who look like me."

"Have a good journey," Taras says. "My brother."

TARAS WALKS up to a two-storey boarding house, its shiplap weathered and needing paint. He knocks on the door and a brisk middle-aged woman in a brown print dress opens it, hears what he wants and points up the dark stairs. Taras takes them two at a time, then hesitates a moment before he knocks. A husky voice tells him to come in. In a moment he knows what Tymko didn't say in his letters.

He sits in a battered easy chair, a plaid blanket over his lower body, his right leg resting on a footstool. He has no right foot, only a stump in a tied-off sock.

Myroslav sits near him on the bed in the small, dark room lit by a single overhead bulb.

"So you're here," Tymko says with a lift of his eyebrows. "There's a chair by the dresser."

Taras makes no move. "What's happened to you? Why didn't you tell me?"

"I was walking a boxcar in the yards. I fell when I tried to jump to the next one." Tymko tries to make it sound matter-of-fact.

"Fell?" Taras can't believe this. Tymko was always so sure-footed. "How?"

Tymko grimaces, leaves the answer to Myro. "Another string of cars came up from behind. They shouldn't have been on that track —"

"I fell," Tymko interrupts. "Happens all the time."

"They bumped into Tymko's string. Just hard enough to knock him sideways."

"A wheel ran over my foot." Tymko gestures just beyond the stump. "My one and only perfect, beautiful, misunderstood right foot."

Taras gets the chair and pulls it near to Tymko. "How was it misunderstood?"

"I never understood how much I needed it." Tymko's laugh booms out for a moment and turns to stifled sobs. "I've begged its pardon a thousand times since. I don't hear much back."

"I guess not. How do you get by?" Taras tries to be matter-of-fact too.

"The railroad has given me a small pension. Enough to live in this place and pay the landlady to feed me. So that's that. But what kind of greeting is this? Give me a hug, Taras. Give the professor a hug. Where are your manners?"

Taras leans over and hugs Tymko. Then Myro. For a few minutes everybody's crying. Taras pulls a thin flask out of his coat pocket, finds three glasses in a cupboard and pours a generous shot of whiskey into each. What a change from potato wine in the laundry shack.

"Don't let Mrs. Plaskett see that." Tymko takes a deep drink and has to pound his chest when he starts to cough and wheeze.

"Sorry. I haven't got used to drinking since they had us locked up all that time." Taras isn't fooled. Tymko's lungs haven't really recovered since he was dragged in the river.

Tymko always used to say, "The capitalist system will find some way to get you." He sits in the scruffy chair amply vindicated.

Clears his throat. "Don't worry. I'm oh-kay, as the boys say down at the yard. Ohhhh-kay!"

Taras sees that Tymko doesn't want to talk about it any more. He turns to Myro. "Professor. Have you found a job worthy of your talents?"

"I have. I teach little kids arithmetic. Just like before. I try to get them to see how easy it is. How much it's going to help them."

"And do they agree that it's easy? And helpful?" Taras hasn't had the chance to tease Myro for a long time now.

"Not always. But what do they know? They're kids."

Everyone laughs. Myro, in tweed pants and a dark jacket looks very respectable, only still too thin, as if his body is holding itself in readiness in case it has to go back to grubbing brush on a wretched diet.

"Myro, if these kids can learn at all, you will teach them." Tymko looks at Myro as if he's his best, smartest son. "The angels would stop to listen."

"I wonder," Taras says, "do the angels know arithmetic?"

"Good question," Tymko says. "Since angels were never people, maybe not."

"They were never people?" Taras realizes he hasn't given angels much thought.

"I don't think so," Tymko says. "I think they were always up there with God. Isn't that right, Professor?"

"To the best of my knowledge," Myro says, "angels were never people. But they know all kinds of things, so maybe that includes arithmetic."

"You're right," Tymko says. "They probably have an instinctive understanding of arithmetic. And socialism."

He smiles sadly. After a year and a half of reading about the revolution in Russia, he's not sure where it's taking people. In fact, he's not sure it's actually begun. The real revolution.

Taras remembers his own questions. What if it doesn't turn out the way you think? How do you make sure it's more than just a bunch of people being killed?

He tries not to notice Tymko's pasty colour, lank hair, diminished mass. Before, he could lift you in the air and spin you around.

"When I'm feeling better, I can maybe get a wooden foot. I'll be able to walk a bit and they'll try to find some job I can do. I can be one of the old buggers who sets out the signals and takes them down again when the train passes."

Taras can't imagine Tymko doing this.

"I'll have time between trains to tell the other old buggers about socialism. We can start the Edmonton Old Buggers Radical Socialist League."

"And the old buggers shall lead them," Myro says.

"Revolution can't be far away when that happens," Taras adds.

"That's right, boys. I see I've taught you well."

"I guess you have," Myro says. "Professor." They laugh, but the laughs are getting thinner.

"Tell me about Shevchenko in that army camp he was in," Tymko asks. "When he was in exile."

"You don't want to hear that now. It's a bit gloomy."

"I do want to hear it. *Because* it's gloomy. It helps me feel better."

"All right. Where to begin? Well, he spent almost ten years in exile, as you know. As ever, he was in trouble because he wasn't careful enough about what he said. His ideas were an offence to the tsar and his family. And remember, the tsar's family had once subscribed to the project to free Shevchenko from serfdom. They expected gratitude and found only revolutionary ideas of Ukrainian nationhood. Even though many of the Russian nobility were westernized and full of liberal ideas, you could only push so far."

Tymko sips whiskey, sighs with pleasure. This is the Myro he loves.

"So it was that when the Brotherhood of Saints Cyril and Methodius fell, he fell with them, and he fell harder because he was a better choice of scapegoat, being a former peasant without an influential family. And because they'd wanted to get him for a long time. And because the tsar never forgave him. It was a complex system of imperial control, but at the centre was a real person, the tsar, and he had the means to punish a former serf for his free-thinking ways."

Tymko settles back in his chair, nods his agreement.

"Our Taras never surrendered his spirit, but there were many terrible times for him. As a writer and artist he was true to his vision – he painted what he saw, and he saw with Ukrainian eyes. As a Ukrainian patriot. And that led to his persecution. He had tried to live the life he believed in, of personal liberty and freedom of expression. But he was essentially a poor man, dependent on others. Being only a freed serf, he didn't have the safety of wealth and position so many of his friends had."

In the camp, Taras remembers, not even the guards had freedom of expression. They had to pretend to believe in what the government said they were doing. Many of them did believe.

"Shevchenko lived his last months, a time when he was already very ill, in hope of hearing the tsar's proclamation of the end of serfdom. Everyone knew it was imminent, but he died in February, 1861, before it took place. I know there must have been times when he sometimes lost hope. I have imagined the disillusion and pain that must sometimes have beset him.

I TRY to understand how my life has gone. How I have ended up in this place.

If I had not left the countryside, had not escaped serfdom, what could I have done? Next to nothing. But I did escape, and it was like a miracle. I met the most illustrious, the most generous people of my time and joined in their conversations. I wrote poems and stories, and created paintings and engravings that will speak for me when I'm gone.

I have been truly loved by many. But I was not one of these wealthy people. Not even among the Ukrainian nobles. I needed their patronage. Without time and enough to eat, you cannot write poems and paint pictures. I needed them to be generous with what they could spare from their comfortable lives.

I think I was their dancing bear. Their performing monkey. The child who sometimes does something unexpectedly clever. The thing about the bear or the monkey or the child is not only that they may perform well, but that you don't expect them to be able to do it at all.

A bear on its hind legs makes an amusing parody of a man. A monkey can look into your eyes as if it knew your heart. It pleases you to cosset and reward that monkey. But it is still a monkey.

Unlike the bear or the monkey, I knew what they were doing, somewhere in my mind where I tried not to dwell, because I needed them.

Or am I wrong? Do the dancing bear and the frisking monkey also understand what's happening to them? Are they simply awaiting the right moment for revenge?

Perhaps I should be proud to have made such an influential enemy. If the tsar hates me, surely that's my highest recommendation. I made him almost angry enough to have me killed. But I was only exiled. And during that exile, I have been reviled and shunned and starved of joy. Forbidden to write or paint or sketch.

I have also been befriended by officers and their families. No, I don't forget the commandant's wife and our shimmering walks through the arid hills. I have gone on expeditions and been given real employment: recording scientific progress through my drawings. People have taken risks to let me work, for even at this great distance from Moscow and Petersburg, the tsar owns vicious curs who will sooner or later growl in his ear.

So here I am. Peasant. Serf. Freeman. Artist. Defender of ideas. And I have made some difference. The most powerful man in the empire hates me and wishes not to kill me but to destroy what makes me human. Surely I'm strong enough to prevent that. The tsar has many concerns, duties, entertainments in his day. He doesn't have the time to hate me with perfection or nuance. He sees my talent and wishes to destroy it. Very well, but I have time to think and to resist. Will people remember that some day? Will they consider it even a little bit brave?

It can't only be my friends – and even they sometimes can't resist patronizing me. Oh, they don't mean it, really, but they think, If only Taras could behave more prudently, if only he could restrain his talk of Ukrainian independence. If only he could concentrate on those objectives which might be achieved. If only he could hang onto money. If only he could moderate his singing, dancing, shouting, drinking and declaiming of poetry. Well, perhaps not entirely. He's great fun to be with. But he doesn't know how to take care of himself. Doesn't know how to look about him.

I do, though, too well. Ever since Englehardt had me beaten because I took his painting and copied it. I don't say Englehardt beat me, perhaps I could understand that he might do so in a flare of rage. No, he had me beaten, by others. I don't know why it didn't break my spirit. I suppose that even then I was able to escape into a world of my own imagining. A world where it meant something to be a man.

"ENOUGH," Tymko says, suddenly weary. "That's enough for one day. Thank you, Professor."

"I told you it was a sad time," Myro says. "But we do remember him. We'll never forget if I can help it."

"He was a glimpse of what we could be without our chains," Tymko says.

"Man was born free and is everywhere in chains," Myro says.

"Who said that?" Taras asks.

"I don't know any more," Tymko admits.

"A French philosopher," Myro says. "I forget the name."

Tymko looks very tired. "Hide the whiskey now," he says. "Mrs. Plaskett will be bringing my supper any minute and she hates liquor. The clothes cupboard will do."

Taras hides the whiskey and rinses out the glasses in the small corner sink, dries them and puts them away in the cupboard. Myro helps Tymko sit up straighter.

The landlady taps at the door and enters without waiting for an answer. She leaves a large tray with a dish of boiled beef and beans and a pot of hot tea with three cups. When Tymko begins to eat, Taras and Myro see how weak he's grown.

Taras is relieved to find that Tymko can make it to the toilet down the hall on his own, using crutches. When he comes back, Myro settles him in bed, propped up with pillows.

"Hey," Tymko says, "what're you looking at? I'm not dead yet."

"Of course not. Nobody said that." Taras realizes he should've just laughed it off.

"Teach me some arithmetic, Professor. I need to figure out how long I've got."

"You don't need arithmetic. You need cheering up. Taras, tell us how your family is. And how Moses the black Ukrainian is faring."

Tymko's eyes brighten during the telling, but soon his eyelids droop and he falls asleep. They tuck in his blankets, turn out the lights and creep from the room. At the bottom of the stairs, they meet Mrs. Plaskett and she watches them out the door. Taras hears a tiny sniff and is sure she smells the whiskey. When they're almost out of earshot, they hear her voice from the dim hallway before she closes the door.

"Come again. He's glad for a bit of company."

"We'll do that," Myro calls back. "Thank you."

Myro insists Taras come home with him. His suite is small but very tidy and it has two bookcases full of worn books, some in English and some in Ukrainian. Taras leafs through them and Myro makes scrambled eggs and toast, taken with more cups of tea. Afterwards Taras feels tired to his bones. Myro makes a bed for him out of lumpy sofa cushions, but the room is warm and Taras is with a friend, who sleeps just beyond the doorway in a room barely large enough to hold the single bed and dresser.

Taras has known Myro as a serious, trustworthy person without realizing, until now, how rare that is. Without Myro and Tymko, and Yuriy and Ihor, and Bohdan, how could he have endured the camp? In the old country only Ruslan was as close to him. But he and Ruslan were only boys. In Canada he's known the friendship of men.

CHAPTER 43

Zenon's story

October, 1918

ZENON, Nestor and Halya are at work in the newspaper office, drinking coffee from an enamelled pot keeping warm on a hotplate. They've just finished proofreading the November edition and sent it to the printer. Halya's contribution was an article on Canadian internment camps. Not the kind of piece she could be arrested for, at least they hope not, but quietly describing and questioning the entire project.

Zenon and Nestor are using the slight lull to go through old files, getting them in chronological order, chucking out duplicate copies of some old issues. Ordering the files is easier now than it used to be, because when Zenon was arrested, the government seized huge swathes of material, boxes and boxes of it, and most of it never came back.

Halya is working on a story they can't publish. Not yet, anyway. As Joel Greenberg said after the police came for Zenon, this isn't a country where you can say what you want.

The story she's writing is Zenon's story, about not only his arrest and imprisonment, but starting back in his childhood. She works away at it whenever there's a bit of time. His family were farmers near Vegreville, Alberta, and when Zenon contracted tuberculosis at the age of four, there wasn't much the local doctor could do for him. Eventually he got better, but the bacillus had by then worked its way into his bones and given him one leg that was shorter than the other. Not the best thing for a farm boy, but it didn't really hinder him.

He went to a small country school, but one with an extraordinary teacher, a man who spoke Ukrainian and English with great fluency and made sure his students did the same. In those days most people thought that finishing elementary school was more than adequate for a farmer's son, but Mr. Dubnyk didn't think that way. And by the time he'd finished grade eight, Zenon didn't think that way either.

He had to spend most of his day doing chores on the farm, especially during harvest, but there was less to do in winter. Afternoons, and in the evenings by the light of a coal oil lamp, he worked his way through high school by correspondence. Mr. Dubnyk would come over once or twice a week to help him with his homework, but mostly Zenon breezed through everything until grade eleven, when Mr. Dubnyk was very useful in explaining Algebra.

He also brought books. Halya was amazed to learn that Zenon had read the same Dickens novels Miss Greeley had lent her. Zenon is the second person she's been able to talk with about Dickens, and it's like being back in school; a really good school.

This is the moment Halya has written up to. The next part will be about how he managed to work his way through university and how, after writing for the local paper in Vegreville, he met Nestor and came to work for him.

She's read through everything she's written a couple of times this morning, but she's having trouble concentrating. A headache started just after breakfast and it's getting worse. She can see the letters on the page, recognizes the words they make up, but sentences are trying to crawl away across the page. Pages are blurring.

Reaching for a cup of tea, Halya misses the handle and spills tea over her tidy stack of papers. She groans and searches in her pockets for a hankie. Zenon looks up, puzzled. Halya doesn't spill things. He comes over to her desk and sees her unfocused eyes. He feels her forehead and is shocked at the heat. Nestor notices and comes over. He and Nestor look at each other and nod.

"What is it?" Halya says a little crossly. "I'm fine. I'm nearly finished this part. I'm..." She looks puzzled. I'm what? she seems to be thinking.

Zenon grabs Halya's coat and Nestor telephones for a taxi. As soon as Halya and Zenon are out the door, he calls a doctor he knows.

Zenon and Nestor have heard a rumour that Spanish flu has appeared in Edmonton, travelling up the rail line from Calgary. If it gets bad, there could be hundreds of people affected, maybe thousands, and many of them could die. They're dying in Calgary, where no one goes out much if they can help it. Schools are closed, and theatres, even churches.

By the time Zenon has settled her into bed in their one-room suite, Halya can't even answer his questions. He brings water she can't drink and bathes her forehead with cloths that he's soaked in cool water and wrung out. Her body is blazing hot, as if she has a small furnace inside her.

If only there were something useful he could do. If only she'd open her eyes.

The doctor arrives two hours later. As soon as he steps into the room, he sees Halya on the bed and pulls a cotton mask from his pocket. When Zenon sees him put it on, he feels terror pushing aside the common sense he always tries to live by.

The doctor takes Halya's pulse and listens to her chest. Wherever he touches her, she moans but doesn't seem to know she's doing it. Zenon watches his every move, as if this will tell him what to do for her. The doctor is a middle-aged man named Houghton. Zenon can't say it right because the letters don't match the sound. It's hard not being able to say it. The serious professional person Zenon's made himself into is reduced to a poor immigrant who can't speak properly.

"Is it the Spanish flu, doctor?" he asks.

The doctor moves away from the bed. "Yes, I'm afraid it is. She must stay in bed and drink lots of water." His voice is muffled but the meaning is clear.

How could he and Nestor have been so stupid? They should have closed the paper down as soon as they heard the rumours. Who cares about a newspaper at a time like this?

"Will she be all right?" Zenon knows how lame his words sound, but he has to ask.

"I can't answer that," the doctor says gently. "Try to bring the fever down. Bathe her with cloths wrung out in cool water."

"I've been doing that already." Zenon feels panic in his chest and throat, a thick, stupid feeling in his head. He sees the doctor won't stay much longer. He has to learn everything he can. "Is that all I can do?"

"I'm afraid so. Oh, and wear this." He hands Zenon a mask.

Zenon holds the mask as if he doesn't understand what it is. "I feel helpless."

"I know," the doctor says.

ZENON SITS by Halya all evening and long into the night, the curtains open to the light from the streetlamps. It paints exaggerated shapes on the walls, on the bed. In the shadows he feels older, weaker. He came out of prison starved and sickly. The thought of her helped keep him going then; what will happen if he loses her?

He strokes her hair, her cheek. Keeps trying to get her to drink water. He has to dribble it into her mouth a few drops at a time.

"It's all right, darling. It's all right." He has to say it, but knows it isn't so.

He keeps applying the wet cloths. Simple things are hard to do. He can't think for the fear in him. Tries to control it by talking to her.

"Halya, darling, please be well. You can't know how much I need you." He wonders if she can possibly hear him, from some place deep inside her fever. "I love the way you look at me, with that tough little smile. When you're going to say something sarcastic about the government. I love the colour of your eyes. Your hair. You've made me so happy."

He takes her hand and feels fresh terror at its heat. She's delirious, moaning or whimpering with pain.

He would pray, but he isn't a believer. Rationality has ruled his life. He wonders what he can do to help her, to make her fight the disease. Wonders how to be rational when everything is suddenly irrational.

His parents are dead. Halya and Nestor are the people he cares for.

"Halya, *liubov,* please listen. You are my darling, my wife, my truest friend. You saved me when I came back from prison. I don't know how I could have survived without you." He needs her to know these things.

Needs her to know she has to come back.

She doesn't answer, but he begins to think she seems calmer, quieter. When this goes on for an hour or so, he allows himself to lie down beside her, takes her hand and absorbs its heat into his own. And falls into sleep.

CHAPTER 44

Pampushkas

SUNSHINE STREAMS in the window. Halya doesn't want to wake up but there's a noise and it's been getting louder. Not a constant noise. It comes and goes, but there's never time to fall back to sleep in between. No choice but to swim up into the light. She realizes her fever's gone down. She turns to look at Zenon, lying beside her – sweat-soaked, eyes shut. The noise is his breathing, it makes a hoarse rattle each time he breathes out.

"Zenon!" His eyes open but he seems not to see her. She's never felt such terror. She knows it's him, but already he's gone somewhere far away from her. She remembers that he was looking after her. She thinks she remembers a doctor.

Now he's much sicker than she was.

"Cold...so cold," he murmurs. But his skin burns. He coughs a sudden spate of hard, wet coughs and his chest shakes with their force. She rummages in a drawer for a handkerchief. When she holds it to his mouth, bright blood stains the cloth.

Halya has no strength, but she has to do something. Although she doesn't want to move, she forces herself to dress, her hands shaking on the buttons of her blouse. She makes herself go out the door and down the steep stairs, light-headed and clinging to the rail.

At the nearby grocery store, they let her use the telephone to call Nestor. After that she makes it home, gasping for breath and struggles up the steep stairs. Her legs feel as if the bones have gone soft. As if they've been taken out and boiled a while, then put back again.

Zenon's hoarse breathing, his unknowing face, are just the same. She tries to see the face with eyes open, his wide, generous mouth smiling at her, but sees only this mask. She begins the business of wringing out wet cloths and applying them to Zenon's forehead. There's no sign he knows she's doing it.

Halya feels desperately tired, but she can't sleep, can't let her guard down. She has to bring Zenon back from the place he's gone to. In the back of her mind she hears his voice, talking to her when she was lost in fever, calling her back.

She takes his hand in hers and talks to him about his kindness, his patience, his bright mind, his warm spirit. She praises his hands, his eyes, his smile. She bends over and kisses his cheeks, his forehead, and finally his lips. Wonders, will he remember any of it when he's better?

NESTOR ARRIVES and finds Zenon still unconscious, except when he wakes for a moment and complains of cold or has another bout of coughing. Then he asks in an injured tone why no one is helping him get warm. Nestor fills the kettle and boils water for tea, makes Halya drink some. He's called the doctor and been told not to expect him for several hours because of the sudden flood of influenza cases in the city.

Halya continues to bathe Zenon's face, or trickle water into his mouth, but he never seems to get any cooler. He has a fit of coughing so fierce it raises him from the bed and he spews blood all over the bedcover. She changes the cover. Between these spells the dreadful breathing goes on and on. Once it seems to stop altogether and then there's a small catch in his throat and he breathes again. His lips are turning pale blue. She tries not to see it.

She hadn't known the disease could strike so swiftly and so hard. Where, where is the doctor?

Around suppertime Nestor makes sandwiches and tries to get

Halya to eat, but she won't. She puts towels around Zenon's head and shoulders, and when they get too bloody she rinses them and wrings them out.

Zenon's skin is now stained blue. His tongue, when she tries to give him water, is brown. Nestor, who's been reading about influenza, says this is caused by lack of oxygen.

It's so unbelievable that Halya thinks she must be going crazy. *Do something!* she wants to scream. *Help him!* But what can Nestor do?

She doesn't know how she's hanging on, and yet if she weren't suffering too, maybe it would be even worse. Since she's so ill herself, she simply does what she has to.

Her own fever doesn't prevent her from thinking what might happen. But it blurs everything, makes it both real and unreal.

It's dark, after eleven at night, when the doctor finally arrives and examines Zenon.

His ragged breathing grows weaker. More time passes between gasps.

"I'm sorry," Dr. Houghton says at midnight, "your husband's dead." He closes Zenon's eyes, writes the death certificate, tells Nestor what arrangements need to be made.

After he leaves, Nestor begs Halya to come home with him; his wife will look after her. She shakes her head.

She understands that even if the doctor had come earlier, it wouldn't have made a difference. The childhood tuberculosis that left one of Zenon's legs shorter than the other also weakened his chest, and the time in jail made it worse. She tries not to think that he died because his family was poor. Or because of his political ideas. But she does think these things.

She's too shocked and hurt to go with Nestor. Too angry. She lost Taras and now she's lost Zenon. She's not going anywhere until she can somehow understand that.

Nestor fills a boiler with cold water and Halya throws in the bloody towels and bedcover. She washes Zenon all over with wrung-out cloths and wraps him in a clean blanket. Pulls away the bloody top sheet and scrubs at spatters on the bottom one.

She won't let Nestor help with any of it in case he becomes infected.

Around two in the morning he has to go home, but promises to come back around noon the next day. Halya stays awake a long time. She touches Zenon's face, his hands, thinking he might not be dead. She knows that must be wrong, but he still seems too warm for death. She strokes his chest and shoulders, his belly and thighs, his genitals. Listens to his chest. Hears nothing.

He grows slowly cold but she finally falls asleep in a chair before that's done. She wakes at dawn, chilled, and knows he is dead and somehow she is not.

Later two men in dark clothes and white masks, undertaker's men, remove Zenon's stiff body. Halya sits in a chair, watching. Their manner of handling him, brisk and impersonal, would tell her everything if she didn't know already.

Nothing in life seems to last.

As the undertakers' men leave, Nestor and Paraska arrive with a basket, make tea and set out food. Paraska keeps up a stream of words that helps fill the emptiness in the room, but they flow right past Halya. Paraska has brought clean sheets and changes the bed while Nestor distracts Halya, making her eat and helping her plan for prayers at Zenon's grave. Funerals are temporarily banned because of the influenza outbreak. Nestor doesn't say that he has purchased the burial plot. Halya hasn't even thought about that. She's still too young to know about all the things that cost money and how much it takes.

After many cups of strong tea they leave, satisfied by her promise to lie down. But she stays in her chair, not even bothering to lock the door behind them.

That night the priest comes to speak with her. Afterwards she remembers none of it. She lies down on the bed, eyes fixed on the ceiling.

At some point she sleeps. She wakens in the same position but with sunlight coming in. She gets up and makes tea, stirs in milk and a lot of sugar. She tastes the sugar with interest; thinks: I like sweet things. She hunts around for the *pampushkas* Paraska left. Each has a flick of icing on top that melts on her tongue. She approves of the sensation. Keeps going till all the little buns are gone.

A COUPLE of weeks pass. Prayers have been said. Nestor paid for everything, because for Halya, undertakers' men are simply people who appear when someone dies. It has nothing to do with her. She doesn't go to work, but Nestor checks on her, brings more baking. Halya promises him she's all right and will return to work in a few days. She keeps drinking tea and eating buttered toast or *pampushkas*. They take away the hollow feeling for a short while.

She realizes she should write to her father and Natalka. She finds paper and pen and begins. It's as if a stranger writes, describing something that happened to an acquaintance. When she's done she forces herself to go out and mail it, and on the way back she picks up some milk, and bread and butter and honey. She catches sight of herself in the store window and thinks, "She looks thin."

As she hangs up her coat, she sees Zenon's shirts and trousers in the closet and now she can weep. When it's dark she realizes she's hungry and makes slice after slice of toast slathered with butter and honey. She eats them between gulps of milky tea, sobbing all the while. Some time after midnight, she falls asleep. In the morning she starts again with toast and milk and sobbing. By bedtime she's exhausted and her tears have stopped.

The next morning she starts tidying the room. She thinks about Nestor and about the paper, wonders how he's managing. Somehow this makes him appear with more baking. She drinks tea with him. Nestor flips the November issue of *The People's Voice* onto the table and she grabs it and starts reading, consuming it the way she's been consuming toast.

Halya says she'll be back at work the following Monday. Nestor acts pleased. He doesn't think this is the moment to tell her the government has shut down the paper.

"Tell Paraska it's enough *pampushkas*," Halya says with the hint of a smile. "Tell her they saved my life."

"I'm glad to hear your life is saved." Nestor looks at her very seriously. The young woman who climbed up those stairs three and a half years ago is now dear to him, almost a daughter. And he could have kept the paper going with her writing and his own.

"I'm too young to want to die," she says. " I think I knew that even when I was sick."

"Would you like me to write to your father?" It's clear he'd do it in an instant.

"No, I've done that," she says. "But thank you for offering."

"Do you want to go home for a visit before you come back to work?"

"Better not. I might get stuck there. Anyway, my father doesn't want me."

"I'm sorry," Nestor says. "He should be proud to have a daughter like you." She smiles again. "Look, why don't you lie down for a while and I'll sit with you."

She surprises herself by agreeing. Wonders fleetingly what she'd be like if Nestor had been her father. He fluffs up her pillow and she settles herself on the bed.

Halya hasn't noticed a second parcel Nestor brought with him and left near the door. When he sees she's asleep, he opens the cardboard box and lifts out a typewriter, the one she used at work. And a large stack of paper. He leaves them on the kitchen table.

After a few more minutes of watching Halya's strong, regular breathing, Nestor goes quietly out the door.

She'll be all right, he thinks. *Pampushkas.*

CHAPTER 45

The sun shone warm
but did not burn

TARAS CONTINUES to visit Tymko each afternoon. He's been here almost two weeks and wonders if he should go to the railroad and ask for a job. It's not costing him anything to stay with Myro, but if it goes on much longer he wants to pay his share of the food; and although he had enough saved up for the journey, he hasn't earned a lot in the year since he went back to Spring Creek.

One day early in November he takes fresh oranges and cuts one in sections for Tymko.

"Oh, that's good isn't it?" Tymko crushes one in his mouth. "Makes you want to believe in God."

Tymko talks less although he seems pleased to have Taras there. They haven't actually said it aloud, but both Taras and Myro think Tymko is weaker than when Taras came.

After school Myro bounds up the stairs with a bag of pecan-studded cinnamon buns. And four plain cotton masks. His school has just closed because of the flu epidemic.

Mrs. Plaskett brings tea and accepts, but doesn't put on, her mask. At Tymko's direction, Taras adds whiskey after she leaves. They find it good. Since the camp they never take food and drink for granted. Or whiskey. It's as if every privation is written in a thick book and any pleasure now is a measure of restitution.

After a while the landlady brings Tymko's supper and more tea.

Taras and Myro watch him eat his pork chop and peas like anxious parents.

Today Tymko does need help going to the bathroom. Myro goes with him, and while they're out of the room, Taras slumps in his chair and wipes away tears.

When they come back, Tymko settles back into his chair. "It's true what I've heard. You can feel pain in a part of your body that isn't there any more. Worse than that, it's an itchy pain. Not a goddamn thing I can do about it, boys."

"More tea?" Myro asks.

"In a while," Tymko says. *"Dyakuyiu.* Right now I'm thirsty for something else. I want to hear more about Shevchenko and that black man, Aldridge. I keep seeing them together. Not a word of each other's language and yet something is understood."

"Very well."

"I want to know how it was. Where they met. What they talked about."

"They had, at best, only a few days together. But they shared something. A kind of understanding that happens in an instant and lives on in the mind afterwards."

"That's right. That's what I need to hear. Show me the scene."

"Douzhe dobre. Apparently they visited Kalnikov's house. The one I told you about, where Taras attended an evening party."

"Ah. The count with the pretty young daughter."

"Exactly. But this is quite a few years later, and the pretty daughter is married. She and her child, a four-year-old girl, have come for a visit."

"Damned aristocrats," Tymko says. "Still, this family sounds better than most. And they did help our poet."

"They did. Although this was *before* Taras got in so much trouble and the tsar sent him into exile. After that, people didn't help as much. They were afraid. And not without reason."

"Tell the story, Myro."

"Dobre." Myro sits up a little straighter. "You'll forgive me if I make some of it up."

"Make up all you like. I'm used to that now. I just want a story.

Truer than life."

"The time is 1848 in St. Petersburg. Taras and his new friend Ira Aldridge have been invited to the Kalnikovs because the old man is curious about this great American actor. And because Tatiana speaks English, learned in childhood from a governess, and can translate for them. I see it all so clearly."

"Tse dobre," Tymko says softly.

"Well, then..." Myro takes a deep breath. "You won't mind if I just tell it as if I'm there? As if I can see into the poet's heart?"

"I not only won't mind," Tymko says firmly, "I insist upon it."

Myro begins.

TATIANA ALEXANDROVNA would once have been the perfect model for an angel, thinks our poet Taras Shevchenko. Or the mother of Jesus before she became with child. Now, ten years after he first saw her, she is, although still youthful looking, more guarded, more divided by conflicting loyalties and cares. A married woman paying a visit to her family.

Her small daughter, Yekaterina, runs in and out of the room. She stops at intervals to gaze at a man with a thick moustache and tightly curled hair, whose skin must look to her like melted chocolate. She runs off again to think about it by herself until curiosity draws her back. This last time she runs to her mother and buries her face in her mother's skirt.

Tatiana kisses the top of her head and sends the small figure in a bright purple dress whirling back to the long corridor beyond the room. Without being aware of it, she sighs.

Yet at this moment Tatiana seems almost to have returned to her fifteen-year-old self. Her simple dress is deep blue, lovely next to her rosy-peach skin and dark eyes. Her brown hair is braided and wound around her head, giving her the look of an artless country girl. Of course she cannot really be artless. At times Taras sees tears in old Kalnikov's eyes when he watches his daughter, but he smiles now as if she's still his child, safe in his house.

Tatiana sits in a ruby velvet-covered chair between Taras and the American. Translator for a former serf and the descendant of slaves. Thrilled at the chance to help.

Seated on a plain wooden chair, Ira Aldridge holds himself with straight-backed dignity. His warm brown skin glows with light that comes from within. His eyes note every detail of the room and the people in it.

Our poet sings a merry folk tune that has Ira nodding his head to the rhythm and applauding when it's done. Tatiana tells him the meaning, and as she speaks the foreign words, Taras realizes how little the song accords with his memories of peasant life. No use telling their visitor that. Perhaps he knows without telling.

Ira will sing next. Tatiana explains that the song is about Moses and the people of Israel, held in bondage by the Egyptians. The song begs God to free the Israelites. Ira stands, a man of medium height and build, and seems to grow larger and more powerful, as he does on stage when he plays Othello the Moor — welcome when he's of use to Venice but despised for his race. Ira draws a breath and seems to take up life from the room, life the others hadn't known was there.

"When Israel was in Egypt land," Ira sings in a deep baritone, "Let my people go. Oppressed so hard they could not stand. Let my people go." The notes saturate the room, the bodies of his listeners. Taras is reckoned a fine singer but knows he could never match this.

Yekaterina creeps back into the room and sits on a stool in a corner as Ira's voice sends waves of emotion toward her.

"Go down, Moses, way down in Egypt land. And tell old Pharaoh: Let my people go."

The song flows through Taras like a river. Tatiana begins to explain it, but her words drift away. Taras has understood. The song is not about Moses and the Israelites. It's about Ira's own people, black people from the west of Africa.

As Ira moves back to his seat, Taras presses the black man's hand, marvelling at the intense colour against his own hand. Yekaterina runs to her mother and pushes onto her lap, pulling at the abundant material of her mother's skirt to make herself a small nest, but keeping her eyes on Taras and Ira.

"Perhaps, my dear Taras Hryhoryvich, you would favour us with one of your poems," Kalnikov says: "Something about youth, for instance."

Taras smiles at his old patron. He recites from memory and Tatiana translates line by line, looking apologetic, as if unsure her words will match the original ideas. She doesn't understand Ukrainian as well as Russian.

She begins with the title, "My thirteenth year was passing," and Ira nods.

"Watching the lambs one day, I walked far past the village. Perhaps the sun shone, or was my joy without a cause? Joy as if at the throne of God." Tatiana sees she can do it and takes the story to heart as if it is her own. Kalnikov watches as if he's never quite seen her before.

"They called us for our midday meal...but I stayed among the weeds and prayed. Why a small boy wished so...fervently...to pray I cannot tell, nor how my happiness came about. But around me, the village and God's sky, the lambs even, all seemed to rejoice. The sun shone warm but did not burn."

She understands, the poet thinks. She recalls some moment of perfect innocence and wonder.

She continues, translating after he speaks, a phrase or two at a time. "It was not for long the sun kept kind and warm...not for long I prayed, when the sun turned to red fire and...now my heaven burned. As one awakened from sleep, I saw the village grow dim...God's blue sky become dark. I saw the lambs...knew they were not mine. In the village no home awaited me."

Tatiana is distressed now, wishes perhaps that she hadn't taken this on. Her arms pull Yekaterina closer as she strains to think of the English words.

"My bitter tears flowed...but by the roadside...a girl was picking hemp and...heard my sorrow. She wiped away my tears, kissed me gently." Now Tatiana finds her way again.

"It seemed once more the sun shone...as if the world were mine... Fields, groves, orchards. Laughing, we drove the lambs to water. Now when I remember, my heart weeps. Why, God, could

I not have lived...my short time in that dear place? I would have died knowing nothing else...never knowing an outcast's life."

The last line is "never cursed men and God," but Tatiana can't bring herself to say it. Kalnikov nods, tears in his eyes.

Ira rises and embraces Taras. Tatiana and her father say nothing to disturb the moment. Yekaterina peers like a small animal from her tangled blue burrow.

Semyon, the butler, stands in the doorway, a silver tray with pastries in his hands. Tears stain his sallow cheeks. Feeling Taras's eyes upon him, he straightens himself and carries the tray to the table where the samovar awaits.

WHEN MYRO STOPS, neither of his listeners can speak for a moment. Then Tymko says, "You should write that down."

And he weeps as though for all the sorrows of life. His land, his people. His wife and daughter. The exile and death of Shevchenko. The millions killed in the war and afterwards. The Revolution. Myroslav and Taras kneel beside his chair, each with a hand on his shoulder.

"There's been too much blood," he says. The younger men nod, but Tymko knows they don't see the things he sees.

Mrs. Plaskett must have a sixth sense. She brings in a kettle of hot water to refresh the teapot. Taking care not to look at Tymko.

"He could use a little whiskey in that," she says as she goes out, and Taras could almost swear she winks at them.

After she shuts the door, Taras takes out his flask and adds whiskey to all their cups.

CHAPTER 46

A man who died

HALYA sits at the typewriter, a pile of neatly typed pages beside it. She has finished writing Zenon's story and now stares blankly at the wall behind the empty bed. She's done what she set out to do, and now everything seems to slow down, a little at a time, until she thinks she might turn to stone. She could sit here for a day, two days, more.

Her work at the newspaper has ended. Nestor doesn't know when, if ever, he can get *The People's Voice* running again. She has a little money in the bank, mostly saved by Zenon during his years at the paper. Enough to live on for a few months. She could stay on in this suite, eating toast and tea and gradually adding things back into her diet. She could look for a job, although she doesn't know who'd want a refugee from a newspaper shut down by the government for its seditious views. Or was that revolutionary views? Treasonous views?

And she's still just a woman who didn't finish high school, because she couldn't do it all in eight months. Mind you, she's a woman who didn't finish high school who won a prize for an essay on the novels of Dickens. That should count for something, shouldn't it? No, probably not.

Nestor says they can take her back waiting tables at his uncle's café. She could make a living.

Or should she try to go back to her father and Natalka? She could write to him, see how he responds. She doesn't think she could go back to being the dependent daughter, someone he thinks he can control. And yet she must see her *baba*. She can't understand how she failed to find a way to visit them until now.

Yes, she's sent letters. But does Viktor even read them to Natalka?

Halya slowly becomes aware of noise outside, coming closer. Then shouting, car horns and what she thinks must be rifle shots. She makes herself get up and look out the window. A wave of people flows down the street. Like lava pouring out of a volcano, she thinks. John Madison at Briarwood taught her the exports of many countries, and about lava, and this is the first time she's found any of it useful. People flow like lava, coming closer.

Sirens shriek. Far away a train whistle blows, on and on. Men run down the street, leaping, bawling, setting off firecrackers. *Laughing.* It takes her a while to understand. They signal not war or danger but something new.

She walks downstairs and out the door. The cheering crowd surges down the street. Men in working clothes and a few in uniform, eyes wild. Women in housedresses who have run into the street without coats. Nobody wears a white mask.

A young soldier calls to Halya. "Hey sweetheart! The war's over!" Other people echo his voice: "War's over! War's over!" The soldier holds his hand out to her. She lets herself be pulled into the torrent. She knows the November air is cold, but doesn't seem to feel it.

The soldier whirls her around, kisses her, his lips burning. She feels tears on her face, his or hers she doesn't know. She kisses him back and for a few seconds they hold each other close. The crowd jolts forward with its own odd, irregular rhythm, pries her fingers loose from the soldier's grasp. Another wave deposits her at the edge of the street, like silt.

She sees a man on the other side and he glances her way across the colliding bodies. He looks like someone she once knew. A man who died. The human tide ebbs for a second and they face each other across the street. It can't be him, but so much has happened to her, she has lost all control of her life, so what if it is? They watch each other, feeling the weight of the years apart, the pain of separation and loss, falling away. Taras crosses over to her.

Up close, he sees how thin she looks, how pale. "What's wrong?" he asks.

She knows she must look like a bag of old sticks. "I had the influenza. My husband too. He died."

A wave of vertigo passes through her brain and for a moment she thinks she'll fall, but he reaches out an arm to steady her and it passes. It is him. It is. Taras.

"I'm all right now," she hears her voice say.

THEY GO UP the stairs to the suite. Taras can't believe the power of his desire, all over his body. It blazes through his arms and legs and belly. They lie down on the bed.

She touches his face, his hair, his chest. She doesn't want to know yet how he can possibly be here. But he's real, not some fevered dream, and somehow they've found each other. That's enough. When she was a girl, she loved him, but now she's a woman. Longing flows through her. She helps him undress, and he helps her. Their clothes fall to the floor.

When he enters her body, deep shudders shake him and their tears break free. He's afraid to move in case it will end too soon, but he can't think about that for long. He feels himself coming closer and closer, feels her moving with him. It seems to go on and on, although there's no way of knowing how long. And then he's still inside her and it begins again.

Afterwards they lie together a long time. For now they don't need to put anything into words.

HALYA HANDS TARAS a cup of hot tea. He drinks and almost scalds his mouth. Across the table he looks at a face he both knows and doesn't know. It must be the same for her. Four and a half years have passed since they came to Canada. They have led separate lives; changed from untried boy and girl to man and woman. Her hair is darker, her face still pinched from fever. He is healthy once more, but he'll never again be so young, so unknowing.

"He told me you were dead," Halya says.

"I know. Don't think about it." He'll tell her all about Viktor soon, but not yet.

"How did you find me?"

"I didn't. I came to see Tymko. He's dying in the hospital. I wandered into the street and saw all the people. I thought they'd gone crazy, and then I realized, it's over now. The war's over. I walked with them until I was tired. I looked across the street —"

"Who is Tymko?"

Of course she doesn't know. She thought he was dead. She doesn't know the men who became his brothers, his teachers.

"Taras?" She takes his hand.

"Tymko is..." He stops as his throat tightens. Tries to smile. "Listen, Halychka. I have a story to tell you."

"*Dobre.* I want to know how it is you're alive."

THEY DECIDE to marry right away and the wedding is very small. The witnesses are Nestor and Paraska. Myro comes, and Miss Greeley. Taras didn't want to wait for his parents to travel so far. And there is no moment for a celebration with Tymko dying in the hospital, but they will do that over time, in their own way.

After Tymko's small funeral, they take the train to Spring Creek. They have written to Viktor, and to Daria and Mykola, to say they're coming.

MOSES MEETS THEM at the train. He and Halya look at each other for a long moment without speaking, as if remembering and verifying what each has been told of the other. Then without either seeming to go first, they hug.

They stop at his house to drink tea and exchange news. Moses has been to see people who look like him — not only in being black, but in countless small ways. The shape of one person's nose or another's eyes; a small gesture or the way a smile forms. The cadence of laughter. Voices that blend like music. No, that are music. When he's with them, he fits. They are his family.

His aunt and uncle wanted him to stay. Find a nice woman and get married. He did meet a woman he liked, named Esther, but she told him from the start she'd never leave her country, especially not to be the second black person in a small town somewhere south of Moose Jaw. He would like to find someone but thinks that if it happens it will have to be here, in these hills.

He reminds Taras of the story of the old man, Ostap, in Shevchana: "Then ask yourselves: Now who are we?" he quotes back to Taras.

It seems that Moses is a black Ukrainian man of Saskatchewan.

He says he had a lot of time to think on the train, watched over by black porters. They often looked puzzled by him; he didn't belong in any category they knew. And he sometimes saw white people look at him the way Stover did.

Lately he's been remembering his time at school, when he was the Orphan Boy. Then he'd had the feeling of being someone special, even if it was for a terrible reason. Even if he mostly felt sad. But he doesn't think anyone noticed Stover much one way or another. Maybe it's all that simple: he wanted to be noticed and no one cared. Racism is always out there, easy to learn if you want to.

He drives them to Viktor's place. Natalka meets them at the door. Halya and her grandmother hold each other a long time, stroke each other's hair and faces. Viktor is ill in bed. Something to do with his heart. Natalka's had the doctor in.

In his room, Halya looks into her father's eyes. Understands that he's dying and that he knows it. He holds his hand out to her and she takes it. He sees Taras standing in the doorway and beckons him in.

"I know you're married already," he says in a hoarse voice. "But I want to give my blessing. May you live a long life. A happy life."

Halya kisses his cheek.

"Tell Mykola I'm sorry."

"I'll tell him, Batko."

"I have made my will. You and Taras will inherit this land.

Will you stay and run the farm?" The question is for both Halya and Taras.

Taras thinks a moment and nods. Halya too. Moments later Viktor sleeps. He is slipping away. His soul, or whatever a person has inside that tells him who he is, is leaving.

Taras realizes that Viktor has achieved one of his goals. He has become a new man.

A few days later they bury him in the town cemetery. A Ukrainian priest comes down from Regina and Moses is cantor. Daria and Mykola stand beside Taras and Halya.

Taras feels something shift inside him and then settle. He is tied now to this land between grass and sky. He is reasonably sure that he will never again be taken away and imprisoned, and that he and Halya can be together as long as both of them live.

As WINTER SETS IN, the farmhouse takes on something of the feel of a village house. Taras buys a grindstone to make flour. He braids leather harness for Smoke and works with him in the yard. Tymko gave Taras the beaded flower from Leah Beaver, and Natalka sews it onto a linen *sorochka* for him. She cooks the most beautiful food, and soon Halya begins to look healthy and strong.

Halya writes articles about Ukrainian issues and mails them to Nestor. They can't be published with the paper shut down, but some day they might be. On Sundays they pick up Moses in town and drive out to see Taras's parents.

Marko Kupiak visits them and enthralls Halya and Natalka with birdsong. Natalka cooks cabbage rolls and roast chicken. Nothing is too good for a man who whistles like that, she tells him. If he were young, and single, she might even try to go after him.

"Ah," he says, "never let a man know things like that unless you're serious."

"Go on," she says, blushing.

Taras writes to Myro, who is seeing a young woman, also a teacher, and to Yuriy at his farm. He writes to Ihor, who is still at the ranch in Alberta.

The Kalynas – Taras and Halya and Daria and Mykola – and

Natalka all spend Christmas in town with Moses.

Moses throws the *kutya* on the ceiling. It will be a prosperous year.

In the New Year, a letter comes for *Pahna* Natalka Antonenko. From Maryna, written for her by Larysa. The first letter Natalka has ever received. Maryna and Larysa, and Larysa's son, Ruslan, are in Canada. So is Lubomyr Heshka.

"I gave you such good advice," Maryna says in her letter, "that I decided to follow it myself. After Ruslan died, we sold everything we had to buy the tickets. The necklace helped." And then, she goes on, seeing what they were doing, Lubomyr said that if two women and a baby could emigrate, surely a strong, more or less young man could do the same.

They left the old country a couple of months after Taras and his parents, just in time for all of them to spend the war in an internment camp at Spirit Lake in Quebec. They survived that, somehow, and now they live in Hamilton, Ontario. Lubomyr has a job in a steel plant and a Canadian sweetheart. Maryna and Larysa run a tailoring business and hope to visit Spring Creek some day.

Maryna has become someone's *baba*.

JUST BEFORE EASTER a parcel arrives, forwarded from Taras's old boarding house in Edmonton – an album of Arthur Lake's photographs. Halya looks at the pictures for hours and Taras tells her about the camp. He's used to making stories now. When he can't remember what happened in a picture or wasn't there when it was taken, he makes something up.

This is what she loves. Stories. She doesn't mind if some are made up. In fact, she likes the things he makes up as much as the things that happened. They're made of the same materials.

And then spring comes and a warm wind blows from the west. The air grows moist from dissolving snow and smells of earth. Taras rides Smoke up into the hills and looks out over the grass. Time to plant their first crop.

PART 7

CHAPTER 47

Going back

August, 1960

THE TEN-FOOT FENCE is gone, might almost never have been, but anyone who knows can tell where the posts were rooted and see ghosts of the peaked white tents against the mountain. Yuriy once said he would come back and climb Castle but in the end only came once to look. Gazing up at the mass of rock, Taras doesn't think he could climb it either, even though he once went halfway up with the Alpine Club. It still seems to deny him entry, despite the months he spent under its cliffs. Like Ihor, he can't find its spirit.

The air smells good. He doesn't remember noticing that.

The road they were building has been finished to a higher standard than any of them could have imagined, and paved. Even so, it's not the main highway between Banff and Lake Louise any more – that's the much newer Trans-Canada. Their old road seems more interesting, more intimate. It has more trees, more bends, more things hidden. The Trans-Canada seems bleak to him, too much at the mercy of sun and wind.

Against all odds, they made something beautiful.

Taras stares at the camp site until he begins to believe he's put his fear to rest. Or does he still feel a wordless unease? Will it always be there? All right, then that's how it's going to be. He smells something pungent, musky, sees a dark shape move in the trees. In all his time here he never saw a bear. This surely must be one. He hopes it's not interested in him. After a minute or so, the shape moves away into the forest.

By the path back to his car, a hank of barbed wire lies coiled like a snake. He picks it up, throws it in the trunk. He'll figure out what to do with it later, but he can't just leave it.

BACK IN TOWN he sees someone he thinks he knows coming out of the drugstore: Kvitka. Flora. Only she looks so much older, the red-gold hair faded and laced with grey, and it upsets him; she should be as he remembers. He knows this is unreasonable. Another woman comes out of the store and catches up to her. This one's like Kvitka as she looked in 1917. So this is her daughter; no, granddaughter.

He wants to call out to her, but what is the point of disturbing her, of bringing back that faraway time? At this moment she's on her way somewhere. How could he have the gall to interrupt that, to force himself on her notice? And what would she think of him now? How old he looks, that's what she'd think.

She disappears into another store; and he realizes that Kvitka would never have thought any of these things. She would have been happy to see him. Now it seems too late. Or he decides it's too late. Why is he thinking this way? he wonders.

He walks up to the drugstore. Sees his reflection in the window. A still-dark-haired man in sturdy trousers and a black leather jacket with a beadwork appliqué in the form of a rose. Leah Beaver's rose. He wonders where the Beavers might be now. On an impulse he asks a man in the drugstore where the office of the *Crag and Canyon* is. It feels strange to go in there, although they treat him politely. Apparently he's now a white man, or maybe whiteness isn't as important as it was. They can't tell him anything about the Beaver family.

He takes a room at the Mount Royal Hotel on Banff Avenue. Remembers shovelling snow from the walk outside it long ago. As the sun slides behind the mountains, he feels his body slowing. Soon after supper he goes to his bed and falls into deep sleep. In the morning he can't tell where he is. For the first time he feels old. Maybe it's from seeing Kvitka and knowing for certain that, like him, she is no longer young. A large breakfast restores his strength, but he wonders how he'll find enough of it to drive himself back through all those mountains. Back to Saskatchewan.

Getting here was the easy part.

THE BUNKHOUSES are gone but the Cave and Basin pool is still there. He feels a longing to bathe in those waters one more time. At the Hudson's Bay Company store he buys black bathing trunks. Back at the pool a young man takes his money and points him toward the change rooms. Already he smells sulphur.

He steps down into the water and lets heat claim his body. A young family splashes each other in a far corner, but otherwise the pool is empty. Except for Yuriy and Ihor floating close by. Except for Tymko when Arthur Lake brought them here after the river. Taras cups his hands and splashes hot water on his face.

Myro was right. Nothing is forgotten.

But he's gone on with his life. He and Halya have built Viktor's farm into a prosperous, orderly place where they've raised four children. Halya still writes articles for Ukrainian journals and for the local weekly newspaper, tapping away at Nestor's old typewriter. She's the head of the committee that built the new library in Spring Creek. She reads novels, more than Taras could ever keep up with; she's even read one by a Ukrainian Canadian woman. When Miss Greeley died, she left Halya her books, and Halya has read all of them as well.

Novels are her horses. She's working on one of her own. She says she's almost done. He did ask if she wanted to come on this trip, but she said, "You have to finish your story."

The three boys live with their families on nearby farms, but it's their daughter Oksana (who married Yuriy's son Taras) who inherited the genius for working with horses. Oksana's daughter Nadia and her husband work with horses too, and they all live at Daria and Mykola's ranch now that the old folks have moved to town. Nadia has a three-year-old, Tymko, the first great-grandchild. Watching the child carry that name around sometimes makes Taras cry, but it was what Nadia wanted because she'd heard so much about Tymko while she was growing up.

In the corral Taras built at the ranch is a smokey grey colt with a blanket of white spots on its rump. Oksana is going to start training him to the halter soon. The first Smoke died twenty years ago, but there are a dozen horses on the place with the look of him. Taras has buyers coming to him all the time wanting them.

Taras sees Yuriy and Ihor at least once a year. Bohdan Koroluk lives in Moose Jaw and has just retired from the railroad. He still makes carvings and has no trouble selling them to friends. He made a beautiful statue of Taras on Smoke as the horse reared high in the air. It sits on a shelf in the farmhouse near Viktor's portrait of Shevchenko.

Taras carves too – horses and birds mostly – and he makes hand-tooled saddles. People buy them.

He keeps a few horses to ride. Picks out one to train each year.

Maryna and Larysa did visit. When they met Moses, he and Larysa couldn't stop looking at each other. Now they're married and have a family of their own. Maryna once said new things could happen if people left the old country for Canada, and that seems to be true. Moses and Larysa's children and grandchildren have married people from all over the south country, down to Willow Bunch and Mankota and Wood Mountain.

Moses is no longer alone. No longer the only black Ukrainian.

Taras sinks further into the water, lets it hold him upright, until only his head and neck remain out of the water. It seems the heat goes through his bones, to the marrow. Sampson Beaver said these were healing waters. Taras hopes it's true for him.

He turns his face so the people at the other end don't see his tears fall into the water. He wants the tears to carry away the pain, but that's not possible. It may be, though, that something eases in his chest and belly. Something hard that's hurt ever since he was sent to the camp. He's been able to forget about it for weeks or months at a time, but it's always come back. He thinks of Viktor, once he knew they'd all forgiven him; the release in his face, his body. Maybe he's finding something like that here.

That night he sleeps once more like the dead. Or like people paralyzed by polio, unable to move in their iron lung machines. That happened to a friend's son in Spring Creek.

The next morning when he wakes, he knows where he is. If he heads out early, he can be home before dark. After eggs and toast he climbs into the maroon 1953 Meteor and sets off down Banff Avenue to the Trans-Canada and turns east for Calgary.

HE REACHES THE FARMYARD, ringed with grassy hills, as light leaves the sky. He sees the row of *kalyna* bushes growing along the road. Soon they'll begin to make berries. As he gets out of the car he hears excited barking and Sobachka, the old sheepdog – for some reason they've always called her by a name that means puppy – leaps up against his chest. She presses her head into his leg and herds him toward the house.

Inside, Halya is waiting. "Tell me about your journey," she says. Telling her takes the whole evening. When he's done, she goes out to the car and brings in the scrap of barbed wire. Hangs it on a nail near the Shevchenko portrait.

A FEW DAYS LATER she comes into the living room after supper, carrying a tall stack of typed sheets of paper. She sets them on the table, centred on the embroidered tablecloth. She looks at him in a way that says he should get up from the rocking chair and come to the table. He comes and sits in a chair by the stack of papers. She stays standing.

Something makes him think of the time in Edmonton when they found each other in the street.

Halya's hands shake a little as she picks up the first page and hands it to him. He begins to read, and in a moment he's back on a train looking into the night, his ghost face staring back at him.

ACKNOWLEDGEMENTS

My thanks to the Canada Council for the Arts and the Saskatchewan Arts Board, whose support provided time for me to
work on this book. Thanks also to the Banff Centre and its self-
directed residency program, which allowed me to spend time
in Banff working on the manuscript and visiting sites which
appear in it.

I want to acknowledge as well the help of the Canadian First
World War Internment Recognition Fund with the publication
of my book.

Thanks also to the Whyte Museum of the Canadian Rockies
for the opportunity to work in their archives, and for permission
to use the photograph that appears on the cover of my book and
four others in the interior. These photographs may have been
taken by a soldier, Sergeant Buck, and I have created a fictional
character, Arthur Lake, who takes them in my story. These internment photographs also came to my attention through *In My
Charge; The Internment Camp Photographs of Sergeant William Buck,*
edited, with a preface, by Lubomyr Y. Luciuk and Borys Sydoruk.

The Whyte Museum contained two other sources that helped
me: the archives of the *Crag and Canyon* newspaper and the
splendid mountain photographs of Byron Harmon.

I also want to acknowledge the marvellous photographs of

Thomas and Lena Gushul in the Glenbow Museum's archives.

I've read many books as part of my research, too many to mention here. I want to acknowledge the importance for my work of *In the Shadow of the Rockies; Diary of the Castle Mountain Internment Camp, 1915 – 17*. It makes available the camp logs from Castle Mountain and Banff, extensively annotated by the editors, Bohdan S. Kordan and Peter Melnycky, who also provide an introduction to the material. Bill Waiser's *Park Prisoners; The Untold Story of Western Canada's National Parks, 1915 – 1946*, was also very helpful.

Blood and Salt, is of course, a work of fiction, although I've tried to ground it in the research I did, while also performing the novelist's job of imagining and re-imagining.

I read many historical works, either in whole or in part. Jaroslav Petryshyn's *Peasants in the Promised Land; Canada and the Ukrainians* was a valuable resource. The paintings and brief stories about them in artist Peter Shostak's *For Our Children* were inspiring. And the stories in *Land of Pain, Land of Promise, First Person Accounts by Ukrainian Pioneers, 1891 – 1914,* translated by Harry Piniuta, provided fascinating glimpses into their times.

Pavlo Zaitsev's *Taras Shevchenko; A Life*, translated by George S. N. Luckyj, helped me immensely. I read translations of Shevchenko's poetry by Watson Kirkconnell and C. H. Andrusyshen from their book, *The Poetical Works of Taras Shevchenko*. One of my characters speaks four lines from "My Friendly Epistle," and another character gives a prose version of "I Was Some Thirteen Years of Age."

Lisa MacFarlane's essay, "Mary Schaffer's 'Comprehending Equal Eyes,'" published in *Trading Gazes; Euro-American Women Photographers and Native North Americans, 1880 – 1940,* helped me develop my own thoughts about Schaffer's famous photograph of Sampson and Leah Beaver and their daughter.

I encountered the story of the bun who ran away in Barbara J. Suwyn's *The Magic Egg and Other Tales from Ukraine* and in

Christina Oparenko's *Ukrainian Folk-tales,* and have drawn on their retellings.

Thanks to George Hupka, who helped my husband and I learn as much as possible during a visit to Ukraine. And to Solomea Pavlychko and Oksana Zabuzhko, wonderful Ukrainian writers who inspired us with their spirit, learning and literary excellence. And to the kind and hospitable Achtemichuk family of Shevchana and Chernivtsi. I have borrowed the name Shevchana for the village in my story, but only the name is the same, the rest is fictional.

Thanks to Mr. Kupiak of Moose Jaw, Saskatchewan, a man I used to see when riding the bus as a child. He would entertain the passengers, especially children, with the most amazing whistled bird calls. Marko Kupiak in this book is of course a different man, although I tried to give him the whistling and the kindness of the original Mr. Kupiak.

Thanks to my cousin Vernon Sapergia, whose brilliant horse-manship inspired my character Taras Kalyna's skills with horses.

Thanks to friends who read all or part of the manuscript, including Ostap Skrypnyk, David Carpenter, Richard Rempel, Bobbi Coulter and Larry Warwaruk. And a huge thank you to Jack Hodgins for his extensive comments, and to Geoffrey Ursell, my editor, critic and support throughout this process.

PHOTOGRAPHIC CREDITS

FRONT COVER AND PAGE 74
Whyte Museum of the Canadian Rockies (V295-lc-35)

PAGE 133
Whyte Museum of the Canadian Rockies (V295-lc-58)

PAGE 202
Whyte Museum of the Canadian Rockies (V295-lc-39)

PAGE 259
Whyte Museum of the Canadian Rockies (V295-lc-66)

PAGE 297
Whyte Museum of the Canadian Rockies (V295-lc-117)

AUTHOR PHOTO
Zach Hauser

ABOUT THE AUTHOR

BARBARA SAPERGIA is a fiction writer and dramatist living in Saskatoon. She has four previous books of fiction, including three novels and a book of short stories. She's had nine professional play productions, including *Matty and Rose,* about the struggles of black railway porters in the 1940s. It was produced by Persephone Theatre the same year she was Playwright in Residence. She's the co-creator of and wrote numerous scripts for the children's television series *Prairie Berry Pie* and wrote for the *Mythquest* TV series as well. She has two published plays and a book of poems, *Dirt Hills Mirage.* She has written ten radio dramas, including an hour-long drama broadcast in Canada and Australia. Poems and stories appear in many periodicals and anthologies. Two of her plays have won the John V. Hicks Long Manuscript Award (*Nell* and *Double Take*).

FSC
www.fsc.org
MIX
Paper from
responsible sources
FSC® C016245